THE DAWNING

A Whispering at Dawn Novel

Melissa Halbert

Dedication:

Dedicated to my loving husband, John, who uplifts me and supports me in everything that I do; to my daughter, Sadie, that is a natural teacher who opens my eyes to new ways of thinking and exploring life; and to my family and friends that are always there for me, even when I have a hard time being there for myself. I'm grateful for each and every one of you! To you, my dear Readers, thank you for reading a story that has brought me a lot of healing by writing Vivienne's story.

DISCLAIMER

This book is for ADULT AUDIENCES ONLY.

WARNING: This book contains profanity, violence, sexual content, and sexual violence inappropriate for individuals under the age of eighteen. Discretion advised for sensitive viewers.

All the names, characters, places, events, and incidents in this book are the product of the author's imagination. Any resemblance to actual persons, living or dead, or actual events is purely coincidental.

CHAPTER 1

FOUND

"You are dying," a voice in my mind screamed at me. "Wake up! Do not let the darkness take you! Wake up, Vivienne!"

It was not cold or warm there, it just simply was. It was the darkness that continued to enrapture me into its intoxicating web, delivering me from the pain in my physical body. I felt so tired. It took everything to fight the darkness, even now that pulled at my consciousness, wanting to settle in like a warm blanket. I heard voices just beyond the thick wooden door, and I found my consciousness slowly stirring from the place that did not have a name.

"Please," I tried to yell out in a failed attempt as my voice caught on itself and I winced in pain as the air moving into my lungs felt like sharp, tiny daggers followed by what felt like a heavy weight placed upon my chest. Did I hear anything at all? I could not help but wonder if this was another strange dream? I have felt lost in a sea of strange dreams, and they have felt so real that I can no longer tell if this is real life, or another dream. I have lost a sense of time in the darkness and feeling lost in the dreams that would unfold and take me to places I knew I had never been. Was I hallucinating or dreaming about this, too?

"Hello," a man's voice called through the door. "Is there anyone there?"

"Plea...sssss...ee," I whimpered in pain, trying to raise more sound this time.

The wet, musty smell overwhelmed my senses as I became more aware of my surroundings. An icy chill settled into my bones as my mind registered that I was lying on the cold cement floor in the cellar. There was the slow and steady drip from a leaking pipe above me. Each plip and plop sounded off like the long hand of a clock announcing that time was my enemy. It would be only a matter of time before death was upon me. Where is she? Why did she leave me here to die?

I grabbed a can of peas that were laying near me and rolled it towards the door. It rolled about two inches from the door and rolled back towards me, following the downward slant towards the drainage hole in the center. I grabbed it again and shifted my weight slightly. I cried out in pain as I flung the can towards the door as hard as I could. I collapsed back onto the floor and clutched at my side, crying out in pain.

A hard thump landed against the heavy wooden door. There it was again. There was a long pause, followed by a splintering thwack as the sharp edge of the blade of an axe breached through. The thwacking continued each time someone behind the door used the head of the axe to punch out more wood until they could bust out the lock.

"I found one," a strange man called out. He wore a suit that reminded me of a science fiction comic, of what a spaceman or an alien would look like. The suit covered him from head to toe.

He approached me cautiously. Kneeling beside me, he lifted my wrist and held it as a doctor would have to check my vitals. All I could see were his eyes through two large eye pieces, while a mouthpiece covered his face with a black tube that wound its way around to his back. I looked from him to the other two men standing in the doorway. The shock of their appearance chills me to the bone. I shook uncontrollably, my eyes widening as the man that was beside me leaned in closer.

"You're safe," he said calmly. "We are here to help."

"Please," I tried again in a barely audible whisper as the darkness sang me its soft lullaby and my eyelids felt so heavy, I could barely hold them open.

"She's alive," he shouted happily, followed by a blinding flashlight entering through the doorway.

"How long have you been in here?" He has such a soothing voice mixed with a slight southern accent. A voice that matched his eyes. I like his eyes. They were kind.

"I don't know," I rasped. "Please, I'm thirsty."

"We will take care of you," he said, motioning to a soldier with the blinding flashlight who stood tall in the doorway with a rifle at his side. I could not understand why they would come to Stony Creek bearing weapons, unless... everyone... was dead. It all came flooding back.

"What do you remember?" He propped me up carefully and helped me sip from a glass of water that another man in a suit brought over to me. The water tasted incredible. The cool liquid went down my throat, and I could feel it settling into my stomach and beyond. The second sip I was not so lucky with as my throat seized, causing me to choke on it, coughing uncontrollably.

The stranger tilted my head up again and brought the cup back to my mouth. "Do you want to try again?"

I took another sip and tried my best to form a coherent thought to answer his question. The brain fog kept me from focusing fully. He wanted to know something. What did he want to know?

"Do you know what's going on in Stony Creek?"

"People are sick. The flu, it's killing people."

"Did you get sick?"

I watched the soldier with his weapon shift his stance, with his weapon at the ready. "No," I said carefully.

"Do you or have you had any flu-like symptoms?"

"No," my voice cracked. "My mother, she is sick. Is she ok?"

"What else do you remember? Please, it's important."

"Our town's preacher said we were at the end of days. I watched as the world went crazy, and I thought the preacher was right. It is the end. The streets filled with the dead and the desperate, while insanity preyed upon others like a disease. Please, where is my mother?"

As he tried to sit me up, I grabbed my side and moaned in pain. He immediately saw the old, stained blood that had seeped through my sheer white blouse.

"Shit," he said with concern as he lifted my blouse. "What happened?"

"A crazy nurse stabbed me," I said as my head lolled to the side, as a wave of nausea hit me. "Please mister, is my mother..."

I crashed back down onto my side as my body rocked with dry heaves, followed by retching up the water I drank.

"Get on the line and tell them we have found a survivor. Looks like a botch job to sew up a stab wound. The wound shows visible signs of infection. No visible signs or symptoms of the virus," he told the soldier behind him. "What shall I call you?"

"Vivienne," I whispered between heaves as another wave of nausea accompanied with dizziness hit me. "You?"

"Hello, Vivienne. My name is Anders," he said as he picked me up. I grunted, holding my side as my weight shifted in his arms. "Don't be afraid. I've got you."

He carried me out into the small room we used as a small family room filled with three other soldiers looking out of place amongst the piles of board games, books, and knitting supplies. Two of the soldiers were laying out a large grayish-green tarp on the ground as the other stood in my line of view.

"Russell, we're going to need help with this one," said the man kneeling on the ground. "We will lift, and you need to shift this under the body."

The body?

Anders turned slightly to shift my view away from what they were doing. As he shifted his weight to turn me again, the soldier blocking my view moved, and I saw what they were doing. My breath caught in my throat as I deep cry caught in my abdomen. A cry felt so deep that it could not face the truth.

She did not leave me. She lay slumped against the concrete wall, with black tar seeping from her mouth, nostrils, and her lifeless eyes that stared up towards the ceiling as if in prayer. Her abdomen distended, and her skin discolored into a lifeless pale gray. The veins on her arms were so black that they were visible through her light stockings as well. Her button up dark navy-blue dress with white flowers set the stage for a surreal scene that refused to register within my fragile brain to what I was seeing. As they shifted her body onto the tarp, her arm dangled out away from her body. Her pearl bracelet caught the light from a lantern.

"Mother," I cried weakly, reaching my hand towards her as we passed by them quickly. Anders' shifted me slightly in his arms, and I curled into his chest as my long black curls draped loosely around his arm. His footsteps stepped heavily on the wood planks up the stairs and the wood groaned beneath us with our combined weight as he lifted me up into a world filled with light and uncertainty.

CHAPTER 2

IT BEGAN IN 1947

A darkened room the size of a small studio apartment deep underground, lays dormant and dark. The mahogany table sits valiantly in the middle of the room with its intricate designs carved along the outer panel by a skilled artisan holds the newspaper clippings that lie scattered across the table. A clipping from the front page of The Stony Creek Gazette, dated October 2nd, 1947, with a handwritten note in red ink catches your eye. It reads:

It has begun.

Title: Journey of Terror from the Middle East Reaches Stony Creek

Subtitle: Man reunited with local family after a journey of terror, asks nation to hold his country accountable for devastating acts of violence.

Mostafa Akir, a young man who comes from a small farming village in the Middle East, has recently reunited with the Akir family that live in Stony Creek. Mostafa has asked our great nation for support in holding his government accountable for their crimes against innocent people. Mr. Akir states that his government ordered soldiers to kill everyone in his tiny village out of fear of a mysterious illness that was sweeping through his village quickly, killing all that it infected, sick, and healthy alike.

Mr. Akir claims he escaped by hiding in the shadows, and out into the fields where he watched soldiers enter his neighbor's homes. He witnessed the soldiers' torches setting fire to homes after they gunned down family after family in execution style. Haunted by the gunshots and their screams, he ran to escape the soldiers' wrath. A camel herder found him, dehydrated and starving. Providing him with food, water, and a means of travel, Mr. Akir reached one of the nearby coastal cities that held a seaport. An elderly couple from Syria allowed him to work for passage on a small cargo ship that traveled to Spain. From there, he stowed away on an international cargo ship that traveled to New York City. For the better part of a month, his journey to the United States was by sea.

The port authority found him during an inspection and held him in customs upon his discovery for over seventy-two hours, questioning him on his identity because of having no identification papers on his person. Port authorities commented that upon hearing an in-depth retelling of his journey into the United States, they released him to health officials for a mental health evaluation while notifying proper officials. His family, residents from Stony Creek, signed for his release into their custody by showing proof of his lineage. The Akir family is living in fear of what this means for their family beyond the sea, and what it means for them if they want to return home to their country of birth.

Mr. Akir stated, "I do not understand why this is happening and I beseech the United States government to hold them accountable as they commit genocide on innocent men, women, and children."

The representative for his country's government has made an official statement that they have no papers or record showing that Mr. Akir is a resident of their sovereign nation and claim that he is fabricating stories for media attention to stay in our country without legal papers of residency. According to Mr. Akir's uncle, individuals in their country only get papers when they are to serve in the military, are international trading merchants, or have high-paying positions in the government. It takes a great deal of effort and money for the average person to get papers to travel internationally.

Community members have expressed concern for the town and the safety of its citizens over retaliation of his claims or the media attention that may develop. A petition posted near City Hall asks for the relocation of the family, where they will not pose a danger or a risk to the community.

Recent reports state that Mr. Akir is presently undergoing a psych evaluation at Stony Creek General Hospital. Bystanders have reported his condition as frantic, and they considered his appearance to be strange and almost inhuman with his behaviors. His family has refused to answer questions but has made a formal statement that the trauma of his experience has left him unwell, and they beg the community for their understanding and respect the family's wishes for privacy during this challenging time.

We will update this story as it develops.

#

A partial clipping lays off to the side, a smaller news headline, dated later that month on October 23rd, 1947. The title grabs your attention.

Title: The Flu Virus Arrives at Stony Creek

The flu has come to Stony Creek earlier than expected, Dr. Mark Kines warns citizens to practice due diligence and stay home when you are not feeling well. Because of how fast the flu is spreading, Dr. Kines calls this a potential epidemic unless the community works together to eradicate its spread. He asks us all to wash our hands, cover our mouths when we cough, and to stay home when we show signs of the flu. Dr. Kines has asked the mayor's office to cancel fall festivities this year out of fear for the health and safety of residents. The mayor has been out of town on business in Washington, D.C. and is unavailable to comment.

"If you are running a fever, you need to stay indoors," reports Dr. Kines. "The hospital has almost reached capacity, and we are running out of beds." Dr. Kines asks for individuals or their family members to call his clinic and his staff will provide further instructions...

CHAPTER 3

THE STONY CREEK VIRUS

Laying on top of a box of files, lays a simple canvas portfolio file organizer containing a small collection of well-kept handwritten loose-leaf pages. The pages themselves are pristine with no folds or creases, and the text is still legible. The only telling sign is the discoloration of the pages. The plainly colored sisal twine cord dangles from the organizer, with two small metallic objects attached to it. One object is a small compass, and the other is a small round metal clasped capsule the size of a marble. Inside it is a small marble that contains a congealed substance that resembles blood. Upon opening the portfolio, a Western Union telegram from the United States Military is on top of the stack of papers. It reads:

November 1, 1947,

Professor Michael Alden

PIP Red Phoenix Emerges

Representatives en route. Expect immediate departure after debriefing.

Major Stevens

CHAPTER 4

WAKING UP

"You're awake," a man's excited voice said in a slight southern drawl with a low hushed tone, while Johnny Mercer sang Zip-A-Dee-Doo Dah over the radio in the background. "Good morning!"

His voice was vaguely familiar, coming from a fading dream. My head turned towards the sound of the voice and my eyes blurred as they tried to focus through the heavy fog of a deep, medically induced sleep. The more I tried, the more the room spun with a nauseating fierceness.

"My eyes don't want to open," I muttered, moving between the comforting blanket of sleep and the waking inhospitable world that felt like a greased-up merry-go-round. I felt like I was waiting for the creepy music to echo and ricochet off the unseen walls of an unseen darkness that crept closer, unwilling to release me from its grasp, making me feel claustrophobic within the realm of my own limitations.

"Let's start slowly," the kind voice continued. "Begin by wiggling your toes."

"My toes have nothing to do with the room spinning," I told him, moaning through a wave of nausea. "Can I try to sit up?"

"You have just had major surgery. Humor me," he said in an amused tone. I could hear the smile on his face. "Start small and don't force it. By the time you get your fingers to wiggle, your eyes will adjust and see more clearly."

"Who are you?"

"You don't remember? Of course not. You were in

terrible shape when we brought you in. My name is Anders," he said with a brief pause. "If anyone heard the story of how we found you, they would send me straight to the funny farm."

"Why is the farm funny?"

"It... Well, it is not really a farm, more so a place that they send people with mental issues to. They sent us into the town to search for survivors. We had almost given up hope of finding anyone alive when we found you. You would not let go of me to let the doctors do surgery until I promised to stay by your side. For someone on death's door, you have spirit. It took six men to keep you from tearing your IV out and trying to leave. I kept my promise, and my superiors have assigned me as your personal guard while you are here. Getting rid of me won't be that easy, although with that kind of natural strength I don't think you'll have too much of a problem if you tire of my company."

"You may well regret your promise to me," I said with a small smile. "I've been told I'm a pain in the ass."

"I will keep that in mind."

"Why can't I remember?"

"The doctor said it was normal. He said people in shock may or may not remember much. It may all come back all at once, or you may get bits and pieces."

"What if it's so terrible that I don't want to remember?"

"Want a highlight of my evening?"

"Is this a trick question?"

"Perhaps," he said, laughing. "You really did not care for the professor, our supreme scientist, on a pedestal. You hit him square in the jaw when he tried to examine you and get you out of your bloodied shirt. It was the shock, I'm sure of it."

"I've been told that I'm an excellent judge of character. If I hit him, it was for a good reason. At least, I... I think so. Are my toes moving? I think they're moving," I said, working my way out of the haze.

"You're doing great, Vivienne."

It surprised me at how difficult it was to tell my body

to do anything. The sound of his voice kept me connected, and I felt grateful for the lifeline back in the present. I could not explain it, but I just did not feel... right. I chalked it up to whatever medication they had me on. I felt completely disoriented.

I continued to drift in and out of the sleeping darkness, only hearing bits and pieces of what Anders was saying and catching the tail end of his story.

"I couldn't manage his drinking anymore, so I threw out every single bottle. My father, in his anger, chased me down, across the two acres, and took a switch to my rear end. I couldn't sit down for the rest of the day."

"That sounds painful. Why did he drink? I'm sorry I can't remember."

"It was his way of coping. My mother's health was failing her and watching her deteriorate broke him. Between caring for both my mother and my father in his drunken stupidity, it left little time for school and friends."

"I'm sorry," I told him sincerely in an aged voice that did not resemble my own. "That sounds like a tough experience and lonely way to grow up."

"The isolation was difficult. With little effort, my father quickly became the town drunk. I lost count of the times the police would bring him home and drag him up onto the bench on the porch. I worked at the hardware store to make ends meet until the factory shut down. My hometown became a bit of a ghost town after that, and Al, my boss, like others, had to close shop and move on. Families moved to towns where the factories produced parts for automobiles, planes, and agricultural equipment. After my mom passed, I signed up for the military. I couldn't run fast enough away from my father."

"What happened to your father? Do you still talk to him?"

"I write to him and send him money every month, but he doesn't bother with writing back. If he were dead, the letters eventually would come back to me. I admit it would be nice to hear that he is well, but I can imagine he is still very cross with me. I did not tell him I was leaving. I just left."

"At least you care enough to ensure he has the means to put some food in his belly."

"When I left, he was wasting away. If my mother would have passed quickly, I would have stuck around and found other work. She did not pass quickly. Her death was long, difficult, and filled with so much pain. I refused to watch my father destroy himself."

My eyes opened, and as my eyes adjusted, I expected to be in a hospital room. The dark fabric of the tent rippled as a slight breeze crept its way in and sent shivers down my spine. The icy chill washed over me in a wave that pierced through my skin and froze me to the bone.

"No hospital?"

"It is. Just not in the traditional sense."

"Could I have an extra blanket?" I asked, as my teeth started chattering. "I'm freezing."

"Of course," he said, getting up. "The weather is definitely taking a turn. Does it normally get this cold here?"

"I don't think so," I said as my teeth chittered through the words. "I don't remember ever being this cold in my life."

Anders pulled a blanket out of a box that was near him. He unfolded the blanket and lifted it into the air in a fell swoosh as it landed softly on top of me. I pulled it as close as I could and tucked it under my chin. Anders sat back down in a metal folding chair at the side of my bed and fumbled with a book with a frayed spine that looked a little worse for wear.

"Are you warm enough? I can grab you another blanket if you need it."

"I'm warm enough. Thank you."

"You just had major surgery," he said matter-of-factly. "Like the doc said, our bodies do strange things after being in shock, and I'm sure we can say the same after surgery or trauma. You've been through a lot."

I stretched out my hand. He sat the book down on my

legs, and he gently took my hands between his. For a moment we became lost in one another's eyes, not saying anything lost in the unspoken agreement between us.

"What are you reading?" I asked him to shift his focus.

"*Wind, Sand, and Stars* by Antoine de Saint-Exupéry," he said with a small smile, picking up his book and turning it around in his hands. "It's an autobiography of a pilot that flew mail routes across the African Sahara and the South American Andes. His story has been an anchor for me and kept me sane through many tough nights."

His southern charm stood out with his tan skin, his light brown hair, and a strong jawline with pouty lips that demanded respect. He shifted his weight towards me, leaning forward, and he looked me directly in the eyes and smiled warmly. I stared and found myself unable to look away. His hazel-green eyes stared back at me, and I became enraptured and held in his gaze as flecks of gold sparkled from the glow of the lantern nearby. My knight in shining armor was as handsome as he was kind. His gaze softened as he looked at my lips.

"Is my mother alright," I asked him, breaking the spell. Why wasn't she here? There would be no way that she would leave me alone, especially after having surgery.

"Shit, you don't remember any of it," he said, as a flash of concern and worry crossed his brow. "Forgive my language, Vivienne."

"I don't remember," I told him as I tried to focus on what happened. A cold veil of thick fog surrounded my mind, neatly wrapped itself around my memory, shielding me from seeing the past. "I... I don't understand."

"I'm not sure if it's my p...pl...place to tell you. I'm so sorry, Vivienne."

"She's dead?" I asked him, choking on a sob as my heart fell into my stomach.

"I'm so sorry," he repeated, as he lowered his head to his chest.

"How long have I been here?"

"We found you on the 2nd of November. You've been unconscious for three days."

A tall, slender man with a medium build and broad shoulders entered the tent, startling me slightly as he cleared his throat. His long blonde locks piled on the top of his cleanly shaven sides fell on his forehead as he reviewed a file in his hands. He casually tried to brush them to the side, which only provoked more hair to fall in front of his eyes.

He wore a long white jacket, a face mask that could not hide his 5 o'clock shadow, and my best guess was that he was a doctor. Anders, startled, stood up at attention, raising his hand to his head in a salute.

"At ease," the man told him with a small pat on his shoulder. "You're lucky to be alive, young lady."

"How am I alive?" I asked him.

"Do you remember what happened to you?" He asked me with his head still poring over his notes.

"Should I be dead?"

"That is a good question, Ms. DuSan. Together, I hope we can find the answers I'm looking for to make sense of you are still alive."

"Vivienne," I told him, adjusting my body weight to sit up. I struggled and moaned loudly as I clutched my side in pain. I laid back down immediately, regretting attempting to move.

"Let us try to rest for a day or two before we attempt any acrobatics, shall we? Have you had the flu recently, Ms. DuSan? Forgive me, Vivienne."

"I did. Before the outbreak, I was one of the first patients affected. Working at the hospital, I pick up every virus that comes through. If there is a virus, it will eventually find its way to me. My boss liked to call me a virus magnet."

"Viruses are tricky. There are those people that can carry them like you would a handbag while the virus seeks the perfect host, and there are those people that activate the virus.

I have a theory that there are a select few that we like to call catalysts of change. They attract viruses to strengthen our species."

"That makes absolutely no sense to me. I do not enjoy getting sick, and I do not enjoy watching people die. How can a virus strengthen our species by claiming so many lives?"

"Nature is chaotic, and it doesn't care for kindness or anger. It simply responds to its programming. To strengthen a species, a virus gives us an advantage to adapt and weed out the weakest link for the strong to survive. As populations grow beyond control, nature has a way of taming it back down to be in balance with the earth. Nature's programming doesn't focus on death, it navigates cycles to bring balance and responds when things are out of balance."

"What do you mean by programming? I survived the flu, but my flu was nothing like what the others had. That was... that was... different."

"Can you tell me more about your case with the flu? What was it like? Was there anything remarkable happening? Did anything in your overall experience stand out?"

"Our hospital is also our clinic and includes two specialists. The first floor holds both the emergency room on one side, and the clinic on the other. The lab and filing are on the second floor, along with three other doctor's offices for rotating physicians that serve the surrounding area, including two other towns. Most days were uneventful except for a random heart attack, fever, or broken bones, but those were just as commonplace as a cooking accident gone wrong to treat burn wounds, to hunting accidents that needed stitches, or a geriatric patient that was close to their time and sent home to pass on. Day in and day out, every day was the same."

"So, nothing remarkable happened during this time?"

"Nothing remarkable ever happened in our small town until the day I caught the flu. That day, it felt ominous, like an omen or portent of what was to come. I did not know how else to explain it, but it felt different. Have you ever had the feeling that there just was not something quite right about the day? That change is in the very air, and there is nothing you can do to change it. All you can do is sit and wait for it all to unfold."

"Yes, I understand. What happened?"

"There was a guy that the entire town was talking about. He was even in the papers. A local police officer brought him into the emergency room, and he did not look right at all. It took four people to sedate him."

"That sounds familiar," Anders said jokingly, with a small nudge on my arm. I smiled warmly at him and then looked back at the doctor, who stood waiting patiently for me to continue.

"Dr. Kines looked out of his element, but he was the one that was lying on top of the guy, trying to calm him down while Margo pinned his legs down. If Stan had not been working, I doubt it would have worked out at all. Stan came in and effortlessly put him in a grip that looked awkward. The man resembled someone living in a nightmare. The way his eyes looked at me, I cannot shake that from my memory. His forehead was dripping with sweat as the blood smeared on his face trickled down like teardrops that wanted to suffocate the world. I am not sure which memory makes me feel as if I have gone down the rabbit hole, like Alice in her Wonderland. The crazy nurse that stabbed me or that man."

"A nurse stabbed you," he asked with increased interest like a gossip monger that arrives at the party partaking in the juiciest of morsels. "Wait, wait. Do not answer that, we will get to that later. Tell me more about the man in the emergency room. Why was the entire town talking about him?"

"I don't remember the story exactly, just that there was concern that our small town would soon swell with national media presence, leaving our private lives exposed. Everyone knew his family. His aunt and uncle worked odd jobs all over town. They were from somewhere in the middle east. Mostafa's claims were serious, and caused a lot of panic in our small community."

"What were his claims?"

"From what the newspaper said, he claimed soldiers killed everyone out of fear of the virus… Oh, God! Do you think he brought the virus from where he is from?"

"We do not have enough information to say if that is true or not. Do you know what happened to this man?"

"He died in the hospital twenty-four hours later from the flu, or whatever this virus is that killed so many."

"Did anything else stand out? You mentioned he had blood on him. Was the blood from someone else or was it self-inflicted?"

"He had a deep gash on his hand, and I overheard Dr. Kines say he would need stitches. He must have smeared the blood all over himself in his state. The things he screamed at me unnerved me to say the very least."

"What did he scream at you? Inappropriate things?"

"He looked at me like he recognized me, and he just kept exclaiming the same thing repeatedly. He said something about the mouth of hell opening and how the dead will rise again. Then he passed out. Like I said, he was not in the right mind. It wasn't the way I wanted to spend my evening in the hospital getting my fever monitored and fluids put in me."

"Do you remember his name?"

"No, I'm sorry I don't. Mostafa something. What do I call you, doctor?"

"My name is Dr. Alden. The men around here like to call me Professor, since that is my day job. Let us have a look at you, shall we?"

"Professor?" I looked over at Anders in a slight panic.

CHAPTER 5

THE TOWN THAT SLEPT

"Yes," Anders told me, stifling his laughter. "That professor."

"I see Anders has caught you up on recent events," Dr. Alden said, slightly amused. "You have a wonderful right hook, and I dare say I do not look forward to getting into another fight with you. May I?"

"Please," I told him nervously as his icy hands touched my skin. His face came closer to mine as he took out his stethoscope and listened to my heart and lungs. His ocean blue eyes investigated mine briefly with a startled look. I felt as if he were seeing me as a woman for the first time rather than as a test subject.

He checked my eyes by having me follow his light, asked me about any headaches or other symptoms, and then lifted my gown to check on the stitched-up stab wound. Anders was kind enough to look away, but I felt extremely uncomfortable having a strange man lifting my hospital gown, especially as I realized I was not wearing any undergarments of any kind. My eyes felt like they were ready to pop out of my head, but it did not seem to bother Dr. Alden in the slightest. He remained focused on my wound and covered up my lower half with the bedsheet.

"I'm going to grab a blood sample from you," he told me calmly in a monotone voice as he took out his needle and set everything up. He gently took my hand and straightened my arm. He grabbed a cotton ball from a small tray that he had brought in with him covered in alcohol, and he cleaned the area. I winced as he inserted the needle into my vein. I closed my eyes, taking in a small breath and holding it as he adjusted the needle slightly.

"Your file says you worked for Dr. Kines as his personal secretary. Is that correct?"

"Yes," I said, as I let all the air out of my lungs. I watched him take out the needle, and he held gauze to the area, applying slight pressure. "Do you know if he survived?"

"When things started getting terrible, he told me to stay at home and take care of my mom. He didn't want to risk exposing her to the flu virus."

"Do you know where he kept all of his blood samples and patient records?"

I watched as he began jotting down notes in the file that he held close to his chest.

"He keeps everything in his office or the lab in the basement. The lab is tiny, but it holds what does not fit in his office. Stacks and stacks of it. He also has a small lab with a desk and files in his home when he wants to hide from everyone."

"Interesting. You are healing much quicker than I would have expected for someone in your condition. You have a knack for surviving insurmountable odds."

"How so?"

"You arrived dehydrated and malnourished. My best guess is that you were in that basement for days, up to more than a week. Your infected wound, along with sepsis, should have killed you long before the body shuts down with no water or food. Your condition would have killed most grown, healthy men in a shorter amount of time. I do not understand how you are alive."

"I... I do not understand! What do you mean?"

"Do you know how long you were in the basement?"

"No," I said, frustrated. "What are you trying to get at?"

"Based on the condition you were in when you arrived, we didn't expect you to survive the surgery or the night. As far as we are aware, you are the lone survivor of a virus that has wiped out your entire town within a matter of days, and you are recuperating as if there were no sepsis. You are healing at a rapid rate. In as little as three days, you have almost recovered completely. The tissue regeneration appears to be taking more time, however. Do you know how you survived?"

"I alone survived?! Oh, God," I exclaimed. "I do not know how I survived! I remember nothing!"

"You are a walking and talking miracle. I've read Private Sullivan's report, and I have a few questions if you're up for them."

"Sure," I whispered, unsure of how to react to all this added information. Should I be happy that I survived? How should I react to all of this? *This is not real! This is NOT real!*

Reality blurred as I felt myself detach from the present, and I curled up into a ball as hot tears streamed down my cold cheeks. The feeling that all of this before me was nothing more than a nightmare overwhelmed me into a pure panic that it may, in fact, be my new reality. Thinking back on the past, none of the events that led up to the here and now seemed real. How could any of it be real? I prayed I would wake up in my bed with the smell of cooked bacon and pancakes coming from the kitchen.

"We had polio to worry about, and now we face something that would take out an entire town in a mere number of days. What do you remember of your last few days wandering around Stony Creek before the basement?" He paused, looking at his notes, then looked up at me with concern, and he continued, "Are you able to recall that time?"

"I do. My mom had to go to the hospital. She is a diabetic, and her kidneys are... were... failing. She started showing signs of the flu," I said as I choked back a sob as the veil lifted and vivid images flooded back into my memory with a great assault as my mind took me backwards in time. Images of my mother's body laying outside of the cellar. I recalled how Anders had found me and broken the door down with his unit. I gasped loudly and closed my eyes shut, overwhelmed by the pain and the remembrance of how much I suffered on the floor. The pain. I wanted to die. "Oh my God, I remember!"

"Sir," Anders said in a low, concerned voice. "Should we wait until she's had some time to rest?"

"It's okay," Dr. Alden said in a compassionate tone. "Take your time, Ms. Vivienne. Would you prefer to wait?"

I took in a deep breath and continued as I rubbed my temples. "No. I want to get this over with. We all heard on the news and in the newspapers that the flu virus was spreading quickly. Our local news station said that the death toll was rising, and the Sheriff advised people to stay inside until the worst was over. The businesses shut down to comply with the Sheriff's order, except the grocery store and gas station. Nobody knew what to expect or why this was happening. Just last year it claimed the Bills' boy, but the flu has never taken so many lives all at once. My mother told me about the Spanish flu when she was a young girl. It killed so many, especially those living in poverty. Is it the Spanish flu?"

"No, this is something else, I'm afraid. Where was the mayor throughout all of this? Isn't he supposed to be communicating with the civilians? Was he compromised?"

"No, the Sheriff stated on the news that he was in contact with Mayor Briggs, who was away on business."

"Back up for me. You and your family live on the edge of town, correct?"

"Only my mother and I, and yes, we live on the edge of town."

I stopped and put my head in my hands and cried.

"If I would have known what would have happened, I would have never stepped out that door. She was all I had left."

"I understand. Please, trust me, I know how difficult all of this must be. Do you want to stop?"

"No, I know it is important that you have the answers you need from me."

"Is your mother originally from the area? What can you tell me about her?"

"My mother is... was... a negro mistress to a wealthy landowner down south, near Raleigh, North Carolina. She lived and worked on the plantation. We were also one of the biggest kept secrets, especially once I arrived. An unmarried colored woman living alone with a child on a plantation stood out. Once my mother became pregnant with me, she had challenges to contend with, including the cruelty of my father's family who knew the truth of it all, even if they never openly said a word.

"I miss waking up early to watch the sunrise above the treeline as I sunk my toes into the soft soil that feels like you are stepping into silky butter. My happiest of memories were when my mother and father could steal away moments together, and we would dance together to music from the radio. My father's eldest son, my half-brother, came after us with a gun the day after my father passed away. They gave us enough money to get out of state, along with a car that my father had left us and told us to never come back. We feared what his family would be capable of if we dared try to stay. We left the only home either of us had ever known, and we never looked back.

"We were transient most of my younger years, living in the automobile my father left her out of what she felt was charity. At least we had a tank full of gas, and my mother had money to call her own that the family never knew about. My father must have known what she would face once he passed on. After having a gun pulled on us by one of the local officials driving through the state, I questioned if we would survive to make the trip up north. My mother used the color of my skin to avoid trouble. She would tell people she was my live-in nanny and mentioned my father's name and his plantation to get us back on the road. She told them she was taking me to a boarding school where I would receive my education.

"Several close calls later, we finally made it up north. It did not take her long to realize we would need charity or kindness to get by. She had difficulty finding work. She could not find care for me, and I spent days where I would do my best to help her, whether it was cleaning homes or doing random jobs that would get us by and to have something in our belly. She did not dare put me in school yet until we found a safe place to settle and belong.

"When we arrived here, she begged a small cafe owner to allow her to work so she could at least feed me. That was the day that someone looked beyond the color of her skin and looked at her like a human being. Big Joe sat us both down for a meal in the back and asked my mom to show him what she could do in the kitchen. The rest is history. He gave us a place to stay, helped us get to know his favorite people in town, and protected us if we ever needed that kind of protection.

"I used to think that if all else fails in my life, there would always be a place for me working alongside my mother in the kitchen. I worked so hard to prove to her we are more than our birthright or circumstance, and it was all for nothing. Now there is nothing left, and I stand alone in a town where I never really knew my identity. Is all this just a terrible dream? I feel as if fate is trying to see just how much I can take before I crack."

"I think you're doing remarkably well," Dr. Alden looked up and over his wire frame reading glasses from his note taking. "Forgive me for saying this, but you don't appear to come from a negro lineage."

"I get that a lot," I told him politely. "My father's lineage traces back to Iraq, although he spoke little about it. My grandfather married a cultured woman from Paris, who was undoubtedly wealthy and cultured. He told everyone his ancestors came from France to avoid conflict. They came here as landowners and created a cotton and tobacco plantation."

"Your mother? Where does her lineage come from?"

"I'm not sure, to be honest. I thought little about it, at least not until now. Color is color, at least around here it is.

"Many people didn't exactly respond in kind with a woman of our color having a young biracial daughter. We just wanted to live life just like everyone else. My mother had darker skin than I did, obviously. Surprisingly, she herself was the daughter of a white woman and a colored farmhand, but according to her, his skin was as deep as the night."

"What happened to your grandparents?"

"They killed my grandfather shortly after they found out my grandmother was pregnant, claiming that he had raped her. After my mother was born, they raised her alongside other servants. They sent my grandmother away once she recovered, and they remarried her into a family that would have her. My mother never knew her.

"I passed easily for Mediterranean descent, which made my life easier to manage than the path my mother had to face all of her life. Life became complicated the instant others found out she was my mother. Parents had enough to say on their own, but then they would tell their children, and the harassment would start. The names that they would call us have never left me. I could never understand in the human experience why we can be so cruel.

"It's hard to explain to a child why she's being treated differently than other children. As a child, I did not see the color of our skin as a hindrance. I saw it as an opportunity to gain experience, to play, and to connect. In today's world, connecting is dangerous unless you know the people well enough. New folks that had moved into town, we simply did not get to know them unless it was through a close friend of our family that we knew we could trust. The list of people we trust is few."

"If you are well enough, I would like to go more in depth of your last day wandering around Stony Creek, before your mother locked you away in the basement. Are you well enough to do that?"

"Yes," I said, taking a deep breath in, dreading to relive the memories all over again. I appreciated the Professor's kindness. Yet there was something about him that did not feel quite right. It was his intellect. I often found highly intelligent men very intimidating, alongside their exceptionally large egos.

"That's a good girl. Please try to remember even the smallest and inconsequential detail. Assume that I know absolutely nothing. Describe as much as you can down to any details that really stand out to you as you recall from memory."

"Well, like I said, my mother was not doing well. I called ahead to the hospital. My mother was weakening every day, and she started running a fever. The receptionist told us we needed to give the police officer at the door our name. She warned us that there were no beds available. I did not recognize her voice, and she hung up before I could ask who she was. I would not have gone if I knew what was happening. The flu cannot kill an entire town, can it? I know there was no way we could have known, but if I had only known. I..."

I wanted to cry, but I knew if I started now, I would not stop until I cried myself into a quiet stillness that ended up with a throbbing headache and exhaustion that would lead to hours of sleep afterwards.

"I'm scared," I whispered, choking back on my words.

"You are safe here," Dr. Alden said softly. "I know reliving this is hard, but the information you give us is vital to piecing together the events of the past few weeks."

"It was like the town just fell asleep and never awakened again," I whispered, fighting the urge to drift back into the darkness to distract me from what I had agreed to do.

"You can do this Vivienne," Dr. Alden told me with sincerity, but underneath it I could feel his curiosity grow like a crushing weight of questions that had yet to leave his mouth. "Please, tell me. What did you see?"

"Death."

CHAPTER 6

ENTER THE NIGHTMARE

"Leaving our home, jumping into my mother's 1937 sky blue Willys, we had no inkling that we would move into a scene that is created in a nightmare. I can only explain it as a book of fiction unfolding before me. A story that I did not realize I played a part in, and yet I did not feel like it was real. Does that make sense?"

"Absolutely. Trauma has a sneaky habit of making our rational minds believe that we've gone insane or lost touch with reality."

"Do you want to hear something funny? I never told my mother this, but our car reminded me of a nosy school mistress. Its rounded nose and sloping grille just always hit me the wrong way. Although its seats are comfortable enough, I always felt like the car had a personality, and she was a grumpy ol' thing, fuming as the steam blew under the hood, erupting into a sizable plume as she puttered about when she did not feel running, which was becoming increasingly common. The car had more personality than most people let on. It is why I isolated myself so much. People scare me, especially when you cannot see what is under the hood. You never know what they're really thinking."

"That is a very astute observation," Dr. Alden said with a crooked smile. "I'm impressed that you can see the truth of how society is conditioning us to hold on to our secrets and present ourselves as the wrapper. What would a day in the life of a Stony Creek resident look like if everything were functioning normally?"

"Oh," I sighed, taking it all in from memory. "It's a remarkable sight! fall heralds a breathtaking presentation of yellow, reds, and oranges mingled with the stark contrast of the various pine trees scattered on the hills that surround the town as the subtle scent of pine settles over the town like a warm blanket. The smell of wood burning from fireplaces after a long sleep reminds me of hot cocoa sitting by the warm hearth. This time of year, there is a hint of winter's chill in the air. You can smell the snow at the higher elevations. Our town, being in a small valley, meant that every fall, a low fog would roll in from the lake. There is nothing quite like the change of seasons in Stony Creek. It is an experience for the senses.

"The township, every year, decorates the main square to celebrate the fall harvest festival. Pumpkins sit on every corner along with random piles of hay bales that make a stark contrast against the colorful displays of pumpkins, tissue paper floral arrangements, and paper cutouts of leaves, gourds, and scarecrows from shop windows. It made decorating Halloween much easier to contend with. Fall is always the prelude to Halloween, and then Thanksgiving. I loved walking around the town square to watch the children moving from door-to-door, dressed up in their small costumes as the hollow eyes of pumpkins flickered in a soft yellow glow. Every year was the same, and I must admit that I felt safe in that certainty of what to expect.

"The trees lining the streets stood tall and proud as they waved their colorful branches. It was such a wonderful delight when a strong breeze would pass through, and the trees would release their leaves to float down like rain on the top of our heads. I used to love playing in the leaves as a child, and now that I am older, I used to sit on a bench and watch children play in piles of leaves. The memory of their laughter is tearing me alive. Their voices muted, like they never existed. Here one moment, and then they are just gone. How does that happen? Are we just dreams moving through time? Do we even really exist at all?"

"That's an exceptionally good question. What do you think?"

"If nothing feels real, then how does it exist? The town itself, with its well-manicured streets, would appear as the perfect place. As the town slept, nightmares dwelled in the swells of the shadows, threatening to linger and devour all in its path. At the breaking of dawn, a shimmer of hope glistens on the morning dew as the sunrise peaks through the cloud barrier in gallant beams of heavenly light in a town waiting to awaken. Can evil linger just below the surface, lying in wait as it crawls up from the depths of hell? A town devoured by darkness, all hope eradicated, and I do not know how I should have felt about any of it! What is true?!"

"I'm not sure how to answer that," he said calmly. "Would you like to take a break and continue this another time?"

"No! I have to do this!" I could not help the feelings that continued to engulf me in waves. I moved between memories of comfort, to anger, to longing, and then I would plummet into the hell abyss of fear, sadness, and overwhelm.

"Continue when you're ready," Dr. Alden told me as he motioned for Anders to stand up and leave his seat so that he could sit near me. Anders moved to stand at the end of my cot. "Anders, please grab our young lady some water."

"Yes, sir," he told him with a small salute. He grabbed a canteen and helped me shift my weight so that I could sit up without doubling back over in pain. He piled pillows and blankets behind me, propping me up so that I was sitting comfortably. Sitting up was a novel experience, and it made me feel nauseous.

"Everything around me whispered of death. What once felt vibrant and alive felt dormant, lifeless, and without joy. Even the vibrant orange in the pumpkins appeared muted. Like a thick wool blanket, it covered Stony Creek with darkness, sadness, and confusion. The closer we drove towards the town square, the heavier that feeling became. It was stifling! I don't know how to explain it, but before we even arrived at the town square, it was a sense of dread that I couldn't shake."

"Did anything stand out on your way there?"

"Yes! With the number of vehicles parked along both sides of main street, you would think there was a festival or parade happening. Eventually, the road itself became blocked by parked cars. We were about a quarter of a mile from the hospital, which was on the other side of the square. My mother said she was well enough to get there if we took our time for her to rest along the way. We did not have a choice except to get out and start walking. When we realized the cars were not moving, we had little choice."

"Did you see anything that stood out as you walked? Were there any people in the cars that you passed by? Anything outside the ordinary?"

"My mother told me not to look in the cars, so I didn't. I could see what looked like a barricade that blocked off the road into the town square up ahead. We heard people yelling off in the distance, and we were not sure what to make of it. It made us both feel nervous. We were close to town square when I looked up and saw a swollen arm hanging out the window of a dusty grey pickup truck. The color of her skin did not look right, and I could not look away. I kept my eyes on the ground until we reached the barricade.

"A grand statue towers over the town square. Her watchful eyes keep sight over a once bustling town center with the old and young alike. The tall figure wrapped in a sheer fabric covering her body, her body plastered in aged marbled white, resembling a time traveler from a time in history long past standing tall and proud at the center of a hauntingly majestic fountain surrounded by wood benches riddled with leaves. She was our town's witness, seeing the young and old alike, first dates, wedding ceremonies, and gatherings to remember a loved one that has passed on. I liked to think of her as a graceful ballerina ready to leap into flight in a beautiful twirl."

Dr. Alden appeared lost in his thoughts, and I wondered what point in my story had him so captivated.

"She sounds beautiful," he whispered. He looked at me with intense sadness. As he stared at me, his eyes stared through me as if he were in a trance. "Untouched by all that exists around her, uncorrupted by the desires of man, by the will of God. Immortal... Untouched..."

"She is truly all of that. I wanted very much to be like her when I grew up, but being graceful was never one of my strong suits. The statue, the graceful ballerina. They erected the stone to resemble the Greek goddess Persephone, queen of the underworld. Our small-town relishes in the change of the seasons. She is forever in mid-dance with her hands stretched out in front of her, ready to twirl her way into her lover, Hades' arms. You could almost feel the way the veil would move around her, and the way she carried her stance."

Dr. Alden's electric ocean blue eyes caught mine and I could not help but shift uncomfortably and bashfully look down as the corner of his mouth lifted slightly.

"What is the main square like?" Dr. Alden asked me, masterfully switching the topic back on point.

"The main square holds several small shops, the town hall, police station, and the hospital that surrounds a park with a white gazebo adorned with twisting twigs of once vibrant ivy. The town square is the perfect example of thoughtful planning. Families could gather to enjoy the change of seasons, as well as come together in times of celebration, but that... that day. They... They..."

"Take a deep breath, Ms. Vivienne," Dr. Alden said gently, leaning in to move closer to me as put his clipboard down on my legs and grabbed my hands to hold in his. I appreciated the gesture, but I could not escape the chill that stemmed not from the cool air moving through the tent, but from within. Something about him was not right. His hands were cool to the touch, pale, long, and slender. They matched his stature perfectly. "You are safe. I will let nothing happen to you. Would you like to stop?"

"No," I said as the tears came freely now. I looked over to Anders for comfort, and he nodded and smiled at me. His genuine warmth and kindness made me feel safe. Dr. Alden seemed kind enough, but vastly different and worlds apart from what I felt emanating from Anders. Dr. Alden scared me. I did not understand why he did, but every cell in my body told me to run away from him.

"Let me know when you are ready to continue." Dr. Alden lingered a moment more, staring strangely at me, and finally turned away from me as withdrew his hands from mine. He stood up and went to stand in the back of the tent, pacing back and forth. Fear threaded its way throughout my abdomen, tightening into a painful spasm, followed by a wave of nausea that swept through my entire body. I felt faint, and I had to shift slightly, grabbing onto Anders' hand that found its way to mine. I took a moment to steady myself, and then nodded at Anders to let him know I was okay to continue.

"We approached one of the wooden benches near the fountain. From behind, we could not tell they were dead. The smell in the air there was unfathomable. I assumed the smell was coming from the... the dead man in the fountain. When we went around the bench, we... we recognized them. It was Mr. and Mrs. Johnson. They were in their seventies, and Mrs. Johnson gave out candy every day after school. It was tradition for the neighborhood kids to go to her house to say hello and grab a sweet treat while Mr. Johnson read his paper on the porch or watered his lawn. She was one of the few people that was always kind to me. Her head lay on her husband's shoulder, her eyes closed, as if she fell asleep dreaming of happier days. His arm wrapped around her, holding her close while the other held his chest. His head lowered to his chest. My mother thought he may have passed from a heart attack. He... He did not look like the others."

"I know this is difficult, but you mentioned he looked different from the others. What did the others look like?

Could you be more specific about what you noticed about Mrs. Johnson?" Dr. Alden stopped pacing and stood in with peaked interest.

"Mrs. Johnson had thick dark blood coming from her eyes, ears, and mouth. Purplish-black veins covered her skin. The dark blood looked more like tar, rather than blood. The others looked the same."

"Interesting," he said while he lowered his head over his clipboard and busily scribbled down notes.

"I can't even imagine what they went through. Why did they go to that bench? Was it special to them? Did they know they were dying? I had so many questions running through my mind! They built their lives here, and then it was just gone. Lost to time. Fragments. What happens to all those memories now?"

"During times of trauma, people will often return to where they have found the fondest memories that bring them peace or happiness," Anders responded as he sat back down next to me, gently squeezing my hands. "Their memories will live on through you."

Dr. Alden interrupted with a slight clearing of his throat. "Did you notice anything peculiar about the body in the fountain?"

"No, unless you count on the fact that his shoes were missing and his feet were a pasty white with purplish bruises or something on them. His arm and hand that were visible were a purplish gray with black lines running through his veins like Mrs. Johnson. I did not touch him. He looked so bloated that if I shifted his weight to roll him over, I feared he would burst like a water balloon.

"The fountain had a lot of leaves from the surrounding foliage in the town square, causing an almost mutated ripple as the water battled against the thickening surface for freedom. He was face down with one hand touching the foot of the statue. It looked like he was worshipping her when he left this life. He was not bobbing for pennies. I made dozens of wishes in that fountain. I understood enough about life to understand that we outgrow childish hopes and dreams, but I cannot help but wonder about the number of wishes that lay under the surface of the floating leaves, in a square once so alive and welcoming, and now swallowed in the mouth of madness. The fog that rolled in as we continued to walk made it all feel so surreal. The nightmare held us in its grips, and it was like we could not wake up.

"As we continued to walk, we noticed that most of the stores had windows broken with evidence of vandalism and destruction. I have never seen anything like this here. These were people that knew one another. These were people they knew their entire lives. It felt like we were all strangers, moving around each other, but not existing together. How can people just suddenly forget who they are?"

"Uncertainty and fear can do strange things, and panic with even the smallest populations can develop quickly into a very scary situation," Dr. Alden responded from his corner of the tent with his head still down as he wrote notes on his clipboard. "It's not uncommon in times of crisis. I know that is not the answer you are looking for. These situations can bring about the most primal of instincts out in humans. I would not view it as a need for logical reasoning in this situation. It's more of an irrational emotional response."

"Whatever the reason is, I don't understand any of what has happened here. In times of crisis, the last thing we should forget is what makes us human."

"Please continue."

"We walked from the fountain and headed for the church that was the highlight of the town square. Its polished white paint set itself apart from the rest of the town square. Instead of usual brick and wood, the building appeared to glow as the sun's rays shifted behind the building. The light hit the roof at the right angle, and the cross on top illuminated its elongated shadow to where we were standing across the street. How we must have looked in the cross's shadow in a town surrounded by the ghosts of the dead. I'm sure we looked like two scared women trying to find something tangible in a new world that felt completely foreign."

"We saw Mrs. Matthews, in her best blue floral church dress, screaming at the top of her lungs, coming out from the alleyway. We tried calling out to her, but she did not hear us. She ran into the church so fast. She was the first person we had come across that was alive, and we hoped she had answers to what was happening. We were trying our best to catch up to her when Larry Mills, the local grocery store clerk, almost ran right into us, buck naked aside from a bra on his head and he was wearing red lipstick like a clown and had on a pearl necklace and high heels. He danced around us in circles, screaming and laughing at the same time. He had the beginning of the black veins running out from his chest, like branches reaching out across the skin. Not as large and apparent as the others we had seen so far, but in what looked like the beginning stages. We were grateful when he eventually lost interest in us and went running in the opposite direction."

I took a deep breath as Larry Mills' face came into my memory. I shivered and held the blankets closer to my chest.

"There was something else about the people that died or had the virus that I can't shake from my mind."

"What's that?" Dr. Alden asked me with peaked interest.

"Their blood-red eyes."

CHAPTER 7

THE CHURCH

"Did you reach the church?" Anders asked with a childlike innocence of a bedtime story filled with fantastic adventure. While I found this trait endearing, the truth of this story did not allow me the same expression or value of wonderment. It was far from an adventure, and it was a tale that I vowed to myself that I would never repeat. I am living in a nightmare, and like the story that I tell them now, that nightmare refused to end. I wanted to wake up. Dr. Alden looked at Anders with annoyance and shook his head. My gut feeling told me they did not like each other much. They were both complete opposites of one another in terms of personality, and I dare to assume upbringing.

"We reached the church, and in all honesty, I wish we hadn't. We found Preacher Evans standing in the middle of the bushes in the church's yard. His light blonde hair was hard to miss amongst the thinning, dark green leaves and wiry branches. My mother called his name, and he waved at us both with a big smile on his face, as if nothing were wrong at all. My mother walked towards him, and then she held up her arm, trying to stop me from getting any closer. It was already too late. I was close enough to see that he was not wearing any pants. He was urinating in the bushes with his legs all scratched up and bleeding. In his mind, it did not appear that he thought there was any wrongdoing. To me, it seemed like he thought he was simply watering the lawn. He beckoned us to join the others and pray for the end of times. His skin was so pale, his eyes were dark, sunken in, and his eyes were red."

"Did anything else stand out to you about him? Did he have the same markings along his veins as the others?"

"No, I saw nothing like that. He was just off, and not acting like himself. He did not look well, and his eyes reminded me of the others. His light blue eyes were no longer visible. His pupils were so big, and the whites were completely red. If he had any markings, they were somewhere on his body that I could not see."

"Did you or your mother have any thoughts about what was happening?"

"Can a virus make people act strangely?"

"There are some viruses that we are aware of that can affect the mind, like rabies, for example. Why do you ask?"

"I asked my mother what was going on, and she said that there must be drugs in the water supply for everyone to lose their minds. I did not think it was drugs, not after... not after we saw them. Please, don't make me remember." I let loose a long sigh and looked towards Dr. Alden pleadingly.

"I know this is hard, to see what you've seen, Ms. Vivienne..."

"You do not know," I snapped at him, cutting him off. Tears rolled down my cheeks, and I felt like a rubber band that had stretched too far and had finally broken. "We did not see them, not until we turned back towards the steps and walked past Preacher Evans. The bushes blocked them from our view. We did not take the main path that runs through the middle, right up the steps into the main entrance. We walked around the far side and went through the park to avoid the gazebo since it was the path we would take if we were walking to the hospital."

"What did you see?"

"Mrs. Matthews, she must have seen them, and that's why she ran into the church with such terror. You do not understand! How could you? You wouldn't be able to understand unless you were there and saw them," I exclaimed with a raised voice bordering on hysterics. "God, I just wanted to run! It... it... was a family, with two small children who passed from this virus. Their skin, covered with the black veins and like the others they had blood coming from their eyes, nose, mouth, and their ears, too. Do you think their insides just melted? Can a virus do that? There was so much blood! The children's mother lay over the top of them, with a gunshot wound on her forehead. The rest of the back of her head splattered against the steps. The father still held the gun in his hand, with his body slumped over against the side of the stairs. They both had signs of the illness, their exposed skin, and the same black colored veins except they were smaller and not all over like the others."

"Vivienne," Dr. Alden said, trailing off, taking his glasses off and rubbing his eyes. "I know how hard this is. Please, believe me."

"I can't even imagine what it would feel like to watch your own child pass before your eyes." I glared angrily at him as the tears let loose. "Hearing you say that you know it is hard triggers me on a level I can't even describe! These were children that once lived with joy in their hearts, playing in the same cursed fountain, and they will never play or hold that joy again! Tell me why! Why did they have to die?! All that remains are bloated bodies that barely resemble the human beings they once were. How can you really know?!"

"Please," he said, looking up at me sincerely. "Forgive me if my words have unsettled you or if I don't appear to be as empathic as I should. My detachment comes from years of training to detach myself from the emotional side of situations such as this. It is my job to search through the data and find answers, and hopefully a means to save lives. I have been through similar situations just like this one, Ms. DuSan, and each is horrible and the experience, if I am honest with you, takes a toll on my mental wellbeing every time. Every time, I feel myself slipping just a little more. The nightmares of my experiences continue to haunt me still. There is a reason I need to detach myself from this, alright? Not that I am not void of feeling, it is because I need to protect my emotional wellbeing so that I can focus on finding answers to ensure this does not happen again. Right now, you are a part of something that goes unseen by the public's eye. If it were, it would produce mass hysteria, and it would create civil unrest that might claim more lives. People out there right now will never understand our role and our jobs in all of this, and they will never know the horrors that you have survived. Every individual in this unit is a silent hero in my eyes, including you. Please believe me, Ms. DuSan, I sincerely empathize."

"I'm... Oh, God! I'm so sorry," I said, feeling overwhelmed with guilt for snapping at him while assuming his role in all of this. I put my face in my hands and cried heavily. What is wrong with me?!

Dr. Alden surprised me with his sincerity as he touched my shoulder softly. "Do you need a break? I would like to go into more detail about what you saw with the family when you are ready. I know asking may seem heartless, but it could give us additional clues to look into."

"No, no, I'm fine. I do not need a break," I told him as I wiped my tears with the bedsheet. "I do not want to go through this again. Will I have to go through this again?"

"Hopefully not. I will do my best to ensure that they are mere follow-up questions to your original statements. Remember to pause when you need to. Robert," he called out. Moments later, another younger man that looked like the perfect likeness to Dr. Alden came into the tent.

"Yes," the man asked in a soft and well-mannered tone that reminded me of what a butler from a rich household would sound like, almost whimsical.

"Please ensure the mess tent has some broth made ready for our Ms. Vivienne first thing in the morning, would you?"

"Of course," Robert said, giving me a small nod and hurrying out of the tent.

I looked at Dr. Alden curiously and looked back at the opening of the tent where Robert left. I repeated the back-and-forth head movement as I tried to place their relationship with one another. It could be happenstance, but the resemblance was uncanny.

"I see you are observant, Vivienne," he said, amused. "Robert is my oldest son and assistant. You might say he's a chip off the old block."

"Forgive me. I hope I was not staring! It is not the first time my curiosity has gotten me into trouble," I mumbled.

"Nonsense," he said with a small chuckle.

"You look rather young to have a child of his age."

"I will take that as a compliment. I like to think of it as good genetics. My father looked a mere age of forty when he was in his seventies. What do you think, Anders? Should we add a new nickname to the pile? Baby face? The soldiers like to think I do not hear the nicknames they have given me. What was the latest one, Anders? Professor Fuddy-Duddy? Or Professor Gobbledygook? Something about the need to give my monotone voice a personality. Apparently, I lost my personality when I was in diapers." He emphasized his tone, dripping with sarcasm. Anders looked like he wanted to melt into the chair he was sitting on. He lowered his head and avoided eye contact with us both. "Are you ready to continue, my dear? I would like to wrap this up so you can get some rest."

How am I going to get through this? A voice that sounded like my mother filled my mind with reason. You are honoring the lives of those who passed by telling your story. Even if the haunted memories came from the heart of a stranger, a woman that remained unnoticed for being different and silently repressed by a culture that knew no better.

"I have faced many hardships in my life, Dr. Alden, but looking at those children who would never again sit in a swing or play in the park surrounded by laughter, it... it destroyed me. I did not want to turn away from them, even though I knew I should. I felt the powerful need to protect them. I felt like I was betraying them by leaving them there. My mother convinced me we needed to keep moving. She held me by the shoulders and guided me up the stairs and into the church. She was weakening. I will never forget that when she... saw... them... she crumbled to her knees and yelled out, asking God why he would allow such a thing to happen. I did not have the heart to tell her God abandoned us long ago. Why would a God that loves us so deeply allow this atrocity to go unnoticed, unpunished, or unheard of to continue to happen? I know that Preacher Evans told me it was all in God's grand design, but I will never understand what has happened here!"

"This is an age-old question, and you're not alone in feeling this way. There are those people that view this as a grave injustice against humanity. Rape, disease and illness, murder, wars, and famine. It brings out the worst in humanity, but it can also bring out our best. There is simply no answer I can provide that will take away the suffering that they have experienced. It is why I went into this field of research, and to get my PhD. I wanted to have influence, regardless of how small, it is a step in the right direction to understanding how this all works. I am more like you than you realize. During the second wave of the Spanish flu, I lost my mother. My wife and our son Robert lived just outside of town. By the time we knew what was happening, my mother was dead, and over half of the town soon followed. We were lucky to have survived when so many died. It left a mark on me." He paused, taking his glasses off and wiping at his eyes again. He cleared his throat and then continued. "Did you know the family?"

"I'm so sorry for your loss, Dr. Alden," I told him as our teary gaze met one another, both of us sharing a connection and lost in our grief. He smiled at me in understanding, and he held me in his gaze until I realized neither one of us was talking. I looked over at Anders, who was staring at me curiously. "No, I didn't know them. With the paper mill just outside of town, the town has seen a great deal of growth in the last five years. Our economy has steadily improved, and with that we have had more shops open along main street and the town square for those that can afford them. When we first moved here, it was nothing like it resembles today. I guess I am eating my words here, right? Our town is nothing like it was not even a month ago."

"What happened when you went into the church? I am assuming you went inside, yes?" I could tell he was trying to keep me focused, and in a small way I appreciated it, but my brain wanted me to pause and take a moment, an exceptionally long moment and allow myself the ability to catch up to the experience, this memory of what had happened. To make sense of it, but I also knew that I just could not. Was there really any sense in any of this?

"Yes, we went inside. We had to step over the family to get into the church to check on Mrs. Matthews. The double doors leading into the church were open. The door held in place by a large brick was slightly off its hinge, titled backwards at an angle. The other door moved back and forth, sensitive to even the slightest breeze moving through. When we stepped inside, it did not remind me of a place of worship. It reminded me more of a haunted house setup with its sole purpose to horrify anyone that steps inside.

"The shadows danced and played with my mind as the gentle wind played with the tree branches just outside, mingling with the colored hues of the stained-glass windows. It shrouded the pews with oddly shaped, moving shadows like long fingers as the fog continued to move in and swirl around our feet. The effect made the main path that led up to the pulpit feel like an eerie nightmare where you know you must get from one place to another, but you also know that there is something alive in the fog and it is watching every move you make waiting for you at your end destination. I do not care to think about it."

"I do not blame you! I would have walked out," Anders said, his eyes wide. "That would have given me such a fright."

"Mrs. Matthews stood in the middle of the aisle with her back to us. The hair on my arms stood up, and I knew something was right. The inner battle between the logical mind and my inner critic that was telling me to get the hell out of there, but my heart interfered with my common sense. I called out to her and asked if she was alright. She turned around to face us and then moved her overweight body into a crouched position. She reminded me of a cat that is surprised by an enemy. She started growling at us, and my gut told me to run. My mother kept calling her by name, Martha, and when we were within her line of sight, her head tilted downwards so that we could not see her face well in the shadows.

"She lunged at us, and my mother and I fell backwards, kicking and hitting at her as we scrambled to get away from her. My mother tore off her oversized pearl necklace and the beads erupted into the air as they scattered across the ground. Mrs. Matthews grabbed at her neck and started screaming. We moved towards the pulpit, and when I looked back, Mrs. Matthews hunched over, her hands outstretched like claws, and she was running towards us like she planned to ram us with her head. I screamed and pulled my mother towards the door off to the side of the pulpit and down the stairs. I slammed the door behind us and used a chair that was sitting off to the side to jam the door by putting the chair at an angle under the handle. It would not buy us the time we needed, but it would buy us precious moments to gain a head start. The other exit was through the basement and out the cellar doors.

"We made our way down into the dark basement. There was only one small light bulb hanging from the ceiling in the basement, and it barely made a dent in a room filled with shadows. We stood in the dark, attempting to find a path through the maze. My mother and I jumped as we heard Mrs. Matthew's weight shift on the wooden stairs nearby, causing them to creak with her heavy, labored breathing, followed by the sounds of Mrs. Matthews breaking the door down with her body weight. Mrs. Mathews screamed in a deep throaty way that sounded more male than female as we heard her tumble into object after object, followed by a loud crash of broken glass. I knocked over boxes and threw chairs over to slow her down. We had to climb over a pile of tables in a rack that was in front of the cellar style doors that led outside. It took longer than I had expected. My mother was not looking well, and she was slowing down.

"My mother reached the cellar door first and opened one door with ease, but the other one wouldn't budge. We would have to climb the steep steps like a ladder and squeeze ourselves through to get out. I was right behind her when a hand grabbed my ankle and began pulling me backwards. I screamed for my mother as I latched onto both sides of the door. My mother grabbed hold of my arm and began pulling while I kept kicking as hard as I could. My foot eventually landed into something that felt more like a head rather than a soft body, and her grip loosened. I fell on top of my mother, and I quickly got up and shut the door with force, and helped my mother get up. Mrs. Matthew's throaty laughter was just on the other side. We left as fast as our clumsy feet could take us. I have never seen my mother look so horrified. My mother said something under her breath that I didn't want to acknowledge, but what if she was right?"

"What did she say?" Dr. Alden asked with a crossed brow, as if he was trying to determine if my story was real or a hallucination. I wish it were a hallucination. They haunt my dreams.

"My mother said at the end of days, the dead shall arise. What if we are at the end of days, and what the crazy man said in the emergency room is true? He told me that the mouth of hell is open. Do you believe the dead can rise, Dr. Alden?"

CHAPTER 8

THE NURSE

"I've studied many cultures, and I have read of possession in religion and superstition of the undead in voodoo, but I have seen nothing in the field that science can't explain. Do not worry yourself with any of that nonsense. What happened next?"

"We passed through the alleyway until we reached the small sidewalk in front of the realtor and travel office. There was a man not much older than I am, sprawled out, lying face down on the sidewalk, dead, surrounded by a pool of his own blood. As we walked by him, a ray of sunlight hit him at an angle, and I noticed his skin looked unusual."

"What do you mean?" Dr. Alden perked right up, his pen at the ready as he leaned forward to listen more intently.

"I mean that his skin did something it shouldn't be doing. Yes, he looked pale and flushed. He was sick with the flu. There appeared to be a fine mesh, like threads of a spider web on his skin. I do not know how else to explain it. Do you know how spider webs look just as the sun hits them after a morning frost or a misty rain? That is exactly what it looked like. The weirdest thing about it though, was when I approached his body to get a closer look, the mesh appeared to shift and shimmer slightly, and then the mesh began moving its way around the corpse! It reminded me of how caterpillars cocoon, but that's simply crazy, right?"

"The team recovering the bodies didn't make any mention of anything like this." He looked over his notes and then looked up at me, a glimmer in his eyes. "Holy mackerel!

That is unusual. I hate to ask this of you, but how did he appear compared to the others in terms of discoloration? The others appeared to have been deceased longer, compared to him?"

"He just looked like he had the flu. He looked very pale. It was his eyes that clued me in that he was dead. They were open, and well, you cannot mistake a dead person's eyes, can you? I did not like how I felt when I looked into his eyes. So empty, like a shell."

"How do you think he died?"

"With that much blood? This is above my pay grade. You are the doctor. A gunshot or a stab wound? The whole town went cockeyed."

"What happened next?"

"When my mother and I saw the mesh move on his skin, she dragged me to my feet, and I was blindly following her across the street. There were roadblocks and cars blocking the road that led to the hospital, so we had to go around and navigate through the grocery store's small parking lot. I tripped over a woman that I did not see because I was too busy looking at everything else around me. There were cries and screaming coming from the direction of the hospital. I kept trying to look and see if I could see anything, but all I could see were the rows of trees and a lot of vehicles blocking my line of sight."

"Was there anything remarkable about the woman?"

"She died with her groceries scattered about her. She did not appear to be like the others. She was bleeding from a gash in her skull. She had a broken leg, with the bone protruding from the skin, and her stockings ripped in multiple locations with evidence that the birds or other local wildlife had found her."

"Were there any clues around her that would suggest what happened to her?"

"A red Ford truck had crashed into the front of the grocery store just a short distance away from where we were. It is highly likely the truck hit her before hitting the store head on. Glass, splintered wood, and boxes of soda crackers strewn all about. We did not go to the truck to see if anyone was inside it or alive. It... it was all too much for both of us by then. We saw looters inside, running around with their shopping carts. Someone from inside the store fired a gun. We heard yelling, so we just kept moving as quickly as we could. My mother could not run at this point. She... She was really having a challenging time. As we weaved our way around all the cars that littered the streets, we entered the hospital parking lot and we both froze, and my mother sat down on the ground and cried."

Anders' hand squeezed mine gently. Looking into his eyes, I felt a small surge of strength, and I smiled at him. I squeezed his hand, thankful he was there. "Your mother was a real moxie!"

"Her courage doesn't end there. What she did for me, I can never repay."

"What did you see as you approached the hospital?" He asked, pressing me further. I could not help but feel he was searching for something. *What is he looking for?* I felt an inner knowing that he knew more than he let on.

"A little over a quarter of the town must have been there. There were so many people trying to get into the hospital or find help. So many were sick and laying on the ground. There were tents up with sleeping bags inside filled with families. Others were angry and yelling while arguing with the police officers guarding the hospital. There were others wandering around, looking confused and so very lost as the blood dripped from their ears, nose, and eyes. The virus was spreading fast, but all I could focus on was my mother. I held her for the longest time as she cried.

"We spotted a young police officer walking through the crowd putting names on a list while handing out numbers. I had to squeeze my way through to get to him. I explained to him why we were there. He warned us that there was no guarantee they would even have time to see us, and he showed us the list of names ahead of us. He explained that the hospital was short staffed, and over half of the staff had already fallen sick or died with the flu virus. I explained to him I was Dr. Kines' secretary, and I convinced him I would help if we could get my mother inside.

"He helped us clear a path, while some people yelled at us while others cried and pleaded. It did not escape my attention that he was coughing as well, and his eyes were turning red. He did not act like he was sick. He kept his head held high, and he just kept moving. I hoped, against all odds, that he would survive, but my gut told me differently. I knew at that moment that we were all going to die. It was only a matter of time. It is why I wanted to go help. The truth that people would die on the steps of the hospital tore at me like a deep wound, and I hated feeling so helpless.

"I turned around to look behind me when I heard a familiar voice, and I saw our neighbor Mrs. Burley. She was begging a police officer at the barricade just down the steps from the main entrance to the hospital. She yelled at him, telling him that her husband was barely breathing, and she could not move him by herself. The officer apologized profusely and told her someone would be with her as soon as they could and explained that they were doing everything that they could to help. She looked up and saw us, and she called our names, begging us to help her. When I turned away from her with her cries following me, I lost a piece of myself right there and then. I keep asking myself what more could I have done, but none of the answers I give myself bring me any peace.

"At the barricade, there were men who were not local and wearing uniforms from neighboring towns. We checked in at the front desk with a teenager working at the desk. She said her father was the doctor on call, and they came in from two towns over. She said that the receptionist that was working the desk fell ill, and she had to take over."

"Private Larson," Dr. Alden called out. I saw an armed soldier enter from the other side of the tent and watched as he saluted everyone present. "Please tell Roger to check with other local police departments to see which towns are missing personnel and medical staff. We need to get a handle on this now."

"Yes, Sir, Dr. Alden, Sir," the private said in a loud, acknowledging voice with a final salute before departing. "Private Andrews is on guard rotation, Sir!"

"Guard rotation? Are you scared I will try to run away?"

"No, no," Dr. Alden lifted his hand in a stop motion. "Nothing like that. This is merely for your own protection. You could not notice, but you are in a camp filled with male soldiers and scientists. This is simply a precaution out of the utmost respect."

"I see," I said, not believing a word of his flashy, charismatic smile. I looked over at Anders, who refused to make eye contact with me. This was not the entire story.

"What do you mean by getting a handle on this?"

"It is nothing for you to be concerned about. We want to make sure the virus hasn't left this town, and that the families or other local law enforcement officials don't wander into a quarantine zone."

"Quarantine zone?" What were they scared of? I felt the familiar pangs of anxiety building in my belly, of yet just one more thing to think about on top of everything else that resembled a long building list of denial.

"This area is off limits until we can see what we are dealing with. It is a precaution to protect other towns from suffering from the same fate. What was the state of the hospital?" he asked with a slight clearing of his throat to grab my attention.

"It wasn't like anything I had ever seen before. Both wards were full. There were people in beds, people on the floor, along with deceased people sharing the same space, covered with bloody blankets, waiting for removal. One of Dr. Kines' nurses, Tanya, she was moving slowly from bed to bed, trying to make everyone as comfortable as possible. She looked like she was ready to collapse. She was sick, covered in black veins, and bleeding like the others. She had a bottle of morphine, and she was telling one patient that this would help put her at ease in her hysterics. I watched as the morphine took effect and her body relaxed and her eyes closed. She looked so peaceful, but by the look of her, she only had a matter of minutes before she succumbed to the virus. The morphine was a blessing in disguise.

"My mother led me down the hall and up the stairs to Dr. Stevens' office."

"I'm sorry to interrupt. Who is Dr. Stevens?"

"He's a specialist at the hospital. He manages those hard cases that require extra care, like my mother."

"Please continue."

"When we got there, we found him. He looked like he was napping on his desk at first. As I approached him asking if he was alright, I noticed the blood. I held onto my mother as we went down the hall to see if we could find another doctor. My mother held onto the wall like it was the only solid thing she understood. A nurse I was not familiar with walked up to us. My mother cried out to her, screaming that Dr. Stevens was dead. The nurse looked at me with wild eyes. I do not know how to describe it.

"She screamed at the top of her lungs, grabbing her head with both of her hands as she dropped to her knees. She crawled towards us, and it was like she could not even see my mom. She told me she was going to give me the gift of life. She was talking one minute and then it was like something inside her just snapped. She just went crazy, leaped towards me, and started screaming at the top of her lungs again. She stopped attacking me, turned around in circles as she cried while laughing at someone that was not there. She raised her hands to her ears and screamed as if she was in pain, telling them to stop yelling at her. Then she looked at me and smiled. She told me I would help the voices to stop."

"Did you attempt to leave?"

"No, we should have. It is difficult to explain, but it

was like we could not look away from her. She was scary and beautiful at the same time. The nurse slashed her wrist with a scalpel, licked the blood on her wrist, and then before I could react, she rushed at me, screaming. I tried to hold her off, but she was stronger than she looked. She moved her arm like she was going to grab my mother, who was standing behind me trying to help, and I shifted my weight and moved my arms ahead of me to shove her back, but she was so fast. I have seen no one alive move that fast.

"She screamed, rushed at me so fast that I did not realize what had happened at first. At least, not until I fell back into my mother and I saw all the blood. Right at that same moment, the crowd outside went crazy. We could hear glass shattering, and all panic ensued. The nurse started laughing, and then ran down the hall, still laughing as she heard the gunshots. We heard people screaming, and my mother knew it was time for us to leave. The pain was nothing like I have ever felt before. It did not register right away. Not until I saw all the blood and realized it was coming from me. My mother, she... she helped me up, and we left through the back entrance.

"The smell wasn't apparent until we left, but as we exited the back entrance, we found a line of bodies leading up to the hospital, like a long, waiting line. I did not notice what they died from. It was a bit of a blur. My mother cried, telling me it was going to be alright, as she supported my body weight as we moved through the trail of bodies. I was shaking uncontrollably by then.

"We heard a loud scream coming from behind us, and we turned to see a screaming naked man missing an arm as he came running out of the hospital building just behind us. As he came running towards us, I noticed his eyes were red, and he had blood coming out of his mouth, ears, and nose like the others. The man ran past us like he did not even see us. He ran right into a brick wall directly ahead of us, as if he could not see it was there or like he was blind. He knocked himself out and just laid on the ground, twitching. We kept moving.

"Things started getting a little foggy after that. I know we walked at least four blocks away from the town square and the hospital. We found a car with the keys still inside, and my mother said they would not mind since it was an emergency. She helped me get into the back, and she started the engine and started making the long way around to get back to our house. We were near the factory when the car came to a screaming halt, followed by a tremendous thud as the car ran over something exceptionally large. The impact had me rolling out of the backseat and onto the floor of the car.

"I sat up as best as I could, and my mother stepped out of the car looking at whatever she ran over. Moments later, she came running back in. I sat up and looked out the back window. I saw someone laying in the street. He looked like Mr. Perkins. He looked like the others that had the flu, except his skin was a pasty whitish gray like the man around my age. My mother was crying and apologizing to him as she drove off. I turned back around to look back out the window, and I know the fever, or the trauma, must have been messing with me because I saw Mr. Perkins get up, set his broken leg back into place, and he started limping as he headed towards the town.

"I blacked out off and on as she drove, but I overheard her praying as she asked God to save her little girl. I tried to tell her to stop worrying, and that I would be fine, but my voice did not want to speak. My entire body felt so heavy and tired. When we made it home, she helped me inside the house and took me down to the basement, where we had all our supplies. She laid me down on the ground and poured whiskey on the wound. She lit a candle, then she held a knife in the open flame. She took the heated knife to my abdomen, and I remember hearing my own screams as if they were not coming from me at all. It was a very odd experience. I must have passed out from all the pain or the blood loss.

"I don't know what time or day it was when I had awakened. It was dark, and I could hear the crickets chirping outside. It was so quiet. Normally, I would hear neighbors or logging trucks passing through the outskirts of town in the evening, but there was nothing except the crickets and empty silence. With the door locked, I banged on the door for what felt like hours as I called out for my mother or for anyone that may hear me. Nobody answered. I was alone.

"When I could not bang on the door anymore, I just knew. My mother was not coming back. I knew then that she was dead, and that I would soon follow. The pain from my wound radiated throughout my entire body. I was hungry, thirsty, and I had all but given up hope that someone would rescue me. As the cold and darkness sank in, I drifted in and out of sleep as I waited for death to claim me. I counted three sunsets and four sunrises. After that, I remember little else other than having strange dreams."

"Is there anything else you can remember or recall that seemed strange or out of the ordinary?"

"I've told you everything I can remember," I told him tiredly. "It would help if I knew what exactly you were looking for."

"That will be all for now," Dr. Alden said, clearing his throat again. "We have just begun clearing out the bodies as we search for more survivors. Let us keep our fingers crossed that there are others.

"When can I go home?"

"When we know it's safe," he replied, jotting down his notes on the clipboard. "Ander's let's help her lay back down so she can get some rest."

I looked over and my eyes locked with Dr. Alden. He was looking at me in a way that left me feeling naked. "Get some rest Ms. Vivienne. We will speak again tomorrow."

"Thank you," I replied, feeling a stirring in my belly. I was not sure if it was a warning or something else.

Anders stood up and helped me get situated back in my cot, and he pulled the blankets up around me. "You're not leaving me, are you?"

"Only when I absolutely have to. Do not worry, Viv. I'm

right here by your side."

"Will you hold my hand until I'm asleep?"

He chuckled and laid down a sleeping bag beside me on the ground. He dimmed the lantern, and without saying a word, he held my hand. I immediately fell asleep remembering my cries in the dark basement. Cries that would go unanswered as death claimed the small town of Stony Creek.

CHAPTER 9

OMENS

Have you ever tasted something that you knew should not taste good, yet it was the most delightful thing you have ever put into your mouth? That moment when it hits your tongue, and you feel your taste buds come alive? I have never been more thankful for food of any kind until that moment. I wanted to savor the simple act and the repeated movements of bringing a simple utensil to my mouth and relishing in its contents.

I wish I could say it was something exotic and tantalizing to the senses in terms of a meal, but no, it was a simple beef broth. Although, it was the most delicious tasting broth on the planet. I could easily pick up that there were meaty bones thrown into the pot to provide additional flavor, along with onions, carrots, celery, and garlic, with a hint of vinegar and bay leaf. Although, there was a flavor I could not place, but it brought out the flavor of everything else. *How strange*, I thought. *How is it I can pick out these individual flavors?* Was I able to do that before?

I never was a big meat eater, but I had to admit that the thought of a juicy medium-rare steak made my mouth water. This was new and, albeit unusual territory for me. I craved protein to where it felt like a toothache that would not abide until my teeth were tearing into its seared flesh. Within minutes, the warm liquid provided warmth in the icy chill that built up throughout the evening and into the early morning. It also helped the cravings.

"You have more color in your cheeks already," Dr. Alden

said in a cheerful voice as he entered the tent. "Let's get a quick look at you and then I'll let you get back to your breakfast."

"I've actually finished the bowl. Would it be possible to get more? Or a steak? I would settle for even a hamburger patty."

"You can have as much broth as you like."

"No actual food?!" I could not believe my ears. "Surely, you are joking!"

"I know this is going to be a painful conversation for you, and I sympathize."

"I'm starving! Can you seriously expect me to live off broth? For how long?!"

"Look, you were without food and water for days. When your body goes through that kind of stress, it is like resetting your digestive system. Too much of anything right away could do more harm than good. We will have to introduce your body to food again slowly. Not to mention, you're recovering from surgery."

"You're still not answering my questions. How long will I be living off broth?"

"When your body is ready for solids, I will treat you to a wonderful meal. Let us put it all into perspective, shall we? You can allow your digestive system to build back up and adjust, or... You will have Anders sitting at your side, holding you up while you're enduring some extreme digestive issues over the bucket."

"You don't mean that he would watch me while I use the facilities, do you?"

"Indeed I am. He would also be the one changing it," he said, smiling as he looked right at Anders. "His medic training needs to be put to effective use. Isn't that right Anders?"

Anders' eyes held daggers, but he said nothing at all. Not even a no sir, or a yes sir. I wanted to remind him that Anders had saved my life, but my vocal cords momentarily stopped working. I could not help the panic building within me over knowing that Anders was about to know me much more intimately than I was prepared for.

The thought of him hearing or seeing me do the deed horrified me! Place me in a room full of spiders, and yes, I would scream bloody murder for a while, but I would survive. Place me in a tent where Anders would be at my side while I work through a bowel movement and, Lord knows what else, and you may as well kill me now! The thought never occurred to me that Anders would have to deal with that as well.

"You're joking, right?! I am not doing anything like that in front of anyone," I exclaimed with relief as I felt a bit of my fiery personality that I kept hidden, bubble up in utter defiance. "It's unfair, and it's an invasion of my privacy."

"Look around you. Life is vastly different here. Privacy is a luxury that you cannot enjoy in a military camp. Do you think you can hold it indefinitely? Or perhaps you would like to go into the makeshift outhouse with all the other men?" Dr. Alden asked me, giving me the hairy eyeball, discouraging me from arguing further.

"Wonderful," I murmured as I crossed my arms in front of my chest, pouting. "I'm so sorry, Anders. This is humiliating."

Dr. Alden nodded in approval at my response. "You will adjust to Anders caring for you. I can see you are quite independent and able to care for yourself, but until you can not only sit up by yourself, but walk around, he will be at your side. If he is not here, for whatever reason, Robert or one of my assistants will be on hand to help you with whatever you need."

That was that. He left the room, leaving both Anders and I looking at each other in a way that suggested we both felt uncomfortable, if not awkward, about the whole thing. At least I was!

"I hate to admit it, because I hate the guy, but he's right," Anders said with a sympathetic smile.

"On which count is he right? The awkward part, or the suffering with endless broth?"

"Both. I know it's not what you want to hear, but I honestly, I know this is all going to be uncomfortable for you as you recover, but I will do my best to help to ensure that it's not as painful as you think it's going to be."

"Thank you, Anders. I appreciate that, really, I do. I never thought I would be in a position like this. You know?"

"I do," he said once again, holding my hand in his. "I never thought I would play nurse to a woman that has defied insurmountable odds."

"I'm glad you're here."

I did not place trust in others so easily. To place that level of trust in someone was a very vulnerable space to be in, and dropping my guard down equated to me feeling like I was standing naked in front of that person. It took me years to trust those I held in confidence, and I needed to move into a space of trust with Anders and Dr. Alden in even less time.

Anders, he was different. I trusted him automatically. It could very well be because he saved my life, as well as how he stayed by my side, but it was him as a person. He kept his promises, and I believed him when he said he would do something. My gut perception told me I could trust him completely. Why then did I have such a tough time trusting Dr. Alden? What was it about him that scared me so much? Was it his ego? His success? He was obviously a powerful man.

I also knew on one level that not knowing what was happening had me feeling terrified. I could not go home, and on another level, Dr. Alden was like a puppeteer pulling all the strings. What was to become of me? Would I become one of his puppets? Not knowing what to expect or what was happening triggered memories of growing up with the same level of uncertainty. When my mother and I were living in the car, moving from town to town, the uncertainty of when our next meal would come or if we would have a warm bed to stay in left a longstanding mark. This time, she would not be there to help me through my fears and wading through unfamiliar territory.

Remember what mom used to tell you? Focus on the one thing that you can do right now. Let everything else drift away. What can you focus on doing right now?

My response was a simple answer. I asked Anders to bring me another bowl of broth, which I took my time with. Feeling full, my body drifted into a dreamless sleep. I spent the day sleeping off and on and eating broth during my wake periods. I asked Anders if he could ask the cook what his secret ingredient was in the broth after I gave him a sip to see if he could recognize what the flavor was that I could not recognize. He shook his head and shrugged his shoulders. When he came back with my next bowl, he said the cook said his secret ingredient was pepper. We both knew it was not pepper, but it is one of those things that will annoy me until I forget about it. At least I am not alone in wanting to know his secrets. According to Anders, he also makes a mean stew that has a similar flavor.

I woke up, and it was evening. Anders was reading by the dimmed lantern. Left alone with my thoughts and dreams, my mind raced on all the what if scenarios of how I could have done things differently? I did not understand how I was alive. If there was meaning behind any of it, I desperately wanted to understand it. This was the only thing keeping me pinned to the bed. I wanted more than anything to get up and get the hell out of here. I wanted to go home to my familiar bed, to the familiar sounds and smells. I did not want to accept that my life as I knew it was a figment of the past, and that the world I knew did not exist any longer. Looking at the reality of my situation made me feel like I was walking in darkness. I felt like I was about ready to crack like an egg. It was not just the physical wounds. It was mental and emotional. The inner torment weaved its way through my psyche, and all I wanted to do was curl up in a ball to cry and hide away from the world.

Why me? What makes me so special that I alone survive? The anger that I heard in hundreds of the voices of those that perished washed over me, and it left me with guilt and shame.

The tears came, but I could release none of it. I wanted to hold on to the pain like a baby blanket. Why? My mother is dead. Families that I had grown up with are dead. An entire town... dead. I was alone. There was no one left. Dr. Alden mentioned they were still scouring the town for survivors, but after everything that I witnessed, what were the chances? Why couldn't I allow myself to feel?

I knew I would need to talk to someone about all of this. I could feel the familiar tugs of depression, the more I allowed my mind to roam on why I was not worthy of surviving. *What can I do? I am here right now!* I did not want to bother Anders with everything that was moving around in my head, so I watched him while he read. I pretended to sleep when he looked up from his reading until he caught me looking at him, lost in thought.

"Hey, are you still with me or did your mind take you somewhere else?" Anders asked, pulling me back into the present with a smile on his face.

"Oh, Anders," I said with a startled sigh. "Forgive me. I was going through this entire ordeal and trying to make sense of it all. I am failing miserably. Nothing makes sense, and I keep thinking that this is a nightmare. Why did I alone survive? Why me? I don't understand!"

"This isn't a simple experience you can deal with like your normal day-to-day life. You have been through a traumatic experience. If you weren't feeling the way you feel, I would be a lot more worried."

"Feeling this way is normal? I feel like I'm losing my mind, Anders," I told him as I covered my face with my hands and the tears finally escaped from their captivity. "I don't know how to cope with all this loss. So many people, my mother... They are all dead! A whole town! How should I be feeling at this moment?"

"Shhhhh," he said in a soothing voice. "It's all right, let it out. You are safe now. Give me your grief. I can take it."

"I can't," I said as the inner resolve set in. "If I give you my grief, then there will be nothing left of me. All I have right now to hold on to is my grief. I have nothing else. If I give it to you, then I will have nothing left. I fear I will be an empty shell, and unable to feel anything at all. I've lost everything! My home, my mother, my life…"

"I understand," he said with so much compassion that I knew what he said was true. I broke down in tears, and he leaned in, kissing my forehead, his eyes filled with tears. He really understood. My heart leaped in my chest as our eyes locked. He once again grabbed my hand in his and held it while his other hand moved through my hair. The simple motion and repetition moving from my forehead and down the length of my head calmed me instantly, and I could barely keep my eyes open.

"I used to do this for my mom when she needed to rest. She was very stubborn and even during her darkest moments, if she had a mind to do something, she would. Your stubbornness, your powerful will, and your humility remind me so much of her. I am grateful that I can be here for you, like I was there for her. I just want you to know you are safe with me."

"I'm sorry," I whispered.

"No, please don't apologize. You have nothing to be sorry for," he said as he continued to stroke my hair.

"I'm sorry for your pain," I said, choking on my words between small sobs. "Losing a parent is the most painful thing I have ever been through. Physical pain has nothing on the pain that I feel losing my mother. Does my reminding you of her bring back that pain?"

"No, not at all. You know, I used to think that caring for my mom was a burden. Even in the end, I blamed her for being so sick and then abandoning me with a drunken father. It took me almost a year to admit that I was just angry that I was so powerless. It was even more difficult to surrender to the fact that no matter what I did, it wouldn't change the outcome or make a difference."

"Do you realize what you did?" I asked him, reaching out for his chin to lift it up so that he was looking into my eyes. "Your sacrifice to care for her is an act of pure and selfless love. You showed her she mattered, regardless of what was happening to her. It takes a lot to ask for help when you're stubborn and independent. How can I ever repay you for the same kindness?"

"How about you rest, and we get you feeling better? Deal?"

"Deal."

This man could bring me to tears and unfold my heart like a warm blanket that wanted nothing more than to wrap around him for safekeeping. I wanted to be in his arms at that very moment, and despite my condition and everything else I faced, I wanted him to hold me. I did not know how to ask. He was already doing so much for me, including doing more than his everyday job of being a soldier to help me. He also did not wear any protective gear around me, which meant that by being near me, he was also risking his life. Why would he do that?

As he continued moving his hand through my hair, I curled up into the blankets that he had wrapped me up in and I closed my eyes. I moaned a little as I put my head closer to Ander's arm. He shifted his chair, and I felt him as he leaned in closer. The smell of Old Spice was comforting. Suddenly, a feeling of dread washed over me like a turbulent wave, followed by nausea as the room started spinning. I closed my eyes and took a deep breath.

"Are you all right, Viv?" I felt his hand brush against my forehead.

"I'm just feeling really dizzy and nauseous."

"Want me to get the doctor?"

"No, it will hopefully pass. I…"

I cracked open my eyes and observed that I was no longer in the tent. I was somewhere dark and cold. It smelled familiar. I allowed my eyes a moment to adjust to the dark. I looked around the familiar cellar I knew so well. *Why am I here? Oh, God! Did I ever leave?*

I wanted to scream, but my vocal cords did not work. I had no control of my body, and yet it was moving to commands that I was not giving it. *What is going on?!* I could almost make out what looked like someone sleeping beside me. My hand is touching him. Touching him in intimate places. He was wearing a military uniform.

My stomach, revolting in severe pain, causing me to grip at my stomach as I feel an almost familiar feeling. Hunger. A hunger so strong that takes over all reasoning. A feeling that accompanies words that are not my own fills my mind. *I do not have a choice! I am so hungry! His sacrifice will help me find her.*

I straddle the man, unbuttoning his pants. I feel the need to possess him and to feel him inside me. The man moans as my hand makes him hard as I insert him inside me, and I rock back and forth. I pick up his hairy arm and I take a huge bite of his flesh as I revel in the blood that sprays in my mouth, followed by the taste of raw flesh. My mind fills with need and pleasure as my ears fill with the sounds of his screams that accompany my own.

A familiar voice fills my head. *Mother, sister, daughter. You are near!*

CHAPTER 10

IN-BETWEEN

"There, there Vivienne. This will help you feel much better."

I heard Dr. Alden's voice, like it was far away. I felt as if I was traveling through a cave with a bright light beckoning me forward at the opposite end. When I reached it, I was looking up at Dr. Alden, hovering over me.

"Tell me specifically what happened," Dr. Alden said with annoyance. "You are not making any sense. Tell me again, and this time, take your time and focus on the details. You are more frantic than you claim she is."

"If you experienced what I did, you would have felt frantic, like a woman who has lost her knickers at a dance. Professor, I am trying to tell you she was not making any sense. What I told you is exactly what she told me."

"Start from the beginning. Take your time," he told him and then he turned his head back towards me. My eyes were open, but I felt depleted, and unable to move. I felt paralyzed. I looked between Dr. Alden and Anders, my eyes pleading for help. The fear boiled to the surface, and I wanted more than anything to get up and run. I felt the tears well up in my eyes, but I could not even lift my hand to wipe them away. My mouth would not open. I could not speak. My stifled screams came out as low moans. What is happening?! Oh God, am I dying?!

"Sir, she doesn't look like she is doing so well."

"Shhhhh, it is alright Vivienne," Dr. Alden told me, laying his hand on my shoulder. His hand moving down my bare arm slowly until he reached my wrist. He was staring down at me, becoming lost in his own thoughts, until Anders interrupted him.

"She looks scared, Professor. What did you give her?" Anders asked, standing over Dr. Alden's shoulder, looking down at me, concerned.

"I have given her an experimental medication to help her relax and stay calm. There is a component in the medication that causes the body to become very relaxed, and even at a lower dose, it appears to be quite potent. It should pass in a few hours. For patients with psychosis or schizophrenia, this may have the potential to be much more humane than the use of physical restraints. If a chemist can produce the right compounds, we may be on to something that can help patients with similar episodes. Not that I expect someone like you to understand."

"Permission to speak my mind, Sir?"

"Please."

"I am an educated man, Sir! I may not have been able to graduate from high school or go to college like you, but I understand the English language. She was not having an episode! How do you justify giving her an experimental medication as humane? You do not even know what it is going to do to her!"

"How would you know if she was having an episode or not? Are you a doctor? Not that it is any of your business, but I am dedicated to this field. My wife suffers from episodes, and I have made it my life's work to not only help her, but those like her."

"My apologies, Sir."

"Look, I understand your concern, but take a moment to see the situation for what it is to a trained eye. When I arrived, she was in hysterics, and you could not control her. If I cannot restrain a patient with two soldiers, including my son, there is no point in risking harming her physically to calm her down. Her strength is quite remarkable. She has every right to feel confused and afraid after having an episode." He paused, looking at me softly, and then continued, "I assure you I have her best intentions at heart. I am quite enamored with our beautiful patient."

"Hey, Viv," Anders said. "I know this is difficult, but you heard him. This will pass in a few hours. Close your eyes and give yourself permission to think of what makes you happy."

I looked in his direction, but I could not easily see him, until I watched him pace back and forth behind Dr. Alden, who had his nose in between his fingers, slowly shaking his head. There would not be any rest if they were both sitting here together. Their mutual annoyance with one another reminded me of a cock fight I once saw as a little girl on the farm. I did not understand why they were fighting then. I just knew they were after the girl hens and one was about to become the evening meal, just like the soldier was an evening meal. Why did I no longer care she ate him?

"Yes," Dr. Alden responded sarcastically. "Individuals suffering through trauma experience nothing but happy thoughts and dreams filled with muffins and tea. My God, man!"

Anders and Dr. Alden were annoying me, and yet, I did not care in the slightest. They were here for something, but I could not remember why. As soon as the question formed within my mind, it became a fleeting thought, lost to the dense fog that lingered like an itchy wool blanket, taking all my thoughts and leaving me with what felt like ants crawling all over my body. Normally, it would annoy me, this feeling all over my body, but I found I was perfectly fine just lying here. That made little sense, or maybe it did? I did not feel the need to move, anyway. It was too much effort to move. Why would I want to do that?

"It will make sense if you understand where I am coming from. My mother faced death without morphine. We could not afford that luxury to help her in her passing. So please, do not patronize me about trauma. My mother, in her last days, would retreat within her mind. She told me about the world that she had built, and it was a place for her to go when she was in so much pain, she could barely stand it. Maybe it would help her, too."

"Anders, I thank you for your heart-wrenching story, and I empathize. Truly, but if you do not sit down right now and stop your pacing, you will lie beside her fully medicated," Dr. Alden practically yelled. "Now, please. Disassociation is not what Vivienne needs right now, and for me to help her I need you to start from the beginning with what happened."

"She was feeling dizzy and nauseous, and I asked her if she wanted me to fetch a doctor. She said no, and then..."

"And then?"

"Well, I can hardly believe it myself, and maybe it is not worth mentioning at all. But..."

"Out with it, Anders!"

Yes! Out with-it Anders! I thought, intrigued, like a child hearing a bedtime story. Only that it was my story, but it did not phase me in the slightest.

"Her skin rippled like a wave that glowed."

"Her skin did what now?"

"I knew if I said something, you would want me evaluated. Maybe I am just tired, but I could have sworn that she started glowing a light blue, and it was like a flash, a wave of the glowing from head to toe, and then nothing. It did not happen again."

"Go on."

"Well, the next thing I know, she's sitting looking horrified. She went pale, and then she started screaming and crying. I asked her what was wrong, and she just looked around her and claimed that she was back in the basement of her house. Then it all unraveled, and she was not making much sense. She claimed she felt like a prisoner in her own body and could not control its movements. She sat there looking like a statue, unable to move, like it was really happening to her. Then she started talking about a soldier being eaten. That's when you came in with Robert and the guard."

"What stood out as unusual to you?"

"You mean besides how strong she is? None of this sounds like her. I don't know how else to explain it. It was like she was living in a nightmare. She was talking to me and able to respond to my questions like we were having a conversation. I'm not sure if she even realizes she was talking to me though, because she lost consciousness once she started eating the soldier. Do you think it could be Smith, Sir? He is part of the search crew and failed to report in at the specified time."

"They did not notify me. When was the last check in?"

"It is three in the morning now, so a little over nine hours ago, Sir."

"Robert," Dr. Alden called out. I could hear shuffled footsteps crossing the soft dirt. "Gather Edwin and his boys. We have a lead."

I closed my eyes and listened to them leave, grateful for the silence that would follow. I could feel Anders holding my hands and his head leaning on my arm. I went into my mind and summoned myself to a place I had become all too familiar with when locked in the basement and dying. It was here that I found solace. Anders was not wrong about the power of our mind, and this was a newly learned skill. I plunged into the deep breathing patterns that resemble sleep. It was very much like being asleep, and yet I was alert enough to know what was happening around me as I floated on the precipice between dreams and the waking world. It was like flying into a daydream and existing there. A world that built itself with no help from me. This space is in-between all things.

Locked away in the basement, I would dream fantastical dreams of places that existed outside of time, and of a man I had never met. When I was at the brink of wanting it all to end, he appeared and pulled me into that place, in the in-between. I would pray to whatever god would hear me to release me from the pain, loneliness, thirst, and starvation. Like an inner knowing that never leaves, he would appear in my dreams and take me away from the pain. His strength reminded me of Anders. It was in this strength that I felt a sense of calm, safety, and the courage to push forward just a little more.

Every day, I would give just a little more of myself to the waking world. I'd given all that I am to live from moment to moment, and yet, I knew my journey was only just beginning. He told me I was on an alternative path, and that it would not be easy.

"Hold on to this life, my love! Help is coming," he would whisper into my ear over and over.

How could he have known? Who was he, if not a figment of my imagination? My heart told me he was so much more, but I knew enough to keep him a secret. I believe in angels. While my relationship with God is on shaky ground, I know they exist. When I was a child, on the road with my mother, an angel kept me safe. Like my angel, they both glowed with that peculiar glow. Could it be the same angel? Maybe. The thought also occurred to me that my mind created him because I was looking to be saved. In a life filled with uncertainty, there was one thing that I have always held onto. Hope. Hope for anything real in a life filled with so much heartbreak, overwhelm, and sadness. I wanted to believe in miracles again, like I did as a child.

Three familiar waterfalls fell behind him into a great clear sky-blue pool, surrounded by foliage, and a beautiful mirage of red and white flowers that set the oasis into a visual splendor. Why does this place feel so familiar? It felt like being home. I learned long ago that home isn't necessarily where we grew up, it's the home we create. It's that feeling that holds love and comfort wrapped in a package that only your home that's made with those qualities can provide.

"Are you here?" I called out as my voice echoed through the fabric of time and space, which held little meaning here.

I closed my eyes and took in a deep breath. With the power of my will, I summoned him to me. I didn't know exactly how I was doing it, but it was an intuitive knowing that mingled with an emotional longing that went deeper than superficial needs. It was a yearning and desire to be loved by him.

Sometimes in this space I couldn't see him, but I could always feel him if I closed my eyes and thought of him. Even in the waking world, I could always feel him like the lingering remnants of a dream. He was familiar. I knew him, and I couldn't explain who he was or why I felt the way I did, but I knew he was mine, as I was his. We had never touched, not once, and yet I would give myself willingly to him so easily. What made this even more uncertain is that I have never seen his face. He is a faceless figment of my imagination. I had not been back to this place since I had awakened in the military camp.

He stood tall in the near distance. His features were barely visible. I could make out his dark hair and his bronze skin, a dark, neatly shaven beard, and broad shoulders with a lean body. He wore a burgundy skirt that swept just to above his ankles, and his belt adorned with gold shimmered in the sunshine. His bare chest held shadows that teased of a muscular upper body.

Even from a distance, my body longed for him in a way I had never allowed myself to know from a man. I longed to know the mystery that stood before me. I wanted him to possess me, and to know me in a way that no one could ever know me. I wanted to be vulnerable, and in his arms, nothing would ever harm me. In some small way, I wanted to feel like a did as a child, the level of innocence that comes with trusting wholeheartedly. I feared losing myself in any relationship, but what I feared most was the cost of that love. In this life, one thing was certain. Everything I did or wanted came at a cost.

"The world is older than you know," he whispered into my ear. "Don't open your eyes."

"Why can't I see you?" I asked him softly as his warm breath teased the skin on my neck.

"It is not yet time for you to know me," he whispered.

"Have you ever heard the story of Cupid and Psyche?"

"I read about them, yes. She betrayed him and endured many trials to prove her love. Is this your authentic form? If you're testing me, it's not fair. I should test you in return."

"This is one of many forms, but you have always known me. What task shall you put before me so that you may know my love for you?"

"Touch me, so that I know you are real."

I felt a silky veil of fabric cover my eyes, and my hands went up to touch the softness of the blindfold. His fingers touched my shoulders gently, and I shivered as he ran them lightly across my collarbone.

He kissed me lightly on the lips as he tilted my chin upwards. I pressed myself into him and reached out my hands to touch his bare chest. I lifted my head in response to him, eagerly wanting more. He kissed me again with more pressure on my lips as his tongue slowly parted mine. I opened my lips to allow him in, and I felt a flood of warmth enter my body as if I was glowing in response to his kiss.

His arms wrapped around me in a tight embrace. I felt something deep inside me stir. Something that felt unfamiliar, awakened, and stirring. Like a spider curls up in a ball to play dead, I felt its many tendrils expand from its center as it lit my body on fire, as his kiss spread into my entire being like a wildfire. I muffled a cry as I buried my face in his chest as pain ignited through my entire being.

"Awaken, my love," he demanded in a voice so powerful that I awoke startled and drenched in a cold sweat. Fear settled into my belly, a fear that I couldn't explain, and I felt a panic stir within me at being alone in the dark in a place I wasn't familiar with. I shifted my weight so I could prop myself up on my elbow, and I looked around me. Shaking, I tuned into the silence, and I heard breathing coming from beneath me.

"Anders," I whispered. "Is that you?"

"Yes, Viv," he whispered sleepily, and reached up to touch my hand that was lingering over the edge. "I am with you. You are safe. Go back to sleep."

Anders' hand drifted back down, and I heard him shifting his weight a bit, followed by the subtle breathing and soft snores that accompanied sleep. The panic within me didn't rest. When I closed my eyes and drifted into sleep, I stood in the middle of the darkness that I feared would lure me away. It was the same darkness that wanted to take me with it when I was in the basement. It didn't call my name. It knew no names, but it summoned me in a way that suggested that it knew me. I didn't want to go with the darkness. I wasn't ready. I screamed as I fought the darkness from grabbing hold, and in the dark I ran, and I ran.

It was Anders' soothing voice that pulled me back. There was something about him that kept me grounded. I feared I would lose myself in the darkness again if he wasn't with me. A memory crept in and filled my mind with hopelessness. When I was lying on the floor in the basement, I knew I was dying, and that the world I once knew was ending. I had accepted that this was the end. Living in a world I could no longer relate to was even more difficult.

"You're alright," he whispered into my ear, gently stroking my forehead. "You're not alone."

"Was I dreaming?" I asked him groggily.

"You were having another nightmare, Viv," he whispered. "Go back to sleep. Don't worry, I'm right here with you."

"Don't leave me," I whispered in a hazy, sleepily fog.

"Never by choice," he whispered, taking me by surprise as he kissed my forehead.

CHAPTER 11

A NEW THREAT

I slept soundly until the morning light crept in through a crack in the tent. My eyelids flickered to adjust to the ray of light playfully blinding me. My hand immediately shot up to shield me from the brightness as my head pounded strongly through my temples. I shifted my weight, which was easier to do this morning, but as I attempted to sit up, a wave of nausea overcame me so fiercely that I had little time to react to the spasm that left me gasping for breath as I gagged and dry heaved. Anders sleepily jumped up from the ground, looking shell-shocked, and immediately started giving me a once over.

"Oh, fuck," he said, one look at me and he was in pure panic mode, putting his hand on my forehead. "You're burning up!"

I tried to respond to Anders, but all I could do was moan. If I tried to open my mouth, I felt like I was going to vomit.

He bent down and looked closely at my arm, turning it over with a puzzled look on his face. "What's this on your skin?"

The surrounding noises sounded like I was underwater. I looked down at my arm through my tunnel vision and saw the familiar glistening mesh on my skin. *Oh shit!* It was not like what I saw on the other bodies, but it was similar. The substance on my skin resembled more of a glittering sweat, rather than the recoiling mesh that covered the body like a shroud. I thought it would feel wet, but all it did was make my skin feel soft, like silk.

Looking back up at Anders, I raised my hands to my

throat and touched my lips and then pointed towards his canteen.

"Water? You want water?"

I nodded and then laid back down, grateful that I did not have to play charades longer than was necessary. He poured me water from a canteen into a tin coffee mug. I lifted myself up slightly as he held the cup to my mouth so I could sip it, but I could not keep it down. It came right back up on his shoes and dripped down my chest. I laid back down and curled up into a ball.

"Shit, shit," he said, sounding panicked. I could not focus on his words. Everything he said jumbled together into a language that held no meaning as the room started spinning. I could not react to anything other than putting my head in my hands and praying it would stop. I wanted so badly to tell Anders how afraid I felt, but I could not get the words out through the pain.

"It's okay," he said, moving his hand through my hair. "Just close your eyes and focus on your breathing. I'm going to see if I can track down Doc Lindberg."

I watched as Anders grabbed his camouflage jacket with signs of worry across his brow, leaving in a hurry. I groaned as I held my head and cried from the searing pain that started from my head and reached out like lightning bolts shooting through every nerve throughout my body. What started in my dream of my body awakening into fire was now a chaotic storm. Would I survive this storm or end up like the others? Dead.

I spent the next two hours curled in a fetal position while I prayed to my pillow for it all to stop. The nausea was easing, along with the dizzy spells, unless I tried to sit up. I felt tired, more than anything. Anders gave up trying to give me water an hour ago, and I could not handle his touch. Everything hurt. The pain radiating throughout my body was now a subtle throbbing ache. My muscles hurt. I must have been so tense during the initial phase of pain that I did not realize the tension I was holding in my body.

I could hear the light drizzle outside of the rain. The moisture in the air smelled refreshing as it washed away all the dust in the air and soaked into the earth. There was nothing like the smell of the wet earth after the heavens cried, leaving the earth replenished. A surge of strength moved through me as the nausea subsided a bit, and it left me feeling disoriented and confused.

I felt as if I was moving outside of my body just enough to not feel as connected to it. I felt like I was more of a passenger rather than sitting in my body. I felt different. Dr. Kines always told me we experience physical and mental trauma differently, and everyone is unique with their own array of symptoms and responses. What if this was just a delayed response? Was I finally getting the illness that killed everyone else?

My angel, where are you? In the basement and throughout my time here at the camp, I could always feel my angel with me, but now that feeling was gone. I felt, for the first time in days, completely alone. What has severed my connection with him? Did I do something wrong? I know he did not exist, but in my heart, I wanted more than anything for him to be real! I did not want to be alone!

A sense of claustrophobia filled me with dread as the fabric walls around me started closing in. The feeling of the fabric from the new gown around my neck suffocated me, and I could not breathe. My breath left me too quickly as anxiety swelled around me like a rising tide. A sharp pain radiated through my chest and down my back, and I felt a new heaviness under the weight of pressure in my chest.

I am not there! I am not in the basement! My mind did not want to listen to reason. Anders leaving me alone triggered the isolation, the fear, and even though I knew I was no longer in the basement. It felt like I was there. *Oh, God! Please, please, please help me! I am not there! Dammit, I am not there! What was wrong with me?! Fuck this! I cannot do this anymore! I need to get out of here now!*

I sat up and flopped my legs over the cot and turned at an angle to use the chair beside it to support my unsteadiness. I stood up as best as I could, hunched over the cot, as I wrapped the top dark gray wool blanket around me like a robe. The flaps of the tent were about a foot away from the corner of the cot. It took several minutes to work my way to the end of the bed, fighting through wave after wave of dizziness and nausea that threatened to change my mind. I hobbled over to the exit of the tent that Anders left through, horrified I was going to fall flat on my face with legs that refused to carry me. I had difficulty moving the flap and tumbled out slightly as I took in a deep breath of fresh air.

"What the fuck?" A soldier outside my tent in full protective gear, startled, took one look at me, and immediately spun around and lifted his gun at my head. I must have looked horrific. The metal shaft of the gun at my forehead felt cold and threatening. I lifted both my hands up, trying to show him I was not a threat.

"Do not take another step," he yelled at me, with his visible eyes darting back and forth frantically. "Don't fucking move! Put your fucking hands behind your head and get down on your knees."

I did as he asked in a sequence that was painful and too slow for the impatient soldier. He used the shaft of his gun to force me down, and I collapsed onto the ground, moaning as I clutched at my side, feeling something tear from inside my healing stab wound. My reaction added to the young man's tension.

"Shit! You are sick, aren't you?" He yelled loudly as he backed away from me, still holding his gun pointed at me. "Don't fucking move!"

"Pl... pl...ea...se," I tried to tell him through big heaving sobs. I vomited, and then curled up into a ball on the ground, pleading as I held one of my shaking hands straight in front of me, my open palm facing him like a shield. The hot streaming tears roll off my cheek and watched each tear that rolled down onto the ground stain the dirt as my throat closed and refused to allow anything else to escape.

"Fuck! Don't fucking move," he cried out, staring wildly at my hand. I turned my hand over, and I saw the fresh blood covering my hand. I looked down and saw blood from my side seeping through my gown. My whole body started trembling uncontrollably.

"St...p," I continued to plead through heavy, choking sobs. "Pl... sssse."

I heard the click of the gun as he turned the safety off.

"Stand down," Anders yelled at the top of his lungs as he came running from an unknown direction, moving through the crowd that had gathered. He wedged himself in front of the soldier. "Stand down! That's an order!"

"Sir, we have direct orders to kill anyone infected without question," said the soldier.

"You have orders to kill those that approach the camp that show signs of infection," Anders said with seething anger. "Dr. Alden's orders are that no harm will come to her. She is a patient under his care."

"Sir, you can't be serious," the soldier questioned him in a mocking tone. "Look at her. She's obviously sick, and I'm not going home in a fucking box!"

Anders lifted and motioned with his hand in a simple gesture. Within a matter of seconds, out of nowhere an exceptionally large older man, clear and void of any emotion and scary as hell with scars all over his face, came up behind the soldier and slammed the base of his gun across the back of the soldier's head with a loud thwack. The soldier's body reacted, and his gun tilted to the side slightly and fired. Anders turned and threw his body over mine as he attempted to shield me. The bullet grazed the side of my shoulder as it went speeding by.

I screamed through my tears as I touched my shoulder. The wound felt warm as the warm blood dripped steadily down my arm. I suddenly felt very heavy and exhausted as I looked up through a small gap between Ander's torso and arm to see the soldier collapse in front of us as he landed on his knees and then fell on his side with his head turned slightly towards us. His eyes stared blankly ahead, unblinking. He was not moving. My ears started ringing and I could not take my eyes off the soldier's face.

"Get the doc," Anders shouted as he shifted his weight to cradle me in his arms.

"Is… he… dead?" I asked him, choking back on my tears. The eerie hum in my ear after the gun fired was my stark reminder that I was not living in a dream.

"Hopefully, he's just in shock from the brunt force of the hit," Anders said, focusing all his attention on me.

Why do people keep dying around me? "Am I death?"

"No, Private Thorne is young and acted irresponsibly. Fear causes us to act out of character. He should have remembered his training. You're safe now."

"Listen up ladies," the stone-cold gargoyle raised his voice loudly, breaking through the silence, booming over the crowd that had formed to watch what was happening. "This young woman's protection is our top priority. Her safety is your responsibility. Even if she shows signs of the virus, you will not engage. If she carried the virus, the simple act of standing here and doing nothing has exposed you. You will guard her with your life. This command comes down from the word of God, and you will not go against the word of God. Understood?"

"Sir, yes, sir," replied the soldiers in unison, standing tall and at attention.

All eyes fell upon me, and I could not explain it, but I could feel them. Their emotions rippled like a wave that washed over me, like a cool shower. I felt their curiosity, their fear, and their anger. I was personally responsible for one of their own brothers taken too soon, and to them, it meant that they were expendable.

"You two," the gargoyle shouted, pointing at two young

men. "Take this man to Doc Lindberg's tent."

Anders took my face in both of his hands to distract me, and he looked me straight in my eyes. His powerful emotions lured me in. They were so strong that I could almost see the energy move around him to cover me in a protective embrace. He kissed my forehead softly and picked me up and took me back inside my tent to rest. He carried me to the cot and laid me carefully back down as he lifted my gown and grabbed clean dressings, using one hand to clean the gunshot wound on my shoulder while he applied pressure on my abdomen.

The gargoyle stood with his back to the open tent, staring at the men that looked beyond him, his arms crossed, daring them to defy him. What worried me about him is that I felt nothing from him. He was as stone cold on the outside as he was on the inside. What did that mean?

The world spun around me like a Merry-Go-Round that wanted to speed up quickly. The nausea increased, and I stared at Anders as the frame around my vision phased in and out of the darkness like a dark halo. My eyelids felt heavy and as I slipped into the realm of darkness, I heard footsteps of someone enter the tent.

"I radioed for you hours ago. Where have you been?"

"Young man, you're lucky I'm here at all. I was knee deep in stitching up a young man's guts."

"Who?"

"Private Stevens."

"Do you expect him to survive his wounds? How was he hurt?"

"If he does not get an infection, he may survive. He ran right into a dangerous situation without observing his surroundings."

"With something sharp enough to slice him open?"

"Remember, my boy, to always be cautious. Even the most innocent-looking young soul can have poisonous venom."

"You found a survivor?"

"Grab my bag, boy."

"Doc, did you find a survivor?"

"Yes."

"Any news on Private Smith?"

"I'm sorry, Anders. He's gone."

I could feel Anders' eyes on me, but my eyelids refused to cooperate. I was getting so tired, and the realization that it really happened had me recoiling even further into the dark depths of my mind. *It was real?! The soldier! She... She killed him! Where is she?*

My mind reached out to her automatically, and I could feel her fear. She felt as I did, trapped. Could it be possible that we were feeling each other's emotions? I could not see through her eyes, but I could sense what she felt. She was weakening, and I had the sense that the surrounding walls were not fabric, but they were more solid. I could also sense the wildness in her. The need to escape, and a deep longing to feed. I felt blinding pain, and the connection to her became severed. I cried out.

"Is she going to be alright?"

"How the hell should I know? I just got here," the older male voice said grumpily. "She shouldn't even be alive."

"Yet, she is alive. How do you explain that? Where is Dr. Alden anyway?"

"Dr. Alden has his hands full with the survivor. You boys have left me with quite the mess. What is this on her skin?"

"I was hoping you could tell me, Doc."

"Dammit all to hell, I can't explain any of this. Dr. Alden will not let me near any of his research, files, or have access to his lab. I am not even supposed to be here now. He is not going to be happy with me. I hope I do not fuck this up, but I will do what I can."

"Hold on, Viv," he whispered into my ear. "Stay with me."

I tried to hold on to his voice, but the tug of the darkness was so welcoming. Its siren's call was too strong to deny, and I succumbed, lulled deeper and deeper into the abyss.

CHAPTER 12

FEELINGS

"There she is," an older man's voice greeted me as my eyes opened and I took in my surroundings. I looked over at my bandaged shoulder and, as I shifted, I felt the familiar pain with a tighter set of stitches.

He was a tall man with broad shoulders and the chiseled face of what I imagined a soldier from the Greek or Roman era to be. His short, midnight black hair was slightly longer on the top than most of the men here in a rebellious fashion.

"Well, well, well, our sleeping beauty finally awakes," the doctor said, smiling as he came into the tent. "How are you feeling?"

"I'm hungry," I whispered.

"That's always a good sign," he chuckled.

"Where is Anders?"

"I kicked him out of the tent to take some time to eat and clean himself up. He needs it."

"I'm still alive," I told him in an odd voice that sounded more musical than my own. I looked up at the man who studied me curiously. "You look like I feel."

"That's an understatement," he said, lighting up a cigarette, and taking a deep inhale and exhaling smoke towards the ceiling. I watched as the smoke swirled briefly before hanging over us like a fog. "We prepped you for surgery, and by the time we were ready, your wounds were already closing on their own. In all my years as a surgeon, I've seen the human body survive many things they shouldn't. You are a walking, talking conundrum, and that is just based on what

I've been able to piece together about you."

"Well, that's a first," I said dryly. "It's what every gal strives for, to be a conundrum."

"Sorry," he said with a small wince. "My bedside manner was left in the last war."

"What do I call you?"

"All the boys around here call me Doc Lindberg, or just Doc. I reckon you can do just the same."

"How long have I been asleep?"

"About sixteen hours," Doc Lindberg said as he fussed with my IV. "Your veins collapsed because of dehydration not once, but three different times."

"I'm glad I slept through that," I said, wincing. "I hate needles."

"Ah, big fear of needles, eh? It would surprise you at how even a grown man will turn into a whimpering child at the sight of a needle."

"I can imagine," I said, giggling. "I'm glad I'm not the only one afraid of those dreadful things."

"You were awake for each IV insertion, but you were pretty out of it. We gave you a sedative so that we could prepare you for surgery. Did you know you swear worse than a drunken soldier?"

"I do," I gasped in shock. "I'm so sorry! I hope I did not offend anyone."

"Please," he said, chuckling. "I found it a wonderful delight that a young woman can express her emotions and tell us how it is and leave a long-lasting impression. I definitely won't forget you."

"So, what you are saying is that you found humor and delight in how others responded to my rather crude and unladylike gestures?"

"Exactly," he said with a snort. "It's been a while since I've laughed that hard."

"Apparently, I have my moments. Is there anything else I should know?"

"You told Dr. Alden to go fly a kite because he left you waiting for over two hours to go in and do your surgery. He apologized and explained that he had good reasons and every intention to make you a priority, to which you showed him your ass and told him to kiss it," he said, chuckling. "Sorry bastard, he looked like he really wanted to. Anders almost fell on you trying to cover you up, and then you proposed to him."

"Oh... Oh, dear," I said, mortified, taking a few deep breaths to steady myself. "Well, that is one way to tell him I am interested. I suppose all I can do now is try not to humiliate myself any further."

"People your age waste way too much time on the dance, and not doing the actual dancing. Well, I do not need to poke you any more than I have already done. You are healing like you just have a scratch rather than a stab wound. The skin has closed together nicely. Since you are hungry, let's have you start with some broth, and if you can keep that down for a few meals, then by tomorrow, you will be ready for some applesauce, and perhaps some toast on the side."

"Lucky me," I said dryly as I eagerly grabbed the cup of water, he held out for me. "When do I get actual food?"

"That will be up to Dr. Alden, as I am reminded constantly that you are his patient. I was never one to follow the rules, mind you. So, if you see me putting my nose where it does not belong, just forget you ever saw me."

"Throw in some extra applesauce, and you have a deal."

"Done," he roared with laughter.

Anders walked into the tent. I looked over at him, mortified, and he looked over warily at the doctor. "You told her."

Doc Lindberg slapped his knee and laughed. "My boy, when you get to be as old as I am, you find that honesty is best served with a side dish of leaving as much chaos as you can in your wake. Life would otherwise be boring. After all, it is my job to stir the pot now and then, is it not? I am keeping you on your toes, and if I keep you guessing then I am doing my job well."

He smacked Anders on the back. Doc Lindberg's eyes were so bright and cheerful, you knew when he was smiling. The masks that people become so accustomed to wearing made it difficult to see the truth, leaving a lot to intuition. Intuition is a learned skill, and in a culture that is built on the media's image of perfection, it leaves us in a space of self-doubt and fear as we grasp for self-acceptance and acceptance from others. Could I trust myself, even now?

"Your job is to be a doctor, and to pretend to nurture a bedside manner."

"We both know that will never happen," he said, smacking Anders across the head lightly.

Doc Lindberg roared with laughter again and gave us both an exaggerated wink. Anders smiled at me playfully. I couldn't help but laugh at them both.

If I had these two around to keep me company off and on, being here would almost be bearable. I knew I could not go home right now, but it never occurred to me I may have to stay longer than necessary. Then what? Would they just release me back into my old life? The real question is, what would I be going back to? An empty town?

If I were the sole survivor of an entire town, it would be like living in a ghost town. How does a town recover from something like this? How does it even work? Would all the jobs that people could no longer do suddenly become available, and it would be the rush to fill a new town waiting for those willing to take a chance at starting over? There was an allure to that possibility. Even I, right now, wanted to just start over and forget what was behind me. My mother loved to remind me we can't outrun the past. It will always find an opportunity to catch up to us. It's better to face the here and now, and accept what is, so we can learn from it and do better tomorrow.

My mother was a wise woman, I thought to myself as the tears welled up. I wished more than anything that I could talk to her right now. I felt blessed to have that wisdom with me now, but more than anything, I wished for the sound of her voice. She knew how to say just the right thing when I needed it the most, in a tone that eased my worries, calmed my fears, and held me steady. Telling myself the same wisdom, even pretending that it was her voice, it didn't hold the same effect. It didn't fill the widening hole in my heart. Instead of tempering all those emotions, I felt everything threatening to overflow like a volcano.

"How do you think I survived the virus?" I asked Doc Lindberg out of the blue. They weren't ready for the serious turn of the conversation, but Anders gave the doctor a look that told him it was time to change the tune of our conversation. "I apologize. I keep thinking that everyone else is dead and not able to enjoy laughter like this. I feel guilty for enjoying this time with you both. It just feels wrong."

"It is normal to feel that way, but let me put this into a different perspective. Breathing is a gift. Do you want to waste what precious time you have on this damn planet grieving the past or living for the now? I have said goodbye to many young men in this line of service, many younger than even you. Learn to move on."

"It is hard to move on when you're kept in a tent and isolated like you are the plague itself."

"If you had the virus," he said with a snort. "I would be dead by now. Do you see me wearing a mask or all dressed up?"

"No," I exclaimed, realizing that he was not wearing a mask. That simple act brought me to tears, and I realized just how much I needed that human interaction outside of the protective gear that many of them wore around me, mostly when Anders' needed to relieve himself or to go to the mess hall to grab a bite to eat. I could not even count how many days ago it was when I last had a decent meal.

"Look, if you had the virus, we would all be dead by now. How you survived, I cannot say. You are a fucking miracle, my girl! The answer is somewhere in your blood. I don't have access to those answers, but in time, we will figure it out. Dr.

Alden is an asshole, but he is good at what he does."

"Speaking highly of me again, Lindberg," Dr. Alden said with a slight hint of annoyance in his monotone voice. He took off his mask as he approached my cot. "How are you doing Vivienne?"

I looked at him, my eyes widening, and my mouth agape with words that refused to come out. I nodded at him and smiled, and then stared at my feet that poked out from under the pile of blankets.

"Good," he said, softly. He bent down slightly, kissed my forehead, and ran the back of his hand lightly across my cheek, his thumb brushing my lips lightly as his hand continued to trail down my neck and to the side of my breast. "Robert will be in shortly with some broth. I will be back in to check on you later this evening. You have my word."

Dr. Alden's light caress sent a wave of warmth through my body, a reaction that I did not expect. There was something different about him. He stood up, walked past Anders without a word, and nodded at Doc Lindberg on his departure.

"This is going to be interesting," he said, looking at Anders and then towards the slit in the tent, where Dr. Alden left. I understood what he meant, but I did not have the mental capacity to take on the full meaning of it all or the implications.

There was a commotion outside of the tent. It sounded like metal trays, possibly from the mess being thrown, followed by the sound of two men shouting and grunting. Dr. Alden's voice yelled loudly over the rest, including those that were cheering one or the other party on in the fight. It did not take long to break up the fight. Dr. Alden's bold assertiveness was an attractive quality. Were arrogance and leadership qualities so closely linked that you could not identify one without the other? What did his arrogance mask? What was so intriguing about him that left me wanting to unmask him to find the real man underneath?

"We have a lot of good men here, and they are risking

their lives to be here," Doc Lindberg told me, helping me sit up as a frazzled-looking Robert entered the tent with a cup of broth. His blonde hair ruffled, his glasses slightly tilted, and covered in patches of dirt on his cheek, pants, and lab coat.

"Did you get caught up in the fight?" I asked him, taking the broth from him. "Are you alright?"

"I... I am fine. I am lucky they pushed me out of the way, away from the hot pots. I apologize, it is not much broth. It would have been more, but they knocked it over. This was all the broth that was left in the pot. Once they have cleaned up their mess, they will make more broth for you."

"Emotions and tension are pretty high. Many of them alternate on doing the clean-up in the town. They see a lot, and what they see can break them. They need to blow off that steam. Every day, they have to pick up the pieces and build themselves back up."

"Thank you," I told him with tears in my eyes, realizing what he meant by cleaning up. He meant they were cleaning up all the dead bodies. My stomach twisted in knots as I remembered. "I never stopped to think of what it must be like for all of you. Seeing what I have seen, knowing that what they will see will be far worse than I can imagine, is incomprehensible. You know what's odd? When I hear the word soldier, I immediately think of words like impenetrable and fortress. How strange is it I only now see the truth behind what a soldier really stands for? Is that what war is like, Doc Lindberg?"

"Each war is different. The virus was an invisible opponent, and yet the devastation is the same with lives lost. Soldiers are more than just warriors. We go in and rebuild, seek survivors, clean up what others cannot, and we will not stand down from any opponent, whether seen or unseen. Not everyone is as kind as you are. Once you become a soldier, it's a soldier's life. I tried to live a normal life when I came back from the war with my wife and children, but I was not the same man I was before the war."

"What happens then? What becomes of you or others like you?"

"They either stay in the military, or the lucky bastards learn how to return to their lives, or they end up on the streets and turning to alcohol and whatever else is available to escape from what their eyes have seen and cannot ever forget. It's easy to become disconnected from society seeing the things we have seen and doing the things we have done in the name of our freedom. I wish we had better support out there for our war veterans."

"Do you feel that civilians, like myself, would not understand?"

"I know you will not understand. I mean no disrespect. They built our society to keep everything on the surface, perfect and believable. Show the truth and everything crumbles. People feel safe in the lie. It's easy for them that way. You just keep on pretending until you believe. What we face, we have to learn to bury deep if we want to live in the world that our families believe in."

"How do we change that?"

"Time," he said with a shrug of his shoulders. "There will come a day when people see others for more than the color of their skin, their jobs, or their social status. We will see one another's life experience as a gift to learn from. One day, life will force us to come together and move into a future that goes beyond the everyday prejudice and bias that exists all around us."

"What will happen to you then?"

"Me? I do not know what will happen. I pray that my family will one day forgive me for becoming a full-time military doctor. I wish my wife all the happiness in the world with the man she has married, and I pray he will be a good father to my boys. They deserve that. After the war, I ceased to be the man I used to be. I cannot in good conscience go back to that life and leave my boys out there in the field. I choose to be here."

"You are sacrificing so much to be here, I cannot even imagine," I said with a small smile. "I understand what you mean about our culture and acceptance. It took my mother and I several years to gain acceptance in our mostly white community. It wasn't easy. My mother liked to remind me we can't change anything around us without trying just a little every day to make a difference."

"I agree wholeheartedly with her, little sailor. Get some rest. I've taken enough of your time."

"Little sailor?"

"Think of all that you have faced until this moment as an ocean. It takes a skilled sailor to survive the storm, and to learn how to navigate through them. Get some rest."

I watched with great admiration as Doc Lindberg left.

"Little sailor," I repeated softly. The minor act of having a nickname made me feel as if I was being accepted and embraced into a new family. Even though I was not part of their world, I was only a visitor in the status quo of things. I would take what small comfort it was to belong in their world.

"He's a great man," Anders said, as he followed my gaze.

"So are you," I said, smiling at him. "They found another survivor?"

"How did you know about that?" he asked as his eyes darted towards me, startled. "You remember?"

"I was in and out of consciousness, but yes, I heard you talking to Doc Lindberg. I do not, however, remember proposing to you."

Anders laughed. "Well, if it's any consolation, I was ready to accept your offer, but I figured there should at least be a time of courtship involved before we took our vows."

"I see," I said, smiling up at him. "When will our first date be?"

"As soon as you're feeling better. It will be the best the mess tent offers."

"Anything that I can sink my teeth into would be delightful. I am so hungry," I told him as I slowly licked my lips as I imagined biting into a juicy steak. I looked up, catching him staring at my lips, and I smiled as I imagined his lips covering mine.

"Look what they brought back for you from town." Anders held up a hospital gown in a light blue with dark blue floral bouquets embroidered into the collar of the gown.

"Thank you," I exclaimed happily as he helped me get the garment on just over my head, looking away so that I could pull it down over the rest of me. "Tell me about the survivor."

"I know little," he said, pulling his attention away from my lips and focusing on his feet. "I only know that there was a survivor, but she is deceased."

"She? She's dead? Who was she, do you know?"

"It was the nurse that attacked you, and she apparently was just as crazy as you said. They shot her down after she sliced open the soldier that was sent in to capture her. But…"

"But, what?"

"The strange thing is that her body is being kept at an unmarked location near our encampment. Why would they need to keep her body there?"

"Maybe they needed a private and safe space to learn more about what happened to her. I mean, how harmful can a gunned down dead psychotic nurse be?"

"True enough," he said, laughing uncomfortably. "My brain likes to create vivid stories, and you will have to remind me to keep me grounded. Otherwise, I will be the one waking you up with a nightmare."

"Only if you keep me grounded in return. Anders, I wanted to thank you. I don't know how I would have gotten through any of this without you being here. I am grateful that you are here."

"I wouldn't want to be anywhere else," he said with the sweetest smile. He sat down next to me and grabbed my hand, and started reading from his book while I sipped on my small serving of broth.

CHAPTER 13

PASSIONS RISING

I spent the next twenty-four hours sleeping, and between resting and being awake, Anders was always at my side. We talked about our lives before the virus, and I found I could no longer relate to who I was before all of this happened. The woman that I spoke about felt more like a faint memory, or someone else's story I read in a novel. I found comfort in daydreams, experiencing the stirrings of the desire that was building within me. I felt betrayed. My past identity slipped into the shadows, a silent grave without so much as a headstone to mourn. A ghost that walks through memories left with time, whispering of dreams lost to childlike innocence.

By the morning of the second day, I was ready to break out of the camp by any means possible. I felt like I was going crazy, partially from the boredom of being stuck in bed with not much to do, but for another reason entirely. I wanted to get outside of my head and experience life again. I did not know what that would be or feel like, but I was almost desperate for something as simple as a walk. It also did not help that Anders and I were locked in what felt like a stalemate regarding our affections with one another. I needed a distraction. I wanted to throw myself into his arms and kiss him in such a manner that it would leave little room for doubt about my feelings for him.

Every time he looked at me, my heart would skip a beat. He would gaze at me a little longer each time, and his clumsiness gave him away. I could not help but smile every time he tripped on his own feet while he was looking at me with that southern boy next door kind of charm. I was not sure I could last another day like this. Being so close and yet unable to touch. It was pure torture! Eventually, one of us had to make the first move, but I also knew what that meant. He would cross a line, and right now, his job was to be my caretaker. He was under orders to watch over me and see that I am well cared for. It was all on me and I was mistaking his affections for more than they were, but something deep within me told me that was not the case.

"Look at you," Anders said, marveling at my movement as I sat myself up on the cot and swung my legs over to stand up and stretch. "You could barely move a few days ago."

"I didn't even think about it," I said, embarrassed. "I'm honestly surprised that it doesn't hurt. Will you read more of your book to me tonight?"

"Definitely. The simplicity of his perception draws me in. Despite what is going on around him, when he is in the air, it all melts away and it is just him exploring the heavens with the earth below him. Could you imagine?"

"No, actually. Flying seems like an unnatural thing. Being that high, and knowing that the only thing holding me up in the air is a metal cage? No thank you, but I will leave the daydreaming up to you and I will simply enjoy the story. How many times have you read this book, by the way? It looks like it is close to falling apart."

"Too many."

"It's time to check your vitals, my dear," Dr. Alden said, startling us both as he entered the tent.

"Any chance you have some reading materials or anything to help pass the time with you?"

"Not this time, my dear. I will see what I can do. I will have to show you the lab sometime."

"I would enjoy your company. What makes the lab so fascinating?"

I looked at Anders, who pretended to be absorbed in his book, but without visible eye movement, he was not fooling anyone. At least not me, but perhaps I was the only one paying attention to him.

"It's the microscope. It always steals the show. It reveals hidden worlds blind to the naked eye, and in the blink of an eye, it can change under the right conditions and become something else entirely."

"Well, that begs the question of what you find fascinating under the microscope right now, doesn't it?"

"I'm afraid that will have to remain a mystery," he said, laughing mischievously. "It goes hand in hand with this line of work."

"Fine," I said, pouting. "Keep your secrets."

His hand grabbed at the bottom of the hospital gown, just above my knees. In a bold move, he lifted the edge of the cotton fabric and trailed it along with his fingers teasingly up my leg. The sensation felt more enhanced than it normally would, amplified to a new height that sent shivers down my spine. His eyes lost their amusement, and there was a seriousness to them as he watched his bare hand move up my bare legs, drifting slowly up along the side of my hips up to my stitches. My breath caught in my throat, and I gasped as the top of his other hand brushed my breast. He looked up and our eyes locked in place. His electric ocean blue eyes shifted in the lighting, and they lured me. I could not help but feel hungry and a familiar warmth between my legs.

Startled by my reaction, I looked over at Anders, who was now staring at us both with an unreadable gaze. It was hard to judge the level of disappointment he was holding, but I could certainly feel it. I could not explain what I was doing, but it felt like I was embracing him, except without touching, and in that embrace, I could feel everything he felt. Immediately, I felt overwhelmed with emotions of betrayal and disappointment, followed by an uprising of anger. There were more emotions that followed. Sadness. Loss. My heart shattered. *I thought she was different.* He did not say a word, and yet I could hear him.

Dr. Alden grabbed my hand lightly with his, distracting me from Anders, and he positioned his fingers on my wrist to check the level of my pulse. His other hand caressed the palm of my hand, and I once again felt the warmth return as my gaze met his. I felt something building within him, something that he was desperately trying to ignore. *What is happening?* His eyes lingered, taking in every detail that suited him to look at. I leaned back slightly and opened my legs just enough to show him an area that I never dared to show to anyone other than our family physician.

With my senses already heightened, I felt a sense of curiosity and intrigue coming from him. Followed by an intense desire that penetrated me in waves. It was as intense as an orgasm. I could feel my breathing quickening with a longing to feel a deeply embedded release. *I want to make love to you.* The thought filled my mind like an intimate seduction. A gentle caress that made the space between my legs ache.

Anders lightly cleared his throat as he shifted in his chair. I did not have the heart to tell him he was reading his book upside down.

"Can you take over for a while, Dr. Alden? I could use a break," he said, setting his book down on his chair as he stood up.

"It would be my pleasure," he said, not once looking at Anders. "Grab her meal personally from the chef. I had asked him to prepare something special for her. How are you feeling this evening, Vivienne?"

"I'm still pretty weak at walking, but I can barely tell I've had stitches. I do, however, feel like a prisoner in this tent. Could you give me permission to walk around? I feel it would help in getting my strength back. Walking around this small space is different from being out in the fresh air. I have to admit, I've walked around this cot so many times that it's weighing heavily on me, and I'm driving poor Anders insane with my incessant pacing."

"I'm sure he can handle it."

I was desperate, and I wanted to at least be able to go outside and walk around. Even if I had to have an armed guard with me.

"Please, Dr. Alden. What is to become of me?"

His hand slid down my arm like butter until it reached the elbow. His hand moved with ease to my breast. I gasped and surprised myself as I widened my legs and pulled him closer to me. I felt his body shiver underneath my touch. He reached up and took his mask down. Seeing him was worth the wait. His chiseled features led to strong cheekbones. A stern upper lip with a pout of a lower lip that I wanted to bite. I looked at him in the eyes, and a sense of ownership overcame me. Not from him, but from me. The mystery of it felt even more exciting. I grabbed his other hand that was on my waist and guided him down to the warmth that was begging to be touched.

My hands moved up his arms, across his shoulders, and to his neck. I pulled him down gently to bring his face a mere inch from mine. I used my fingertips to touch his bottom lip.

"Will you taste me?" I asked him in a whisper.

"I want to taste all of you."

I could feel his breath on my face, and I watched as whatever personal doubts he held melted as he kissed me deeply. I arched my back slightly as his hand explored inside me. He lifted my gown to expose my breast, and his head bent down to suckle my nipple. He lifted my gown over my head, and then continued to move down until his head was between my legs and his tongue joined his fingers in exploration. My hips moved in tandem with the luscious movement of his swirling tongue while his fingers playfully teased me. One of his hands draped under and over my leg to feel my hip, while the other stretched across my body to grasp at my bare breast. I moaned as quietly as I could, biting my lip as the buildup increased, and for the first time, I experienced what an orgasm was like with someone else.

I wanted to scream and cry at the same time. Was it

always like this? I had nothing to compare it to, but it felt like a combination of dying in the most pleasurable way possible. Like a little death. My heart felt as if it wanted to leap right out of my chest. He lifted me up off the bed and put me on my knees. I looked up at him, confused.

"This is fair game," he said with a smile. "Have you ever done this before?"

"No," I whispered, looking up at him, feeling vulnerable.

"I will go easy on you," he whispered as he touched my face. "Allow yourself to be just as curious about me as I was with you."

I had no flipping clue what he meant by that. He grabbed his zipper, pulling it down and reaching inside to pull out a formidable sized penis. I looked back up at him like he was crazy. He grabbed one of my hands and wrapped it around his member as he slid it in and out of my hand slowly, showing me what he wanted. He tilted my chin to look up at him, and he smiled down at me.

"Keep looking at me," he said in a heavy, seductive voice. "I want to see you as you devour me."

Opening my mouth with his thumb, he gently pulled my head forward to enclose my mouth around the tip of his penis while he loosened the bun in my hair, allowing my long black curly hair to dangle freely around my face and loose down my back. He moaned as he made small forward and back hip movements, with each small thrust gaining increased momentum until he pushed into my throat so far that I almost gagged while he exploded in my mouth. I looked up at him as I swallowed what was in my mouth and smiled at him.

"Dr. Alden?"

"I believe you have earned the right to call me, Michael."

"Michael," I said with a small whisper, feeling vulnerable and wondering if what just happened really happened. "I do not really know how this all happened so quickly. I... I have never done this. I am a... Well, I am a."

"A virgin?" He asked me with a relaxed smile.

"Yes, how did you know?"

"I am a skilled lover. I will not take you until you are ready to open yourself to me."

"I have heard it hurts," I told him with a feeble smile. "I really do not want my first time to be on a cot. I want it to be special. I have been saving myself for my... my future husband, whoever that may be."

"That is understandable, and I respect your decision a great deal. It shows your character and makes you even more special in my eyes."

"Why would you want to be with me when you have a wife at home?"

"That is a much larger conversation for another time. Know that you are safe with me, and I will take care of you. I have not felt this way in an exceptionally long time."

I was not sure of how I wanted to respond to him. Did I want to go to that next level with him? A vast majority of the women I grew up with had married or already messed around, but unlike them, I had little interest in anyone local. So why am I now interested in two men? A doctor and a soldier? Nobody else interested me in the slightest, and now I could not seem to get enough of either of them. I wanted them both. Anders, I could imagine tasted like honey and I deeply cared for him, except now I was with Dr. Alden, Michael, intimately, and none of it made any sense.

I watched as Michael cleaned himself up with a small towel near my bedside that I would have used to wash up for the evening. I lowered my gown just as Anders walked back in with two trays of food. He almost dropped both trays when he saw that Michael no longer had his mask on and was adjusting his zipper. Anders said nothing. He just stood there, looking indecisive and very pissed. Michael noticed his behavior and refused to even acknowledge him.

"Perfect timing. You're bound to be hungry after such an extensive examination," he told me as he gently lifted my chin and kissed me on the lips. "I'll leave you to eat, my dear. Ensure that Anders helps you with a warm sponge bath," he said as he finally acknowledged Anders' presence. "Ensure that the water is warm."

"Yes, Sir!" Anders exclaimed sarcastically, holding nothing back. A look of understanding passed over Michael's face. Anders looked down at the trays in his hands and then looked straight ahead at the space between us to avoid eye contact.

"Is there something you want to say, Anders?"

"May I speak frankly, sir?"

"By all means," Michael said, amused, as he crossed his hands over his chest.

"You are a married man! Your son is right outside!"

"I do not see how that is any business of yours."

"She doesn't belong to you."

"Calm your nerves, Anders. She does not belong to you, either. If you so much as touch her or take her virtue, you will regret the day you did. Do you understand me?"

The heat rose to my cheeks, and I wanted more than anything to run outside of the tent and not look back.

"Sir," he said, saluting, looking a bit more hopeful and even more upset than he was when he left the first time.

"Finally, his simple mind understands. Now, my dear," he said as he grabbed both my hands in his and kissed them. "I'll have Robert deliver some items for you to use at your pleasure."

"Thank you, that's most generous."

"Not at all," he said with a lopsided grin as he left the tent to go into the lab. "I'll ensure you have regular clothing as well. You will want for nothing."

I looked over at Anders, who said nothing as he angrily sat my dinner tray on the bed as peas ran over the plate and across the tray as they threatened to make a run for it. I wished I were the pea, escaping from the small confines of the plate. He refused to look at me, and I did not know what to say. This was going to be a long night. I felt so much shame. I have never in my life done anything like this. Why would I start now?!

I did not understand Anders' sacrifice by being with me. It did not register until the thought of losing him was weighing over my head. He made a choice to be here, and he risked his life from the very beginning, just to be at my side to keep his promise to me. He cared about me a great deal, and I was repaying him in the worst way possible. How could I care for someone and hurt them like this at the same time?

"Anders," I said, barely above an audible whisper.

"Stop," he said, shifting his peas from one side of his plate to the other.

CHAPTER 14

CHANGES

A sponge bath is something I experienced when I was a child, when my mother and I were living in the car and trying to find a place to settle. I loathed them. They filled my childhood with memories of using gas station bathrooms or in the back of the car with a sheet pinned as a curtain. Even the smell of a gas station took me back in time, reminding me of the uncertainty of the road ahead. I would have given anything for a warm shower.

Anders disappeared for almost two hours without touching his dinner. To be honest, I was not sure he was coming back. When he entered the tent with two other soldiers carrying a metal washing tub filled with steamy hot water and towels, I found myself in tears over something as simple as this. As soon as the soldier departed, I asked Anders to turn around, and I undressed.

"Hello? It's me, Robert," a nervous voice called out from just outside the tent. "May I come in?"

"One second," I called out as I grabbed a towel to cover myself. Anders was facing the wall of the tent and shifted his weight uncomfortably. "You may come in."

"I have a gift for you from my father," he said with a smile, setting a large white garment box down my cot. "You've made quite an impression on my father."

"What is all this?"

"My father sent the patrol out to grab you a few things."

"Your father is very kind," I murmured quietly.

"You don't know my father well," he said with a small

nervous laugh and clearing his throat. "Pay no attention to me."

I looked at the box with what I assumed were the items Michael mentioned I could use at my pleasure and wondered at what price these items would cost. Robert took his time leaving, shifting his weight as if he wanted to say more, but decided to not say anything at all. I grabbed a sheet from the cot and sat down. He acted nothing like his father in terms of confidence. Dr. Alden held a certain natural power and sway that accompanied his self-confidence. Robert acted unsure, reserved, and very shy. These were traits from his mother, obviously.

"Thank you, Robert," I said, trying to hurry him along. "Please give my sincerest thanks to your father. If you would not mind terribly, I would like to enjoy the warm water while it lasts."

"Of course, how silly of me. Enjoy your evening, Vivienne." I watched with a dreadful feeling in my belly as he rushed out of the tent. The entire scene was awkward, but the unspoken words that lingered left me with knots in my stomach.

I looked at the oversized white box with a satin green ribbon tied in a bow sitting next to me. Once upon a time, I would watch women from the town square carrying such boxes after visiting the shops I did not even dare walk into. I always wondered what it would feel like to walk out of the shop with a sense of pride at owning something luxurious. I could not help but wonder what it would feel like to live in their world. The simplest of truths is that I ignored it all, since it held no place for me in my life.

I opened the box and lifted the tissue paper off the contents. I gasped and gently fingered the items that were within. A simple, elegant long sleeve blue wool dress with embroidered flowers along the bottom with a matching sash. A pair of walking flats were under the dress, along with a small matching handbag with a comb, a vibrant red lipstick, and a small mirror. There was a soft satin nightgown and robe under the dress, along with delicate undergarments, and a bottle of perfumed oil for my skin and hair.

I picked up the dress, holding it up gently, fearful of ruining it, and held it close to my body. The boutique in the town square had this outfit in the window in late September. I walked by it on my way to work at the hospital, admiring its color and simplicity. Seeing the price tag in the window was enough to deter me from going in, but it was one of those boutiques that I would never enter. Now, here it was, in my hands.

"That's quite the gift," Anders said with venom. I turned around, startled. "What did you do to gain such a gift?"

I looked away, ashamed of what I did. *Way to go, Vivienne, he views you as a kept prostitute and the lover of a married man.*

"I'm so glad that my virtue means nothing," I angrily replied.

Placing the dress back in the box, I stepped into the warm water and grabbed the sponge, which forced him to turn back around. I looked over at Anders, and my heart immediately started pounding hard at the thought of him touching me. Every time his head turned slightly, I would catch my breath at the thought of him standing before me and seeing me as I am, naked and willing to show him what I was feeling. I did not want him to view me as his duty. I wanted to be more than that to him. Duty. The word felt cold and venomous on the tip of my tongue. What if that is all that I was now to him? What then?

"How could you let someone like him touch you?"

His words stung, sharp as needles, and I felt the scab being removed from a familiar old wound that I had spent my teen years trying to understand. I could only stare at the floor and wonder what was wrong with me. The confusion surrounding being touched and sex was a delicate and confusing line that I was not ready to cross, and yet, here I was. Confused as ever. Is it good? Is it bad? Why am I feeling so much shame for a few moments of pleasure? Is it because deep down, I knew there was no genuine attraction with a married older man? Or was it because it was fleeting and only temporary? On some level, I knew there was a deeper truth. I feared becoming my mother. I buried my shame in the dark forest of my mind and focused on Anders.

"Why did you not tell me how you felt about me?" I asked him boldly in return.

I watched as his back stiffened. I grabbed the oil and massaged it into my skin. I felt so alive, decadent, and my heightened senses made the experience very pleasurable. My skin responded with goosebumps as my fingertips moved slowly up my arm to my shoulder, moving across my collarbone, and up my neck with a soft caress ending at my jawbone. I could feel the touch lingering, and I swear I could almost see it! There was a soft, subtle illumination to my skin. The oil smelled heavenly of vanilla and a floral note I was not familiar with. It smelled a bit like lily, but it was too woodsy, with a hint of amber. Should I feel shame for this too? Or would I allow myself a moment to feel something that was real, even if it was by my own hands?

I watched Anders shift his weight from one foot to the other with building impatience and tense up as the smell filled the tent. I admired the view of his backside, but feeling his anger was a constant reminder that it was a one-way street. I felt so alone, and without his support, I felt a madness stirring within me, ready to crack like an eggshell, and I was not sure if I could pick up the pieces and put myself back together again. Not after everything!

"Anders, would you mind helping me wash my back?" I asked him to break down the wall between us as I grabbed my towel to cover as much as I could.

"Fine," he said through gritted teeth. He turned and looked up and paused. He took in a deep breath, and I tried to imagine myself in his eyes. My long, black curly hair draping my body like curtains. I could imagine that I looked wild, exotic, and resembled nothing of this world. Deep inside, I felt seductive, alluring, and powerful. It was a sensation I was unaccustomed to feeling, and yet, I continued to feel vulnerable, shy, and reserved. When I was around Anders, I was simply a girl falling in love with a boy.

He regained his composure and grabbed the sponge from me. I heard Anders as he bent down to steep the sponge in the water. As he stood up slowly, I allowed my towel to drop. There was another pause. He eased my hair over my shoulder, and in slow circular motions, he washed my back. He walked around me slowly and handed me the sponge, our hands touching momentarily. He looked at me with angry eyes that also held desire and a hunger that I knew was only for me.

I lightly covered myself with my hands, and he bent down slowly to grab my towel. He took in every inch of me as he did. I could feel his anger dissipate into a deep desire and longing to touch me. He handed me my towel and continued to look up at me. I handed him the oil.

"Would you mind?" I asked shyly.

Without a word, he grabbed the oil and poured a small amount into his hands. He handed me the oil as I turned my back to him. His hands were warm, and he used a gentle pressure as he massaged the oils into my back, rubbing my shoulders and arms. I turned my head to look back at him, and he moved in front of me.

"Tell me that nothing happened," he asked, ruining the spell we were creating together.

"Why?" I yelled at him, catching him off guard. "Why ask me when you already know the answer?!"

"I cannot stand the thought of him touching you," he said, lowering his head with a long sigh. "To even think about it makes me feel sick! How can I even look at you?"

"How can I look at myself in the mirror? I do not know who I am anymore, and I regret what I allowed him to do to me. Can trauma cause people to act out of character? I feel like I do not even know myself right now. I mean, I would never... I have allowed no one to touch me, not intimately. I am saving myself for my future husband."

"What he said about your virtue? That's true?"

"It is true."

"I have no reason to be upset. You're not my wife," he said as he shifted his weight uncomfortably. "Or my girlfriend, but if I had my way, you would be. What happened between you two?"

"He touched me, and I touched him."

"What you did is a conscious choice," he told me, looking up at me, irritated and eyes smoldering.

"I know that! I am going to tell you this right now, so there is no question. I have wanted nothing more than to be in your arms. I have fantasized about you nonstop, and I cannot help if my emotions are running higher than normal because of it. I have been waiting for you to make the first move, and when you did not, I assumed that what I thought was between us was just in my head. I do not want Michael. I want you!"

"Michael?!" He asked, his voice rough and low, clenching his fists. He paced back and forth with his hands behind his head as he mumbled to himself. When he finally said something, I realized I was holding my breath because of the awkward silence. "You don't want Dr. Alden? You also cannot put that all on me. What you do with him has nothing to do with me. What happens when two people come together is an agreement made between them. I do not even know how you are going to get yourself out of that mess."

"Thank you for your support," I told him angrily. "I know I hurt you, but I have been trying to tell you this whole time that there is something wrong with me! I am changing..."

"What do you mean, you are changing? If this is some lame excuse to get out of what you did with him..."

"God, it is not!"

"Then what kind of change could you possibly be going through that would have you parting your legs for him?"

I gasped. "Forget it." I turned away from him as grief overwhelmed me and the tears stung my eyes.

"Hey," he whispered as he reached out, touching my shoulder. "I am sorry that was not fair. Please, tell me."

"I'm not attracted to Dr. Alden," I said as he let out a long sigh. "But... Something was different about him. I do not understand any of it. I do not know what is happening to me. I wanted him, in the same way that I want you."

"This is not helping you."

"I'm being honest. I do not know why, but it is there, and it is not normal. There is something about him that lures me in a way that makes no sense. When I first met him, there was zero attraction. That is why I asked you if people that have been through what I have, do they change? I feel it in my bones. There is something not right about him, and I do not trust him."

"Yet you two were getting acquainted intimately? Vivienne, that makes no sense!" He said, getting clearly annoyed. "What does that mean for me? For us? I will not sit by and play second fiddle why you and the doctor have a grand old time and flaunt it in my face that I will be nothing more than what I am."

"I do not want him. I want you for all that you are, and that is more than enough for me. What I want with you could last a long, long time. You are someone that I..."

"What?"

"You are someone that I could see myself settling down with. Please do not hate me! I am so ashamed of what I allowed him to do to me."

"I... I don't hate you," he said, thinking it through. "I'm hurt. If I misread your intentions that you were into me as much as I am into you, then I apologize. I want you so badly it hurts."

"Please, I want you just as badly! I feel like I am changing from the inside out. I do not know how else to explain it to you without sounding crazy. I can feel what you feel, and I feel so lost in how to navigate what you are feeling versus what I am feeling. Where do my emotions begin and yours end?" I put my hands up to my face. I was afraid. "This isn't me! You know me more than anyone has ever known me my entire life. When I investigate my future, all I want to see is a place with you in it."

"If that's true, what if you were feeling his attraction to you and became confused?" He asked me thoughtfully.

"Do you think that could explain why I let him touch me?"

"I do not know, but we will figure this out. Together. What can I say that would erase this day?"

"I do not know. I am so sorry, Anders. I did not mean to hurt you," I said as the tears continued to roll down my cheeks. "No wonder everyone fears me! What if I become a monster, like that nurse that stabbed me and ate that soldier?"

"You must see there is more to all this. There is something bigger going on, and whatever it is, it has all the camps gossiping like a bunch of chipmunks. This much I know for certain, you are still you. You are beautiful, and one of the kindest women I know."

"I am so kind that I betrayed your trust," I said through sobs. "You thought I was different."

Anders looked up at me more intently and with a look of confusion. "Did I tell you that?"

"No, you were thinking about it earlier before you left to go on your break," I told him, using the towel to wipe my face. "I want more than anything to leave this all behind. I wish we could run away from here and start our lives over."

"We cannot run from our problems."

"Do you think there is no future for a couple like us? Your pale skin is a huge contrast to my darker skin. We would stand out, and you know what happens to couples like us? They end up ostracized, put in prison, or killed. Does that sound like a fun relationship? What could I give you other than the here and now? Maybe you are right in just assuming I'm like all the others and you should stay away from me so I can save you a lifetime of challenges and hardships."

He closed the small gap between us, and he held my face in his hands. "You can't choose my life for me."

"I know that," I told him, as his face came closer. His eyes locked on my lips, and my hands reached out to touch his chest.

"I want you," he said, his breathing quickened. "More than I have ever wanted anything."

"Let me prove it to you. Please kiss me?" I asked him as I looked up and pleadingly explored his eyes as I bunched his shirt into my hands, drawing him in closer.

He kissed me lightly on the forehead. "No."

"No?"

"Viv, I cannot do that. Not after knowing your lips were on his. It is not right, Viv."

"I... I understand. I was not thinking," I told him as my insides twisted and I placed my face in my hands. "I'm sorry. I should have known better. I do not even know what I am doing anymore. What the hell is wrong with me?!"

"Nothing is wrong with you. You have been through hell. The day I first laid eyes on you, I knew you were the one for me," he said, leaving me open-mouthed. "You are worth the wait."

With little else to say, I dressed quickly and tucked myself in my cot while Anders called out for help to take the tub out of the tent. I turned down the lantern that was sitting on the chair beside me, turning over so that he would not see my tears of shame when he came back in. I was not sure when he came back. I must have fallen asleep quickly. I woke up, wide awake, and wondering if the day had happened at all. The smooth feeling of fabric from the nightgown was a reminder that it had.

I was not even sure if Anders, who laid on the ground beside me, was fully asleep. His breathing was steady and shallow, but his anxiety and frustration were like an overwhelming undertow that threatened to sweep me under fighting the current. No matter how I tried to disconnect from him, his powerful emotions threatened to take me against my will. I could not decipher where his feelings began and where my own ended.

I could hear Michael and Robert working late into the night, messing around with glass vials, and talking to one another in hushed tones. I could not help but be curious about what was keeping them up so late and deep in conversation. If they had any news on the virus, I deserved the right to know what was going on. I threw my legs over the side of the bed opposite Anders and got up as quietly as I could. Lifting my long nightgown to avoid it getting the fabric entangled with my feet, I stepped over Anders' feet, and I moved into the small adjoined space between the tents and peeked through the flap into the space they were using as a lab.

"Did you think we wouldn't see you?" Michael raised his voice on the far side of the tent with his back to me.

I froze. How did he know I was there? *Oh shit!*

CHAPTER 15

NO LONGER HUMAN

I tried to think quickly of a cover story, but all I could produce was I heard his voice and that it would be nice to say hello since I could not sleep. I was walking into dangerous territory, especially with Anders not being present to save me from myself. I felt the butterflies building in my stomach. *You can do this, Viv! Think of Anders.*

"You sneaky thing! You had us fooled! Using another virus like your candy wrapper is plain clever, with you at its center," Michael muttered under his breath as he jotted down notes. I slowly let out a small sigh of relief, realizing he was talking to himself. "What are you?"

He shifted his weight to his right and opened a suitcase near his feet and took out a mystery vial, added a drop onto the slide that he was looking at, and put it back under the microscope.

"Fascinating," he gasped. "You're invading and mimicking the other virus. Where did you come from, you little copycat?"

His son, Robert, entered through the main entrance into the tent, handing his father a cup of coffee.

"Oh, good! You are back! Robert, look at this," he said with a smile. "You won't believe it if you don't see it for yourself."

Robert walked up to the microscope as his father stepped aside and looked into the eyepiece.

"What the hell is this?" Robert asked, turning white as he looked up at his father.

"Evolution at its finest. This is the virus integrated with the blood sample from our latest sample. Given her state, what we are looking at is unprecedented. A new species of human."

"You can't possibly mean it relates them to humans," he snickered. "She is far from human. She is… She is…"

"I know what she is," he said in a condescending voice. "Yet, she exists."

"Yes," he said with fear filling his voice. "But how does she exist?"

"I've written out a few scenarios based on my theories. We need to look at it as more than a virus. We need to view it like a parasite. It is using a flu virus to infect, multiply, and spread. It completely mimicked and then eradicated the actual flu virus, taking on its properties to conduct its function, which we have yet to identify. It changed itself so rapidly that not even the healthy cells had time to react. This virus reminds me of… No, it couldn't be."

"You can't possibly mean it's the virus you studied in Germany?"

"I have an inkling that it is the same, or a branch from the same family. We will not know until we have time to study this further with controlled experiments in the lab."

Robert prepared three slides and then looked into the eyepiece on his microscope at the first one. He turned and began flipping through a pile of his notes on another table. Confused, he sorted through at least ten pages before giving up and setting the clipboard down.

"What did you do? I can't replicate this."

"I exposed the Stony Creek virus to the latest flu virus, gave it time to sit, and then added a drop of the nurse's blood as a catalyst."

"Fascinating," he exclaimed with his back to me as he added a new drop to the slide. "I wonder what happens when we throw in a disease or two."

"I have a feeling that they will end up just like the nurse. Hand me Vivienne's blood from when she first arrived, would you? Let us see what happens when we add her blood as a catalyst."

The nurse?!

Robert handed him my blood, and he grabbed a new slide and used a dropper to place a drop of blood on the slide. He placed it on the microscope stage and moved the knob on the side of the microscope. He then grabbed another vial that was already on the counter and added the drop to the slide with my blood on it. For a split second, I felt like I was seeing things, except Michael saw it as well. An explosion of light flooded the small area around the microscope. Michael jumped back, and he grunted as he bumped into the sharp edge of the metal table behind him.

"Robert," he asked loudly.

"Yeah," Robert answered, turning around, and looking up from the notes his father had given him.

"Do you see that?" he exclaimed, pointing at the microscope.

Robert looked over towards the microscope, dropped the clipboard that held the notes, and slowly began walking backing towards the exit. "What the hell is that?!"

We all watched frozen in place with mouths gaping wide as small wispy tendrils of light radiated out from the slide like an ephemeral star seeking to latch onto a life source. If I could describe it in a word, that word would be beautiful. Whatever it was, I felt drawn to it in a way that I could not explain in words. Like a mother's lullaby, it sang to me.

Michael approached the microscope with caution as the light and wispy tendrils slowly dissipated like a flashlight battery that was losing its charge. He grabbed the stool from beside him and sat down, drifting his head towards the eyepiece to observe the slide. His son was not as convinced and stayed by the door. Michael excitedly grabbed his notes and began writing out what he was seeing.

"This is unlike anything I've ever seen. It is like an engineered delivery system. It is delivering material to the cells. The question is, what is it encoding into the cell? The cells are going through a rapid cell division, changing like a beautiful dance. What is this? What would we become if these mutations completed the process? Hand me the other subject's blood."

"I'm scared to find out," Robert said, still looking frazzled. "I looked over the notes you brought over from the other lab assistant working on corpse intake, and he had done complete workups on two corpses brought in from the edge of town. They both appeared to die from organ failure. What if the virus rejects the host, causing the body to attack itself like an immune response against itself?"

"Our little virus is a messenger. Have they been able to track down the medical files we needed from the hospital?"

"No, they're still clearing bodies. Why?"

"There are vital facts that we are missing. If Dr. Kines or any of his staff documented any stage of the virus, we will need those files. It will help further our research along. We need that information sooner than later," he said with an annoyed sense of urgency.

"Dad, don't worry," Robert said in a way that showed just how he loved and admired his father. "We will contain the virus."

He looked back into the microscope with my blood. "We are only now on the frontier of going deeper to understand that process of a standard flu virus. Imagine the possibilities with what we can uncover with this. If we can understand whatever this is, we will just call it a parasite for now. We could use it to eradicate all illnesses and potentially all diseases on the planet."

"Is it safe to look at her sample now?"

"It is," Michael smiled at his son warmly. "Have a look."

Robert inched his way towards the microscope and took three nervous head bobs down before allowing himself to come into full contact with the eyepiece. Once he did, both of his hands flailed about, attempting to get his father's attention.

"Did you tamper with Vivienne's latest blood sample?" Robert asked his father.

"No, why do you ask?"

"This can't be right," he said, standing up, taking off his glasses, and then rubbing his eyes. "Can you look at this and tell me what you see?"

Robert moved aside and Michael moved to the other side of his son and looked into the microscope. I watched as his body tensed up, and he stood up and looked at his son with wide eyes.

"Dad, is... Is she..."?

"She didn't just have the virus. She is the evolution of the virus. This is fascinating!"

"Dad, these are not human cells."

"She's no longer human."

I am no longer human?!

"Oh my God," he said, taking in a deep breath, putting his hands on the top of his head as he paced back and forth. "Hand me the slide with the nurse's blood and the virus."

He quickly switched out the slide and investigated the eyepiece. "Fascinating. These cells do not appear alive at all, and yet they are continuing to function as if they were. It is like they lost the electrical charge to light up. What would happen if we added a drop of Vivienne's blood?"

"We should wait until we have a more secure and controlled environment setup, Dad. You saw what happened with Vivienne's blood sample when exposed to more of it. Should we... Should we start quarantine procedures?"

"No, there's no need. We have already passed the seventy-two-hour evaluation period when we were all exposed to her blood. We will counter protocol with mandatory testing to those exposed to her or the nurse. Robert, send a message to the Major. Tell him the Red Phoenix has taken flight."

"Dad," he said nervously. "Per protocol and regulation, we base quarantine on our findings. How do you propose we explain this to the Major?"

"You do not need to remind me of protocols and regulations. I will not risk the spread of the virus beyond this area. After you send the Major the message, gather the equipment we will need," Michael told Robert as he turned around, causing me to back away from the opening. "We will leave within the hour."

"Where are we going?"

"We are going to take a small road trip."

"Alright," Robert said nervously.

"We need to visit the nurse that stabbed Vivienne. Based on what we have found, the nurse may be more than a rabid dog that needs something to play with."

"You think she's the carrier? The catalyst? What does that make Vivienne?"

"Time will answer that for us. Vivienne is more than we could have imagined. We will need more of her blood to know for certain. Get the message sent and meet me at the holding site. I will grab nonessential personnel to aid us in collecting our sample. I have an inkling that we are witnessing something truly unprecedented. We are watching history in the making, the birth of not just one, but perhaps two new species, if my hypothesis is accurate."

"Why do you even try to communicate with it? Whatever you think it is, it appears to be less human with each passing day. It made no sense the last time we spoke to it. Why is it drawn to human flesh? It complains incessantly about her hunger and that we are keeping it away from her mother, was it? Or was it its sister or daughter? The entire conversation was confusing. I could not make any sense of it."

"We can still refer to it as her since there is obvious female anatomy, Robert."

"What?"

"Never mind," he said with a long sigh. "Off you go, Robert."

She... She is alive? No! Oh, God! What does all this mean? A new species? What did that even mean? Would I be like her?

Feeling overwhelmed with anxiety, fear, and concern, I turned around and as I gasped as Anders put his hand over my mouth.

"Shhhhh," he whispered, holding his finger to his mouth. He grabbed my hand and led me back to the cot and he sat me down. My lack of sleep was creating fresh stories for my brain to follow. They were not stories made of rainbows, puppies, cute little fluffy bunnies, or kittens. They were horrifying. I sat there, staring at my hands as I rocked myself. Anders paced back and forth, which did not help my nerves at all. I wanted to scream at the top of my lungs and ask God or whomever was listening what was going on. How could I not be human? I looked human, right?!

"I'm not human," I said as I choked back tears. "I'm not human."

Anders stopped pacing, and he kneeled on one knee in front of me. He grabbed my hands in his and he let out a deep sigh.

"Look, I don't know what they mean when they say you're not human, but this much I know. You're special, and a miracle."

"I knew something was wrong. I... I... I felt different. I could feel myself changing, its inside of me. It's becoming a part of me, Anders!"

"Look at me," he said, pulling my chin towards him. "You are still you. Whatever is going on, we will figure this out. I won't let you do this alone."

"If I am not human, then my life hangs in the balance. How long do you think they will allow me to live before they make me a science experiment?! At some point, they will reassign you, and where will that leave me?"

He stood up and pulled me into his arms. I held onto him like he was the only thing in this life that made sense. I breathed in the smell of spicy aftershave, with notes of sage. He smelled like home.

"We will figure this out." He cleared his throat, breaking the spell between us. "I am going to see if any of the guys have heard anything. I will be back as soon as I can."

"Please, please don't go," I pleaded with him as I grabbed his arm.

"Hey," he told me softly as he moved the hair out of my eyes. "I will be right back. Promise."

I cannot do this journey alone. Not like this. I cannot imagine him not being by my side, but how could I protect him from something I did not even understand? Could we ever live in a world where we could be more than we are? Sneaking in a kiss was one thing, but what I wanted was to set the world on fire with our love. The world would never understand a love like ours, especially if I ended up craving his flesh. How can I protect him from me?

Anders had become my anchor, my rock, and now he was putting himself in a position to be a willing sacrifice. Anders did not deserve any of this. I do not want to become a monster like that woman! Her desire. God, is that why I wanted Michael so badly? Or was it a mix of my need to satiate a hunger I did not understand mingled with his own desire to dominate my body? *Dammit! Would anything make sense?!*

CHAPTER 16

THE CABIN IN THE WOODS

"I have confirmed that she is indeed very much alive. They captured her. She is also off her cracker. They're holding her at an undisclosed location near another camp," he told me, handing me a canteen filled with water.

"She's alive," I repeated to myself. "I'm not sure how I feel about her being alive. I know she is of significance, especially now with what they have discovered. I will never leave this place, will I?"

"I do not know what is going to happen next. Even if you could escape, where would you go? As much as I hate Dr. Alden, he is the best one here to help you understand what is going on within you. It sounds like they cannot get many answers from the nurse," he said, shaking his head. "I wonder if it's because of everything that she saw early on with so many people dying around her. Or if it was the virus that changed her, that explains partially what you are feeling? Right? She was mentally unstable to begin with, and this experience took her to the edge. This kind of thing can break anyone."

"When she stabbed me, she was... She was not right in the mind. I cannot imagine anyone with a sane mind reacting the same way."

"You never said what the nurse yelled at you when she stabbed you."

"She called me her sister, daughter, and mother. I do not know why she chose those exact words, but if I am becoming like her, then perhaps in a grotesque capacity, I am all those things. At least to her. Will I crave human flesh as she does?

What... What if I hurt you?!"

"I will take that chance," he said, taking my hands into his and squeezing them. "She called you her sister, daughter, and mother? From what Robert was saying, it sounds like she is not happy they are keeping you from her. What do you think she wants from you?"

"I do not know. How do you stand all of this?"

"We see a lot in the military," he said with a sigh, rubbing the stubble on his face with his hands. "This is by far one of the worst that I've seen. I helped with recovery after the big earthquake in Alaska last year that sent a tsunami over to Hawaii that decimated all in its path. They sent me with my unit to Hilo. Each experience is unique."

"How was it different from Stony Creek?"

"Here, the buildings still stand. It is the bodies, and so many of them, that make it unreal. It is like standing in the middle of a story that has lost its voice. Each body is an echo of what gave the town life."

"What about Hawaii?"

"To see the devastation and the buildings that once stood tall in rubble and working hours on end to fish bodies of men, women, and children out of the debris, all the while praying we would find someone alive. When we did, it made all our efforts worth it. There were few survivors."

"Isn't it like that now?"

"Yes, but here, it's an unseen threat that has taken everything in its path. In Hawaii, we knew there was more of a chance for survival if the individual was lucky. Here..."

"What?"

"We didn't expect to find any survivors."

"What's going to become of me, Anders?"

"I honestly don't know, but I will do whatever I can to ensure that you are safe. I am not going anywhere."

"Promise me, Anders?" I asked him as I looked up into his eyes. He wiped away my tears with his thumbs, and he leaned in and brushed his lips against mine so softly that it barely registered. "Promise me!"

"I promise," he said as he looked into the distance. "No matter what, I will always find my way back to you. We need to rest. Let us try this again."

I laid down, curling up into the blankets as Anders tucked me in, adding an extra blanket to keep me warm. He laid down, bunching up his jacket to use under his head, as he laid down on a folded blanket and wrapped himself up in another. The blankets were deceptively warm, even though they did not look like much from their appearance.

I drifted off to sleep more quickly than I thought I would. Once Anders turned the lantern down, I was drifting in a dreamless sleep. A noise startled me wide awake. I laid there listening intently to see if the noise was something to be concerned about or if I was merely dreaming it. It would not have been the first time that I had a night terror that had awakened me, but I had not had one for years. Not since I was a young child. I felt like I was in the middle of a waking dream. The kind where you know you are awake, yet you are still asleep and entangled in a dream you cannot escape. The merging of two worlds, and the only way to get out is to fall back to sleep.

Unsure of the time that had passed since I had fallen asleep, but knowing it could not have been long. It was still dark. I reached down and grabbed the Winchester flashlight and turned it on, moving the light away from Anders, who slept peacefully on the ground beside me. I sat up and walked over to the flap of the tent, and I peeked outside. I walked out into the frosty night, surprised that there was no guard on duty, which could have meant a bathroom break or a shift change, but it was out of pattern. They would normally wake up Anders, regardless.

There it was again! I turned, pointing the flashlight toward the dark forest that loomed before me. The creaking branches and the icy wind that picked up around my bare feet left me clutching my naked arms to my chest. Whatever it was, it chilled me to the bone. It did not sound human. Without thinking, I walked in the sound's direction. I could not remember a recent time when the camp was this quiet. It was eerie.

As I approached the forest, an owl swooped over my head, startling me as it landed gracefully on a thick branch above me. It sang softly with a low-pitched who-who-who as it watched me move through the forest. There was another cry in the chilly evening air that caused a sense of dread as my blood boiled with fear. The cold snap in the air drew my attention to the waking world as another gust of wind threatened to lift my nightgown. I rubbed my arms as I tried to warm myself. Another cry swallows the night, swollen and overripe against the waning of the wind that now batters against my body, chilling me to the bone. My bare feet exposed on the hard, sharp ground stumble as my feet land on sharp pine needles, sticks and jagged rocks. My feet crunch on the dried leaves that have long since lost their lustrous color. My lungs take in the icy chill in the air announcing the snow at higher elevations. I stopped and stared into the dark forest around me, only illuminated by a band of light coming from the flashlight. The cloud cover moving in threatened to trap me.

What am I doing?!

The urge to rush to the source, like a mother, would rush in to protect and ensure the safety of her child was overwhelming. Whatever this was, it was not my child, yet I felt myself being summoned to it by its need. The pull became stronger and stronger with each step that I had taken since leaving the tent.

The cells within me vibrated in a way that I have never felt before. With every tortured scream, my blood burned, and fear overwhelmed. It was terrifying. I could no longer tell if I was shaking from fear or shaking from the cold. It sounded like a demon. Not male, nor female. Twisted and corrupt by an unseen force that mutates its very nature. Whatever it is, it is not human. How could it be? *Monsters do not exist, Vivienne!* Is it...? Could it be the nurse?

I ran full speed back to the tent. I needed to wake up Anders. He was a part of this. I did not want to do this alone and knowing that he will walk this path with me, regardless of where it led, meant the world to me. It also meant that if I were going to be stupid, at least he would be my voice of reason.

I could have been more tactful. Instead, I landed right on top of him and raised my voice louder than I should have. "Anders!"

"Whatshafunit," he said, slurring his words together as our bodies scrambled together as he made heads or tails of what was happening.

"Shhhhh," I whispered as I pulled myself back up towards his face.

"Viv, what's going on?" He asked, eyeing me strangely and looking around the room.

"Wait," I told him with my fingers to his lips. I needed him to just listen so he could hear it. If he could hear it, then I was not losing my mind. "Do you hear that?"

Anders grabbed my shoulders and was shifting our combined weight to move me off him when he looked unpleasantly startled as he listened intently to the wailing scream that continued the wind. He shifted uncomfortably, nudging me off him gently as he stood up and cautiously looked around the tent. I did not blame him, even though I knew that the tent, while durable, would not keep whatever that was out if it wanted to find a way in. "What the hell was that? Have you ever heard anything like that around here?"

"No," I said, feeling relieved, grabbing my robe, and wrapping it tightly around me, along with the blanket as protective shielding. "Never. There are also no guards on duty!"

"What?! That can't be!"

"Shhhhh," I whispered. "What do you think is going on?"

"I don't know," he whispered, standing up quickly and getting his jacket on and grabbing his weapon that I did not realize until now that he kept directly under my cot as he slept.

"Stay here. I need to find out what is happening."

"You are not leaving me alone," I exclaimed as I put on the shoes that Michael had Robert pick out for me.

"Fine, but stay close to me."

"Wait!"

"What?"

"You need to help me find whatever that is... out there."

"You want me to do what? Forgive me for what I'm about to say, Viv," he paused, taking in a deep breath, and releasing it. "There's no fucking way I am taking you towards whatever the hell that is!"

"Anders," I pleaded. "I have to go! It... It is calling me, and I need to know why. I think it might be her. The nurse."

"No," he told me, his eyes stern and his arms crossed as held his ground.

"I either go with you or I go without you, pick one," I told him as I crossed my arms and returned his glare.

"Dammit, Viv," he whispered under his breath. "You're going to get us both arrested or shot."

"Does that mean you will help me?"

"If we leave and they find out, we may as well sign our freedom over to them. I do not want to face a court martial over this, and your future is already uncertain as it is. Do you really want to add more fuel to the fire? If you end up causing mistrust, it could lead to further restrictions you may not like. The only way we avoid both is that we do not go waltzing off in the middle of the night to God knows where to God knows what. If a patrol catches us coming back towards the camp, not knowing that we left the camp, they will not ask questions. They will shoot us on site. Think this through!"

I closed my eyes and reached out with my mind moving beyond the camp and allowing my mind to dictate where the screams were coming from. Like a bee to a flower, it drew me to its darkness. I felt a longing to escape, to find something. Yes, to find the source! It must find the source and drink. Drink to survive. A hunger. A need to bite into human flesh and give into deeply seeded passions. A deep desire to feel life, to feel pain, pleasure...

"No," I exclaimed as I severed the connection, and the brute energetic force of it knocked me off balance.

"Are you going to explain this now?" He asked me as he held my arms steady. "What's going on? What did you just do?"

"I reached out to it, to connect with it. I... It... It is hungry."

"Do you want to explain why your body lit up like a candle?"

"What?" I watched his hands flap around as he attempted to mimic what my body was doing. I did not know what he was trying to say, but it reminded me of a young girl running from a spider, only without the frantic screams and running. I raised an eyebrow at him, stating my confusion.

"Your body did this thing. It glowed, only slightly, like a candle that was just lit. Then it was like something covered you in black fog, and you were barely visible. I am not describing this right. What is going on? Did you slip something in my canteen before I went to sleep?" He asked me as he picked it up and sniffed it.

"Anders, can you seriously ask me that? Look. I am asking you to stretch your mind and help me figure this all out. I can feel it wants to kill. It strongly needs to satisfy its hunger and fill its twisted desires. What we are going to find is dangerous. It's deadly, and all I know is that it is connected to me."

"How do you know? Did it ever occur to you that maybe why you are feeling this way is so that you turn around and run the other way?"

"Look, I can't explain right now. Please, we need to go. I need to know how I fit into all of this. If you are right and she is dangerous and my going backfires, we will run like hell. Deal?"

"I have learned to trust my intuition, and my intuition is telling me this is a bad idea, Viv!"

I walked up to him and put his face in my hands. "I can

feel what she is feeling. I can feel her pain. They are torturing her. Trying to discover what makes her work. I cannot explain it, but I know she is something different, and yet, she is of me as I am of her. How can I prepare myself for the changes that are happening within me if I cannot understand them? Or at least try to."

"I can't believe I am doing this. Dammit, Viv! You have some serious explaining to do when we get back. We must be careful. I don't feel like either of us dying today."

"There's no guard on duty, so we have that going for us."

I watched as Anders stormed out of the tent, swearing under his breath. I followed him out.

"Something's wrong. There should be a guard here and over there watching his flank," he whispered as he looked around. "Stay here. I need to check on something. Don't worry, I won't be but a few steps away."

I waited patiently as he disappeared behind the tent. If he knew there was a problem, then that was undeniably disconcerting. A slight tremor of fear worked its way from my belly as I looked around the camp. The soft snores of sleeping men filled the surrounding air. The hush of the camp a reminder that not all was what it seemed. Not tonight. I sighed a sigh of relief when I saw Anders walking back towards me.

"See, I told you I was only a few steps away," he said, looking pale with concern written all over his face. "Something is definitely wrong. There is no perimeter patrol, either. I woke up the late-night shift who were still sleeping and asked them why they were not at their posts. They have the night off. They did not focus on the details. A night off from graveyard means they can catch up on sleep, and it's not exactly our job to question orders."

"Ordered by whom? Who would order something like that?"

"I'm not sure, but it leaves our camp exposed and wide open. There are only two people I know of that could give an order like that, and one of them is at headquarters. The other you know as Michael. It makes no sense, but I have a few ideas. We need to be extra cautious."

"Why? What are you thinking?"

CHAPTER 17

HUNGER

"This has to be a test!"

"A test of what?!"

"A test to see what she will do or what she is capable of if she knows the camp is open and you are accessible. She obviously wants to get to you, and they know I would guard you with my life, but why leave you so defenseless? If she's as tough as they say, and it took four guards to take her down, then I would not stand much of a chance against her, unless..."

"Unless they are testing me as well to see what I'm capable of in return."

"I will bet he is trying to get rid of me, or at least hoping I will be the innocent bystander taken out by the crossfire. I bet he has had his spies eavesdropping on us the entire time."

"Don't say that! I will not let that happen. I refuse to lose you, too! I have already lost enough!"

The rest of the camp remained silent as we cautiously stepped out beyond the boundaries that provided a false sense of security, with only the sounds of the dark forest to welcome us. I turned on my flashlight, and he lowered it immediately.

"No," he whispered. "We have to do this right. We go in the dark. Give your eyes some time, they will adjust."

An inner knowing stirred within me. No place was safe. The trees resembled dark shadows, their contrast giving the forest a presence that suggested a sinister force lurked hidden and unseen as the branches reached out like long crooked claws.

Anders placed me behind him as we walked slowly,

pausing briefly here and there to move over thick roots on the ground or avoid ditches that did not appear to be as steep as they were. They trained him well. He was more observant than I was, and I kept tripping on tree roots. Each time I stumbled, I watched as a wave of tension stiffened his entire body. He was used to stealth and tactics, and then he met me. What an odd pair we were.

As we continued to walk towards the wailing screams that continued to draw us in like a beacon, I felt myself weakening slightly. This was the most active I had been in days. I took in a deep breath of fresh air and held onto the moment long enough to revel in the simple freedom of being anywhere but a closed in space. I turned around and saw our camp behind us. It looked so small. I turned back to Anders and nodded my head to give him the okay as I willed my legs to go on. Ahead of us was a ranger's outpost. Unremarkable, smaller than a vacation cabin but only slightly larger than a shack, it would hold little interest to even those even remotely curious about it. Just beyond it, I would see the lighting of another camp. This camp was much busier than ours, with more activity going on well into the night.

"What are they doing at that camp?"

"Corpse retrieval and processing," he whispered. "This camp does not sleep. It works around the clock like a well-oiled contraption and keeps going until its job is complete."

"What do you mean by processing?" I asked him, coming to a halt, and pulling on his shirt to stop.

"We can't give the bodies a proper burial because of the virus. They will identify the bodies, and then burn them in a mass grave."

"Including my mother," I asked him, choking on the words.

"Yes," he told me, looking apologetic. "I'm so sorry, Viv. Its procedure. We can't risk the spread of the virus."

I could not look away from the camp, as I imagined my mother placed in a mass grave, along with all the other faces that entered my mind. People that I watched grow year after year, adult and child alike. The mental image of them all lying in the ground, some with shocked looks on their faces and others wracked with pain. All of them waiting to be burned. The mental imagery had me grabbing my sides as I hunched over slightly as I tried to hold back the sadness and pain that wanted to break free.

I felt a wave of nausea wash over me like tar, followed by a mind-piercing pain that poured searing pain through my skull, followed by the torturous scream. It was coming from the small wood cabin. I grabbed my head with both of my hands and moaned in pain as I tried to focus through the pain as my vision scrambled and my ears rang loudly.

"Viv," he whispered, pulling me into his arms. "What's wrong?"

"The pain! So much pain," I cried.

"Let's turn around," he told me, looking around with wide eyes. "This doesn't feel right."

"I can't," I whispered to him. "I have to do this."

He held onto me and helped me walk. We were about ten feet from the cabin when he had me stop and sit down by a large tree. We could see part of the front and the side of the cabin. He held up his fingers to his mouth and pointed towards the front of the cabin. They positioned a guard outside the door, walking back and forth with a lantern in his hand. He would lift it up every now and again to illuminate the darkness ahead of him.

"We need to double back and go around to the other side," he whispered into my ear.

I nodded at him, and we turned around to double back, moving in a wide circle, and into a thicker grove of trees to avoid being seen. We approached the opposite side of the cabin, and there was a decent size tree with a wide trunk that obscured the view from the front of the cabin. The only way he would see us is if he walked all the way around the tree. The guard on duty would not waste his time walking all the way around the tree. He was not expecting any trouble, because everyone else was dead.

There was a small, illuminated window on the dark side of the cabin. We moved quickly and quietly to the window. Anders had us keep our backs to the wall so we could see everything happening around us and then inched his way to the window. He lingered until he could look inside and ensure anyone would not see us from the inside. He gave me the thumbs up, and I walked to where he was standing to see through the small, barred window.

"Oh my God," I exclaimed in a breathless whisper. I looked up at Anders, at a loss for words. "It's her."

"Who?" He asked, peeking in the window behind me. "The nurse?"

I nodded. Her back was to us, but there was no mistaking who she was. She stood there. Her body hunched over in an unnatural position. I gasped, and I jumped back into Anders as her body shifted in a sharp, unnatural movement. Her neck jerked to the side, and then her body twitched like ungreased gears that continued to catch with each notch. As her head turned to look at us, I could not look away as her body awkwardly twisted to be in the same position. I stood there with my hands on the window, unable to believe what I was seeing.

"Anders," I whispered. I started trembling as the nurse wobbled like a small child that would walk towards its mother, unable to control the body movement and lack of coordination. She came towards us with open arms and an enormous smile that did not fit her face right.

She wore her nurse's uniform, now torn in multiple places that exposed a bare breast and her upper leg and the region between her legs. The white uniform had blood stains splattered on it like she walked through a sprinkler. Her hair was wild and disheveled, with strands of her blonde hair framing her face. The color of her skin was bluish white, her cheekbones protruded out awkwardly, and her eyes were dark, sunken in and revealed an opaque, deep blue. She looked like she died from starvation, but if that was the case, how was she moving?

She reached the window and put up her hands to match mine. "Mother," she said through the glass pane in a voice that was not feminine. "I'm hungry."

One of her hands jerked back. In a motion that was faster than a human's speed, she broke through the glass and grabbed my hand. She dragged my wrist through a sharp edge of the broken glass and then let me go. I cried out from the pain and watched as she licked the blood hungrily from the glass. Whatever was in my blood almost had an immediate effect on her. I blinked as I watched her skin glow with an almost fleshy pink and her flesh fill out just enough to be deceiving. I could not believe what I was seeing!

"More," she yelled as she reached for me through the window, scraping her own arm. I watched in horror as a thick tar-like substance oozed to the surface to fill the wound. It did not move beyond the wound. Instead, it became coagulated and adhered to the wound. She used her finger to grab the blood from the other side of the glass, and I watched her lick her fingers with pleasure. As she did, the cut on her arm slowly disappeared.

"More," she yelled at me, her eyes looking wildly at me.

"Hey," shouted the soldier from the front of the cabin. "Who's there?"

"Anders," I said, nudging him in the gut with my elbow. He grabbed me and we ran at full speed, as fast as my legs would carry me through the forest, as my blood dripped down my hand and onto the forest floor.

We stopped by the extremely large tree that we had stopped at prior that would hide us well enough. He took off his jacket, and then took off his shirt and wrapped it around my wrist. He looked at me with concern and then looked back towards the cabin. Even in the dark of night, seeing him half naked and being so close to me. I could not help but admire his natural beauty. We saw movement approaching from the other camp and he ducked down low beside me. We watched as the two soldiers carried another unconscious soldier and took him into the cabin.

An eerie laughter cried out into the night, followed by the other two soldiers scrambling out, swearing, and falling over their own feet. They ran past a tall, slender man wearing a long overcoat and a hat that stood unmoving on the path. I could not make out his features because his back was facing the moonlight. As he turned his head slightly, I could see the metal of his wire-rimmed glasses reflect on the moonlight.

"Is that Dr. Alden?"

"What were they doing with that soldier?" Anders asked, as we both watched the other two soldiers run as fast as they could from the cabin.

I reached out with my mind, and immediately I connected to her. The soldier was underneath her. She had a shard of glass in her hand. The sleeping soldier, drugged, slept softly, unaware of the danger he was in as he laid on a floor that had seen better days and showered with small fragments of glass and furniture that she had destroyed in one of her rampages. She took the sharp edge of the glass to his arm, allowing a slow stream of blood to pool up, and then she licked it slowly, seductively. His blood did not satisfy her. The life force she took from him was minimal compared to her mother's blood. Unbuttoning his pants, she straddled on top of him and moved her hips back and forth. She could no longer feel it in a way that she used to. My blood did something to her. It helped her to feel more. She desperately wanted to feel again. She craved me. I could feel her drawing her connection to me, and I could feel her smiling as she fondled her breasts and continued to straddle the poor man that I knew in my heart would not make it through the night. *Mother.*

Shit! I thought, my eyes going wide.

"Hey, Viv," he whispered as he took my face in his hands. Startled, I practically fell backwards. "Are you with me? We have to go."

He grabbed my hand, and we worked our way back through the forest, keeping to the densest areas to avoid detection. When we reached the outskirts of the camp, he left me near a small cluster of trees as he snuck back into camp to check to see if they had set up a new rotation or patrol, and just as before, nothing had changed, and the camp still slept.

I looked back in the cabin's direction. I could have sworn that someone was watching us from the forest. It could have been my imagination, but after tonight's events, I knew it may be better to trust my intuition. I lived in a new world. One with creatures of legends and campfire stories meant to thrill you as late-night giggles wavered over hushed voices. Monsters were very real, and I was becoming one of them.

We entered the tent, and Anders sat me down as he wrapped a blanket around me.

"Okay," Anders said, his voice and hands trembling as he lit the lantern. He removed his shirt and looked at my wrist. "I'm going to run to the medic tent and grab some supplies. That cut is deep. You are going to need stitches. If anyone asks, you cut yourself when the lantern broke."

"But the lantern is…"

He picked up the lantern, turned it down, and then dropped it in the dirt, avoiding fabric and shattering the glass.

"Never mind."

He picked up the larger pieces and put them in his shirt as he used his foot to move the smaller fragments with the dirt off to the corner of the tent before he left. I have never seen him scared. If I was being honest with myself, I was just as scared. In fact, I wanted to stay in my tent and pretend the evening never happened. Next time, I will listen to Anders when he speaks the obvious of do not go walking into a known danger, and we will just stay put or walk in the other direction.

How can they even remotely explain the evening's events, even if there was someone to tell it to? We just saw a walking, talking dead thing that used to resemble a person.

The woman I met in the hospital was insane. Did the virus make her insane? Was this into what I would turn? I had already acted out of character with Michael, as well as with Anders. What was I truly capable of? My future was even more uncertain than it was before. I should have left well enough alone and realized the blessing in ignorance is in fact fucking bliss. I wanted my world to return to normal.

"Fuck," I yelled as I put my hands through my long curly hair and threatened to pull the strands I grabbed onto as I looked up to the unseen heavens above me. "Why?! What do you want from me? What more can you take?!"

"Viv, are you alright?" Anders asked as he came rushing into the tent with bandages, rags, water, a bottle of what I hoped was whiskey, and a needle with thread. "Christ, you scared me! You're going to wake the entire camp."

"How can either of us be fine after what we saw?"

"Here, drink this. Drink it like water and you will feel a lot better."

I took the bottle from him and took a big gulp. I almost dropped the bottle as I gagged on the contents of the bottle. It was so strong, and it burned the back of my throat. "Are you trying to kill me with that stuff?"

"Yes, that is my goal. Take another drink."

I rolled my eyes at his sarcasm and took another small sip.

"The last time I saw her, she still resembled a human being. Am I going to end up like that? Like her?" I asked, wincing as he began cleaning up the wound. The tears welled up in my eyes and I felt a sadness that I did not feel before. What kind of acceptance was this? What kind of surrender? To know that my life was no longer my own. It was only a matter of time before what was growing inside of me consumed me completely. Would I still exist in that kind of state?

"I refuse to believe that! Whatever she is... I do not know how to explain it, but when I looked at her, all I could think was that there was something about her that was missing. There is something not right about her. How can you end up like her? No, there's no way!"

"We don't know that."

"No, we don't," he said as he put everything down and pulled me into his arms. "If faith only came with a slice of hope, it wouldn't be much of a pie."

"That makes absolutely no sense," I whimpered as I buried my face into his neck.

"It means that there is more to all of this than just hope. Trust in yourself and place your trust in me. I am not going anywhere. Believe in the impossible. You are already doing it, and you will continue to defy those odds. Whatever that was back in that cabin, it was not you! Do you hear me! I made a promise to you."

"You didn't promise to be at my side while I become a monster!"

"What if it meant you were to be something more?"

"What do you mean? That is the only other survivor and look at what she turned into. She exposed me to her blood. The evidence is outweighing odds. I turn into something else."

"Maybe, but I'm not convinced it's the truth. Wouldn't you already be looking worse for wear like she was? She looked... dead."

"I'm not sure. Right now, all I can see is the way she smiled at me while she licked my blood from the glass, and how her body moved. Please Anders, don't let me turn into that."

"You are nothing like her."

"What if I turned into that? What would you do?"

"How can you even ask me that? Let's turn the tables. What would you do if I turned into something like her?"

"I... I would never let you go. I would stay by your side."

"Exactly my sentiments," he said, kissing my forehead and sitting me back down on the cot. "Let us get you patched up. Drink more whiskey. You're going to need it."

"Shit," I groaned as he held up the needle and the

medical grade thread.

"That's nothing. I am also trying to get you naked. After this, take your clothes off, and I will take them down to the creek to get the bloodstains out."

"So, you are trying to get me drunk to see me naked again?" I asked him, slurring my words slightly. "Smooth."

I took another big gulp of the whiskey, which no longer burned my throat but warmed my body and made me feel very sleepy. Anders tilted my head up toward his and he kissed me gently on the lips. His lips were warm, so soft, and they were as eager as mine were to greet him.

"Create a happy place in your mind for you to go to so you do not focus on what I am doing. Are we together? Close your eyes."

"Yes," I said, closing my eyes and imagining what it would be like to have Anders to myself without prying eyes.

"Where are we? What are we doing?"

"Ouch! Dammit! That hurts!" I opened my eyes and saw the needle and thread coming out of my skin. My eyes popped out of their sockets and a little cry escaped from my lips.

"Viv, it is alright. Take a deep breath. Close your eyes. Where are we?"

"We are far away from here. We are alone, like we are the only two people on the planet at that moment. There is a tent near us, but we are not inside it. We are laying on the grass near a stream, and you are holding me. Our skin is glistening with sweat, and we look content. Happy."

"Tell me more."

"I think I need to lie down," I said, hiccupping and taking another big gulp of whiskey. My head felt very heavy, and my eyelids wanted to shut without my permission.

CHAPTER 18

DANCE FOR ME

"Oh, my head," I moaned as I rolled myself up to a seated position.

I lost my brain in a dense fog of a slight hangover, and I could not focus on any details beyond the immediate needs of slow and subtle movement. I looked around the empty tent, squinting my eyes. The natural light coming in the tent was a bit too much for me. I stood up and immediately sat back down, placing my head in my hands. I did not think I drank that much. Although, I did not drink, not really. I drank on holidays with my mother, but that was eggnog.

"Whiskey, you are a powerful burden," I said aloud, rubbing my throbbing temples.

I stood up again, this time more slowly, and saw a note on Ander's chair with the whiskey bottle. The note read: *Have a swig! It will help your head clear.*

He cannot be serious! Can he? I opened the bottle and sniffed it, and the immediate gag response reflex surprised me as I gripped my stomach. My temples roared with confusion from the unexpected excitement. It felt like my heart moved in and was fighting my brain for a place to stay. Obviously, that was not the case, but it sure felt like there was a fighting match taking place in my head.

I looked down at the bottle and noticed the neatly done stitches on my wrist peeking out from underneath the makeshift bandage. I honestly remembered little of getting the actual stitches. I remember drinking, seeing the needle, and then nothing. I do not think I dreamed, either. That was for the best, considering my fear of needles and recent events. I had enough to fill my mind. I did not need any nightmares as reminders.

I took a swig from the bottle and immediately gagged. I hoped Anders knew what he was talking about, and it would help the pain, and hopefully the nausea, while it was at it. It was not as soothing as it was last night. Not at all. I heard the clanging of pots coming from the mess tent. I felt misplaced, out of time, with no idea of what time or day it was. Did drinking always feel that way? If it did, I was not in any rush to do it again. At least not with whiskey.

I did a double take, as I saw a flash of white come through the opening that led into the lab. I walked towards it and saw that my nightgown was hanging between the two tents. I reached out and grabbed it. The fabric was cold to the touch. I rolled it up and placed it inside the blankets on my cot. I looked down at what I was wearing as it all fell into place. If my robe was on me, and my nightgown was out there, then did that mean...

"Oh no," I whispered. Did we do something? I did not feel like we did. Did he undress me? I vaguely remember him saying something about washing the blood out of my nightgown. He has seen enough of me from the sponge bath, but being drunk or passed out drooling all over myself was not exactly seductive or intimate. I hope it was all innocent enough. It was always something. I had this nasty habit of getting myself into trouble. It never used to be that way, but now? Now I was a walking khaki wacky doll sharing her crop with two men, and I was flipping my wig!

I stepped just outside of the tent, pulling my robe around me more tightly, and breathed in deeply. The crisp, chilly air was helping me clear the fog and feel more like I belonged in this reality. The smell of fried bacon and onion were lingering on the air. The memory brought comfort, followed by sadness, as I remembered my mother in the kitchen. Her warm smile and open arms were ready to embrace me regardless of what she was doing. I did not know how to not miss her, or how to stop the sadness from engulfing me completely. The late afternoon sunbathed the horizon just over the tents with a backsplash of treetops in a deep orange glow.

I did not expect to see anyone guarding our tent. This time, however, there was a guard just outside the tent. He nodded at me but said nothing. I did not recognize him, but then again, I did not know everyone at the camp. Just the random faces I could remember while having a gun held to my head. I paid little attention to who was normally outside of the tent, given that my experiences have been traumatic so far. It surprised me. I gave it no thought as I stepped outside.

I took in another deep breath, realizing how hungry I was. I hoped it was the beef stew that Anders told me was on the meal list for the week. Anders mentioned the men have been making the same recipe since before the civil war. A simple one pot recipe of beef roast cut into chunks smothered in flour, bacon grease for frying it up with chopped onion, peeled and diced root vegetables like potatoes, parsnips, rutabaga, and carrots, along with salt, pepper, and about a tablespoon of vinegar along with enough water to cover it all. Thinking about it made my mouth water. My mother had her secret ingredients. She liked to toss in diced stewed tomato and throw in a bay leaf. Although she called her version of it Hungarian goulash, either way it was a delicious stew to me.

"Finally awake, Ms. DuSan?"

I gasped, turning around, startled, and grabbing my chest. "You startled me, Dr. Alden. Forgive me, I'm a bit... restless this... this evening."

"I see that," he whispered, his eyes twinkling as his gaze took in the sheer satin robe he had given me and lingered on the exposed cleavage. I felt suddenly self-conscious, and I pulled my robe tighter across my chest, holding it shut. "Please, call me Michael. We are more than friends after all. Are you unwell? Anders mentioned in passing that you did not sleep well last night."

"Yes," I said uncomfortably, without knowing what else to say. I did not like how he was looking at me. He continued to smile at me in a way that reminded me of how a cat plays with an injured mouse. The hunger was not from a drive of need for sustenance. It was in the enjoyment of sinister pleasure of willingly knowing that it held a helpless creature captive. The thrill of knowing that it could not escape. Was this the same man I thought I knew? He felt different, and not in the physical sense, but in the sense that whatever this ability was, that helped me to tune in and understand the unspoken. Michael did not feel like the same man. Whoever this was, he was dangerous. My gut told me to run, but where would I go?

"Have a good evening, Michael," I told him as sincerely as I could to avoid unwanted attention, as I felt my body tremble with fear.

"Vivienne," he purred, unmoving and still smiling. As I turned to go into the tent, I could still feel his eyes on my back. As I approached the flaps of the tent, my knees became unstable and buckled beneath me. He was at my side instantly and caught me with ease with one arm as his hand still held onto the lantern with the other. I gasped, looking at him with wide eyes.

"Let me help you back to bed," he said, his smile growing wide.

"Thank you," I told him, stumbling over the words. What could happen? Anders would come in at any minute, and he would save me. Fear stirred in my gut, and Michael's large presence overwhelmed me. My entire body was on alert. We entered the tent. He sat his lantern down on the chair next to the cot.

Keeping me pressed against him, he brought both of his hands to my shoulders and traced my collar bone. I froze. Considering that we had already had an intimate moment together, what could I say to him that would make a lick of sense? I already opened the door for him to come in. What would happen if I rejected him? I feared what he would do.

One of his hands continued to roam down my shoulder as it trailed down my arm and his fingers lightly grazed the side of my breast. He pulled me towards his body more aggressively, and my throat became constricted, and I felt like I could not breathe. He moved in like he was going to kiss me.

"Good evening, Sir," Anders said loudly.

Thank God!

"Good evening," Michael said, stepping away just enough to regain his composure. His upper body posture stiffened when he heard Anders' voice. "You realize you have left Ms. Vivienne without an escort."

"I apologize, Sir! I took the time for self-care as she slept, Sir."

"Tsk, tsk. Were you not told? She is not to be left alone," he said, without taking his eyes away from mine. "I do not want my precious flower to be in harm's way. Go grab our Ms. Vivienne dinner, would you Anders? I'm sure she's quite hungry."

"Yes, Sir," Anders said, saluting. He eyed me warily as he left the tent to go outside, leaving me alone with Michael. I took a deep breath and looked at him, wondering what he was going to do next. Surely Anders would not just leave me here with him? He would produce an excuse to get me away from him. I felt sick to my stomach with his hands on me. His touch did not feel right at all. It felt nothing like before. I could not explain why, but it felt like an invasion that made my skin crawl. His other hand moved down to my injured arm, and he stopped. He stepped back slightly, as if confronting me about something profoundly serious.

"How did you hurt yourself?"

He let go of my arm and went outside the tent. He said something I could not hear to the guard, and then walked back in and stood before me.

"A lantern broke," I told him as I tried to hold his gaze to show a quality of inner resolve. I failed miserably as I looked down at my hands. When I looked up, his eyes held venom like a snake. I hastily looked back down and lowered my head. I feared that if I were to look into his eyes for too long, he would strike without warning.

"Let's see how badly you have hurt yourself," he told me as he unwrapped the bandage.

"Did you sew this up yourself?" he asked, looking over the stitching and rubbing his fingertips over the sensitive area and applying pressure.

"No," I whispered in pain, still avoiding his gaze. "Anders helped me."

"He is under orders to notify me immediately."

"You weren't around," I said quickly, defending him.

"I see. Well, tell me how you so clumsily dropped a lit oil lantern and caused such a deep wound. There are no burn marks from the oil, he said, looking around. No other obvious damage to your person. How did such a deep wound come about?"

When I did not respond, he continued.

"If only you would be more honest with me. In the meantime, it is in your best interest to remain in your tent for the time being," Michael said, looking at me coldly. He dropped my hand and looked around the tent. "It would be best if we kept you indoors, especially as you are taking great lengths to end your life."

"I am not suicidal," I told him defensively, and immediately looked back down when his piercing eyes bore into mine threateningly.

"My dear, you must learn to lie better. It is obvious by your injury that you have meant harm to yourself. Why else would you hide the truth of your condition from me? This entire experience has traumatized you deeply. It's understandable."

"Please," I whispered. "I do not want to be kept as a prisoner. What do you want from me?"

"You will remain in this tent," he yelled at me, his voice devoid of all emotion as he looked at me in a way that chilled me to the bone. He took a deep breath and pressed his arms down with such force as he punched the sides of his legs. The impact made me jump slightly. "You do not deserve my kindness, and yet you have my heart. Until you gain my forgiveness, you will do as I say without question. You are a lying little bitch, and I will punish you."

"I... I do not understand. What did I do?" My entire body was shaking, and my eyes filled with tears. I felt I could not move. Frozen in place, in fear. He was terrifying!

"Do you really not know, little bitch? Tell me you understand?"

He grabbed my chin and held it up so that it forced me to look at him.

"Yes," I said, gasping loudly as he pulled me into him.

"Yes, what?" He asked me, growling.

"I understand, Michael."

"That's a good girl," he whispered as a small smile formed on his lips. His grip did not loosen from my chin as his other hand slipped into my robe to hold my breast. He opened my mouth slightly with his thumb, moving it in and out of my mouth. "You'll make this up for me, won't you? You've caused me enough trouble for one evening."

One skill I learned to master early on was to hide my feelings. Whether I did this out of fear because of how others would respond or showing others that their cruel jokes and slanderous words would not affect me. Either way, I did not want to give others that kind of power over me. Fear was always surrounding me in everything that I did, and now I was face to face with something entirely different. Michael would be no different. I would not give him the pleasure of a reaction.

"Tell me you want me."

I refused to respond, and he grabbed my wounded wrist and squeezed it. I yelled out in pain. "Tell me!"

"I... I want... want... you," I said through sobbing gasps.

"Yes, my little fox," he pulled me back into him as he smelled my hair. "You smell of alcohol. Did she scare you to where you wanted to take your life? Could you feel her pleasure as she took the soldier in ways you have not yet explored?"

"Wh... what?" I looked up at him in shock as hot droplets of lava rolled down my cheeks. "You know?"

He was watching us! It was him! I could not control the anger that was boiling up inside me. I slapped his hand away from my chin and looked at him with how I truly felt. I looked at him with disgust. He responded by pulling me into him with his hand around my waist, our bodies pressing together as his other hand moved from my breast to my throat.

"You will learn your place, little bitch," he told me, as he lightly bit my lower lip as he opened my robe wider to explore the area between my legs that met him with resistance.

"You have no right to keep me here. I am not your prisoner! You expect me to be your gracious ballerina? Hm? Shall I dance for you?"

He watched me with humor in his eyes. I did not see it before, but he was pressing my buttons on purpose. He enjoyed riling me up, and yet my gut told me it was a dangerous game. If he did not win, I knew without a doubt that I would not like the consequences. No, he was a man used to winning.

"Would you dance for me?" He asked, purring as he reached his hand down from my throat and lowered his pants just enough.

"No," I told him through the tears. "I will not dance for my jailor."

"You will. They always dance, and open wider than they thought they would."

This is not happening!

He grabbed my hand and wrapped it around the bulging hard on that pressed into my abdomen, and he moved my hand back and forth rhythmically, kissing me forcefully until he moaned deeply as he orgasmed. He released me, and I plopped heavily on my knees. I could hear Anders outside yelling at the guard.

"Let him in," Michael called out. "I'm quite done here."

Anders came in and took one look at me and stopped in his tracks. Michael looked at Anders with an evil grin. He stopped right behind Anders, who tensed up. "Do you enjoy sloppy seconds, Anders? That's all you will ever have."

"What happened?" Anders asked me as soon as Michael was out of earshot. Concern riddled his face, his eyes wide, and his stance threatening to drop the trays that carried our dinner.

"You left me alone with him," I said, blinking through the tears that stung my eyes. "The way he touched me tonight, it felt like he was taking everything that I am and squeezing the life out of me. You left me alone with him!"

"Shhhh," he said, setting the trays down on the cot and rushing over to me and pulling me into his arms. I did not want him or anyone else touching me, not after... not after that.

"No," I told him as I pushed him away from me.

"I wish I knew what to say. He is my superior and if I do anything without justification and proof to my superiors, it could end badly for us both. I promise you I will figure this out. We just need to wait for the right moment and for the right superior to show up. Right now, Dr. Alden's word is God."

"So, what you are saying is that he can take me whenever he wants. I am his, regardless of what I may feel or want."

"No, that is not what I am saying. You are not alone, and I will do whatever I can that is in my power to keep you safe without jeopardizing my role to protect you. If I go after him, he will have me court-martialed. What happens to you, then?"

"I..." I lowered my head and sobbed.

"When the Major arrives, he will make this right. You just have to hold on."

"I see," I told him, feeling completely helpless. Whatever hope remained was slowly slipping away from me. I felt the overwhelming nudge of despair reach its long fingers around my heart. "You are his bitch just as much as I am."

"Viv, I..."

We both heard feet shuffling loudly just outside of the tent, followed by Michael's raised voice. "Grab Edwin, would you, and get me a cup of mud? Black, mind you. It is going to be another late night."

In an awkward silence, he handed me my tray, and I sat staring at my meal, lost in the moment, as a perfectly delicious meal of beef stew with buttered bread grew cold. Anders ate quickly and left the tent for a while, leaving me alone with thoughts that would not form and the ever so watchful gargoyle until the camp wound down for the evening. I was grateful when Anders gave up trying to speak with me upon his return and turned down the lantern. What more was there to say?

Tonight, the air felt heavy with my grief. There were no wailing tortured cries cutting through the silence tonight, only the screams that I held within my tortured body surrounded by the soft sounds of Ander's deep slumber.

CHAPTER 19

GONE

My entire world came crashing in on itself, like a dizzy spell gone wrong, and I jolted upright as I became adjusted to being back in my body with the aftereffects of too much alcohol. My whole body was shaking from the emotional response that begged for release. My face and the bedding around my head were soaking wet from the sweat and tears I did not realize were there. The light shifted in through the flap of the tent, bringing with it an abundance of light and what little warmth it could provide from the icy sting in the air. I moaned loudly as I held my head.

"Anders?" I called out into empty silence.

I sat up slightly, still closing my eyes to avoid the light that was coming in, and reached out, expecting to touch him, and instead felt only the softness of the dirt. I looked over the side, surprised that he was not there, and looked around the small space.

"Oh my God, what is that? Is that blood?" The dirt held a small splatter of what looked like blood, along with an imprint of someone dragged out of the tent. "Anders. Oh, God."

I pulled on a pair of the army issued pants that Anders scrounged up for me after a riveting argument when I demanded he act on my behalf. He grabbed the pants, along with a solid t-shirt and an oversized matching jacket. I wanted nothing from Michael. Not his clothes, trinkets, or to even acknowledge him by his first name. I stepped out into the cold, lung-seizing chill of an overcast day, and ran into the back of the gargoyle.

"What the hell?" he yelled, turning around quickly in a stance prepared to block me.

"I didn't expect you to be blocking the door with your... your..."

"Go back inside," he told me coldly, and turned back around. "Get used to seeing my backside, lady."

"Where is Anders? What have you done with him?!"

"I did nothing," he grunted rudely. "Dr. Alden will answer questions you have when he is available to see you."

"Do you know what time it is?"

"Close to breakfast time by the smell of it."

It was not like Anders to not wake me up before he went and showered. He would always wake me up, and then on his way back, he would bring breakfast back with him. One of my favorite parts of the day was when we would sit and enjoy our meals together. Nor would he leave without letting me know.

The gargoyle gave me an annoyed and disgruntled sigh. "Are you still there?"

"Will you fetch me something to eat? I'm quite famished," I asked him as my nerves betrayed me and my voice quivered. I hoped he would see Anders in the mess tent grabbing our breakfast, and this was all a misunderstanding on my part. The blood was not actual blood, and they did not drag him from the tent unconscious.

"Fuck," he whispered under his breath. "He didn't tell me I would be babysitting."

"Who? Anders?"

"No, ma'am," he said, scoffing. "I report directly to Dr. Alden. Fuck, fuck, fuck. When did I become a houseboy, and I bet I will be your servant or nurse before the day is out? Fuck!"

"I'm more than happy to do this myself," I told him in the most annoyed voice I could muster. "Who did you piss off to get this job?"

"Nobody," he said, grimacing. "They assign me where they need me. You are a threat or of some immense importance. Either way, we are stuck with each other. Fuck!

Private Charlie, front and center," he yelled at the top of his lungs. "Take over for me while I go play fetch."

"Sir," the private asked nervously as he ran up to the tent. He took one look at me and went white as a sheet. "Sir?!"

"Did I tell you to question me, boy? Are you too much of a pansy to guard a woman?"

"No Sir," he shouted a little too loudly, looking mortified, and took his position in front of me like I did not exist. I sighed, and I watched as his butt cheeks clenched together and he stood tensely, like he wanted to scream or run, both.

I watched as the gargoyle stormed off, and I felt my heart plummet. Well, clearly everyone knew I was Michael's whore, or I was a monster. Did I feel less than human? I did not think so, but even I had to admit that I was changing. I was healing quickly. I glowed when I was excited or connected to someone, and I could feel what they felt. If I were lucky, I could even hear them. My list of strangeness was growing. I did not want to consider my connection to the nurse as a skill or a gift. That was a curse. Anders likes to think that I am a miracle for surviving, but what if it wasn't a miracle? What if it was a mistake, an accident that became a contradiction? A joyous surprise.

I could not help but think about what I would become. Anders told me repeatedly that I would not end up like her, but what if I did? Would I go crazy and look dead until I fed on the blood of someone that was like me? What if whatever I was turning into amplified the gifts that already existed? I was always keen on inner knowing that I could never explain. Or the random times where I would know where lost things were, or I knew something would happen before it did. That did not make me special, though, at least not from my point of view. It made me a bit of a freak, but it was a family trait. We were all freaks.

Not much has changed for me. Not here or my life in the town if I am honest with myself. The truth of it all was simple. I had no friends. I was quite the loner, and I did not date. Nobody wanted to date a woman of mixed blood. There were many people that had no trouble reminding me I was Satan reincarnated because my white father was with a black woman. There were good people, too. Dr. Kines was about as close to a friend as I ever had. Growing up different from others did one amazing thing, though. It gave me a set of armor that words could no longer penetrate unless I allowed them to. It did not mean that I was not naïve, or that I did not experience fear. Right now, that is all I felt. Fear. Fear of what Michael has done to Anders because of me.

I reached out into my thoughts to see if I could feel Anders or anything coming from him. All I could hear were the mixed emotions of everyone else. Boredom, anger regarding delays on why we are still here, daydreams of loved ones, and there were one or two that were homesick. I could not hear Anders, and if I could not hear him what if that meant they killed him? I did not want to think about it, but it was something that I needed to consider. The evidence was damning.

I spent the day laying in my cot, occasionally pacing back and forth when I could not stand being stuck with myself for company. I eventually annoyed the gargoyle to where he began making threats of what he would do to my fingers and toes if I did not shut up. When Anders did not come back as the day carried endlessly on, leaving me alone with my thoughts, I felt despair creeping its way back into my chest and gripping tightly and unwilling to depart. My inner voices wreaked havoc with self-blame and scenarios of Anders tortured by the nurse, constructed by Michael's devious mind to get him out of the way. I tried to connect to her again, but nothing worked.

Would Michael go that far to have me all to himself? I felt as if I was about ready to lose my mind when Michael came waltzing in, whistling a random melody. I do not think I had ever seen him as a cheerful man. He was in an excellent mood as he looked at me and smiled his very white teeth. If last night did not scare me out, this did. He was far, far too happy.

I glared at him. I was afraid of being alone with him, and I did not trust him, but enough was enough. I needed to know what happened to Anders.

"Where is Anders," I demanded.

"Right to the point. He is not here. Sit up, would you? I need to check your vitals."

"Fine," I said, eyeing him warily. "Where is he?"

"His whereabouts are unknown. How are you feeling today, Vivienne," he said, lifting his eyes from his stethoscope long enough to meet my eyes directly. He lowered them as he focused on listening as he moved the stethoscope to various places on my body.

"How can you not know?! You are the one in charge!"

"Yes, I am," he said as he walked over to his notes that he placed on the chair near me.

"Is Anders alive?"

"Yes," he said, barely paying attention as he reviewed his notes. How could he be one way, like last night, and then today, acting like nothing had happened between us last night? Like there was nothing between us at all. What if he was a serial killer that used his position to torture and kill others? What did he say to me yesterday? I told him I would not dance for my jailor. He told me I would, and that they always dance. What did that even mean?!

"Can I get my own meals?" I asked him, waiting for him to acknowledge that he was listening to me.

"Edwin is your full-time guard from this point on. He can take you for your meals. I will meet all your other needs. You have but to ask."

"Does that mean I can take a walk around the camp? Edwin? Well, I am glad the mysterious gargoyle has a name. That makes him almost human."

"As long as Edwin is with you," he said as he turned to leave. "You and Edwin will join me in my tent for dinner this evening. My personal chef will make us something nice. We will celebrate a new beginning."

"Why? New beginning? You are a married man, and it would not look appropriate for you to be seen dining with me."

"My darling," he said, clearly annoyed. "You will not question me again. My wife is no longer of any concern. You, however, are my concern."

"I see," I told him as I looked down at my hands. The thought of Anders not being with me felt like he had taken my heart out of my chest and stomped on. How is it I survived such horrific experiences, and yet I feel as if I am in a living hell? Was life the punishment? Michael maneuvered himself in front of me, and I felt oddly uncomfortable being under his gaze.

"There's one more thing we need to do. I know how much you love needles, so I'm going to give you enough fair warning that I'm going to give you a shot of something that will help you," he told me as he kept the syringe hidden in his hand that he pulled out from his coat pocket.

"What is it?"

"I told you not to question me," he shouted angrily as he slapped me across the face so hard that my ear rang as I fell backwards onto the cot. I could feel the burning outline of his handprint on my cheek. I held my face and tried to scurry away from him. He grabbed me aggressively as I continued to struggle away from his grasp. "Do as you are told."

His fingers squeezed into my flesh, and I cried out. I stopped struggling and stared down at my knees, avoiding any chance of eye contact to set him off again. I hoped my actions would not cause him to react. Despair's grip was getting stronger, lulling me into its firm grasp, and I felt myself wondering if living at all was worth it. I had nothing, and Michael was trying to destroy what little I had left. My will to live.

"You are like a wild horse that needs to be tamed, my dear. I look forward to taming you. I've made this especially for you," he said matter-of-factly. "I believe it's given you an added benefit in your healing. Are you ready?"

"No," I told him with a hint of sarcasm in an act of rebelliousness. "Do I have a choice?"

"No."

He cleaned my arm, and I looked away as he gave me the injection. Whatever was entering my body did not feel right. It felt cold and drifted in my veins like mud trickling down a slow stream.

"I don't feel so good," I told him as a wave of nausea hit as I grabbed onto his arms.

"It will pass," he said as he pulled my hands away and put his fingers on my wrist to track my pulse. "This is a new experimental drug that I've been working on, made specifically just for you. There will be side effects. Close your eyes and breathe through the nausea. It will clear in time."

"I'm not human," I told him as I eyed his reaction warily from the corner of my eye. He paused what he was doing and then regained his composure while he put pressure on my arm, using one piece after another of thick cotton gauze until he was content that it was enough.

"I will make a mental note to be more cognizant of how my conversations develop in the lab. You have a knack for eavesdropping, you naughty girl," he said in a monotone voice, giving nothing away. "Perhaps an evening sedative will ensure that you are resting properly."

"What am I?" I asked him as my knees felt weaker, and the room spun. I grabbed his arm and held onto him for dear life.

"You are a miracle," he said as he caught me in his arms. The frame around my vision went black, and the darkness swallowed me whole. There was something dark and twisted within him and as the darkness closed in around me, I could feel the weight of that evil within him suffocating me.

"My love, you are so beautiful," his whisper pierced through the darkness. "What a beautiful bride you will be."

I felt myself floating back up, up towards the light that was just above me. I felt the crushing weight of the darkness pressing down on me as Michael's breathing quickened and he moaned with pleasure.

What... did he... is he... are we...

"You are mine," he said breathlessly.

I sat up, realizing as I sleepily sat up that I was naked before him with blood between my legs, dripping down onto the cot. I looked around me in confusion.

"What did you... Did you?" I asked him, unable to make heads or tails of what was happening.

I looked up at Michael and felt strangely drawn to him, but it was different. It was not a physical attraction that lured me. It was something else. Something... was... different. "What did you do to me?"

"Vivienne," he said with a sweet smile. "Everything is as it should be between a husband and wife. Are you here with me or daydreaming?"

"Daydreaming," I said in a daze that sounded a little less unsure of myself. I raised my hand to my head and realized that my hand was wet and clammy. I stared down at my palm like it was something foreign and did not belong there. "I am sorry, did you say *wife*?"

"Let's celebrate," he said with a shy smile that surprised me as he grabbed my hand and put it between both of his hands. "You have such lovely hands. They are so soft and feel like the sweetness of tender lips ready to be kissed."

Was all this some Jekyll and Hyde thing playing out? He stood before me and looked at me. As our eyes connected, I felt something strange. It was a connection. One that I was not ready to accept. It was familiar.

In every way possible, I felt lost and disconnected. Confused! *What is happening?!* Anders was my anchor, and while I know it is not fair to expect that of him or to expect that I could always be with him, we were something more than we were. I know Michael will do anything to consume every inch of me. Did he genuinely love me? No, I do not think he would ever know in his twisted mind what love is.

When authors of long ago spoke of demons that roamed the night, I could not help but wonder if they were referring to him. As he came closer, removing the small distance between us, the hairs on my body stood up and screamed with warning. I recoiled from him and he aggressively pulled me into his arms.

"Please, I can't breathe."

I did not want to upset him. He seemed like he was hanging on by a loose thread. His moods switched back and forth so aggressively I felt forced into the submission. The way he was holding me, his grip was too tight, and his skin was so cold it made my skin crawl.

"You are so cold," I whispered in a panic, really looking at him, as if for the first time. "Are you not feeling well?"

I looked him straight in his face and noticed the dark circles underneath his eyes. The sullen sunken in cheeks and his pale lips. Did he have the virus?

"Oh my God, it's happening again, isn't it?!"

"I want to love you forever," he whispered in my ear.

"Please," I whispered, as his grip continued to tighten. "Let me go."

He did not move, and as the seconds rolled by, I felt his body tense and stiffen. He kissed me and pushed his tongue into my mouth. He loosened his grip just enough to grope me as he kissed me. A voice came from the lab, and he let me out of his grip.

"You are mine," he said in a deep, throaty voice as he turned away from me, leaving me in tears and gasping for breath. "You will join me for dinner. This is not a request. Robert will bring you something appropriate to wear."

He walked out of the tent, leaving me shaken and wondering what he was going to do next.

What is to become of my life? I asked myself as I touched the blood between my legs, looking at the space from where he retreated. *What more can he take from me?*

CHAPTER 20

PUPPET

Commotion outside of my tent pulled me out of a restless sleep. I wanted to escape to the realm of endless dreams where Michael could not touch me. I did not want to be awake. I did not want to be here! I tried several times to pull myself into a memory as before or to reach out to my mysterious angel in our special place, but nothing worked. I felt defeated. Broken more now than I was the day I woke up in this very tent. I found more comfort laying on a cold basement floor knowing I was going to die. *Anders, where are you?*

Heightened voices brought me back into reality, the place I did not want to be. The day appeared to be without end, despite my best efforts to escape it. Edwin was arguing with Robert about something that I did not care to listen to. I covered my head with my pillow and moaned. I did not want to see anyone. I wanted to be left alone, and most of all, I wanted them to shut it.

"Do you both mind?" I screamed out as loud as I could.

What I didn't want was to be trapped at the will of a mentally disturbed man. They were both drawing attention, which would eventually lead to me. I cannot stand this! The worst part of it all was that I brought this all on myself. I opened the door for him to enter, and when he entered someone's life, he didn't do it with subtlety. I couldn't imagine being his wife. I felt very sorry for her as I imagined her feeling as trapped as I was. The only difference being that she was stuck with him for a lifetime of servitude. Why did she not run when he was away? Did he take over her very mind and make her numb to what he was? It would also explain why Robert was the opposite of his father. I'm sure growing up with a dad like that would be its own form of trauma. I could not imagine what Robert must have endured, but it was clear he knew he would never be good enough in his daddy's eyes.

"My... My d... d... dad sent me to hand d... deliver this to her, Edwin," Robert said, clearly panicked. "You do not know what he will do if I do not follow his instructions."

"Not my problem. Let me tell you this one last time. She may not have any male visitors without Michael being present or his verbal consent. Which you have neither his consent, nor is he with you. So, make like a tree and get the fuck out of here."

"Do you want to suffer his wrath for not fulfilling his wishes? He's been very moody the last few days, as you well know. Look, all I have to do is deliver this box directly into her hands and state his wishes. That is all! I beg you! Come on, Edwin, please."

"No."

"I will owe you a favor."

"I will call that in for a box of cigars to barter with. Make it quick."

"Done," Robert said, sounding relieved.

I sat un grumpily as Robert entered the tent, with my gargoyle following close behind. Edwin held a permanent scowl on his face, and it made me curious if he had any other facial expressions. Robert handed me another white box, adorned with the same colored ribbon, and he looked at me with pity.

"Well, what are the instructions you are to deliver, Robert? I do not have all day! Oh wait, I do! Please thank your father for my endless boredom! The least he can do is provide me with a nice steak dinner with a very sharp knife to enjoy myself when he comes around later."

"I will pretend I did not hear you say that, nor should you allow him to hear you talk like that! Trust me! You do not want to get on his bad side. My father said you need to

157

wear each item that is in the box. He's left carefully laid out instructions on his wishes. If you don't follow his wishes, he will punish Anders on your behalf. You can think of him as your new whipping boy. If you follow his wishes, he will return Anders to you based on your behavior."

"Fine," I said, taking the box with contempt. The thought of having Anders back filled me with hope that I might find some resemblance of happiness in this nightmare. If it meant that I would see Anders again, I would do whatever it took to survive.

"I tried to warn you," Robert said as he looked at his feet. "My father has not been himself for the past few days. His anger dwells near the surface, and he is very much like a sleeping volcano that erupts when you least expect it. Please, just give him what he wants. Be careful."

He turned his head slightly, and I saw the fresh bruise on his cheekbone. I looked at him with wide eyes, and when he turned to look back at me, he realized what I was looking at. He dabbed his cheek shyly and sheepishly smiled at me.

"Like I said, father's anger lives on the surface. Especially since he met you. I will not be around to look out for you, or to distract my father. I have been trying to do that to protect you, but he is aware of my efforts. He is sending me home in the morning. We both know by now that when my father wants something, he will stop at nothing to get it. Heed my warning. Just play along. When you don't play, he taps into a darkness that will eventually destroy you. Do not end up like the others."

"Why? What happened to the others?"

"I've already said too much," he told me as he rushed past Edwin, who swiftly followed him out. I heard mumbling going on between them outside, followed by Edwin raising his voice, but I still could not make out what was being said. I do not know if anything anyone said to me or around me would make much sense right now. Was I going to end up like the others? Were they all dead?!

Opening the box, the piece of paper holding detailed

instructions was on top of the contents, wrapped in off white tissue paper. I looked at the instructions and laughed out loud. He was dressing me up like I was a doll. I was to bathe, brush my hair in exactly one hundred and eleven strokes, followed by applying the oils and applying perfume to specific locations labeled on a handwritten diagram of what my body looked like. I felt as if I was more than just a puppet for his amusement. I felt like I was an offering for something far more sinister.

Within minutes of Robert's departure, two men brought in a large washing basin big enough to sit in, followed by several trips with steaming hot water. One man delivering the water paused and looked at me curiously. It was the first sign of interaction from anyone other than Robert and Edwin.

"Levi, stop! You are under orders. If he finds out you have looked at her, you will end up like Anders."

Levi looked down immediately to stare at his now empty bucket and spun around to leave. I grabbed the one who did the talking by the arm and watched as his body stiffened. He did not continue walking, but he refused to look at me.

"What do you mean you will end up like Anders? Please tell me! Where is he? Is he alright?!"

"How can you live with yourself?" the man asked me angrily as he turned to look at me, sinking his glare deep into the pit of my stomach that rocked violently with earth shattering waves that threatened to take my breath away, and my legs along with it.

"What do you mean?" I pleaded. "Please, is he safe?" Tears filled my eyes, and I felt all that I had been trying to hold in let loose.

"What do you think, you bitch? Is it not enough that you killed Timmy?"

"Who?"

"Of course, you would not even know his name!" He was angry now, moving his body very close to mine, his fists at his side. "Anders is suffering because of you!"

"What?" I asked him, grabbing hold of his jacket, which

infuriated him more. "What do you mean?!"

"Fuck! Dammit Phil, that is enough," Levi exclaimed as he grabbed him aggressively and threw him backwards towards the exit, and pushed him again outside of the tent, yelling at him. Edwin came in, looking at me with what I almost assumed was a facial expression of concern. Without saying a word, he turned and left.

I sat there staring at the basin, allowing my thoughts to drift as my eyes relaxed, watching the steam rise as it filled the tent with warm and moist mist. It was relaxing as I imagined myself to be one with the steam, drifting and curling into a spiral as I continued to rise, moving through fabric, and weaving around obstacles. I wanted to leave, to escape, and I could not do it alone.

I took my time sitting in the washing tub, enjoying the warmth of the water. My hands gently touched the outer areas of my vagina. The area felt tender and ripped, sensitive to the touch. I know something happened, but my mind wasn't willing to cooperate with me on the details. I was not stupid. He did something and took what was priceless. It was not enough that he wanted to devour me. No, he wanted to destroy all that I was first.

I did not find comfort in my bathing. My mind would not allow me to escape the many scenarios that played out on what he was going to do with me when he finished with me. After I dried off, I applied the oils to his specifications. I felt almost numb, doing through the motions like someone else was pulling the strings. Was I detaching to protect myself? Where was the strong-willed and stubborn woman that I knew? Did she still exist?

I lifted the peacock blue satin dress out of the box. I imagined myself wearing the cocktail dress for an evening out on the town, with Anders at my side. I cried as I daydreamed about being in his arms and covered in his kisses. I took a deep breath and sat down, fingering the white lacy undergarments. Who was I kidding? This was hell. My personal hell. Michael was the devil, and I literally welcomed him in! Anders is suffering? *I am so sorry, Anders!*

The dress was short, just above the knee, with a simple front and back v-neckline with a fitted bodice. The material felt good against my bare skin. I could never afford such a dress. Like the other clothing he had given me, the dress came with matching shoes and an evening bag, which carried the same shade of vibrant red lipstick. Per his specifications, I swept up my hair neatly into a simple bun. I looked in the small handheld mirror, and I looked at myself with disgust. This wasn't me! I'm not a doll for any man to dress up and play with. I threw the mirror across the room and screamed in frustration.

"Good, you're ready," the gargoyle said, eying me warily and looking around the small tent. "It's time for your dinner with Dr. Alden."

We walked clear across the camp to a medium-sized tent, much larger than my small one. In the middle of the space was a small, intimate dining table for two that was setup with a burgundy tablecloth, candles, formal dinnerware, and a single rose in a vase. Off to the side in the corner was a proper size twin bed with sheets, a burgundy comforter, and fluffy pillows that begged to be laid on. Comfortable enough for two lovers to be intertwined. Being that close to him all night long made me feel sick to my stomach.

Edwin grumbled something about babysitting as he left the tent, and I walked over to the bed and sat down on it, feeling myself sink into what I imagined clouds to feel like. I almost giggled! Despite everything, something as simple as feeling the soft mattress was enough to bring out my inner child that wanted more than anything to kick off the heels and begin jumping on the bed. In an all-or-nothing gesture of rebelliousness to my captor, I took my shoes off and jumped a few times on the bed. It was just as I remembered. It felt like forever since I felt the comfort of an actual bed from a life that no longer seemed real. I wanted to curl up and fall asleep on its cool sheets and drift away without a care in the world to remember what that other world felt like.

I could hear Edwin outside shuffling his feet, which made me feel even more anxious. I went from sitting awkwardly on the hard chairs to laying down on the bed and back to sitting down in the chair. I felt like I was waiting for what seemed like forever for a dinner that I was no longer sure was happening. I sat down at the table, tapping my manicured nails against the hard surface while my other hand felt the smooth fabric of the tablecloth.

In the silence, a new sound formed. One that made me sit up straight and my eyes alert. The crying wails of the nurse filled the quiet spaces in my mind, filling me with panic as I once again sensed her need. Her hunger. There was no place for me to hide. Her banshee cries were like a warning that shook me to the core. I did not know what was more frightening, her, or the warning that I could feel vibrating through every cell of my being to run!

My breathing quickened as I heard several sets of footsteps coming up to the tent. I took a deep breath in, wondering who was going to come in first. I stood up next to the table as Michael walked in with power and confidence as if he owned the place, dressed in a formal black suit with a white-collared shirt and bow tie, his hair oiled back, and he looked rather handsome for a monster. Behind him, Levi entered the tent with two covered plates, which he dutifully sat on each side of the table.

"Please, forgive me for being late, my dear," Michael said in a casual and unapologetic tone. "Shall we sit and dine?"

"I heard her. The nurse, is she close by?"

"Leave us," he told Levi with a flick of his hand, as if he was a servant. I looked at Levi, who avoided eye contact. He looked terrified. He stood off to the side of the tent, waiting to be summoned.

Michael swooped behind me and pulled out my chair. I sat down, turning my head as I watched his eyes look hungrily at my bare neck. He lingered just enough to run his fingers down my arms.

As he sat down across from me and leaned back comfortably as he propped his leg across the other leaning into the table. Lost in his own thoughts, his fingers began tapping the table. I sat there, silently, waiting for him to speak. I feared what his plans were with this visual display. Nothing felt authentic about any of it. How could it be?

"Bring us something to drink, would you?" He asked Levi, snapping his fingers.

"Yes, Sir," he said, leaving the tent eagerly.

"Shall we?" He asked as he lifted the round top cover off his plate revealing a seared to perfection steak with a baked potato smothered in butter.

Drooling, I lifted my cover, ready to dive into a steak in a very unladylike fashion. I gasped as I looked at my plate, dropping the lid on the ground. On my plate was a huge, very raw cow's liver. He couldn't be serious, could he? "What the hell is this? Is this a joke?"

"You will eat this. The liver has essential vitamins and minerals your body will need."

"For what?! I will not eat this."

"You will," he said, slamming his fist on the table. "Edwin, let them in."

Two soldiers came in, dragging Anders, handcuffed, and badly bruised, with a black eye, and several minor cuts into the tent.

"Oh my God," I screamed. "Anders!" I ran over to him and hugged his torso. "Why?!"

"He is your whipping boy," he said without moving from his seated position as he cut into his steak. "When you mess up, he will receive your punishment."

"How could you be so cruel?"

"I can be very lenient and accommodating if you do as you're told," he said, smiling at me. He continued to speak to me as if he was soothing a child. "I would expect this much to

163

be blatantly obvious. Now please sit down and eat your meal."

"Please don't hurt him anymore," I cried, touching his bruised face. Anders looked at me, searching my eyes. When he looked at Michael, his eyes shifted into pure hatred.

"You obviously care a great deal about him. I have to make myself clear, and because of your disregard of my wishes, you have given me no other choice but to prove my point," he spoke matter-of-factly as he stood up and walked over to Anders and held his face up, admiring the bruises. "When you displease me, he will pay for your mistakes. Choose your next steps wisely."

He approached me, pulling me from Anders, and pinned my arms behind me as he pushed me against the table as Anders struggled behind me. "You are mine. If you wish to save your precious Anders from his suffering, you will do as I say. Sit down and eat the liver."

I sat down and looked at Anders. His expression was now a look of pure blind rage. If he had the strength, I believe he would kill him.

"I will give you both some time to discuss my wishes, and I ask that you both choose wisely. A human body can only handle so much torture. He may end up paying the price with his life if you are not careful."

Michael leaned down and kissed me harshly, and I could hear Anders squirming against the two soldiers as he did.

"Stop, please," I cried out as I tried to squirm myself out of his arms. The more I tried, the more he seemed to enjoy it as his grip tightened. He grabbed my breast and rubbed my nipple with his thumb. He grabbed my hand and put it to the throbbing bulge in his pants, but he did not go any further.

"You have until sunset tomorrow to decide."

"What do you mean?"

"I mean, my dear girl, that you have until tomorrow at sunset to determine if Anders will live or die."

"Why are you doing this?"

"I shall give you the simplest of answers, so there is no

confusion. I'm doing this because I can. Leave him," he told the men holding him. As they set him down on the ground, Michael looked at them, annoyed that he had to wait. "Look at and admire your handiwork. Enjoy your time together. I hope there's no internal bleeding, Anders. I hope she misbehaves often. I have so many plans for how I want to torture you."

Levi came into the tent with a bottle of wine, looking confused as Michael was leaving.

"Leave them the wine," he said, turning back at us with an evil smile spreading across his face. "After all, I am a reasonable man."

CHAPTER 21

I WANT TO LOVE YOU, FOREVER

I stood there for what seemed like several minutes, looking in the direction that Michael had left. My mind reeled in shock, unable to believe how the evening's events had transpired.

Anders groaned as he tried to stand up. I quickly made my way to his side and helped get him over to the bed. It took effort, but he laid down on his back, and I lifted his shirt to look at his body. He had nasty bruises, but nothing too severe. *Thank God!*

"I can't believe he's done this to you," I cried, getting on the bed, and laying down close to his warmth with my head on his chest. "I'm so, so, sorry! If I would have known what he would do to you..."

"I do not blame you, Viv. I want to kill that fucking asshole," he grunted in pain. "He's even more fucking insane than the nurse."

"You saw her?"

"He threatened to make me her next plaything."

"He did what?!" I asked him, astounded that he would go so far. "She does not play with you without killing you. Can he do that and get away with it?"

"You tell me, it sounds like she's already killed at least two that we are aware of. Lord knows how many of our men will end up dead while she has Dr. Alden's interest. You should have seen him. He looked like he enjoyed it all as much as she did."

"What did she do to you?"

"That is the thing. She refused."

"Refused? Did she give a reason?"

"No, but I could tell she recognized me. She saw us together. Whatever bond that you have with her, it prevented her from hurting me."

"You think she knows how I feel about you? Like she knows in her odd way that we are together?"

"I thought about that. Animals often imprint with who they view as a protector or guardian, like a parent or a mate. What if she thinks I am your guardian or mate? I know we are not animals, but considering how she responds and acts..."

"That makes better sense than what I have going on in my head. Let us go with that. What happened next?"

"Dr. Alden enjoys playing the role of the torturer, reminding me you were his and that I would only have what he allowed me to experience with you. She looked sad, and you could tell she was not happy to be missing the fun. Like a child forced to sit idly by while the others play while her nose is stuck in the corner on a timeout. Once the asshole drew blood, she looked like she could barely contain herself. She paced back and forth like a rabid dog. She looked more far gone than when we saw her at the cabin. Her body refused to move in the right way. I am not wrong when I assume she is dead, right? The living dead. God, I cannot even believe I am saying any of this."

"You need to rest," I told him, looking up at him and caressing his chin. "I should do as he told me and eat that..."

"I don't want to let you go."

"Then don't," I whispered, leaning back into him. I felt him taking out the bobby pins, one at a time, allowing my hair to fall all around me.

We laid there for a while, saying nothing, just holding one another. Eventually, his breathing softened, becoming slower and deeper, as he succumbed to sleep. I was grateful that he had allowed himself the opportunity to rest. I know he would not allow himself much of that luxury, given the situation with Michael. Even if it was just tonight, I wanted him to have it. To feel safe in knowing that we are together.

I got up quietly, being careful to not disturb him. I sat at the table and sliced up the raw liver. I gagged and felt what I just swallowed came back up. I took a sip of water from the canteen, quickly washing it back down. The texture was enough to make this experience a thing of nightmares, but considering my life until now, this was just another slash in my nightmarish diary. I cut it into smaller pieces so that I could just swallow it. My stomach rumbled and turned in rebellion, but it was much more bearable.

I knew better than to drink too much this time around, but one or two glasses to numb my brain long enough to enjoy a mindless rest did not sound so bad. I slowly sipped a glass of wine as I picked at the liver. I had to admit, accompanied with wine, it was not so bad and made the experience almost bearable. I ate as much as I could, but the meat was drying out and was no longer fresh, which sent me into another mindful tirade of leathery decomposing flesh rotting away in my stomach.

I used to fear the mysterious noises in the night or the imaginary monsters under my bed. Now I feared the truth so much more. Monsters were real, and they hid in plain sight in our neighbors, our siblings, our children, or our parents. I now understood why fairytales existed. Any one person who could harm another, torture them, and do something so hideous that they could only do it using supernatural means. It was the only thing that made sense to our irrational minds, riddled with fear. I do not think anyone could ever truly wrap their minds around anyone that harbored the devil inside. What then of Michael? Did he always have a devil within him?

Several hours had passed, as I took my time eating the liver. The camp was completely silent, and I could hear the early morning Robins waking up with small chirps as they prepared to greet the day with their vibrant song. They were the same birds that would flock to the town square in the winter months and take shelter under the swoops of buildings' roofs to keep warm, and in the spring, they would build their nests there as well.

I laid back down beside Anders and curled up into him. He moaned slightly as he turned on his side and pulled me into him. The familiar fatigue overtook me, but I would not allow myself to rest. I did not want to fall asleep again, only to wake up and he would not be there. Besides, he would stand guard over me, no matter what. It was only fair that I do the same for him.

As morning quickly approached, and daylight's soft glow entered through the crack in the tent, I studied Anders' features, moving my fingers along every aspect that caught my eye, every line that became visibly prominent. I could not help but fall madly in love with him. He not only saved me from the basement. He has saved me every single day since.

I wanted more than anything to breathe him in and touch him in a way that I held onto in my fantasies. I wanted to feel what it meant to love, outside of infatuation or hormones. To make love. Pleasure amplified with a sincere and deep connection. I wanted to give myself freely to Anders. I wanted to share my body, my heart, and my soul. I wanted something real! I wanted one thing that I could hold on to that Michael could not control or take from me.

I explored Anders' body in my mind as I lightly caressed his chest. I thought of the way his eyes lingered a few seconds longer than they should, or the fire that I felt emanating from us when we both felt conflicted and tortured by our own desires. He made me feel warm in all the right places. I laid on my back and made sure the blanket covered me just enough so that it was not overly obvious of what I was doing.

I removed the fabric over one of my breasts as my other hand trailed down my leg and lightly pulled my dress up. I explored my body, pretending he was touching me. I lingered on his lips as I imagined their softness, and the way his eyes held me in a container filled with adoration and love. I was close to an orgasm when I heard him clear his throat.

"Viv, are you okay? What's wrong?" He asked, panicked,

as he bolted upright, removing the blanket from on top of me with a sheer force that sent it tumbling off the bed.

This is not happening.

"Oh," he said, as his eyes widened. "Oh, God, I'm so sorry! Shit, Viv, I did not know. I did not mean to interrupt... what... that... I... I heard your breathing change and I thought something was wrong or you were having a nightmare, or that nurse was drawing you back into her mind, or... I do not know what I was thinking. I am sorry, Viv."

There it is. His eyes betrayed him. My eyes raised to meet his, and I licked my lips as I grabbed his hand, bringing it to my lips. I watched as he went through an internal dialog. All I could do was look at him, as I took his finger into my mouth and slowly took him inside me, imagining that it was all that he wanted to offer me. My desire for him left me speechless, and my breathing quickened. He shifted his weight on the bed, continuing his personal debate, and then, with a resigned sigh, he turned away from me.

"Don't," I said, sitting up removing the dress from my body. I reached for his arm, and pulled myself into him, lifting his shirt so that my naked breasts pressed into the flesh of his back. "Please, don't turn away from me. Not this time."

A small gasp escaped from his parted lips. He partially turned his head to look back at me. He turned himself back around towards me, and I watched as he slowly took in the sight of me and he gulped deeply as he said in a raspy voice, "It's my duty to keep you safe. Please cover up."

"Is that what you really want?"

He was fighting against his training, but I knew he needed something more. He wanted me, just as I wanted him. He turned again with slow movements that looked almost painful, as if it weighed him down like a lead weight. I grabbed his arm. He sat motionless on the side of the bed, but he did not refuse me as I pushed my weight into him, forcing him to lie back down on the bed. I lowered my head to his as I beckoned his lips to meet mine.

His lips were warm, and his mouth welcomed me with a longing I could have never imagined as his mouth opened and our tongues met. My body ached with anticipation as his hands pulled me to him. With a quick maneuver, he turned our bodies and flipped me onto my back. His wide frame hovered over mine and I gasped as his hips pressed back into my body with urgency as his hands moved with curiosity to seek without boundaries. His lips and his tongue moved from my neck to my exposed breast, and my hands moved under his shirt to feel the muscles that tensed under my touch along his abdomen and chest. His tongue flipped over my nipple, teasing me long enough to get a small brief moan, and I held his head in my hands as he moved down between my legs.

"Be as silent as you can," he said, looking up at me with a rebellious grin. "We don't want to alert the enemy forces."

I looked at him puzzlingly, but he just smiled as his hands gently touched my lips and then moved down to tease my nipples. He took his time, drifting his mouth in random places I did not even know were sensitive areas until he reached my clitoris. As his tongue moved while his warm mouth lightly suckled, he sent me into a blissful wave after wave of pleasure. My hands grabbed at the sheets for support as my back arched with a thunderous orgasm. I caught myself whimpering and buried my face in the pillow as the space between my legs became moist and welcoming.

"May I make love to you?" He asked in a low whisper, his eyes glazed over with need and urgency.

His pants were already down, and I looked at him appreciatively. I did not say a word. I opened my legs wider as I reached for him. I wanted him to be my everything. He took his time entering me. It was its own seductive dance until I lay spread open, moaning with matching urgency and ready to receive him as my hands pushed into his hips, pulling him forward. He slid in and pushed himself fully into me. I moaned with pleasure of feeling him fill me. I welcomed him repeatedly and eagerly. Our hips moved in unison, with intensity, until my body shook uncontrollably as my body became alive with an explosion of pleasure that filled my entire being like a parade on the fourth of July. His pace quickened, and I felt his release inside me, our bodies trembling as we gasped for breath.

I moved from under him so he could lie on his back, and I draped my body over the top of him. Our bodies intertwined, glistening from passionate lovemaking, and he held me closely. As my head lazily rested upon his chest, my fingers caressed his upper arms, delighting in his rippling muscle tone. If I close my eyes and allow the stillness to settle in, I can still hear his pounding heartbeat. He playfully teased my hair as his fingers wound their way, turning the long ends through his fingers.

"I want to love you forever. You are so beautiful," he said in a barely audible feeble whisper. "I am in love with you. You know that, right?"

I froze as a memory came crashing down on me. Michael said something similar. It was like a dream on the tip of my tongue, almost ready to be revealed, and yet I could not bring it forth. The logical aspects of my mind could not wrap around the flood of emotions as the undeveloped memory attempted to surface unsuccessfully. My body tensed up and Anders looked up into my face.

"What's wrong? Did I hurt you?"

He eased me to his side and then looked at the mattress, confused. He looked down between both of our legs, and then looked at me as he studied my face.

"There's no blood, Viv," he said. His expression expressing his disappointment as his eyes reminded me of my betrayal.

"What do you mean? I do not understand. I am a virgin. I've never... I... I... Oh, God..."

Confused, I pushed myself back to the edge of the bed, knocking the pillows off as I looked at the sheets and I reached down between my legs and looked at the clear fluid on my fingers. A mingling of our lovemaking. Everything that I wanted to deny to myself in that moment came rushing forward as the memory broke free to the surface of feeling Michael on top of me, and then acting as if nothing had happened. What did he give me in that syringe?!

"What? What is it?" Anders asked with his face filled with concern as my eyes filled with shock and horror. "Did something happen when I was away?"

"Michael."

"What? What about him?"

"He... He gave me a shot of something. I was dizzy and then it was like I blacked out or something."

"What are you saying?"

Anders' heart held me in a safe space, and I knew nothing could ever truly harm me if he held me there. Hope existed there, but would he stop loving me knowing what Michael had done?

"What the fuck is going on here?" Michael shouted, shattering the moment into thousands of shards, echoing what was a moment in time that held the closest thing to happiness that I have ever felt.

The papers he was holding dropped to the ground, scattering. He rushed over towards the bed and grabbed Anders by the throat and practically threw him to the ground with little effort. I screamed as I scrambled to grab the comforter on the ground and place it around me. Anders did not put up a fight.

"Michael, please stop," I screamed at him.

"She is mine," he yelled forcefully at Anders, spitting in his face as his rage consumed him. "I was her first, and you are nothing!"

Anders, under Michael's grip, looked over at me with a mixed expression of hurt and anger. I should have told him immediately what I suspected, rather than waiting for him to find out this way, but I was not even sure it was all real or had happened at all. I should have told him last night. Then perhaps his conscience would be clear, and he would have rejected me, and he would not be at the mercy of Michael now. This was my fault. What was Michael going to do to him?

I looked down at my feet in the dirt underneath me. I watched my tears drop onto the comforter, turning the deep burgundy into black circular spots. I became absorbed with the pattern as the realization set in that I was a prisoner to the passions of a man that could not be human. He was an actual monster. A monster that held no remorse for his actions and escapes the consequences with his position, and obvious charm. If they only knew of the monster within him.

"I will be yours, Michael," I shouted. "Stop!"

Michael stopped assaulting Anders and stood up, leaving Anders on the ground, clutching his side as his face swelled.

"Yes, you are mine," he said, coming over to me and looking at me appreciatively. "You are my divine goddess. Regardless of the situation, I know you are mine."

"Did you take me without my permission?" I asked him through the burning tears.

"How can you rape your spouse? We are married. Did you not realize, my wife? I gave you a sedative mixed with a gift to celebrate our union so that it would not be painful," he told me through his seething rage. "A gift you do not deserve."

"Married?" I asked him gently with both of my hands up in surrender, my eyes wide as the room felt overbearing and it became increasingly difficult to breathe. I could not feel the oxygen moving through my lungs at all, and the tent felt stifling as everything came crashing in around me.

"Yes, we are married. I may grant you a plaything while I am busy with other affairs, but your whipping boy may not be one of them. There are rules of conduct, sweetheart."

"Please do not hurt him," I said through the heaving sobs. "Allow me to accept my punishment if you are upset with me. I will do whatever you want."

"I know you will, darling. My dancing ballerina," he said as he stroked my hair. "Edwin, take him to the lab. Do not think about trying anything, Anders. You know there are men posted at each exit point. There is nowhere for you to run."

I looked up as Levi entered the tent and grabbed Anders' things while Edwin helped Anders to stand up. Edwin looked over at me and I saw a flash of concern move across his face as he looked from me to Anders. Anders, having difficulty steadying himself, looked up at me. His bloodied face, swollen and bruised, he reached his hand out towards me. Edwin steadied him and grabbed his arm before Michael could see it. I wondered if he realized just how we were both at the whim of a madman that would make us both pay for our love for one another. Levi helped him get his pants on, and as they took him out, he looked at me one last time and he mouthed the words I wanted to hear over and over from his lips. *I love you.* It felt like he was saying goodbye.

Michael paced the small tent in silence for what seemed like hours, and when he finally sat down beside me, he took a few minutes more to catch his breath and complete his thoughts.

"You will never be with him again," he said, expressionless and cold. "I would see you dead before watching my child raised by someone like him."

CHAPTER 22

BIRTHRIGHT

"Your child?" I asked him, shocked. "I'm not pregnant."

"You may very well be," he said as he grabbed my chin and then pushed my head to the side. "Regardless of who fathered it, the child will be mine."

Panicked, I dropped the comforter, exposing my breasts, and scrambling to get it back up, all the while feeling like I was about ready to faint. He stood up and pulled me to my feet as he grabbed me towards him in a rage, and tore the comforter from my arms, leaving me exposed. I cried out as I struggled against him. He threw me down onto the bed.

"What do you have to say for yourself?" He yelled at the top of his lungs. "Look what you've made me do!"

I scrambled backwards, getting my bearing, and using the bed to counter his attacks. If he moved, I would move, and we would be in an endless dance until I either submitted to his rage or I paid for my escape with my life. Submitting to him either way meant that I would know about suffering.

An internal rage that had been boiling for days had finally reached the surface. He was planning to trap me in a relationship by impregnating me. His manipulation knew no bounds. He wanted to consume all that I was. My hands went into clenched fists, and my anger left me shaking uncontrollably as the tears continued to roll down my cheeks.

"What am I supposed to do, then?" I asked him in a voice much louder than I had meant to. "I will not allow you to control my life! I may end up carrying your child, but I am not your property!"

"The courts will see differently," he said in a manipulative tone. "I will take the child away from you, and you know I can. Know your place and you will have everything you need to lead a comfortable life while you raise our child."

"Get out," I yelled at him, pretending that I had control.

"I allowed you time to say goodbye to your precious Anders. You should thank me for my kindness in knowing that you were quite fond of him. I give you my word I will not touch him. Think about what I have said," he said calmly with his back facing me as he quietly departed, leaving me standing there stark naked and my anger had turned into helpless sobs. "I will come back when you have calmed yourself."

I fell into a pile on the floor and cried for what seemed like an eternity. When I reached the point where I could not cry any more, I listened to the noises of the surrounding forest. The camp was eerily quiet for the daytime, except for the whispers.

I waited for what seemed like an eternity. Michael did not return, nor did anyone else, except the two guards posted outside of the tent. One stood guard at the entrance while the other slowly circled the tent. Nobody could get in or out without one of them seeing. Michael must really fear what Anders meant to me, otherwise why would he put on such a display? Beating him was the threat. What then would be the follow through? Would he really kill him? I knew it had nothing to do with his feeling threatened. Michael took whatever he wanted, and this had everything to do with his own twisted desires.

I thought for sure that he would punish me as well, but he did not have plans to starve me. Although, the menu choices were punishment enough. Levi was the only one allowed in or out of the tent, and each time he looked at me unapologetically. He brought in a boiled chicken neck in a broth for breakfast. For lunch, the tongue of a cow with carrots. My heart was fragile after losing my mother and the entire town to whatever I carried within me. It needed little to shatter.

I felt like I was stuck in an oubliette, broken, looking up at the small sliver of light above me that held all my hopes and dreams. They were nonexistent, only a small sliver remained. Did I deserve to be there for feeling something for Michael that was not my own? Did Anders deserve his punishment?

I still had the bottle of wine from the evening prior, and I had every intention of drinking all of it. I grabbed the comforter and drank the rest of the bottle in three large gulps. I could still smell him on the mattress and on the comforter. I laid down and surrounded myself with Anders' scent and cried. I did not think I had more tears left in me, but there they were. I mourned the loss of him. More deeply this time, because deep down, I knew Michael would end him to fulfill the darkness he carried. Why would he allow him to live?

Later in the evening, when I heard the guards outside changing rotation, I heard Anders' name mentioned. I quietly picked myself up from the bed where I had lain for hours, wrapped up in the comforter that smelled of everything that I wanted and a reminder of all that I have lost. I moved near the exit of the tent to where I could sit on the ground silently and eavesdrop without calling attention to myself.

"What is the buzzin', cousin? What did they do with Anders?"

"Nothing good. He came out with more bruising and bloodied cuts than he had going in. He looks awful. I hope they will let the doc look at him. I just got back from escorting him and Dr. Alden to the other camp. Dr. Alden took him straight to the wailing banshee. He's stuck in there with that thing," Levi whispered to the other soldiers. "I can't imagine a worse punishment. With all the stories passing around the camps about what happens in that cabin, it's the last place I would want to be."

"I heard that anyone that goes inside that cabin doesn't leave intact. Except for Dr. Alden, he is the only one that comes back unscathed. Unfortunate. I am a patient man, however. I just hope I am there when the guy earns his just rewards.

Did you hear what he is doing to this poor girl? To survive something like this, and then to be at the whims of the mad scientist himself."

"The entire camp is talking about her and Anders and their forbidden love. Does she look like a negro to you? Leroy said he was there during her rescue, and he said her mama was a negro."

"There is no way she is a negro. Anders would never risk his military career by bedding one. It is all he has. Have you seen Andrew?"

"He had to deliver the blows on Anders. He is in Doc's tent, nursing his hand and working through what he had to do. I heard the Doc pulled out his scotch."

"Shit..."

I was proud of my heritage. I admit there was a time or two that I would daydream of knowing what it was like to live in a white man's world, but my love of my mother kept me honest. It was not a punishment to have a distinct color of skin. Should we also punish those that have a distinct color of eyes?

If they wanted to call me a negro, I no longer cared. They would see what they wanted to see. Right now, in their eyes, I was a helpless woman. The color of my skin or the knowledge of my lineage would determine my worth and dictate how others would treat me. If they believe me to be a negro, would that just help them decide to look away and do nothing?

I could not find it in my heart to hate them. I pitied anyone that could hold on to a one-sided view that our skin color was no better than currency. Our belief systems are a learned skill. We teach our children how to love and how to hate. Only hatred of each other will continue to divide us.

My mother often asked me when I was having a difficult day after being bullied by children on the playground or harassed by one of my teachers, "Are we not a miracle, Vivienne?" Her argument was about the miracle of birthing a child into the world. She loved to remind me that one day, we would live in an age where the word negro would be part of history books, and the color of our skin will be only a matter of lineage, but it would not define our status to represent what it meant to be human. She told me of her foretelling of the future, and I believed her. I continue to hold on to that hope. We all want a place to fit in. A place to belong. Where does it all leave me now? I am damned, regardless. I was no longer human.

If they needed to label me as something less than I was, so be it. My heritage never meant as much as it did right now by honoring my ancestors. All those that came before me endured times I can never fathom, just to bring me into being. What an amazing thought?! Their suffering, their pain, and their joy, their happiness birthed me into being. I am all that they are, and if I try to change who I am, I deny their right to be honored. I refuse to feel shame for their sacrifice. I am here now, and I will rise.

I had to be honest with myself that what upset me more than anything was their blind assumptions that Anders would not risk everything for the woman he loved, regardless of what color she was. Would their brains shut down if they knew he had risked everything for a negro woman? I wanted to scream it at them, but what would be the point? Then I would just confirm it all for them. They would have an excuse to ignore my helpless cries, and the next level of harassment would begin. I continued to listen to their conversation.

"Makes you wonder what that crazy cock-eyed asshole is capable of. I will bet you he will place the bum rap on any of us to get away with murder."

"You know Lawrence from the other camp, right? Lawrence told me while I was waiting by the jeep that he served with Dr. Alden on another mission about five years ago in Georgia for brain-eating parasites that infected the water supply and made the entire town go nuts. The crazies killed the people that did not go nuts. He said it was quite the mess. Dr. Alden developed a case of infatuation with one of the local nurses that came in to help. They had an affair. She went missing shortly after she ended their affair. Nobody said anything about it, and even the police that questioned him just walked away."

"They ever find her body?"

"No, but come on, a single nurse with her entire family living in the town just up and leaves everything? Including all of her belongings?"

"You think he's a murderer?" Asked one of the other men, absorbed in the gossip.

"If he can get away with that nurse in Georgia and Lord knows what else, there's no doubt in my mind that he doesn't have the money or the connections to cover up anything that comes at him. I bet he does it for some twisted and sick sport to feel more like a man because he's bored with his perfect fucking life."

"I heard he's running experiments on the soldiers that go into the wailing banshee's hut," Levi said quietly.

"Where the fuck did you hear that? That explains why they never come out intact," one said nervously. "Did you hear what happened to James? He got into serious shit with his superior and he had to watch that thing in the cabin. He never came back out."

The wailing banshee was fitting. Would she leave Anders alone as she did before? Or would Michael manipulate her into hurting him? I easily remembered the screams of the soldier that she had her way with. I silently prayed that she would not torture or harm Anders. God, what would become of him? If you are listening, please help me! I continued to silently pray for his safety as I cried to the Almighty. I asked him why he would take everything from me. What purpose did it serve? An entire town, my home, and now he was going to take the one miracle that brought me back to life?

"You are not serious?! That did not really happen, did it?"

"Toby saw him go in. He was spooking around. Said he was not the same after that and asked for a transfer. He said the woman that is in there is not like any kind of woman he has ever seen. He said she is a monster..."

The others laughed. "A monster, eh? Now we are just getting into campfire tales that spook the cookies into a little cuddling action."

"No, he was serious. I have never seen him so scared. He saw her chewing on a fucking leg."

"I believe him," Levi said with all seriousness. "I have seen her, it, whatever that thing is. It is not a woman."

"You cannot be serious! What the fuck does this all mean?"

"It means we stay clear of that hut, and try not to piss Dr. Alden off," Levi said with fair warning.

"He is a fucking dick. Ronald brought him his dinner the other night, and he was not happy with how overcooked his steak was. He threw the meal at him. Plate and all. I can't stand feeling like I'm walking on eggshells every time the jackass comes around."

"You are not alone. I can't wait for the Major to get back," Levi said with a small smidgen of hope tinged in his voice. "The Major will make things right."

"We can't say anything to the Major. Seriously, I thought you boys had more noodles in your noggins. If he sides with Dr. Alden, we may as well hand ourselves over to the wailing banshee right now. Never mix politics with the military, especially scientists and consultants. It gets messy really fast."

I tuned them out as I cradled my legs. It was hopeless. There were men ready to speak out, but fear kept them in check. Would this Major even listen to me if I could speak to him or were they right? Would he already know what was going on here and allow it because of who Dr. Alden was to them? What did I offer over a well-educated scientist that the military depended on to help them understand the nature of viruses and other deadly diseases?

CHAPTER 23

INTO THE ABYSS

The naïve side of me wanted to believe the best in people, to hold on to a sliver of hope that I could survive this and lead a happy life with Anders. The mature side of me that learned from experience knew that there was a darker side to humanity, and that if I wanted to survive, I had to play Michael's game. The soldiers' continued whispers made the crisp air stale, filled with the foreboding feeling of danger lurking in every dark corner. I was now completely alone. There was no one left I could confide in, nor trust.

Anders, I am so sorry. What I would not give to feel your arms wrapped around me. To feel your sweet kisses. I am so sorry! I should have left well enough alone. If I forced myself to stop loving you, then you would endure none of this.

I nestled my head into my arms against my knees and cried. This was my fault. Anything that happened to him was my fault. If he died because of my love for him, I would never forgive myself. When would I ever learn? My mother always reminded me to keep my head down, to not call attention to myself, and to avoid trouble at all costs. How did I do so much damage from a small tent?! What would I be capable of once my change was complete?

Anders told me what the men endure during basic training. Not all men made the cut to become a soldier. Those that succeeded, became reborn into a soldier, and while they kept their memories and their hearts under a protected lock and key, they had to have an empty cup to rebuild their bodies

183

and their minds to endure the toughest situations that many of us could never imagine. Like me, they too had to endure a change. In the end, like me, they also had to find a new way to fit into the world. Would I still have a place in this world?

In the distance, I heard a scream that left me in fear as I held my breath. It was her! This time, her screams ricocheted through the forest like a warning. As she cried out her battle cry, the hair on my arms stood up on end. Within moments, I heard men screaming, followed by gunshots echoing from the same direction of where the cabin was, followed by bells ringing. I could feel her. She was close!

"She's coming!" I screamed at the top of my lungs as I searched the tent for a place to hide. There was not a place to hide. If I could feel her, then I knew without a doubt that she could feel me right back.

"Shit," said Levi, who was standing guard in front of the tent. "The camp will head towards the danger on the other side of the camp. Unlock your safety just in case! Be fucking ready!"

"Fuck," said the other guard nervously. "Fuck! The thing is coming here, isn't it?"

"That is exactly why Dr. Alden has her under special guard."

"Fuck! Do you see anything?!"

Within moments, the surrounding area erupted into chaos. One guard fired his gun. The gunshot was so close that my ears started ringing. Levi came running into the tent, his dark hair hanging over his wild eyes. He looked terrified as he put himself directly in front of me to shield me from what was coming. He tried telling me something, but my ears were ringing, and the sound muffled, so I could make nothing out. He looked at me in desperation and then moved back in front of me.

Just outside of the tent, the sounds of a struggle ensued with grunting sounds, followed by the thud of a body hitting the hard dirt. I looked at the soldier that was ready to risk his life for me. We both did not breathe. We did not move as we stood in the middle of the tent with no idea of what was coming from the outside. What followed was the blood-curdling scream of the guard that was outside.

"Fuck," Levi yelled as he held his gun up as his hands trembled. "I'm just out of training. I'm not ready for this shit."

The confines of my tent suddenly became unbearably small. The heat from my body felt stifling, and I could smell the perspiration that the stress and fear hit me in waves of sweat and tears. I closed my eyes, trying to displace myself from the moment. The shouts continued around me, echoing in my ears.

"No," Levi screamed as he started firing his weapon after something landed at his feet. I screamed in reflex. He shot one round after the other at the unseen threat. I crouched down by the bed with my hands over my ears. I tried to blink through my blurring vision. As my eyes cleared, I focused on the arm laying in front of the soldier. Ripped from his body with the sleeve still attached. Bile came to the surface of my throat as I quickly turned away, holding my stomach as my body trembled uncontrollably with fear.

Oh, God!

Levi fired his remaining rounds, and he clumsily dropped his extra ammo as he dropped to the ground to grab them. Outside, I heard the shouts of men in the far distance. We were on the other side of the camp. The brutal reality of it all set in. They would not get here in time, not until we were both dead.

The nurse flung herself through the flap of the tent, catching Levi off guard. He fell backwards after trying to get back up onto his feet as he dropped his ammo again. I watched with terror as the nurse's body jerked sharply with each motion she made as she approached. Each step looked awkward as one of her legs appeared to be shorter than the other. Her skin had altered more since I saw her last. It resembled wrinkled leather. Her eyes were completely sunken in. She looked through Levi, without fear. She looked at me and smiled.

"Mo...ther," she croaked.

"Don't fucking move," Levi screamed at her as he held up his empty weapon.

Her body curved, and she went into a crouched position like a feline ready to pounce on its prey. As her head dropped slightly, her body shook, and then she looked up and howled. How was she still alive, and how could she move like that?! I heard enough from working at the hospital that if something was not alive, it did not move like that. In fact, it does not move at all!

"Do it," she hissed at Levi with her arms stretched out. "We play?"

Behind her, another soldier appeared with Michael. I surprised even myself that I was happy to see him! They both appeared to be out of breath. He had a syringe filled with what I assumed was a tranquilizer or something that was going to either put her or me out of our misery. She dodged them so fast that I saw a blur of activity as she rushed against the guard at an angle that sent him flying backwards as a shot fired in Michael's direction. A soldier that came running in behind them cried out in pain, grabbing his shoulder as blood splattered in contrast against the dark green of the tent. I screamed, my ears ringing as Levi grabbed the gun from the unconscious soldier nearest to him and fired another round.

Her slight frame was much too small for the torn white nurse's uniform she was wearing and when she bent at an angle, the uniform opened to show her protruding rib bones with full breasts and sunken in stomach. She looked a pasty whitish gray, and it was obvious she had not eaten in some time. A slow and building growl emerged from her small stature as she dodged their attempts.

The noise grew with intensity, followed by the nurse screaming in pain as her body twisted in a way only a contortionist could achieve. Her hands twisted as her head jerked violently. The soldier in front of Michael jumped back into him, fearful of her.

The nurse's body calmed, and her head lifted as her gaze pinpointed directly on me. She lifted her hand that held a pocket knife, and she slashed at her wrist. I watched as the blood oozed slowly, like a thick molasses from her wound, and rolled down the blade as she raised them high above her head. Her lips lifted high above her gum line, baring her teeth like a rabid dog. She knocked Levi out of the way with ease, and she collided into me. We both fell to the ground upon impact, with my hands in front of me, as I frantically started pushing her away from me. Her face came close to mine. Her eyes held the visage of death.

I tried to grab hold of her arm with the knife and missed as she cut into the palm of my hand. Her once blue eyes stared at me as she suckled the blood from my hand. The blinding pain radiated from where she cut me, and I screamed in agony as I tried to get my hand away from her. She lifted the blade that held our combined blood to her mouth, and she licked the blood.

"Yes," she whispered, like it was an orgasm. "Mother."

She placed her head on the side of mine, and she whispered into my ear as the shouts of men from outside continued to surround us.

"Anders will come for you."

"What?" I asked her. Oh my God, what did she mean? Was Anders alive? Or was he now like her? Oh God, what did she mean?

The nurse raised herself off me as she turned to fight off the several men now filling the room. She drove the blade through the air as a warning to those around her.

"Laura," Michael's voice rang out into the air. "It's time to go back to the cabin. Do it willingly or you will see firsthand what it means to cross me."

"Please," Laura said, looking at him with pleading eyes. "No more hurt. You promised no more hurt. You broke promise."

"If you do not allow us to give you your sedative, you will know more pain than any human has ever endured by my hands. Choose wisely, Laura. You can't fight all of us at once."

Laura turned to look at me, void of expression, then she looked back at Michael. "You broke your promise."

"Come to me," he ordered her, snapping his fingers, and pointing down at his feet like he would scold a dog that was disobeying its master. "Submit to me now, or I will break another promise. This one you will not want me to break. Do you wish for your mother to be safe?"

"Yes," she said, trailing off and looking at me with wide eyes. "Safe. Mother feed baby."

The soldier with the sedative slammed the syringe into her neck as she slowly crawled over to him. I watched her melt into the ground like butter. Michael approached me with another syringe. I screamed, pounding my fists against him as I failed to escape his firm grasp, as another soldier helped him to hold me down. I looked over at Levi, with pleading eyes as my vision faded into black as the contents of the syringe moved quickly like a toxin through my veins, forcing me to welcome the fold of nothingness and deep into the abyss.

CHAPTER 24

THE MESSENGER

"Vivienne," a familiar voice called out to me like a soothing melody being carried in the wind. The gentle warm breeze embraced me like the warm mist that comes before the summer's storm. His voice was the sweet nectar that soothed my wary spirit. My mind reached out, seeking his.

"Is it really you? You left me all alone!"

"You are never alone," he whispered to me, knowing my thoughts as if they were his own. "In this place, you are safe from harm."

"You cannot keep my physical body safe," I cried out as I opened my eyes slowly to the welcoming light that surrounded me in its warmth. It felt like I was on a beach. I could hear the waves all around me. I wiggled my toes as they sifted through the warm sand. "How is this place any safer? How can I trust even you? I do not even know your name! Are you with me when he takes my body? Uses it for his own twisted pleasures?"

"Look within yourself. Your blood sings with the same essence as mine. That man will pay for his actions against you," he said with anger in his voice. "I am with you even then. Be brave. Be strong. Do not allow him to break you."

"Why have I not been able to see you? To be with you until now? I... I tried."

I felt myself cracking like an egg under the weight of something heavy. Even in this place, I could not escape the pain or the tears.

"Your transformation is not yet complete. You are weak. I can only get through to you when you are in a deep sleep. Like now."

"He injected me with something to make me sleep. I feel so lost. So broken…"

"In this place, you are whole, and you are safe. Know this place and allow your mind to come within to free yourself from any mortal pain you may experience. Even at your weakest, there is always a way if you give yourself permission to go within. You must let go of the physical realm. It will take practice."

"I am not sure I can. You are asking me to believe in something that I do not believe in the waking world. Is this like dreaming?"

"You are between the realms of the dream and the waking mind. It's in this realm where we thrive."

I am the Messenger for that which binds us together, his mind whispered within mine.

"Is that what I am to call you, then? Messenger? Where are you?" I asked, looking around, trying to find him. He is always unseen, like a remnant of a memory I could not place. "You tell me I'm not alone, yet I am. You tease me with your physical touch like a fading memory. Will you not allow me to see you? To touch you?"

"I am beyond the veil, Vivienne. When you are ready, you will have the power to lift that veil, and you will come to me. I long to hold you in my arms."

I heard what sounded like a soft lullaby coming from behind me. I stood up, turning away from the rolling waves, and I stepped through the shadows into an opening in a thickly wooded forest, heavily scented with pine. Surprised by the sudden change in scenery, I looked back and gave a startled gasp. I turned around to look back into the darkness to find more trees behind me instead of the calming ocean waves and the warm beach. I took a step forward into the dark trees that moaned and creaked as the winds violently shifted this way and that way, as the thick branches reached out like gnarled fingers reaching out to catch its prey. The chill in the air gripped me and I crossed my arms over myself as I attempted to keep myself warm. It was impossible without shelter and more warm clothes or blankets.

"Messenger," I screamed. "Where are you?!"

Large rocks surrounded the small clearing, and the jagged points of the trees created a dark halo against the night sky illuminated by the ominous glow of the milky way. The stars flickered above me, and I looked up as my mind's eye reached up into the sky, daring to explore the realm above me. I felt myself lift off the ground, and I welcomed the excitement of losing myself in the stars and departing my miserable mortal life.

"Come back to me, Vivienne," he whispered as if he was behind me. "It's not yet your time to explore beyond this realm."

"What does that mean?" I asked him, confused. "Why will you not allow me to be free?"

"You have the power to save yourself, Vivienne! Give yourself permission to allow the process of transformation to begin."

"Transformation? What will I become?"

"You will become more than you imagined. The choice must be yours."

"What happens if I cannot do this? I refuse to be like Laura!"

"You will remain as you are, changed, but incomplete. Until you choose to become more, that part of you will remain dormant. Sleeping."

"Can you promise me I will still be me? Please, I do not want to become a monster. A thing that is feared and hunted for the rest of my days. I do not know how to do any of this! I cannot!"

"You can! You are more special than you know. You are the missing piece of an ancient puzzle. The entity within you is as a part of you as you are part of it. The entity within you binds us together. I've been waiting for what seems like an eternity to find you."

"Entity... you mean Dr. Alden is right? It's like a parasite?"

"Yes, and no. Parasites take more than they give. The entity within you will offer you more than it takes. You must know how special you are for this merger to take place!"

"How can I be all of that and remain who I am?"

"How can we be anything at all? It begins with one step. When you embrace all that you are, you embrace the potential to set in motion a future that you would have never thought possible. Do you not know that you are already complete? What has happened to you is a part of you. It challenges you in a constant state of creation, beckoning you to move forward. Will you embrace your future?"

"How can something so horrible be something that challenges me to move forward and embrace my future?! That makes no sense! I have been through hell!!! Whatever this is inside me has taken everything away from me!!!"

"My love, you have a choice in how you choose to respond to that hell. You can choose to walk through the flames and be reborn, or you can stand within the flames and allow them to engulf you as they burn you alive. What will you choose?"

"Will it bring my mother back? What about Anders? Will he continue to suffer? I cannot change anything, can I?!"

"No, but her memory is alive within you, just as the memory of your beloved Anders will be alive within you. You have already experienced what we can do. To live in our memories is but one gift of many."

"Will you be a part of my future? I cannot go into this alone!"

"You are never alone. I am always with you, singing of my undying love. If you listen closely, and give yourself just enough of a pause, you will hear me. One day, you will even be able to feel my presence within you. When the timing is right, I will reveal myself to you."

"Do you exist outside of this place? You are real?"

"Yes," he said. I could hear the smile in his spoken words. "I exist, and I long for you to be in my arms once again, my love."

My love. I repeated his words in my mind as I felt my heart open. The love that I felt for him was as familiar as the gentle winds accompanying the spring storm. It differed from what I felt for Anders. My love for Anders made me feel human. What I felt for my angel I could not even describe. I felt connected to him in a way that I did not understand. *How is that even possible?*

"Time is running short," he said with urgency. "Will you join with your entity and begin the process of transformation?"

"I... I... will."

A small whirlwind whipped around me, and I floated above the forest as my white chemise's sheer layers lifted and surrounded me like wings in flight. The mysterious force drew me back down into the center of the clearing with a group of stones.

Four stones surrounded me in a horseshoe pattern, with one in the center. The long rectangular stone at the center held an impression in the middle that collected rainwater that mirrored the evening sky above me. The pine trees resembled a wave of jagged shapes and sizes, never fully touching between the darkness, and yet completely connected. United by the earth and the roots that bound them. The sound of a small river or large stream was nearby. I could smell the moisture in the air amongst the smell of the damp soil under my feet and earthy pine.

I looked down at my toes, allowing my feet to sink into the soft volcanic-like red soil that surrounded the clearing. I could not help but find it odd to find such soil in the middle of a forest. I felt as if this entire setting just somehow appeared randomly in this place and time for this purpose. How could something that felt this ancient exist in a realm overtaken by progress and the increasing need for lumber and all the related production plants that went with it? Paper mills and factories that made gadgets and furniture were back in demand. This place was pristine. Untouched.

This is the realm of secrets. A forbidden history long forgotten.

I stood before the first stone to my left that held an engraving of an upside-down triangle with a line running through the middle of the symbol. When I touched the symbol, branches snapped around me as the trees groaned and swayed to an invisible force. I felt the heaviness of the trees, bound by gravity, as an unseen force shifted its weight upon my physical body. My body felt tired. The burden of holding onto recent memories of Michael's abuse, of witnessing the town's demise, losing my mother, knowing that Anders suffered or would end up dead because of me, and of every other dreadful thing that I refused to let go of felt like a giant boulder. I could not move. I became a prisoner in my mind as my burdens became my chains.

My body ached. The fatigue overwhelmed me as I dropped to my knees and laid my head down to rest upon the soft soil. I held so much in my body, much more than I thought possible. Each memory that I could not release became a burden within my body, manifesting in an overwhelming fatigue. My heart responded by beating at a faster pace. My shoulders and neck were aching, my lower back felt like I spent a day in a labor camp rather than a tent with a cot. My body was living with everything I was feeling. *It is all connected. Was it always this way?* Trying to focus on the positive was difficult, especially as I felt the burden of the recent days taking its toll and moving over and over in my mind like a plague.

"Healing is inevitable when you allow yourself to remember those moments that make you feel alive. Whole. Remember, you are."

I filled my heart with honoring my mother's love. I could not explain it, but I felt as if she was at my side. I could almost see her form, standing beside me, her gentle smile that told me everything would be all right. On the other side, I imagined Anders. The way his eyes held me with such love and tenderness, and how he urged me to move forward regardless of the challenges I faced. The essence of true love moved through me, and I felt everything that I was holding onto melt away from me like a second skin. At that moment, I learned to let go. A wave moved through my body like an energetic sigh.

The fatigue dissipated as I sat up and looked around me as a low humming noise grew from underneath me. I turned in circles, trying to pinpoint its location as the noise level continued to increase to a deafening roar. I screamed as I put my hands over my ears. It sounded like an earthquake that was about to shatter the surface and destroy everything around it. As quickly as it came, it stopped. It left me in silence with no other noise other than the quickening of my breath.

The dark forest was closer than it was before, with an eagerness to engulf me. I immediately thought of Michael, and in my mind, he was the black wolf, hiding in shadows, snarling and feral, as he waited for his opportunity to strike!

I am alone. He will consume me!

"You are never alone. You can do this!"

I looked wearily to the next stone. I approached the stone cautiously as my hand raised slowly to touch the upside-down triangle. This one did not have a line running through it. Just as before, when I touched the engraving, the air shimmered, and I became startled when a loud crack of thunder announced its arrival above me.

Looking up, I watched as the clouds formed above me, swelling like ripe berries boiling under elevated temperatures, ready to burst. The thunder rolled through the clouds as lightning lit up the sky, exposing the rolling waves in the cloud mass. One drop. Two drops, and then another dropped upon my skin as the sky unleashed its tears. I lifted my face and hands, feeling each drop fall gently upon me and roll down my bare skin. Each drop sang an ethereal tune like a key on a heavenly piano.

"Tears of the earth join yours as you mourn the past to embrace a new future. Water is the life force. Allow it to rejuvenate you."

"Is it as simple as that?"

"It's as simple as making the choice to wake up in the morning. It is a conscious choice to join with the lifeblood of the earth. To be one with yourself, with the earth, and with the embodiment of spirit. As simple as breathing."

"I make the choice to be rejuvenated. I make the choice for my spirit to be healed so that my body will follow," I whispered as the rain dissipated.

I walked to the next stone, feeling drawn by it. I touched the open triangle, whose point stood proudly at the top as if pointing towards the sun. As my fingers touched the indented outline of the stone, recent memories resurfaced, leaving me gasping for breath. My body came alive, heat upon heat, until I felt as if my body was on fire. I screamed as my memories of all the dead people in our town fell around me as if they were dying all over again. I grabbed my head and fell to my knees, screaming out. More images fell into my mind of Michael's abuse as I watched myself from the outside looking in. I looked so young and innocent. I felt so much older. How is that even possible? I could no longer resonate with the young girl that I saw. How could this even be me?!

"I'm broken," I screamed out through the pain, choking on my tears. "I don't even know who I am anymore!"

"Do not allow the actions of others to define you," he whispered. "Who you are within has never changed. Seek her out!"

"I am still me," I cried. The flames rose out around me, but there was no pain. I rose and walked in the fire to the center stone. "I am still me."

You are complete, a soft feminine voice whispered within me. *You are not alone.*

"I am complete," I whispered through heavy tears as the

flames vanished. "Please, no more. I can't do this!"

You can, he whispered in my mind. *You are capable of more than you know. Let go of the rules that entrap your mind into thinking a room only has one door. In the realm of possibilities, you will always see over one opening where before* there *was only one obvious one.*

"You mean through a wall?" I asked him, confused.

"The answer is within you."

Wiping my teary eyes with the sleeve of my nightgown, I walked over to the next stone that held an upright triangle with a line that crossed through its middle.

"What is your choice?"

"I choose to be complete. To be whole."

A whirlwind gathered around me, lifting me off the ground and carrying me to the long rectangular stone. Standing before the cold, hard stone with an uneven surface. The stone vibrated as soon as my hands touched it. I gasped, and my hands snapped back. How strange it was to touch an inanimate object that responded to touch like a purring cat.

I reached my hands into the small impression of the stone that held the rainwater and took a drink of the water. The water felt cool as it went down my throat. I could feel my veins come alive as my body tingled with a warming sensation. Looking at my hands, I watched in a childlike wonderment as they glowed.

Something in my blood called to me. A vision of a place that I have never seen, yet I vividly remember as if it was in my lifetime. Tall green grass like a rolling sea where each wave rolls with the wind through the rolling hills surrounded me. I wanted to lie down, lost in long green strands as I looked up into the endless blue sky. Along with the soil, there is also sand, and patches of wildflowers in yellow and red as far as the eye can see. The air is untouched by industry and modern engineering. A stone temple stands proudly amongst the soft hills with majestic horrifying cherubs guarding its gates overlooking rocky hills in the distance. Ancient. Priceless.

What you see is the past. This temple still stands, but only amongst the rubble will you find its foundation. It's waiting for you.

I am with you, a light musical feminine voice says in a barely audible whisper. "Join with me."

"I will join with you."

I found something magical in the sweet surrender of letting go. Just as I knew that this life would continue to hold challenges for me to overcome, but this time, I would walk in life knowing that I was not alone. Just as I knew that one day, I would walk in the soil of those ancient places I had never been. *Life is the storm.* I knew I would walk in a land where each stone held elaborate markings and the walls told their stories. I would walk with the ancient ones.

My emotions flowed like the ebb and tide of the ocean's waters. As the water moved peacefully around me, so too did the water flow within me. For the first time in a long while, I felt fulfilled. Complete.

The sound of heavy footsteps echoed from the dark forest that was now encroaching on the clearing, coming from every direction. The familiar snarls of the wolf that I imagined Michael to be seemed to come from all around me.

"Viv," Anders screamed. "Viv, where are you?"

"Anders," I cried out, startled that he was here with me in this place.

His scream pierced through the air on the other side of me, and then again from behind me. I turned towards each scream that became louder and louder until I felt engulfed by their burden, absorbing their pain. My heart pounded in my chest like a drum.

"No," I whispered through the tears. "No, no more! I am whole. I am whole. I am whole. This is not real! Dammit! This is not real!"

"Focus, focus on me, my love," he whispered from behind me. "Close your eyes."

I closed my eyes as I turned towards the sound of his voice and reached my arms out to embrace him. "I trust you."

He entered my arms, drawing his arms around me, and pulling me into his warm embrace. I tilted my head up, my lips parted eagerly as his lips met mine. An intense wave of energy burst from within me. I felt like an octopus with many arms that could reach, touch, and explore. My eyes remained closed, knowing that once open, he would disappear. I allowed my new hands to explore his body. His body responded as his own energy responded in kind, our many energetic hands intermingling, like long-lost lovers, in an immortal embrace. An eternal kiss.

CHAPTER 25

DEMONS

"No," Michael screamed, breaking my attention away from my messenger. I looked over to the side as he came barreling towards us. He tackled us both to the ground. My angel, my messenger, disappeared upon impact. He vanished quickly as he had appeared before me, unseen. "She's mine, you fool! My blood calls to her, as hers does to mine. The vow of our blood binds her to me. You will never have her."

"No," I screamed.

"Please don't leave me here with him!"

"You're mine," Michael whispered into my ear as he grabbed a hold of me. His hands explored my resistant body as I continued to fight him.

"No! No!!!" My screams and cries filled the night all around me, as my screams echoed through the eerie silence that filled the forest, replacing Anders' cries that filled the forest. *Vivienne*, the voice of my angel, pierced through my mind like a thousand needles. *Wake up!!!*

I awoke, startled, with my entire body vibrating and on high alert as my heart pounded out of my chest. My entire body felt as if it was on fire. I screamed, as my nerve endings begged for mercy.

"Shhhh, my darling," Michael whispered as he slowly started moving towards me. "You are safe now."

"Not... safe," I struggled to say the words. "Not... safe!"

My eyes darted around the tent. I recognized the bed. The very bed that Anders and I had made love on. Candles and flowers surrounded me, and I felt like I was at my funeral.

Something was not right. What was it? I looked around, moving my eyes more slowly this time, allowing my eyes to take in my surroundings with more detail. It looked like a bottle of thick blood that moved down into my arm.

"What... is... that?" I asked him with significant effort as spit flew from my mouth. My teeth were chattering loudly as if I was cold, and yet I was not as my jaw locked painfully together.

"Shhhh," Michael whispered into my ear. "It is a simple ritual, my darling. The final consummation of blood between us, solidifying our marriage. It will be over soon, and when the pain subsides, you will be... just... like... me."

As my eyelids fluttered, my vision blurred, and I could almost make out his outline against the sharp contrast of the light above me. I fought against my heavy eyelids. My body felt like it was shutting down. Giving up. His fingertips lightly brushed my cheek like an intimate lover as they trailed down my neck. I attempted to fight him but found something that I did not expect. There were restraints across my chest, waist, and legs. The more I struggled, the more they chafed against my bare skin. I was naked and helpless.

"No," I screamed out. "Please, Michael. Please."

I watched as his blurred image pulled something out of his lab coat. I did not have to see it well to know it was a syringe. He injected something into my IV as he continued to hum the song *Ballerina*.

"Dance Ballerina, dance," he crooned Bob Carroll's song. "You mustn't forget the dancer has to dance the part."

The room with his blurred smiling face spun rapidly round and round as my stomach contracted and seized as the bile came up my throat. I closed my eyes tightly to force his image from my mind as I fought wave after wave of nausea. My mind slipped effortlessly into that space in between the waking mind and subconscious. The very space I could not seem to gain access to when I was awake. My confidence in my own abilities was dropping by the hour. In this place, it differed from the realm created by the Messenger. He could create a realm that felt alive and vast. On my own, I found an unfamiliar darkness that resembled how I felt. Lost. Trapped.

Here, in this place, I existed, and yet I did not. I was a mirage. My body glowed with wispy threads, like a silkworm weaving thousands of threads woven into a cocoon all at once within a blue flame. The threads flowed with an intensity resembling a hummingbird's heartbeat. I did not understand, nor could I comprehend fully, what was happening to me, but I knew this was the entity that was now a part of me. The energetic threads that merged from us both were so intertwined that I could not tell where I began, and it ended. It reminded me of the reflection of a water spider. It was then I realized that there was no turning back. Whatever I was to become was already happening. Being simply human was no longer an option.

In this realm, there was no curiosity, only that which exists without the shell, bound to something more that I could not yet reach. I felt a longing to take flight, to reach out beyond this realm and to connect to others like myself. I was not alone. I could feel that! How strange to realize something that excited and terrified me at the same time. There were others! But... There was something. A block, something that isolated me from reaching them.

I felt myself yanked back into the waking realm, thrust back into my physical body that felt confusion, weighed down by painful memories, and filled with pain. I felt Michael's hand on my lower abdomen.

"Hush now, little baby," Michael crooned a lullaby to our unborn child. "You will bridge the gap between what makes us human and what will turn us into gods. You will be the future that leads us to immortality."

I felt the sharp sting of a needle as it entered my belly. I tried to scream out, but no sound escaped my vocal cords. My mind was alert, but my body refused to respond at all. Paralyzed, I found I could not fight back. I could not even speak. All my other senses felt heightened. I could smell Michael and knew he was close. There was another scent with him, and it smelled of death. There was someone else in the room, hiding in a corner somewhere nearby. My awareness of what was happening around me faded in and out of my waking consciousness. Drifting, drifting... I floated on the dark waters of the subconscious. Drifting, trapped, waiting...

"My darling," Michael whispers in my ear. "I love you, my beautiful wife. Together we will bring in a new era. When you awake, you will be at my side, and together we will do wonderful things."

I felt an icy hand as it caressed my breast, then a sharp sting as something cut at my breast just above the nipple, followed by the sensation of a mouth and tongue suckling at my nipple. Her voice bled through in a soft moan. My legs parted, and I felt the weight of someone laying on top of me between my legs. A rhythmic movement started as his penis penetrated me. He continued to rock my body up and down, gaining momentum as the penetration deepened and his moans accompanied each deepening thrust. I could feel the pain radiating out from my entire body like a lightning storm. I screamed into the abyss. All the while, the tongue and mouth kept at my breast like a nursing babe, as I felt her cold, icy hands touch me in clumsy, jerky movements.

"Mother, sister, daughter," she moaned between suckling.

"Yes," Michael moaned with pleasure. "Let her feed you."

I could feel his climax, followed by the shift in his weight as his head rested upon my chest. I felt another gash just above the nipple on the other breast, followed by his mouth lowering down upon my breast and taking in my blood. The overwhelming feeling of dread covered me like a thick blanket. Hatred filled me up and consumed me. I wanted them both to pay.

The pull of the darkness was deep and enticing, and I longed to be there. I did not want to be in this nightmare.

Regardless of what my mind wanted, my body refused to respond. The only control I had was the tear that came down my cheek. I called out to the Messenger, hoping that he would find a way to respond. My emotions prevented me from joining him in our special place, where I knew he had waited. My anger was like a bright burning flame that threatened to consume everything in its path.

As my anger washed over me like the force of a tidal wave, my eyes fluttered. I could see Michael laying on one side of me on the wide bed, naked and appearing content as he suckled on my breast that dripped red. Laura lay next to me on the other side of the bed, curled into me like a serpent holding onto its prey.

Fatigue was settling in again, either by blood loss or me not knowing the time I spent drifting in and out of the dark. Something deep within me called out to me like a longing. A small, very faint whisper. She wanted me to live. To survive.

The energy within me pulsed, and I envisioned all that energy gathered. I summoned all my anger and pointed it directly at them both. An electric shock emanated from my body as it came alive with tiny tendrils that reached out to them, and I watched with sincere pleasure as they both jumped off me, hissing in pain.

"Did you feel that?" he said excitedly, which infuriated me further. His own pain was short-lived and appeared to be inconsequential next to his favorite science experiment.

"Mommy is waking up," she said, jumping up and down and clapping happily.

"Bend over," he commanded her.

"Yes, daddy," she murmured playfully.

I heard Michael grunting for a brief time, followed by a moan of his release. Whatever I did to them exhausted me and had an insignificant effect on either of them. I felt depleted. I turned my vision within and sought the small heartbeat that summoned me as it beckoned me to find the courage to continue to fight. She glowed brightly with small energetic tendrils that reached out to my own. One soul split into two.

How beautiful you are!

My body once again felt the odd sensation of drifting on top of waves. I did not dream in the darkness. There was nothing at all, and I was perfectly happily feeling the comforting blanket of nothingness envelop me in its protective cocoon as I waited, biding my time to escape.

Drifting. Floating. Waiting.

The surrounding air crackled with a loud clap as my mind, and body joined in unison. *I am awake!* I can hear Michael talking softly in the background, but my brain is so foggy I cannot understand what he is saying. I lifted my hand slowly to avoid hurting myself from the rough restraints. They are no longer there.

My perception of having not just one, but two hands overlapping each other in front of my face with a slow swaying motion looked fascinating. I found myself fixated on the tape with a tube in my hand and kept trying to take my other hand and try to touch the tube. I failed miserably as my body fumbled with simple coordination. *What the hell was it?*

"Stop messing with your IV, Vivienne. You will only pull it out again and we both know how you despise needles. You were so dehydrated that it has taken more than one attempt to find a stable vein that would not collapse. According to Doc Lindberg, you may have difficulty moving into your pregnancy by hydrating properly with your morning sickness. You need to keep that in. Your body needs fluids, and a lot of iron along with other nutrients," Michael said in a chipper tone.

He put something into my IV that helped the fog clear, and he helped me sit up while another man I did not recognize helped me from the other side. I could smell vinegar mingled in with the scent of earth and pine. I could also smell something else, a delightful smell coming from the mess tent.

"The baby," I asked hoarsely.

"Our baby is perfectly fine."

"I'm hungry."

"I have a wonderful meal coming for you, my darling."

Levi entered the tent with a simple broth, with nothing else on the tray. He looked at me with a quick flash of concern before lowering his eyes.

"You're joking? Broth?!"

"You need to start slowly on solid foods. Your pregnancy has been hard on you," Michael said, looking at my abdomen.

I followed his eyes down and looked in shock at my slightly swollen and bruised abdomen. The skin looked like someone had kicked me.

"What did you do to me?" I asked, yelling at him with such fierceness that it caused him to stop what he was doing and look at me in surprise. Levi almost dropped his tray while his new helper looked like he was going to vomit.

"I did nothing more than a husband would in caring for his sick wife," he said with an innocent look of false concern that left me wishing I could take a swipe at him.

"The only thing that is making me sick is you," I spat at him. "You're poisoning me!"

"Now, now," Michael said with a soft laugh. "Those pregnancy hormones are on hyper-drive this morning."

"Who are you?" I asked the lanky man on the other side of the bed. He could not have been much older than I was. His shaggy black hair had a mind of its own. His bright brown eyes looked bigger than they were in his thick glasses that had seen better days. He looked upon me with horror, his eyes darted from me to Michael. I feared he would pass out.

"I'm Alex," he said nervously, as he purposely looked away from me. I could smell the beef broth, and I grabbed the bowl from Levi like an animal, snatching something away from a human it did not trust.

He looked over at Michael, his eyes still wide as he backed away slowly, never once turning his back to either of us as he disappeared out of the tent more quickly than he entered.

"What happened to your little pet?" I asked Michael with a sneer as I sipped my broth.

"You have no reason to be jealous, my darling. You are the only one for me. She was inappropriate to a soldier that found himself at the wrong end of a pencil. She's chained up in isolation, learning a valuable lesson."

"Chained up? Like a dog," I asked him with disgust. "Are you going to chain me up and treat me like a dog when I do something you dislike? Are we so beneath you?"

"If you want people to learn, my dear, you must ensure they are listening. Some learn with a soft voice and gentle persuasion, and others, like you and Laura, are more erratic and feral. It takes a special finesse to train you both on how to appreciate your master."

"Master? You will never be my master," I told him hatefully through gritted teeth.

"You and Laura are so different from the others. The others faced my hands with a gentle mercy," he said, looking at his hands. He became lost in thought, and his hands reenacted a series of motions that chilled me to the bone. Alex, his assistant, gulped loudly and turned a pale shade of white, and looked as if he may pass out.

"You are a monster."

"Yes," he said with a snakelike smile. "I am capable of anything. Keep this in mind that I have given you the world, and in a heartbeat, I will take it all away from you. Do you not want to be a mother to our child?"

"Stop threatening me. Your threats will not work on me like they did with the others. I am not your precious pet!"

"No, you are my wife," he said with clenched teeth and an evil glare. His hands moved as if he was taking the life essence from a poor unseen spirit, clutching at their bare neck, and squeezing until there was nothing left. "They were imperfect beings. The others. Oh, my darling, they were nothing like you."

I looked away from him and looked down at my bandaged hand. A shiny metal object on my finger caught my attention. A simple gold ring was on my wedding finger.

"Don't worry, Vivienne. I will buy you a more elaborate one once we are back within civilization. You will have nothing but the finest that money can buy."

Nightmarish scenarios filled my mind. I lifted my nightgown up to expose my bare breasts. I looked down upon the fresh razor-edge cuts along both of my breasts. I trembled, unable to hold my bowl any longer before it dropped, bouncing off the bed and onto the floor, spilling the remaining contents onto the fresh earth. Michael immediately came to me like a protective mother hen and pulled out the syringe. I could not look him in the face. I wanted to kill him, and I longed to be away from him. The contents of his syringe were now my addiction. My escape.

"This has been too much for you. It is time for you to sleep, my darling. Alex, clean this up now!"

My anger filled me, and like a familiar friend, I could feel my skin prickle with energy. It is a miracle that the pregnancy is still holding strong despite everything that has happened. I feared everything, but the fear of losing my child took center stage. My unborn child's safety was all on which I could focus. I knew I would have to endure Michael and his creature, his pet, but that would not be forever. Eventually, I would find my escape. One day… One day he would pay for what he had done to me, and I would make damn sure he would pay for the others as well!

I woke up several hours later with Edwin watching me. It was a very unnerving way to wake up from a groggy, pharmaceutically induced sleep. Thankfully, Michael was nowhere in sight. The tent was dark save for the lantern on the small table that was dimly lit. Outside of the tent, the sound of soft snores greeted me like an old friend as the camp slept on an uneventful evening.

"Would you be so kind as to get me some broth?"

He stood up and left the tent, mumbling under his breath about something regarding being a nursemaid. Levi came into the tent and sat down in the same chair as Edwin. He would not look me directly in the eye, and he shifted his weight nervously with his hand on his rifle. Was he afraid of me? Or was he afraid of Michael?

"Please," my voice said, cracking. "Have you heard anything about Anders?"

"No," he whispered, his eyes wide as he held up his forefinger to his mouth. "He is still missing."

"Missing?" My mind reeled. Was he alive? Dead?

Levi nodded and again put his finger up to his lips. Moments later, Edwin returned with my broth in hand and his scowl had deepened.

Between the dreams, Anders, the pregnancy, Michael's assault, the fear, and the pain... All of it, the whole bundle of overwhelm I placed into a box to deal with later was now overflowing. As a thorn lodges under the skin, it will eventually resurface. I turned away from them both and I cried. Edwin sat the tray down on the bed with the broth and relieved Levi and sat back down. He did not stare at me this time. This time, he looked at his feet.

My teary eyes looked over my surroundings, looking for anything to catch my attention to distract me. My eyes landed on a telegraph on top of a newspaper from the town that was sixty-seven miles away from Stony Creek. I shifted my weight to get up from the bed and wobbled over to the makeshift table made of boxes. My legs did not work like they used to. The date on the telegraph and newspaper was November 18th, 1947.

"What is the date?" I asked Edwin frantically. "Tell me!"

"It's November 18th," he said through gritted teeth.

"That cannot be!" I exclaimed wildly, unbelieving that it was true. "The last I remember it was November the 14th. What happened to me from that time until now? What has he done to me?"

I asked Edwin, not expecting any kind of response, and my eyes widened in shock when he did. "Be grateful you do not remember."

CHAPTER 26

NEW ALLIANCES

I dreamed of him, of Anders. I dreamed he came to my rescue, and we both escaped to live in a small town far, far away from here. We both picked alternative names after a passionate evening of lovemaking and waking up in each other's arms. I do not remember the names we chose, and a part of me keeps trying to recall them as if the simple act of remembering would keep me connected to Anders. I could be a Sadie, an Amanda, a Linda, a Susan, or even an Elizabeth. I could see Anders picking the name of John or Alexander. They were two of his favorite names from books he had read when he was small.

The screaming match outside of the tent startled me fully awake. I was moving between daydreaming and dozing back off to sleep, where my unconscious mind deliciously picked up where I left off. *Anders.* All I wanted was to be back in my dreams with him. Dreaming about him was much better than my recent endless loop of nightmares that filled with Michael and Laura. These precious few priceless dreams pulled from endearing memories filled with tiny slivers of hope stemmed from the place where love dwells. It was in those tiny slivers that I clung desperately to.

The yelling went up an octave as it came closer to the tent. Edwin looked cautiously at me and then at the entrance to the tent. Whatever was going on, it was enough to make even him, the big bad gargoyle, fidget like a little girl about to face the principal.

It did not take me long to discern to whom one of the

voices belonged. Michael's voice sounded weak compared to the other man, whose voice held absolute authority. His voice did not sound familiar. I had become accustomed to everyone fearing Michael. Knowing that there was someone out there that caused Michael to cower in fear left me hopeful that I may find a potential ally.

"You fucked up! This is a fucking catastrophe! You can forget funding from the United States Military after this freak show."

"If you take a moment to read my notes, you will find..."

"You disobeyed direct orders and failed to report all of this," the man yelled at him.

"She's pregnant with my child. What would you have me do?"

"I would expect you to keep your penis in your fucking pants! You risk our entire operation to dip your pen in small-town ink. Do you have any comprehension of the implications your actions have caused?"

He paused for a moment, giving Michael a small chance to answer.

"Answer me," he yelled.

"Major, there is more to this than you are aware of. I could not report the situation of what is happening here without the risk of prying eyes," he lowered his voice slightly. "Please, look at this. Do you recall the project we worked on during World War II, along with the discovery we made in Antarctica? This virus has comparable properties, but the virus appears to be in an earlier state, one that has not mutated and lost all its potential. What we have hoped for is about to become a reality. The King's List. All of it! It's in our hands!"

"Continue," the Major demanded. I looked over at Edwin. He held an odd expression on his face as he looked back at me. He stood up and faced the tent flap, ready to be at attention when they walked through the opening.

"The virus we discovered in Germany was but a taste of its potential. Our test subject experienced a memory recall of memories from previous lifetimes long before his own, but he could not sustain the transference of those memories. He also showed proof of psychic abilities. While those gifts did not last, he became stronger. He showed vast improvements without using the steroids we have been testing in control groups. He appears healthier than he ever has in his life. The muscle mass alone tripled. It was because the strain of the virus we gave him was not complete. What we received was only a small taste of what could be possible with the origin of the virus."

"Tell me what I do not know," he responded, clearly annoyed. "Tell me or show me one thing that will save your sorry ass."

"The virus we've been looking for is in our hands. Vivienne shows promise at unlocking amazing potential in new abilities! Inhuman abilities. The virus is more powerful than anything I have ever seen! Once Vivienne has full access to unlocking the hidden knowledge that we seek within her expanded memory, we may discover the source. The very key we have been searching for may, in fact, be in our hands. Imagine the possibilities!"

"The soldier you injected with the strain found in Germany is here in the camp, is that correct? Are there plans to inject him with the strain that your patient has? Have you witnessed any interactions between the two? This Vivienne and our soldier? How does he respond to her?"

"He arrived at a most opportune time. He feels very protective of her. Were you the one that assigned him to watch over her? His military conditioning ensures that he follows our orders, but I worry about the part of him that is not under our control. The way he looks at me sometimes, I feel as if he wants to kill me," Michael said with genuine concern.

"Interesting," the man said. I could almost hear the wheels in his mind churning. My own included. Who were they referring to? They could not mean Anders, could they? So far, he was the only one that I knew that was overprotective of me. If he was alive, that meant he was somewhere in this camp. I had to find him! I also had to prepare myself for the possibility that if it was not Anders, then there was a potential ally out there. I needed to find him. This person may be my only hope of escaping this hell! "I did not assign him. That order game from God himself."

"If you review my notes, you will see how Vivienne's blood acting as the catalyst alone will advance modern medicine. She is our holy grail! Now, you will understand why I must protect her at all costs! Under my protection, I will monitor her unique gifts and document their progression. God forbid, but if something happens to her, then we will have the child as Plan B. I can already see the potential to eradicate the mutated bloodlines that have resulted in our own genetic downfall. Can you imagine?!"

"With what information I have on hand and firsthand witness accounts? No, I cannot imagine! Right now, I have accounts of walking corpses, and of men going missing. You have a lot to answer for, and you have yet to convince me you are acting in our group's best interests."

"Let us not focus on the here and now. I have already learned so much. The research material I have gathered is worth its weight in gold. Think of the future, instead, Major! With her blood, we could advance our vaccine. It will also help us to identify those with weaker bloodlines. A side effect of the virus if you will."

"What kind of side effect?"

"It will kill those that are not a match, like Vivienne versus the entire town of Stony Creek. Out of all the individuals, it only found one worthy to survive."

"How would it destroy them?"

"We will engineer the doses in such a way that they will have passed because of complications of an illness, like the flu or the common cold. Or better yet, from preexisting health conditions. How much harm could there be in a vaccine?"

"Vaccines are meant to save lives, Dr. Alden," he said,

sounding annoyed. "How can you assume that this virus is our future? What makes you the arbitrator of who will live or die?"

"The virus will dictate that decision, by its natural design. We will save the future of humanity by fulfilling our genetic destiny and repairing what we have lost."

Oh my God! What is he saying?! Is he saying that my blood will destroy millions of people? It will be Stony Creek all over again! *Oh, my God!* I must get out of here. He cannot get away with this. He will destroy countless lives, all in the name of what? Potential to be less than human? Who would ever want that?

What I have become is no longer a representation of what it means to be human. I am the question that lingers within men's minds of what we could become if we could become more. These people around me did not understand just how special they were. Humanity, in their own simplicity of being, could move through life from one thing to another without worry of being hunted like a monster from children's nightmares. No, they are simply just human. Humanity is worth more than the future that Dr. Alden wants to bring into being! What am I? An accident. How I exist right now at all is nothing short of a miracle, but I refuse to play a part in mass genocide! Has history taught us nothing?! Nothing at all?!

"We still do not fully understand what we have lost, Dr. Alden. Are you really saying that you are ready to murder millions of people over the same mentality that Hitler held? It is not our job to create a master race."

"Major, think of..."

"There is a reason we removed his chair on the board of Elders. Origin, as you well know, will not abide by any methods or plans that would cause harm to humanity. You are following along the same path. I cannot protect you, should you choose to continue to follow that path. Your plan would lead to genocide! We are not God, Dr. Alden! Or are we going to recreate Hitler's steps on killing millions of people while he creates a pure master race with a virus that will only strengthen a small percentage of the population? We already know what it can do, and how deadly even a mutated version of the virus can be. Look at what it has done to this town! Until we understand what it's looking for..."

"Major, it's looking for its match. A host with which it can bond. We will continue to lose lives until we can perfect the science to alter how it takes over a host. One day we engineer it to leave the body entirely intact without doing harm if its host is not a match, or a way to detect if an individual has the right makeup to be a host and avoid any risks. Longevity is in our grasp."

"You mean it is a parasite?!"

"Yes, just like a parasite. It joins with the host and changes the host from the inside out. The parasite mimics a virus to invade and grow within the host. The ultimate takeover. It is, in fact, something more. The virus is like a candy wrapper to the parasite, which is the chocolate inside of the wrapper. What we are interested in is what is inside the center of that chocolate."

"How do you know that this virus, parasite, or whatever the hell it is, is the key to longevity? We have been seeking the answer to this age-old question for hundreds of years. What makes this thing so different?"

"What did your report say, Major? Walking corpses, was it? That is your first clue, but to understand what her blood can do for those individuals that could not complete the transformation is incredible and shows the potential of what dwells within her! To believe it, you will need to witness it."

"I can understand why you kept this out of your report. Our sole mission is to identify and retrieve the source of the virus and prevent it from spreading. Have you identified the source of where the virus or parasite came from?"

"It did not originate here, and based on our findings, it originated from a land filled with a colorful history. An ancient land like that is bound to have secrets. Not even war could prevent those secrets from resurfacing after all this time. You are welcome to review my findings."

"I intend to. God, what are we doing? How can we play God like this? It is not right."

"You're right, Major. We are not God, but we will learn as much as we can. When," he paused. "When we can control it, we will do wonderful things, and hopefully save lives. Can you imagine curing even the deadliest of diseases with a single vaccine? What happened in Stony Creek is horrible, but it led us to Vivienne. What we have is as close to the source as we can get. Let me prove my case to you. Please come with me. I need to show you something."

"Sergeant Thomas," the Major called out.

"Sir! Yes, Sir," a voice answered.

"Sergeant Thomas, begin final preparations. The red phoenix is returning home."

"Yes, Sir!"

"Alright, Dr. Alden. Convince me," the Major said as I heard multiple footsteps shuffling as they departed.

What are they messing around with? Who would take accountability if this virus became a pandemic and destroyed civilization? The questions continued to build until my brain hurt. I drifted in and out of calculating thoughts as I waited for Michael and the Major to return. Edwin got up and left to grab me breakfast, and I imagined snooping while he was at it. Edwin entered the tent with a tray filled with pancakes covered in butter and syrup, along with two sausage links. I had never seen such a beautiful tray of food. He handed it to me, and I almost cried. Pancakes. They were a sight for eyes that had forgotten how such a simple breakfast could mean so much.

Edwin moved to the chair across from me, giving the on-edge soldier a pat on the shoulder, which almost sent him flying backwards into the tent. I should consider myself blessed he did not fire his gun. I have not been incredibly lucky around guns. I could not help but greedily care less what the soldier was doing as I dug into my breakfast. I wondered what Edwin thought of it all. He was a bit of a mystery, but I had a feeling there was more to him than just an expressionless being that he functioned as bodyguard or assassin, depending on what his orders were. I wanted to think there could be more to him than being a potential killer who held no emotions. All he did around me was stare off into space, and he rarely looked me in the eye, but when he did, I felt strange in a way that I felt exposed and vulnerable. I did not feel threatened, but more in a way, he knew all my secrets.

I just wanted to pretend there was more to him, so I would not go insane at the thought of sharing space with someone that was extremely dangerous. The soldiers around here gave him a wide berth, and that was enough for me to be wary of him. Especially with how easily he could take another soldier down with no reservation or hesitation. Given my choices of whom to spend my time with, I guess a girl could not be too meticulous. The psychotic doctor, the undead girl, or the gargoyle. Yes, my chances were all limited, and I could not judge myself for the type of company I kept. I had little choice in the matter.

My mind raced with endless scenarios of torture until I died or of escaping. What choice did I have now? My blood would endanger millions of lives. I thought of what it would feel like to be homeless and wandering from town to town with little to my name except for the clothing on my back. It triggered old feelings of fear and shame that I had not thought about for an exceptionally long time.

When my mother and I were driving across the country and living out of our car, I could remember how it felt when we had money to survive on, and I could also remember how it felt to wonder where our next meal would come from or if we would find an ounce of kindness in the town we were passing through. The overall feeling left me feeling scared of the uncertainty. Having any kind of stability, food in my stomach, and a place to call home was too much to ask for during that time of my life. I am thankful that we ended up here when we did. This became our home, but now? Now I had no home, and I had no choice but to remain hidden so that they would never find me. I refused to be Michael's puppet, and I would do everything in my power to ensure that neither I nor my child would willingly be part of any plan that would harm. If I could not escape, I would choose to end my life.

My mind drifted as memories played around me all at once. Powerful emotions overwhelmed me, and I could feel the energy building up around me as the air crackled with intensity. Fear of losing the child growing within me, and fear of losing what precious time I had left to feel the child growing within my body. My body glowed in a vibrant blue hue, and everything around me lifted into the air. Edwin stood up, steady as ever, with a look of surprise on his face as he looked around the room. He approached me calmly and without fear as he grabbed the IV bottle to keep it from breaking.

"How can I do any of this?" I asked him, with tears filling my eyes.

I huddled my legs into my arms and rocked to soothe myself. I had so much to fear right now. If I could not escape, to live away from Michael, my child would never know what it means to live. There was so much to fear, but now I feared something even greater. I feared myself. What was I capable of? I knew deep down that whatever was happening to me was far from ever. This was only the beginning. What would I become? Would I still be me? Would I end up like Laura? Right now, I am no better than Michael if I will take the life of myself and my child. *Who the hell am I?!*

"We will find a way so that it does not come to that," he whispered as he put a hand gently on my shoulder. "You need to calm yourself before he comes back."

I did not expect him to answer, and when he did, hearing him talk back caused me to gasp.

"You can hear my thoughts?"

"Yes."

"You do not trust, Michael?"

"No," he said as he shifted his weight to lean towards me

a bit more. "He sent me here to watch over you."

"Who sent you?"

"I'm not at liberty to say. All I can tell you is that he keeps his promises."

My angel? Is he real?

"I dreamed of a man. A man that said he would keep his promises and send help. I'm probably not making any sense right now."

"He exists, Vivienne. I dreamed of him when I was sick in Germany."

"What do I call him? Our mystery man."

"I'm not at liberty to say. He wants to have that honor himself when he greets you personally."

"Do you trust the Major?"

"I trust Major Stevens with my life," he told me with his hand still on my shoulder.

Edwin lifted my hand and pressed his palm into mine. As our hands touched, I heard a familiar song. I gasped. A faint singing that came from deep within him reached out to touch that which dwelled within me, but it was different. It felt like a ghost of who he could have been. It was like he was an echo of me.

"Who are you really?"

"You already know," he said with a sly grin.

CHAPTER 27

ENTER THE MAJOR

I heard the soft murmur of voices coming towards the tent. The voices became louder and more heated as they entered the tent. They started where they began, this time entering the tent, carrying the heated debate with them regardless of the audience and what I could imagine a steady stream of onlookers pretending to not pay attention.

I pretended to stir like I was waking up. I wanted to pretend to be asleep, but there was a song in my mind that made me curious. A song that I thought was Edwin or Laura, but this song was different. Its notes made no sense, stemming from a sense of chaos, like fingers that did not know the direction if they wanted to lead on the keys of a piano. It was more of a feeling than a song. A warning. It reminded me of a swirling darkness that hid in the shadows, watching and watching until it strikes out and squeezes the life out of its prey before it engulfs it whole like a snake. Was it Michael? Did everyone have a unique song? Or just those that I felt tuned into? What changed?

I looked up at Major Stevens, and I did a double take. I expected someone much older. He could not have been much older than my mother, and she had me when she was quite young. His bald head glistened in the soft glow of the lamp hanging above us as he took off his hat when he entered the tent. His eyes held the story of someone that has seen too much, and yet there was something beautiful in how he greeted his men, as they saluted one another, I could almost sense the love and respect that he held for every one of his men. I could almost understand why Edwin trusted him. He stood tall, like a reed that would never break in the wind, and there was no doubting the muscular form he held underneath his clothing. He did not allow the woes of his age to define him, and I could not help but want to place trust in him. In his strength.

"That thing is dangerous and a perversion of nature! You allow something like that to live?! It has claimed the lives of three of my boys! Are you even aware of how many lives I lost in the line of duty trying to contain that thing?!"

"Technically, she is not alive. Major, I understand your concerns..."

"You understand nothing, Dr. Alden! Do you hear me?! You will understand only what I allow you to understand, and right now you are but one signature shy of losing all your funding. I have lost nine young men to contain that thing. I cannot, for the life of me, understand what you have done and what you have allowed to happen here in such a short amount of time. Three lives lost on a recovery and clean up mission is unacceptable!"

"We need to take this opportunity to study her. Even if you tried killing her the traditional way, it will not work, Major. I have tried. Her tissue remains alive even though, by any logical sense, she is by all intents and purposes very much dead. Technically, she is decaying, but her rate of decay will be expediently much longer than the average rate of decay for a corpse. Given that she is alert and aware, we will witness firsthand the process of death from a mind that is aware of each stage of decay. Are we aware after death? It is a question that has filled the minds of scientists and philosophers alike for decades," he responded passionately.

"There will be no further testing or experiments until we return to home base. Is this understood, Dr. Alden?"

"Did you not hear what I just said, Major? You are shutting me down now? We are right in the middle of important findings and breakthroughs. To stop my work now…"

"Pack up and prepare to return to home base. Your future will depend on what we uncover in the debriefing, and after I go through all your research and findings."

"Major, we lost three lives, but their sacrifice helped further my research. I understand you are upset about your men, but that is no reason to shut down essential tests that are already in progress. It is crucial to my research that I complete these experiments and have access to the environment for further testing, as well as to Laura and Vivienne, without risking their emotional wellbeing in a closed lab. We do not have all the answers!"

"What are you talking about? I am upset about the lives of five-hundred-and-eighty-seven civilians and three of my soldiers. Five hundred and ninety human beings, Dr. Alden. Have you lost all compassion with that big brain of yours?"

"No, Major. I have not lost compassion, but I am, however, practical. I know to not allow my feelings to impede my job, and I side with the logical aspects of the situation."

"I wonder what would happen if your own emotions entangled you in their vast web? I can imagine it would not be a pretty sight. Tell me, Dr. Alden. What is Laura?"

"She is," he paused, creating an awkward yet purposeful silence that lasted several seconds as he contemplated on how to answer him for maximum impact, "undead."

Michael's eyes twinkled mischievously. It did not escape my notice that he was trying to manipulate the situation to get his way.

"How has rigor mortis not set in?"

"As you have seen, it has, but not in the way we would expect. She is constantly in a state of flux, moving between the state of repair and decay. This fluctuation, like I have stated earlier, leaves in her slow process of decay. Eventually, yes, she will die completely. How long that will take, I do not know."

"How is that possible? Why is she not like Ms. DuSan?"

"I believe it was the drug she was taking for her

condition," he said thoughtfully. "I believe it delayed the process enough for her to remain cognitively intact and slow the process of decay during her transition. Her overall mental state is questionable, but her conversation is quite enjoyable should you give her the opportunity. Her condition may be why the virus rejected her. We do not fully understand it yet, but the reason she is alive is the mystery we need to solve. When we can identify what links her to Vivienne, we will have a much better understanding of the virus."

"What are you thinking in terms of this link?"

"If she had any living relatives that were alive, they would have provided an opportunity to become a host. It is unfortunate that Laura does not. Like a needle in the haystack, the parasite is searching for a unique genetic sequence, using any method in which to replicate itself in order to find a host. The parasite recognizes something within her, but her diseased state has caused an error in what it is attempting to rewrite. Vivienne, however, has a family, but with a child on the way, we may not need them."

My family? He cannot mean my father's family?!

"English, please, doctor."

"Think of it as a story being rewritten. In her case, her story is being rewritten on pages where the erased words are still visible. That information is still being shared and translated. The parasite then replicates attempting to repair its error and seek the code in which to repair to further the process of transition. Have you ever had the hiccups?"

"Sure."

"Imagine trying to share an important piece of information, but you keep hiccupping. Start all over and share what you were trying to say again, only to go through the same cycle repeatedly."

"I must admit, this is intriguing. You said that the undead woman would react more human once we give her this drug," he asked. "You are saying that this drug is keeping her alive and connected to that part of herself that makes her human? For how long?"

"Unfortunately, the drug on its own no longer works without utilizing Vivienne's blood. Vivienne's blood acts as a type of battery that activates her ability to rejuvenate. How long will she hold on to that piece within her that is her humanity? I am not sure. Her mental state has already shifted drastically as the level of decay continues. I have a theory. If she continues to receive blood from a host that has integrated with the virus, she will continue to thrive and be able to rejuvenate her tissue and organs.

The rate of success and regeneration depend at what stage of transition the host is in. Vivienne's blood cannot keep her unaffected because of the delay in treatment, and without regular feedings, she will eventually be nothing more but a walking corpse. The question is how much blood she will need to maintain resembling something almost human. I have no way of gauging any of this without further testing. It is a high probability that she will continue to need higher doses as the decay rate speeds up. I had hoped we could reverse the process completely, but we now know that is unlikely."

I felt sick to my stomach as I remembered Laura feeding from me like a babe at my breast. How much longer would I have to endure her feeding from me?! Was it not enough that I am the very thing that killed my mother, an entire town? No, it was not enough, not to him! Michael wanted to create what? Could they create a monster army that survives on my blood? Then what?!

"We are lucky enough to have a host intact without these mutations. Based on the reports that you sent, Ms. DuSan comes from a colored background?"

"Yes, that is correct."

"The council will not take that lightly. What are our chances of obtaining a host that is more promising without risking an entire town?"

"Leave that to me," he said with a tone of satisfaction. "I need more time to find those answers, Major. The council will be extremely pleased when I do."

"They better be, Dr. Alden. My ass is on the line, just as much as yours is."

"Come, Major. Meet the miracle."

Michael looked over at me with an expression of pride, like he would over a prized experiment.

"I would like to introduce you to my wife. Major, this is Vivienne Alden," Michael said with arrogance. "Vivienne, this is Major Stevens."

Michael looked at me in a way that told me I had to play along. He patted his pocket that held the syringe, maintaining a look of innocence on his face. The last thing I wanted was to be in a vulnerable position to where he and his pet could have their way with me again. From the sounds of it, I was feeding her, and I had no way of knowing what the feeding schedule was. It could be tonight, tomorrow, or next week. I dreaded the next time.

"Hello, Vivienne. Please, call me Robert. I apologize for not referring to you by your proper name in our conversation. It must be quite the change, considering all that you have been through. Do you prefer Mrs. Alden, or shall I call you Vivienne?"

"Hello," I responded softly, keeping my eyes down lest they betray me for the raging anger that was boiling over beneath the surface. "Please, call me Vivienne."

"I've heard congratulations are in order for your marriage and the child on the way," he whispered. "Please forgive our frank conversation, Vivienne. That was unkind of me. I hope you will find it in your heart to forgive me. How are you feeling?"

"Tired."

"I understand. My wife went through a rough trimester with each of our three children. I know we are all extremely excited to meet this miracle child of yours."

Alarm bells went off in my mind. I grabbed my abdomen as if trying to protect my unborn baby from harm.

"You are too kind, Major Stevens," I said with my voice quivering, giving me away. "Forgive me, this pregnancy is quite hard on me, and I am tired. You would both find more interest in Laura for all your *needs* for the time being. I am still healing from my injuries, and with the pregnancy, I am feeling quite overwhelmed."

I surprised myself by talking so pragmatically, even though my voice continued to quiver, and my hands were now shaking. I slowly raised my eyes to look at Michael and allowed my mind to dream of the day I would take a knife and slit it across his throat. I would enjoy that day. I have never known hatred like this that could take a human life so easily. I knew without a doubt I would enjoy watching him die, but could I live with myself afterwards? I do not know, but I could not help but imagine his death repeatedly in my mind. I almost smiled at the thought.

"Sir, we should let her rest," Michael said, his eyes widening as if he could sense the threat within me building. He was studying me in a way that sent shivers up my spine. His face held a look of longing, and one of contemplation. I did not have it in me to think of what he would do with me next, given the opportunity, or to my baby. Fear returned, and I could not control the trembling or the energetic surge that gripped my entire body in a fierce wave. My body came alive with what felt like static electricity tingling all over my skin. My body glowed in a light blue hue as the energetic tentacles emerged from my body.

The Major stumbled back into his escort who fell backwards into the table. His escort pointed his gun at me and stepped in front of him. Levi, who was on the other side of Michael, stared at me with his brown eyes open wide and his mouth hanging open as he backed away towards the exit of the tent. I stood up from the bed and walked towards the Major. Michael looked between me and the Major in a blind panic and immediately stepped between me and the Major.

"Vivienne, what are you doing?! Stop it now! Stop it!"

"You will not harm my child, nor will you take my child from me. I will not allow it!"

The Major and his escort helped each other up, while his escort kept his gun pointed at my head. The anger within me gripped me as if it caught me in a wave that pulled me further and further out to sea. I did not know how to stop what I was feeling. I did not know what I was capable of, but at this point, I did not seem to care that he had a gun pointed at my heart.

"Please," Michael said, turning towards the Major and the escorts. He faced them and held his hands up. "She is not a threat. Lower your weapons. Major, please, trust me. Major!"

"Do as he says," the Major told the armed soldier as he looked at me wearily, and then a look of understanding washed over his face. "Of course, you have overheard us talking. This must be terrifying for you."

"Don't you mean studied and used like a biology project? Tell me, Major, is my life worth having any kind of respect at all? Does my life not matter? Do my feelings not matter? Do I not feel pain? Sadness? Fear? Do you think I'm such a monster? Do you know what it is like to be raped and impregnated in the name of your precious science?!"

"Vivienne," Michael raised his voice in a strong warning that had me wincing. "That... is... enough!"

Help me, I focused my energy towards the general and sent my thoughts amplified by my rage. I felt the energetic pull as the energy surrounding my body went through me and poured out to the major. The major stood upright in shock and then barreled over and grabbed his knees as if someone had punched him in the stomach. He grabbed his head and looked up at me, wide eyed.

"Major, are you alright?" Michael asked, looking at me cautiously. "You must forgive, Vivienne. This pregnancy has her acting out of sorts. She is not herself."

"I'm fine," he said as he regained his composure. "I'm tired from my trip, and I have been fighting a bit of a migraine."

He looked at me in a way that confirmed that he

understood, followed by a slight nod. He lightly rubbed his fingertips together as if they tingled, and then rubbed at his forehead. "If you will both excuse me, I need to lie down for a bit."

I did not mean to hurt him! The entity calmed and recoiled back within me. What a strange feeling it was to feel how easily we responded to one another. I could feel that energy within me, like a static charge. How could that defend me? Could I defend myself in a way that I could injure them just enough to get away? Was it possible that I may escape?

I would have to work on how I brought that energy into my being and how quickly it came out. I needed to learn and understand what I was becoming. If Edwin could not help me, I would have to figure out the mysteries of my new life. Would my child be like me? How can I instruct my child anything if I do not even know? Was the entity inside me supposed to teach me something? Say something? I remember hearing her in our binding ritual, but she has said nothing to me since. I did not want to harm anyone, especially the one person who could help me out of an impossible situation. I found myself tired of all the questions that continued to race through my mind, leaving me feeling vulnerable and confused.

I watched as Michael walked the Major back towards the lab, and as their backs turned, I let out a big, long sigh. I did not realize that I was holding in my breath.

"Michael, my friend, you do not look well," the Major said as they departed, still rubbing his head. "Have you not been taking care of yourself?"

"I haven't been sleeping well," he said with a slight edge of nervousness, which surprised me. "You know how I become invested in my projects. Sleep will come eventually. After you rest, I will take you on a tour of the camps and our efforts in the town."

Monster, my mind screamed at him! I wished I could have saved whatever that charge was to send Michael flying far enough that I would never see him again. *Dammit*! I feel like

I'm losing my mind. I could not help but wonder what it felt like to feel a sliver of hope. Hope felt more like a memory of a sunny day, now engulfed by looming, dark, turbulent storm clouds. I wake up to fight to live in the land filled with chaos and pain. Michael haunts me in my dreams. I cannot escape him!

God, I miss Anders. If he were here with me, I feel like I could endure more, but without him, even with Edwin at my side, it is simply different. To hold on to love is something that propels you forward through the abyss of war and beyond. With love at your side, anything is possible. Without it, I feel a coldness growing within my heart, and I fear losing myself in it.

I have hated myself for being the monster that I am. I have lost my freedom, and while the Major has made promises of my child's safety, I know I will never be free. Nor will my child. What kind of future would my child have?

I am so sorry, my little one. I have failed you before you are even born. Will you ever be able to forgive me?

"She will," Edwin responded.

"Thank you," I whispered, and he smiled.

CHAPTER 28

THE MISSING

Michael's new lab assistant, Alex, came in to take a blood sample late in the evening. I was still wide awake and contemplating my life and probable future for myself and my child without the hierarchy of fantasy that I found myself drawn to. If my blood rejuvenated Laura, did that mean I could not die? Surely, I could? What if that was my only way out to save myself and my unborn child from a life of medical experiments and torture?

Alex looked out of place. He looked even taller today, if that was possible, and his shaggy, disheveled black hair with dark circles under his eyes made him appear like how I felt. Today he was wearing smaller reading glasses, which emphasized his long nose, reminding me of the typical scientist or doctor who spent endless hours looking over their research. I could not picture him as anything more than a researcher, but he was in a military uniform which suggested he had been through their rigorous training endeavors. It was his brown eyes that held my attention. He looked like the person who wore his heart on his sleeve, and yet, there was something behind that shyness, an animal that was waiting to show his wild inhibitions and inner nature. I can imagine Michael noticed that as well and was looking for a kindred spirit. Yet, Alex was not and would be nothing like Michael.

"Alex," Michael called from outside. "Finish up and come help me with Laura. I will need samples from her." I heard Michael's footsteps, along with another set of footsteps, walk away. There was a nice crunch on the grass and leaves that were on the ground. Winter is coming quickly. Oddly enough, the chill in the air did not bother me as much as it used to.

"Shit," he mumbled under his breath.

I looked up at him and smiled.

"I'm alm… almoosssss…ssst almost done," he yelled back, stuttering. His hands shook as finished the last vial of blood that he would need from my arm. He tied a strip of cloth around my arm and held the knot above where the needle entered.

"Don't enjoy visiting Laura," I asked him politely. "I do not blame you. It does not seem quite real, does it?"

"No," he answered me and looked up at me, surprised by our moment of understanding one another. "I feel as if I am trapped in someone else's nightmare. Do you feel that way?"

I looked down at my hands in my lap. I could not articulate a response that did not include unleashing a torrential downpour of tears. I simply nodded while biting my tongue.

"Professor Alden has been looking at me all day like I am his next experiment. I have heard the rumor mill that people go missing when they see Laura. Three soldiers so far are missing from what Levi has told me. Do you know him? He is Michael's personal guard. He has been looking out for me. I am not feeling very confiddd… confiddd… confident in my place here."

"Are you scared?"

"I am terrified," he said quickly, looking relieved and shocked at the same time to have stated as much aloud.

"Do you fear being Laura's next plaything? What would you have done to suffer his wrath?"

"I really shouldn't be talking to you about any of this," he said, eyeing towards the exit of the tent as if he feared Michael having superhuman hearing.

"Who am I going to tell? Come on, if you need to talk to someone, it might as well be me. Besides, it gives me something to do, and human conversation is rare for me these days."

"I suppose so," he smiled shyly. "If we had ever met in different circumstances, I would have invited you out for brunch."

"That's very sweet," I said, smiling at him. "So, tell me, what did you uncover that would make you his target?"

"Professor Alden's research just stops at a certain point, and there are so many questions and large gaps in his research," he said quietly and moving more closely to me so I could hear him barely above a low whisper as if we were close childhood friends sharing secrets. "He spends most of his time with Laura, so I went through all his notes and files to help me understand the virus. I have always dreamed of continuing Louis Pasteur's work of understanding how viruses signal each other to spread."

"Is Louis Pasteur a famous scientist then?"

"Oh, yes! He was instrumental in the discovery of how bacteria contribute to the disease process, including viruses. He developed a vaccine for rabies. If we can unravel this virus, we can find a vaccine to ensure we protect the population in the future. I have a theory of how viruses communicate."

"Like people?"

"I know it sounds crazy," he said, his eyes twinkling with excitement. Edwin shifted forward in his seat, eavesdropping, and I could swear the conversation intrigued him. I could not picture Edwin interested in science, and yet, here he sat, intrigued. My mother always reminded me to judge no one before getting to know them, and this was yet another reminder that people will always surprise you. "If we can understand how to communicate with the virus, we could attempt to understand its purpose on a deeper level, and then prevent the virus from destroying other towns."

"What if this virus is not actually a virus?"

"That, I would believe. Nothing makes any sense here. Look, the future is not about physical weapons. If I am right, based on my hypothesis and study of wars, the future will be about what we cannot see. The sooner we develop this understanding as a collective, the more we can improve our chances of withstanding an attack of this magnitude."

"You think that is happening now?"

"Would that be surprising?"

"Like my town? Just wiped out of existence. You do not seriously think what happened here was on purpose?" I asked him with a look of horror in my eyes.

"This was an accident of opportunity. Considering how far away the town is from everything, we were lucky it was not more central to other communities with how rapidly the virus, or whatever it is, spreads. Incredibly lucky."

"What if it was a parasite?" I asked as I gauged his reaction to how much he may have already figured out. He looked at me with wide eyes as a nod of understanding and internal calculations began.

"That is... I hate to say it considering how much devastation it has caused, but it is..."

"Yes, it is fascinating. What else have you uncovered?" Edwin asked curiously, startling us both.

"I read newspaper clippings about a man from the Middle East that came to the town, and shortly after, there was a flu outbreak. If he brought it here, then it was possible that he unknowingly released the virus or parasite into the population in each location he stopped on the way. Was it contained? Did it remain dormant?"

"All very good questions," Edwin told him. "For now, you best keep your thoughts to yourself. You are safe to talk to me or Vivienne, but do not share any of this with Michael."

"I have already shared a few of my theories with him, which is why I fear what he may do with me. He did not appear to be pleased with my extracurricular activities outside of my assigned duties. With the Major away, accidents seem to just happen."

"The Major is away? Where is he?" I asked, terrified of losing the only sliver of hope that I could get away from

Michael.

"Look, if anything happens to me, I have compiled as much as I can in my notes. They are under my cot, wrapped in a sweater. Michael should have had the military looking into this immediately. I am honestly surprised that he has not. It goes against procedure and places the entire nation at risk."

"Couldn't we consider that if there was a risk, we would have all heard about it already? Considering how fast it destroyed the town. If the man was a carrier, the question should be *when* the parasite was released and why? What was the catalyst in this town, or was it active in other areas as well?" Edwin asked him, rubbing his chin.

"That's... that's actually," he looked at Edwin curiously, and then turned his attention back towards me. "I'll have to add that to my investigation notes."

"The catalyst would need to be something so simple, right? We know there was a flu outbreak shortly after he arrived. Wouldn't that trigger the immune system into an immune response, with a high fever, and it gave the mystery parasite an opportunity to invade? This all makes my head hurt."

I looked at Edwin, shocked that he had hidden such an amazing and contemplative brain. No one would have guessed that he was secretly an erudite hiding a learned mind.

"I better get back to what I was doing. I have been in here long enough. He is going to suspect something if he does not already," he said, shifting his weight nervously as he picked up his clipboard and my vial of blood.

"Are we out of cotton?" I asked him, pointing at the strip of fabric tied across my arm as he was turning to leave.

"We are out of everything. There are no more supply drops since we are getting ready to pack up. We must make do with what we have," he responded quickly as he made his way out of the tent without looking at Edwin. "Make sure you put anything that gets blood on it in the bucket by your bed."

I watched as he left, and immediately took off the strip

of fabric and placed it in the bucket. There was no need to stand on ceremony. I listened and waited until I heard Alex leave before initiating a conversation with Edwin.

"He looked extremely nervous when Michael mentioned Laura. Not that I can blame him," I said, looking over at Edwin.

"She's a perversion of our kind."

"Our kind? Do you know what they were talking about regarding her condition? They hoped she would end up like me, didn't they?"

"I have been thumbing through the Professor's stacks of papers, telegrams, research notes and file folders while he is busy with Laura. Michael has hidden or destroyed much of his research. The question is why? We are lucky that his new research assistant took the initiative and hid his notes. I was looking for anything that could help me make sense of all of this, so I had something to report back. I found Laura's clinical file at the bottom of the trash pile that he did not destroy, yet. I must admit, looking at her photograph, if I met her long ago when I was younger on the sidewalk, I would have stopped her and begged for a date."

"She was beautiful and almost wild when I met her, but even then, I knew something was not right. There was something off about her. She was different, and from the sounds of it, she was not well. My first instinct when I met her was to run. She was already undead when I met her. Nobody in their right mind would mutilate other people like that, would they?"

"Based on her medical file, her name is Laura Donnelly. She was a cancer patient with leukemia. Laura was taking a cancer drug. It surprised me that this small town had access to it. She must have connections, or she pulled in serious favors to get a hold of it. Since she is a nurse, I guess it would be easier for her to have those connections. The drug works its magic by preventing cancer cells from multiplying. This must have allowed the parasite to stay controlled within her body. Even upon death, it would alter the process, albeit temporarily. She was dying, just at a slower rate."

"You know you're really smart," I said, in awe of his intellectual ability. "Sly fellow, you are!"

"It's part of the job," he said, tapping his forehead. "Never let them see you coming, and always keep them guessing."

"So, the drug hid her condition as the parasite changed her, but the changes mutated because of her condition and the drug? Trying to sort all that out makes my head hurt."

"Yes, she was a walking time bomb. It would only be a matter of time before the parasite recognized she was not a healthy host. I agree with Michael that there is a hidden connection that links you both, whether it is somewhere through your family ancestry or another factor of which we are not yet aware. I am guessing she could not get hold of her medication via a shipment when the town shut down. Which caused her state of rapid decline, which then affected what was happening within her with the parasite. The drug causes damage to the DNA and causes cell death. It is how we know it can kill cancer."

"How is she still alive? Did the parasite repair her, or does it keep trying to repair her? Or is it my blood? What makes her unique?"

"That is the mystery. I need to get access to her blood samples that come back with Alex. Michael has a nasty habit of destroying any evidence, apart from your blood. Alex will make a wonderful ally if he survives. Michael is spending more time with Laura, and away from the lab. He has done no official work in days. One of my specialties is being able to move with ease like a thief in the night. I will enter the lab and run my own tests. I will not have access to the equipment once we arrive at home base, and my time is running short. It is worth the risk if it means getting answers."

"Are you a scientist?"

"I am many things," he told me with a sly grin. "Being a scientist was my original profession until I went on a mission in Germany to study a similar matter involving what we assumed then was a virus. I became infected with a similar strain, thanks to Michael. It was the day I became many things, many people. It is difficult to explain, but when you are ready, I will tell you more."

An owl screeched over the tent, and I stood up and walked towards the opening. The late evening air was cold, and along with the frost on the ground, I could smell snow in the air. I had the sudden urge to get outside and enjoy the fresh air.

"Edwin, can we take a walk? I cannot stay here another minute."

He nodded, and I grabbed a blanket to wrap around me. I did not care that Michael forbade me from any kind of freedom. We weaved our way around the camp. The men in the camp were busily preparing to move, and they were far too busy with their own duties to pay us much attention. More likely, it was Edwin. If they knew I was with him, they did not need to fear Michael's wrath. They did not question Edwin, and they all avoided direct eye contact, except for the small few that appeared to know him well enough to smile and wave in greeting or pat him on the back in passing. It felt comforting and familiar to be unseen.

We walked around the surrounding woods, moving our way back towards the tent that now held Michael's pet, Laura, and we heard sounds of struggling. The guards posted at each corner of the tent shifted their weight nervously as their white knuckles gripped tightly on their guns. Edwin grabbed my elbow and guided me quickly past. My gut feeling told me something was not right. A dark shadow like mass hung over the tent, like locusts taking flight as they prepared to land to decimate everything in their path.

"Edwin," I whispered as he headed past the tent. "Something's not right."

CHAPTER 29

DEVIL IN HIDING

"It is not our business. Let us keep moving."

"Whatever Laura is, whatever she is becoming, feeds something else besides just her. There's more than just undead walking through the forest here. It attached itself to her. I cannot explain it, and I am not sure what to call it, but I do not want to go near it. I do not want to call its attention. It feels like it is… hungry, and whatever is going on in there, it is about ready to enjoy a meal. Do you think… Alex…"

Without a word, Edwin guided me as we walked more quickly out into the forest, moving swiftly around trees and being careful to avoid large tree roots raised up from the cold ground. I could barely keep up. The further we went in, the denser it became. We entered a small open patch where a majestic large solitary oak tree stood. Its gnarled ancient branches spread out from the ground and reached their way towards heaven in an immortal embrace.

Stepping onto the crisp colored leaves of orange and red, our footsteps lightly crunched as we slipped slightly to sit upon one of the large earthbound arms from the oak. We sat for what felt like hours. I took in the forest's beauty, now dimly lit by the almost full moon that rose above us. The stars twinkled like glitter across the sky. They took my breath away! How often had I forgotten to stop and look up at the stars?

Tall conifers and deciduous trees sheltered the area with a spring in their step as they walked over an expansive root system riddled with moss and mushrooms of varying types. In this moment, I felt connected on a level that I had long since forgotten. The oak itself hummed with a song that lit up the rest of the forest in a beautiful harmony. I could not help but wonder if I stopped long enough, in my human life, if I could hear its song. Not every human had a song, but most had strong emotions which were more like ocean waves rather than a song. Shifting and changing based on their mood and experiences. Why was I different? Or Edwin? Why did our blood sing like the earth? Like nature? What was it that made us different?

When I was small, I loved looking up at the stars, filled with wonderment of life. Standing here in the middle of the forest, I felt transported back into that moment. Dancing and twirling below the stars with my mother, as we both laughed and fell to the ground as the world became a magical spell that spun around us.

"Vivienne, are you alright?" Edwin asked, steadying my shoulders. "You need to be mindful of your healing and reserve your strength for the walk back. Michael and Laura take too much from you."

"Sorry, I am lost in thought," I replied. "I was reminiscing about a time like this with my mother. It is funny how when we become adults, we forget to look up at the stars and dream."

"You were doing more than that," he whispered nervously. "You were glowing like a blue glow bug. We do not want to bring any unwarranted attention. Which we may have already done by just leaving the camp. There are also patrols in these woods."

"Why are you not scared of me?"

"My... superior. He has placed his trust in me and allowed me to see who he really is. He is like me, and yet completely different. He is like you, but he is so much more."

"Like me," I repeated softly. "What is he? What am I?"

"You are the beginning," he whispered. "He has searched for you for such a very long time."

"The beginning? The beginning of what?"

"An evolution and bridge for your species," he smiled at me knowingly. "Which apparently hasn't happened for a very long time."

"Will I ever know him?"

"One day, when you are ready. He told me you were special, and to do whatever it took to ensure you were safe. I failed you. I cannot stop that son of a bitch from touching you without risking my position to watch over you. Michael cannot feed me to Laura without me putting up one hell of a fight. If it comes to that or a danger to your safety, I will do what is necessary to get you out. For now, we must both endure this nightmare. Please, just know you are not alone. I have done my best to make suggestive comments to distract him from you. So far, it is working, but I do not know for how long."

"You know about what he's doing to the men?"

"I do, and it is more than he is reporting. I am sure he has a plan to say there was a minor outbreak. When the Major comes back, you need to tell him everything. Verbally, tell him. You could have killed him."

A panic settled within me, as fear gripped hold of my core, along with a deeply settled shame. "I did not mean to hurt him. I understand nothing that is happening to me, or how to control any of it. Can you teach me?"

"We are very much different, you and me. The only advice I can give you is to talk to everyone around you in a whisper if you use that power again. The smallest, tiniest whisper is like a suggestive thought. The louder you are, the more harm you can do to them without realizing it. I learned the hard way, but the power I had was very short-lived. I am surprised and glad that we can at least hear one another."

"What if I told the Major, and it solves nothing? If Michael found out, it would only anger him further. I do not want anyone else to die because of me."

"You are thinking of Anders?"

"Yes," I told him as I swallowed back tears. "Whatever has happened to him is because I fell in love with him. Anyone

I care about dies or disappears. Have you heard anything? I mean, about Anders?"

"No, I have not. I am so sorry."

"I have never blamed you or felt that you failed me," I whispered as I touched his arm. "Will you be with me when I talk to the Major?"

"I've got you."

The smell of fall was quickly changing to winter. The fallen leaves on the ground crunched under our feet as we walked, and the scent of pine was heavy on the crisp air. The bite of frost teased my lungs, and it was one of the most wonderful feelings. I heard a small stream nearby, and we walked over to it. I sat there for what seemed like an hour enjoying this small amount of freedom from my captivity, surrounded by the deep greens of the pines, and the barren browns, tans, and whites of the trees that had given up their leaves for a sleepy winter.

We heard a group of men coming through the woods, and we both stood up. Edwin did not appear worried at all, but I felt a steady stream of unease when approached by a group of men that feared me more than anything else. The four men approached us cautiously with guns raised.

"Report," Edwin said with absolute authority.

"Dr. Alden has ordered you both found and returned immediately, Sir," the one in the lead saluted him. He had a lock of black hair peeking out from under his helmet. His eyes were a bright blue. I remembered him. He was a friend of Anders.

"Hello, Phil. I would say it is nice to see you again, but we both know that would be untrue. Have you heard anything about Anders?"

"No," he said, looking at Edwin with wide eyes, followed by looking down at his feet. "He's one of the missing men."

"Missing," I repeated after him as my heart fell into my stomach and a lump fell into my throat. My world slowly slipped away as my mind tried to fathom what he was saying. I remembered Laura's words that Anders would come for me, and fear filled me with a sense of dread. Was he like her? Undead? Or was he dead, like the others? "I do not blame you for your anger towards me. I cannot change the past, but I will do whatever is necessary to help find Anders if I am able."

"Is there something you want to tell me, Private?" Edwin asked Phil, stepping in front of me protectively. He stood over Phil in a menacing way, glaring down at him, and boy, it was intimidating. I was certainly thankful I was not at the receiving end of that glare.

"Sir?"

"You will hold Vivienne with the utmost respect, do you understand me, Private?"

"Yes, Sir!"

"Is this about his friend Tim?" Edwin rolled his head to the side to ask me.

"Yes, but it is not just him. Anders is also his friend. I do not hold it against him that he blames me. If it was not for me, they would both still be here with us."

"Private, Tim was my responsibility, and he died in the line of duty. He died a soldier. Treat his death as such."

"Yes, Sir!"

The men started walking again, and Edwin knowingly put his arm around me and guided me to follow him. We did not speak as we walked, and the silence felt deafening as my heart ached for Anders. As we walked back towards the camp, I did not realize just how far out we had walked into the middle of nowhere, heading away from any form of civilization. I took more time taking in the scenery as we walked back out of fear that they would deny me any freedom in the future for this little escape.

Lost in my thoughts, I stopped dead in my tracks as my feet shuffled against dead pine needles muddled in a lost sea of dried leaves. I became overwhelmed with a sense of nausea as a familiar song entered my mind. Edwin must have heard it as well. He stood tall as he pushed me behind him, grabbing with his sidearm and raising his arms in front of us. He motioned to the guards with a hand signal, and I watched them quickly gather in formation with me at its center.

"Is it Laura?" I asked Edwin, feeling fear catch me like I somehow ate a brick and it weighed heavily on my abdomen. What if it was Anders?! Am I really prepared to see him be like her? Soulless and no longer like the man I loved?

"It is hungry," he said, looking at me wide eyed. He knew exactly what that meant. Whoever it was, was coming for me, for my blood.

The last time Laura went on a rampage, it was messy. She fed regularly from me, so what would have caused such a change in her behavior? I turned in small slow circles, fearful of when the attack would begin.

"What the fuck are we doing?" The soldier, who had a grimace on his face the entire time, asked, breaking the silence.

"Private," Edwin said, with a seething warning. "Do your job, be quiet and pay attention, or you may not survive this encounter."

"What fucking encounter, Sir? Aren't we a little old to be afraid of the dark?" He asked as he was getting ready to turn towards us, showing us his sarcastic version of being scared in the dark when something came running swiftly from out of the shadows of the trees.

A dark figure that danced like the wind tackled him to the ground like a hawk swooping down for the kill. The soldier's screams of pain echoed through the darkness, scarring my soul as I heard his throat gurgling cries damper into silence. We all stood there, staring in shock at the event that had just unfolded right in front of us. I did not know about any of them, but my mind refused to register that something had just killed him so quickly that they had little or no time to even react.

I screamed when blood erupted like a volcano from his torn torso, splattering on all of us. Edwin dropped me to my knees and hovered over me like a shield as gunshots popped like large ceramic planters dropped from high above me and shattering down on the ground all around me towards an unseen target that moved too quickly for the human eye.

The attacker turned slowly towards us, crouched like an animal ready to take on its next target of prey. He looked so much like Laura in her decayed state, his dark hair was matted with dried blood and dirt, his leathery grey skin covered with purple bruising as blood pooled under the surface, torn grey slacks, his once decent white long sleeve button-up shirt was now hanging loosely, covered in old blood, as well as freshly splattered red from the man he just killed. His all too familiar name tag still hanging above his right breast gave him away. That and his long and wide mustache that draped down to his chin.

"Oh, God," I cried out.

CHAPTER 30

TRANSITION

"I thought my mother killed him," I whispered through the tears that came on quickly as my mind worked its way through the shock of seeing him again. "Mr. Perkins?"

Mr. Perkins stood up slightly as he cocked his head at me, as if he were trying to understand me. He looked towards me in a way that suggested he was more animal than human as he sniffed the air and a throaty war cry erupted from his undead body.

The soldiers jumped into action to subdue him as he lunged forward, and they quickly surrounded him with their guns drawn. Phil, too eager to get the job done, rushed towards him. He tossed him as if he weighed nothing more than a rag doll. Phil hit the tree trunk and landed with a loud thump. He screamed in agony as he grabbed his leg. Mr. Perkins came running towards us, and Edwin, moving just as fast as Mr. Perkins had, countered his attack, throwing Mr. Perkins into the air. He landed swiftly on his feet and crouched back down, squatting as he shifted his weight.

"Oh, God," I whispered in a panic, scrambling backwards. My mind was on fire, screaming at me to run.

Edwin shifted his weight effortlessly and moved back in front of me, his stance set and prepared to block him again without hesitation. Once again, gun fire erupted towards Mr. Perkins, and in a matter of seconds, he disappeared back into the shadows of the forest, moving at an incredible speed.

"What the fuck was that?" One soldier asked.

"We should all be afraid of the dark," Edwin replied

solemnly. "You two grab Phil and let us get him to Doc Lindberg. Vivienne, are you all right?"

"I'm fine," I said, pretending to be braver than I felt. If they could see my shaking knees, it would have given away the simple truth that I was terrified.

"Good," he said as he grabbed the body of the dead soldier, lifting him over his shoulder. I forced myself to look away. Death's face continued to remind me I was alive, while so many continued to die. It was not exactly fair, was it?

We trekked slowly back towards the camp. The other two that were helping with Phil looked around warily, fearing there may be a secondary attack. I, and I am sure Edwin could as well, knew he was already miles away. For a corpse, he moved faster than any human being could. Edwin moved just as quickly during the fight. Did that mean I had the potential to move just as fast? I was not ready to assess that theory and risk scaring them more than they already were of me.

How many were out there like Laura? Laura, at least on some level, wanted to protect me, but Mr. Perkins, he did not. His hunger had become a driving force of its own, and I knew without question that he wanted to drain every bit of my blood. I am being hunted, and everyone around me is in danger. Would Laura hunt me as well if she did not have a steady supply for my blood? I did not like my mind's responses to my own questions.

When we made it back to the camp, I did not think I would be so grateful for the confines of the fabric walls. We took Phil and the dead soldier to Doc Lindberg. He lit a cigarette as soon as he saw us.

"What the fuck did you all get yourselves into this time?"

"Fuck," cried Phil as they helped him lay down on the stretcher. Doc Lindberg, without even needing to assess his condition, grabbed a syringe, and filled it with a clear substance and quickly jabbed into his hip. Phil went from being red-in-the-face and sweating profusely from the pain he was in, to looking calm and serene as he entered a deep sleep.

I wonder if that was what Michael gave me. Did I look just as calm and serene as when he invaded my body with that thing?

The Doc lowered the lantern down to look at Phil's leg and we all gasped as we saw the jagged edges of bone sticking out of his leg.

"We ran into something that did not want to die," Edwin replied, which made the Doc stand up straight as his eyes went wide and he became very pale.

"Another creature?" He asked Edwin as he drew in a long inhale from his cigarette.

Edwin nodded.

"Wonderful. Just the fucking news I needed. As I needed another excuse to battle my raging insomnia. Another fucking abstract of nature."

Edwin herded us out of the tent. I heard the Doc muttering under his breath as we left.

"Prepare yourself," Edwin whispered in my ear. "I doubt Michael will be in a forgiving mood. No doubt he has already heard about the attack."

We walked into the lab tent, and Michael was pacing frantically back and forth. He looked furious! He also did not look like he was feeling very well, and he did not look at all like his charming self. He looked worse than he had just hours prior. The color of his skin was pale, his eyes held dark shadows underneath, and he walked in a manner that reflected a man of an elderly demeanor. Something was going on with him. His health was deteriorating, but I could not find it within myself to pity him.

"What happened? I heard gunshots and screams, and the patrol notified me there was an attack! Vivienne, are you hurt?!"

He raced over to me and turned me around and around to ensure that I did not have so much as a scratch, including lifting my clothes up so that he could peer under them. My feeble attempts to bat his hands away were unnoticed by him.

"Sir, a... a... man attacked us. Not a normal man. He is

like the woman you are holding prisoner, Sir," one of the patrol soldiers said nervously avoiding eye contact while staring straight ahead and through Michael.

"Any injuries?" Michael asked him, pausing his pacing just long enough to look him in the eye.

"He killed Johnson, Sir. Phil is with Doc Lindberg now. Broken leg, but he will live, Sir."

"I want the man found," Michael yelled at the men. He was red in face, and he was spitting on whoever was in front of him during his pacing. "Now! Do whatever is necessary to apprehend that son of a bitch! Grab extra patrols from the surrounding camps if you must."

I watched as the men left, scurrying frantically with looks of fear on their faces.

"Leave," he told Edwin. Edwin looked at me as if to say to stay strong. I did not know how much stronger I could be. I was honestly hanging on by a thread, and pretending to be strong, hoping my pretending was enough and would somehow become a reality. Deep down, I felt like a frail and weak creature, and I hated it! I would keep doing what I needed to if, one day, Michael would pay for his crimes. *I will see this through to the end*, I told myself. *I must try!*

My need for vengeance was an anchor, and it fueled me to keep going. If I gave up hope, it would be too easy to surrender into feeling exhausted and lost. He would pay for what he had done. I did not hide my obvious feelings of disdain for him. *I am done hiding!*

As soon as Edwin was outside of the tent, Michael walked right up to me and slapped me right in the face. The sheer force knocked me backwards as I fell on my back with a hard thud. I sat up and grabbed hold of my cheek. The sting of his handprint burned my face, and the force left my cheek and eye throbbing.

"Never do that to me again," he seethed, attempting to keep his voice down. "You cannot leave this encampment and go wandering off. We have creatures coming out of the darkness hunting you. You put our child at risk by leaving the safety of this camp! I could have lost everything in the blink of an eye! Did you even think of how your actions may have cost me everything?!"

I watched the vision in my left eye leave me as the swelling set in and it swelled itself shut. I wanted to cry, but I would never, and I mean never, let him know he had any power over me. *Never again!* I regained my composure, picking myself up off the floor and standing tall, and glared at him as I allowed my rage to carry me above the pain.

"What do you have to say for yourself, Vivienne?"

When I did not answer, he growled with rage and came at me like he was going to hit me again. He looked at my face and turned around and kicked the metal garbage bin so hard it bounced off the fabric wall of the tent and landed on its side as it discarded its contents.

"You fucking bitch! You will learn your place," he ranted, taking my chin into his long fingers, and then shoving my chin aggressively to the side

He walked up to me and grabbed my hand, placing it on the bulge that was forming in his pants. He moved my hand back and forth and then unzipped his pants. He placed himself in my unwilling hand, using his own hand to guide and control the movement of my hand while he used his other hand to fondle my breast.

I stood, stiff as a board, unmoving. I mentally checked out. He may manipulate my body, but I refused to take any conscious part of it. I was getting good at escaping into the realm of my inner mind. It was a new talent that was once upon a time reserved for daydreamers and those lost in love and working through those wonderful feelings and being high on life, but in my case, it was something I did out of survival, to protect myself from unraveling and losing my mind.

"You dirty little whore." He held onto my shoulder to keep himself upright as he moaned, and I felt the warmth and wetness of his ejaculation in my hand. He cleaned himself up, cleaned my hand as he would a messy child, and then continued rambling on.

"I will have additional guards placed outside of your tent to ensure that tonight's events do not repeat themselves. Thankfully, Edwin was with you, or tonight could have gone much worse."

Again, I did not respond. I lost the ability to move, to respond. He stood before me like a stranger in a strange land. From behind the veil within my mind, his words held little meaning, and everything felt foreign, including my body.

"Well? What do we say about my kindness in protecting you and your child?" When I said nothing, his face came so close to mine that our noses were touching. "You are an ungrateful whore," he spat in my face, and then he turned around and stormed out.

"Edwin, you will ensure she does not leave this encampment again," he yelled from just outside the tent. "Your connections will only get you so far. Do not compromise our mission again."

"Yes, Sir," I heard Edwin say.

Edwin walked into the tent a moment later, and as he looked me over with genuine concern in his eyes, I let go of all the sadness I was holding onto in trying to be strong. Seeing his sincerity touched something within me, the parts of me that were completely broken. My tears trickled down my cheek, and I held my arms out to him. Edwin swooped me up like a child and I melted into his arms, sobbing heavily.

"Edwin, can you get a message to Major Stevens to come and meet with me as soon as possible?"

"When he arrives, I will be happy to give him your message. I am looking forward to having a conversation with him myself. He is offsite and not due back until morning."

I needed to survive until dawn. Could I make it that long? Would Michael remain infatuated with his pet and give me a moment of peace? Laura had yet to feed from me, so I knew it was only a matter of time, and Michael would not let her go that long between feedings.

"Can you do this for one more night?" He asked me as he wiped the tears from my eyes.

"I will try," I responded as I looked up, sensing Michael returning to the lab with Laura in tow. "Put me down, they are coming."

Edwin put me down, and I sat down in the chair at the small table riddled with papers with notes that made no sense to the general observer. His notes looked more like riddles than anything that came from scientific observation. Was that on purpose? Or was Michael that far gone, and nobody had cared to notice? Michael entered with Laura, and Edwin nodded at me as he crossed behind Michael to exit the tent.

"Mother, sister, daughter," she whispered in a barely audible hiss.

I looked at her, and I could see the life force that she had taken from me was now faint. There was something different about her, darker, and the black fog surrounded her, waiting for its next meal to eat away at another person's pain, their essence, happiness. All the things that made up their life force. The fog moved around her like a shadow, shifting its form based on what its prey was feeling. It mimicked my sadness and grew with anticipation, which I knew was not coming from me. It shifted back and forth from shapelessness to what looked like the shadows of people standing around huddled together. Yes, that is what I would call them. Shadow people. I did not know what else to call it, or them. I did not exactly understand what they were. Was it part of Laura? Or was it drawn to her? I felt as though it was part of the latter, but my mind was not ready to accept there were more things out there that went bump in the night.

I did not know what to expect from either of them, but I could feel Michael's excitement, and yet, I could also feel his fear. He was afraid! What was he afraid of? Of me? He approached me slowly, looking at me with yearning and desire. His hand caressed my cheek, moving down my neck to the opening of my gown. He placed his hand inside and grasped by breast, playing with my nipples with his thumb. I glared at him, which excited him more. He grabbed my hand and pressed it back into his groin.

"Michael, please do not do this to me, not again. Haven't you done enough today?"

"You are mine," he whispered into my ear as he nibbled on my earlobe and down my neck. "I will do with you as I please."

I wanted to fight back, but who would help me? Everyone now feared Michael and feared Laura. All I would risk now would be another black eye from Michael. With the threat of another undead creature lurking, the camps were bound to be on edge, and I would be the last thing they would want to protect. My daydreams of escaping with Anders were a reminder of my naivety and felt like a lifetime ago. Yet, there was something.

What is it? It is there on the tip of my tongue. What is it? Something...

A dawning of realization came over me, a revelation.

You have more to hide than we all realize. You little devil. You have a secret!

Yes, I see it now. He is like Laura. He is in transition.

I can hear him!

Dear God, what was he thinking?! He thought my successful transition could do what? Grant him the gift to be like me? I did not even know what I was!

Edwin, if you can hear me! It is Michael! He is in transition! We need to find help before he becomes more dangerous than he already is!

Michael withdrew the syringe from his coat and quickly grabbed my arm and pushed their contents to lull me into the darkness.

Edwin, please... help me...

Once again, in the darkness, I was still observant and stuck between realms of consciousness and unconsciousness.

It was a space I resented. Were the recent changes of what I was becoming the reason someone could not properly drug me into a dreamless sleep? In so many ways, it would be so much easier if I could check out and forget. The last thing I wanted was to be aware of what they were doing. One day, I would find the strength within me to fight back. One day...

"You've had your playtime," I heard Michael say to Laura in a tone that was scolding as if she were an animal. His pet. I could feel him pick me up. I could feel the cold late evening air. The camp was silent, and with all that had happened, I could imagine it was well into the early hours of the morning. We must have entered another tent. The light fluctuated behind my eyelids and became much brighter as we entered the space. Michael laid me down on the bed.

"Yes, Alex was pleasant," she murmured dreamily. "You need to bring me toys that won't break so easily."

"Now, it's feeding time," Michael said, as I felt him undoing the buttons on my gown to undress me.

"Sir, I'm sorry for interrupting, but you're needed in the Major's tent," Edwin said, but he sounded as if he was extremely far away.

The major. I drifted into a dreamless sleep, waiting for my opportunity to arise.

CHAPTER 31

CHOICES

Later that morning, the Major sat across from me in the empty mess tent. The smell of overcooked oatmeal and maple syrup permeated the air. The dark circles under his eyes suggested he had little sleep, and his demeanor was a serious one. Nothing about his physical appearance helped to calm my nerves, which continued to heighten with every passing moment.

"Have you developed any gifts?"

"Will my response determine my fate?"

"Your honesty will determine your fate."

"Why don't I show you? It is difficult to explain my newfound abilities," I told him, as I felt nervous. I could not help but feel like I was a circus act. Edwin trusted him, and I was holding onto his judgement of character. I took a deep breath and connected with the entity that existed within me. "Keep in mind, I still do not know enough about how this all works, and I am still learning what I may or may not be capable of."

"Do the best you can, and please, no repeat of what you did with your mind trying to communicate with mine. I am still recovering from that one."

"I am so sorry for that! Like I said, I am still learning. Just give me a minute to focus and let us see what I can do."

"You are still unaware of your capabilities? Completely?"

"Yes. Should it be different? Should I be aware?"

"Yes, based on what we know about this type of parasite and the transformation involved based on ancient texts, you should have access to ancient knowledge, past lifetimes, and training. We do not know exactly how it works, but we know that whatever it is inside you, you should be able to communicate with it."

"With it, you mean…"

"Yes."

"The communication I have with it is nothing like that. When I dream, sometimes I am living in a different time and in places I would never know about. They are mixed images, more like imprints. Does it take more time to access this knowledge? Or could the trauma of everything I have experienced prevent me from accessing it? Is there something wrong with me?"

The thought of being alone and left in the dark was terrifying. I could not do this alone. If the entity within me could not communicate with me, how could we coexist? I refused to live in a world where I would always question myself and my abilities.

You do that every day, Edwin's mind interjected. *Each step we take will bring more answers. Please be patient.*

Stop eavesdropping on my private inner dialogue! Edwin simply smiled at me like an older brother would at a younger sibling he was poking fun at. I almost rolled my eyes at him, but the Major was watching my every move to learn more about me.

"Those are all relevant questions that I hope we can find out together. Please focus and try to show me what you can do. Safely."

I looked at him and gave him a weak smile as he pushed his chair back a little farther away from me. I could not blame him for not being able to trust me, considering I almost fried his brain like an egg.

"Focus, Vivienne," I whispered to myself.

I closed my eyes and brought myself back to the forest that held its own ethereal glow and moved myself into that moment, remembering what it was to be free. I opened my eyes slowly as I witnessed my body glow a now familiar auric blue. I looked at the Major straight in his eyes, and he stood up slowly from his side of the table, backing up slightly as if he could not trust the table between us to protect him. Willing the energy and my mind to be as one, I closed my eyes again, and remembered what it was like to fly in my dream of joining with my entity. I willed myself to fly. I surprised myself when I felt myself levitate off the ground slightly. I could feel myself weakening. This act alone was an enormous drain of energy. Parlor acts were not just for show, but best reserved for survival tactics.

"Uh, Vivienne," I heard Edwin say, sounding concerned.

"What?" I asked him as I opened one of my eyes, setting myself back down on the ground. I followed his gaze behind me and turned around. I gasped as both my eyes opened wide and I stared at all the potatoes that were floating. "I do not know how I am doing this."

"How do you get it to stop?" The Major asked as walked up and grabbed a potato, looking at it in awe.

"Stop," I told the potatoes.

Just like that, they fell and rolled across the ground.

"Fascinating," he said, walking back to the table and holding onto the back of his chair. "Is that all?"

"No. My senses are more heightened. For example, I can hear things more clearly, which makes eavesdropping quite entertaining. I can also connect to another individual and pick up insights or impressions of what others feel. My mind is also more vivid, and I can take my mind to various places in time that I have experienced, clear as day. It is not something I can do on command, and it takes concentrated effort. Will I become more? It is difficult to say. You mentioned ancient texts. Do you think it worked differently for those that underwent this type of change back then? Or that they were supposed to do it in a certain way?"

"I do not have answers to your questions. We are in the dark as much as you are."

"It could be your pregnancy," Edwin interjected.

"Pregnancy is a miracle in and of itself, and it takes a lot to build a little one."

"True. Is it not strange that I fear what I am capable of? I fear becoming like Laura or Mr. Perkins."

"You are not like either of them," Edwin told me. He grabbed my shoulder and smiled warmly at me. I was still getting acquainted with this compassionate side of him.

"We do not fully know that, do we?"

"No, we do not, but if you were to be like they are. Technically, it would have happened already."

"That provides a small comfort. There is also one other thing, Major."

"Yes?"

"I can also sense others that are like me, whether they are like Laura or like myself. It is difficult to describe, but I can sense Laura, Mr. Perkins, Edwin, and—"

"And?"

"I can also sense Michael. He has fed from me with Laura. They drug me, feed from me, and they... they..."

I could not find the words. My head lowered, and I cried. Admitting this to him made it feel even more real, and I wanted to pretend that it was a dream. A nightmare. At least a nightmare was easier to accept, but having it out in the open and admitting these events meant it really happened, and I could not pretend or hide any longer. Major Stevens did not interrupt or ask me to go into details. His silence showed me a great deal of patience and respect, a luxury Michael would have never afforded me.

"He's physically abusive and a rapist," I blurted out. "I never agreed to marry him. He has forced all of this upon me, and he had to drug me to do it!"

"This is very serious," he told me as he took his hat off and rubbed his bald head. "He will answer to these allegations, I promise you! Can we backtrack? This is all very overwhelming and alarming news. Are you saying he is like you?"

"No, he is nothing like me. His transition is almost complete, and I can sense he will be like Laura, but he is not like Laura either. I do not know how to explain it, but it is something more that I feel. He is far more dangerous than you realize. He is smart and manipulative, and he has murdered other women. I do not know who you thought he was, but you are wrong. Now that he is changing, the darkness that lives within him is coming forward. He will become a perversion of nature, and he will live to fulfill his own twisted desires."

"Good Lord," the Major said, sitting back slowly, taking all the information in.

"Not to mention, he has been destroying evidence of his research to protect himself. Alex knew something was not right and kept his own research. He was secretly recording his findings and hid them from Michael. Michael took Alex to Laura last night, and they murdered him like he did the others that either found out too much, or they were simply in the way, like Anders."

"They have confirmed Alex is missing. Was this around the same time Mr. Perkins, the other undead creature, assaulted you?"

"Yes. Have they found him?" I looked up, questioning Edwin.

"No," Edwin replied grimly.

"Edwin, lock it down. You will tag men you can trust from our unit," he whispered. "Secure Michael and Laura and put them under enough sedation that they will not be a problem and reinforced restraints until we can transport them to a secure location. The question is, what will we do with you?"

"Sedation will not work for long, just ample warning. It does not keep me under for exceptionally long. Michael spent a great deal of time mastering a concoction that would work. Do you know where he keeps it, Edwin?"

"I do," he said with a sly grin. "I made a copy of his notes on how he made it before he destroyed them."

"Major, would you be willing to reinstate Edwin as a lead researcher and scientist? I want to figure this out as much as you do. It is imperative that I find answers to all the questions that I have."

"You want to bargain?"

"Yes," I told him, matching his seriousness. "I know I lost my freedom the moment I entered this camp. I know fully that I am no longer human. I do not think the United States government would let that go unnoticed if you released me to my own devices, would they?"

"Are you willing to collaborate with our unit under my guidance, undergo testing, and be a part of this project, including your child, with no questions asked of you? In return, you will have my personal protection."

"I do not see that I have any other choice. You are aware of the virus from Germany, not that it was a real virus, obviously? Did the parasite destroy everything in its path like it did here?"

"Not of this magnitude, no. This is the most potent form of the parasite we have seen yet. If you compared the parasite from Germany to Stony Creek, it would resemble a minor cold in comparison."

"What do you plan to do with me?"

"We cannot allow you to leave our protection. We do not understand fully what you are capable of. We also do not understand the risk you pose to others once exposed to your blood. You are a liability and considered a threat to our interests. I hope you can understand my position. All we can do is make you as comfortable as we can and ask for your patience as we learn more about all of this together."

"You cannot ask this of me. I cannot sit idly by and do nothing. I am bored out of my mind! Look, I understand your position, but you are wasting a resource. I have experience being a personal secretary to a doctor. I learn quickly, and I need to do something more than sit idly by doing nothing. Could I help Edwin? He and I work well and understand one another. Please? I need to understand what I am, especially with a child coming into this world who may be just like me, or more than I am. I need to protect her. We need to protect the world from what happened here and ensure it will not happen again."

"Her?"

"I am having a daughter."

"How could you possibly know?"

"How am I able to do everything else?"

"Fine. I am taking an enormous risk allowing you to be a part of this project. Do not make me regret my decision."

"We should do a full sweep of the town again, including the woods," Edwin said as he paced slightly. "If there are more out there, like Mr. Perkins, we need to ensure we have a way to track them, or at least get them to a specific location with bait and then torch it. Do we know of the other locations that patient zero entered have experienced an outbreak?"

"Not of which I am aware. I had assumed that the Professor was managing all this. Imagine my surprise to learn he has done absolutely nothing aside from his own agenda. Very well, Edwin, consider yourself Michael's permanent replacement. Private, please come in," he said to the soldier standing outside the tent.

"Send this to HQ immediately," he said as he wrote something down on the paper. "Bring the response to me, and only to me, without hesitation."

"Yes, Sir," the soldier saluted him and left the tent.

"I will have control look into the gentleman and the areas he claimed to have traveled to. If anything has happened, it will be in various news sources and difficult to hide like this incident will be once they release the cover story. Edwin," he said. "Let's get this done."

Knowing that Edwin and his men were on their way to contain Michael gripped me in absolute fear and panic. Not that I did not trust Edwin, it was more out of fear that he may be strong and fast, like Laura or Mr. Perkins. If he escaped

Edwin, what chance did I have? I sat by the Major who was busy working on paperwork and talking to another soldier about what needed to happen next to get the camp ready to move out. I could not pay attention to what they were saying, and my mind wandered as we waited for Edwin to return with news.

My nerves were about to go haywire when we heard shouts, followed by several rounds of gunfire. I stopped my pacing, and I stood frozen, looking at the entrance of the tent. I looked over at the Major with fear in my eyes. If Michael were free, it would be a matter of seconds before he came for me.

"Stay here," the Major exclaimed as he rushed out of the tent with the other soldier to see what the commotion was all about.

I paced back and forth nervously, biting my fingernails as I did. I wished high to heaven that they had not left me alone in the tent. My building anxiety that was close to having me jumping clear out of my skin when Edwin came barging in, catching me off guard. I screamed as I grabbed the chair and held it up in front of me for protection.

"A chair will not help you if he comes for you, sis. Not to be the harbinger of unwelcome news, but there it is."

He motioned for me to follow.

"What happened? Is everything all right? I heard gunshots."

"We took Michael down quickly. Laura, however, took down two of our men and put up one hell of a fight. We had to shoot her down. She is still... I do not know how to describe it, but she is still animated. She is asking for you."

I followed Edwin with dread as we approached Laura. Her distorted body lay twisted on the ground. Her neck looked twisted like a pastry. It was unlike anything I had ever seen before. Laura attempted to look at everyone around her. Thick blood oozed like tar from her bullet wounds. She appeared weakened from the overall blood loss, but her wounds that were visible were already closing, which was remarkable.

"Feed me," she whispered in a voice that struggled to

speak, licking her lips and her eyes wide with desperation.

"Major Stevens?"

"Do it," he said, frowning. "Edwin, restrain her."

"Let them bind you, Laura," I told her as she watched the men approach her. She looked at them as if they were nothing but ants. It made me wonder just how easily she could get out of the restraints they placed her in.

I asked the private next to me for his pocketknife, and with a quick slice, I cringed from the pain as I cut the palm of my hand and allowed my blood to trickle down into her mouth while Edwin double checked each of her restraints and placed the whole of his body weight on top of her. I was now no better than Michael, preserving this beast to understand more about who I might become in the name of science.

"Do you like it?" She asked me, amused, lifting her dress showing me the male anatomy between her legs. It was then that I saw the large stitches around her waist. The lower half of her body was not hers. I felt vomit rise from my stomach and into my throat. "We chose it to enjoy with you together. He promised me you would love it."

The thought of her and Michael touching me erupted into waves of anger moving through me. Another soldier I did not know that stood beside me began making heaving noises and ran out past the tents as we heard his retching sounds. By the looks on the other soldiers' faces, they felt the same way. I watched as others covered their mouths, messed with their helmets, or simply turned away.

"How long can she survive like this with various levels of decay in the body?" The Major asked. He crept up on us and I did not know how long he was standing there.

"It's difficult to say," Edwin said, looking disgusted. He had his arm protectively around me.

"My boys," the Major said in a tired voice that betrayed his emotions. "My boys did not deserve any of this."

Edwin went back to the lab tent to grab a syringe and a sampling vial, as two soldiers cautiously added more restraints to Laura as she smiled at them. When he tried to use the syringe, the needle had difficulty penetrating her skin, which now felt more leatherlike than human. He took blood samples from the blood that remained leftover from the now closed wounds.

"Can you feel this?" Edwin asked her, touching her new leg and moving my hand up.

"No. I no longer feel," she moaned. "I can remember the feeling. The mind remembers, but the body has forgotten. Fleeting. All fleeting. The body does not respond as it once did, but he promised me he would make it better."

"Then why take someone's life and use their body parts?"

"In the promise to feel. Michael promised I would feel again. Through the gift of their flesh, he promised me."

"Is this what happened to Michael's lab assistant?"

"Michael brought me a man, a man with a needle, and we played with him. We played with him to feel."

"You must no longer trust Michael. Michael lied to you. You must never hurt another human being. Do you agree?"

"Yes, for you," she hissed in disdain. I could feel her enjoyment as her mind fondly remembered fragments of killing. Torturing them and enjoying her twisted pleasures with them. Twisted fragments filled her mind. I tuned into her mind, and they were incomplete. Shattered, like a mirror. Is her mind truly breaking down? How much longer until they deemed her too great a threat to our lives?

CHAPTER 32

PROMISE

"Where's Michael?" I asked Edwin, wanting to ensure he was as secure as possible.

"He's locked up and chained up tighter than Laura," Edwin gave me a small smile.

"He fed from me recently. How can we ensure he will not be like Mr. Perkins or Laura?"

"He's tied up in chains, and I am the only one holding the key," he told me reassuringly as he patted his jacket. "It would amaze me if he could break through all those restraints, at least not all at once. Even if he gets through a one or two layers, it will be noisy and obvious. Let us get this sample to the lab while we still have use of it."

The men immediately took Laura to a separate holding area at the other end of the camp. We were halfway there when gunfire erupted near the lab. We saw a flash of activity as men ran towards the lab. One man, we could not see who, went flying across the open path between the tents. That is when a collective of gunshots opened fire and continued out into the forest.

Edwin called out to his men, Andrews, and Parker outside to guard the tent as he ran outside. I heard yells come from just outside, followed by another gunshot, as Mr. Perkins blew through the entrance of the mess tent. I fell back onto the table and landed swiftly on my back as I fell back over a chair. He stopped when he saw me, frozen. He carried a gun. He approached me slowly, handing me the gun and pointed the gun towards his head.

"Please," he hissed in a barely recognizable voice. "End my pain."

"Mr. Perkins," I gasped, horrified. "You're still in there, aren't you?"

"Please," he whimpered. "End me."

"I... I do not know how."

"I do not want to hurt anyone else. I can feel myself slipping away. I crave... I crave your blood, but the smell of any blood draws me in."

"If you can resist the blood, perhaps, like Laura, you will simply decompose until you're gone."

"I will wait then," he cried, small black tears that crept down his face. I am not like that woman, Vivienne. My mind continues to exist in this body, and with blood, I am made whole again. I do not want this to be my life, Vivienne! I want to die."

"I do not know how to end your suffering, but I promise you I will find those answers we both need. I promise I will come back and help you end it," I whispered to him.

"I will hold you to your promise."

We heard heavy footsteps approaching and left so fast that I barely registered him leaving. It was a blur of motion that left me sitting on the cold ground with more questions than where my already inquisitive mind had started. The gun was still in my hand as Edwin came tearing in. I looked up at him, wide eyed.

"Shit," he yelled, coming towards me. "Vivienne, are you hurt?!"

"I am... I am fine," I told him with my hands still shaking.

"Thank God he didn't kill anyone else and that you're safe," he told me as he took the gun from my hands and held them. "Did he make demands?"

"He wanted to die. He wanted me to end his life, but I... I... do not know how. He is still alive in that body. He is... He is different, and not like Laura. He is not a killer."

"He did not come after you directly?" Edwin asked, setting up the equipment that he dropped when he came into the tent on the table in the mess hall. "He took the vials of your blood that were set aside for study. He took nothing else, just your blood."

"How did he know to go after the blood and not me?"

"I am not sure," he said, scratching his chin. "It is like a drug to them. If his mind is still intact, then he does not want to hurt you, and we may reason with him. At least until he needs his next fix."

"Do you hear them as well? Laura, Michael, and Mr. Perkins, I mean."

"I… I used to. Now, it is just a feeling, like an echo. Since you have come along, it is a feeling I know to trust."

We were silent for a while as he prepared the slides and messed with them under the microscope as he worked alongside his notes. I did not know what to think. My mind felt numb. Knowing that I had two predators, one on each side of the camp and another that was somewhere out in the forest, each craving my blood, kept my defenses up.

"Holy shit," Edwin yelled out, startling me out of my trance. "Her blood is not blood at all, but congealed and clotted. Whatever held her together will not be doing it for much longer by the looks of it," he sighed, rubbing the bridge of his nose. "We see this same makeup looking at a corpse. My guess is that she is slowly breaking down. With her… alterations, she has unknowingly sped up the process."

Major Stevens came into the tent with a worrisome look on his face. "We have a problem. Vivienne, what do you know about the young man that was brought here to your town from the Middle East?"

"Mostafa? He is one man I will have a grim time forgetting. The memory of him…"

"That would be the one. Are you all right to talk about him?"

"Yes." I took in a deep breath and sighed loudly as I

prepared myself to recall those memories I longed to forget. "I was there when the medics brought him to the hospital. He was shouting some very crazy things."

"Do you believe he was a terrorist?" Edwin asked, his face grim.

"We are unsure of the details, but no, we did not think he was a terrorist. What we know now is that a deadly contagion landed on American soil and took out an entire town. We assume it was an accident. There is a sense of urgency to get this cleaned up by all governments."

"I understand."

He handed Edwin the telegram, which Edwin and I read together.

"Based on our intelligence, they found a boat adrift at sea in waters located off the coast of Spain. Per their government officials, they found an elderly couple deceased and showed signs of plague. The boat and bodies were burned at sea. This is only the first report that has come in, and it has taken weeks to get it. We may have a problem. What if he unknowingly released this parasite in every place that he stopped?" Major Steven reiterated the message with more detail, looking at me for answers I did not yet have, and then I remembered.

"Where did he stop after Spain?" I asked him, fearing that more would perish.

"New York City."

"We would have heard by now if he took out New York, right? What if he trusted something so sacred, so private with the elderly couple before he left them? We need to get back into the town," I said with urgency.

"Why?" Edwin asked with peaked curiosity.

"After they released Mostafa from the hospital, a lot of gossip started that his relatives were seeking to institutionalize him. He claimed he was the harbinger of death and that he would open the gates of the underworld to rejoin his family, united forever."

"What does that have to do with going back into the town?"

"He claimed the power he held was the blood of a god. If we find the blood, or whatever the blood was in, we may find answers we all desperately need. I know it could end up being nothing, and we are chasing ghosts, but it beats sitting around and wondering what if, right? We should track down every possibility, even if it does not seem like one. Were all the bodies removed from the homes and the surrounding areas around the town? What do you think, Major Stevens?"

"Please, call me Robert," Major Stevens said with a warm, fatherly smile on his face. "Yes, we have burned all the bodies except those marked by Michael for further study. We have the man identified as the source on ice. Michael planned to investigate his blood work pending approval from Mr. Akir's government. Did you find his lab assistant's notes?"

"I found a small notebook. It will take me a bit to make sense of his notes, but what I have put together so far is very intriguing."

"Why would his government need to give permission to take a blood sample or perform an autopsy when he is here in our country?"

"Their religion and culture prohibit any action taken to the body without approval from the family. Since he has no remaining family left, his last rites and his body are the property of his state. If we were to compromise that agreement, they would consider it a hostile act. Regardless, we will have to smooth over relations and begin negotiations for our two countries to trade information. A favor for a favor. His government has requested that we bury his body immediately untouched. We do not have authorization to take blood from the corpse or to perform an autopsy. Our governments have ongoing political challenges, and his country is making threats if we refuse. Threatening existing trade agreements, which are already strained, for resources we desperately need is a hotbed of debate as it is. Make that your next priority upon returning.

You have twenty-four hours to get what you need from his corpse. Get creative in a way that cannot come back and bite us in the ass later."

"Understood, Sir," Edwin said, continuing to write notes.

"They would deny us information, even if its risking countless lives by doing so?"

"Welcome to war and politics, Vivienne. The stakes include trade and money and sometimes, people. It is as old as our civilization."

"That's inhumane and unfair!"

"Such is the weight of the world. Get into town before dusk. We have already been here longer than we need to be. It takes a generous amount of logistics and resources to make an operation like this work, and my superiors will have my head if we delay it any further."

"I would like to go as soon as possible."

"We are still under quarantine based on when you return to camp from the town. After that, we are leaving this place and never coming back. I will have provisions dropped to last us a few extra days."

A small group of us went into the town. Edwin drove while I sat in the passenger seat with two of our escorts, who sat uncomfortably in the back of an olive-green Willy's jeep. It did not take Edwin long to find the home. He had a photographic memory, and he could recall the exact details based on studying the map for one to two minutes. I admired his ability to do it with such ease.

This time of year, I could almost imagine the scent of wood burning fires, the homes lit up with a welcoming light, and delicious meals roasting in the ovens while keeping the homes warm with its lofty aroma. Looking at the homes passing by us, I had almost forgotten the comforts of things like plumbing. What I would not give for a hot bath with bubbles. I missed having a place, a place I knew I could be long and call home. For now, home would be where they allowed me to be. I did not know what the future would hold for me or my child, but I had to hold on to something. Hope was the only thing keeping me going.

It did not matter that I did not have many people in my life. I had the people that mattered, and life, even though back then it seemed so trivial and boring, held the most prized memories I will cherish and hold close to my heart. We passed by my home on the way, and a crushing weight stooped upon my heart like a barn owl bearing its weight on a small branch. I could almost visualize my mother standing in the open doorway, waving at me with her old, stained apron that covered her yellow dress with little blue flowers.

CHAPTER 33

FAITH

It had not been that long since I woke up in the camp, and yet, it has seemed like a lifetime. This place, this town, no longer felt like my home. It felt like a nightmare that beckoned heartfelt memories of easier and simpler times. It was I who had changed, and not the town. I became the nightmare. I do not even recognize myself in the mirror any longer. I have stopped looking. One day, I will find the courage to look at myself again, but for now, I am comfortable enough to keep myself in the dark. The dark feels warm, like a soft blanket after a hot bath. Right now, I need the dark.

I was thankful when we passed through the town square to see it cleaned up and the bodies removed. I knew Anders was part of that crew, even if for a short while. My heart ached to think about him and so many others carrying the bodies of all those people. Who thought about them? Who would tell them thanks for their efforts? Or was it merely that the world wanted to forget, and their roles lay in the realm of the forgotten?

Was Anders still alive, or would he end up like the others? Forgotten? While my mind told me stories of varying degrees, filled with fear, shame, and sadness. My stories, and the voices that filled them, had me clinging to them like a child's teddy bear. I hated myself for it, but I wanted to punish myself for all that had happened. I lived, and they all died. Anders was missing because of me. My inner voice, that small voice that met with the being that dwelled within me, kept telling me to let it all go. I just do not know how to. At least, not yet.

I patiently waited in the jeep while Edwin and Levi did a perimeter check and entered the home to ensure there were no wild animals nesting in the home, or something else. I could sense nothing out of the ordinary, but like the last encounter with Mr. Perkins, I did not feel him coming at all. I could not discern who was what or where, which left me doubting myself and my newly developing abilities. Michael and Laura filled my head when I was in the camp. I had to admit it was a relief to leave that for even a short while. The silence in my mind was a welcomed respite.

They did not readily equip us to deal with anything other than small animals. I felt we should have come in more equipped, but they felt they needed all the big guns and people to ensure the safety of the camp from Michael and Laura. I did not blame them. There was a great deal to fear with both being in the same camp, but I could not help but feel wary heading into a town that created three undead creatures if I were to count Michael, and well, me. What if there were more surprises waiting for us? Why did I always find the need to take my mind to the darkest places?! *Dammit, Vivienne! Stop it!*

"Vivienne," Edwin called out to me, waving his flashlight from the doorway. "It's clear."

I stood up in the jeep, turned on my flashlight, and jumped down with a loud thud on the pavement that felt funny beneath my feet. Something so small as walking on pavement was a curiosity, as if I had never done it a hundred times before. The feel of the overgrown grass beneath my feet felt like sponges I wanted to burrow my bare feet into. I approached the small, older, pale white home. The front window shutters hung slightly off their hinges, with an ominous foreboding of its long history. I drew my flashlight to the darkened patches where the paint was peeling. It stood eerily against the contrast of the darkening overcast sky.

I hesitated as I went up the cracked cement steps to the small front porch with a groaning awning as the wind whistled by and walked past Edwin. It pleasantly surprised me when I walked into the living room to find such a small and cozy space. The well-loved furniture, with ragged corners exposing its inner frame, had seen better days, and the highlight of the room was its collection of books. Despite the family having lived in a foreign country, they had a better collection of novels than many of the most literate people I knew. Edgar Allan Poe and Victor Hugo immediately stood out on the first shelf.

I entered the kitchen, and I admired the rustic look of it. The outdated cabinets reminded me of where I grew up. Being in my mother's kitchen was one of my fondest memories. It was not perfect. It was not modern, but it held a style that reflected the woman behind it. It may have been small, but small also could be very efficient if you wanted it to be. My mother used to joke with me she would eventually outgrow the kitchen if her pies became any more popular. This was but one of a list of many things that I would miss. How odd to consider all this my old life? In the past, unmoving, and forever imprinted as a memory.

I moved back out into the living room, and down the small hallway that held three doors. There was a bathroom plastered with floral wallpaper to my immediate left. I entered the room next to the bathroom, and it was a decent sized bedroom. The pictures on the chest of drawers showed an older couple. The man's hair was graying, and his wife's hair, covered in a headscarf. They were both smiling and holding one another on the small front porch just outside. It felt strange to be in their room, to have entered a space that they shared their lives in. Mostafa's aunt and uncle. They were kind people, and if his aunt ever saw me in town, she never hesitated to say hello.

I went through the other door and there was a single bed pushed against the wall, with an altar on the floor. The room itself was plain and colorless. The bed had sheets and a blanket. No suitcase or chest of drawers, but there was a box under the bed that held men's clothing. I used my pencil to thumb through the contents of two to three changes of clothing with undergarments. The altar was the highlight of the room.

As I approached the altar, my hands tingled oddly. I did not exactly know what I was doing, but I reached out my hands to feel the air. I moved my hands towards the bed and the sensation immediately stopped. As I moved back to the altar, my hands once again became alive. I got down on my hands and knees and put my flashlight over the contents. The entity within me responded as my skin glowed and the energetic tentacles emerged.

"I am never getting used to that," Levi said with his eyes wide as he turned around slowly, backing away with his eyes still on me, and left the room.

"He will get used to it," Edwin said, chuckling. "He is funny to watch, though. You would think it would have lost its element of surprise. Not with him, though. Every time is like the first time. Bittersweet."

"Why bittersweet?"

"Sweetest moment of your life, and you are bitter when it has to end."

"So instead of being terrified, you are saying Levi enjoys my... natural... way of being? Like he secretly wants to have intimacy with me while I am like this?"

Edwin started laughing so hard, he snorted!

"No, Vivienne! That would put him into an institution! I should ask him though," he said, winking at me.

"Do not even dare! That is just cruel!"

"Yeah," he replied excitedly.

"I do not even get it."

Edwin chuckled to himself.

I placed my focus back on the altar on the floor. Mostafa made the altar out of a slab of stone, a small incense burner, and several candles. There was a scrap of yellowed paper, its edges ripped, and only the size of my hand. On the paper was a phrase handwritten in dark ink, in a language that I was not familiar with, with a hand drawn portrait of a woman with wings surrounded by what looked to be owls.

Next to the paper, a small perfume bottle that laid on its side next to the statue. I moved my hand over the altar, and my hand immediately felt as if it was on fire as I hovered over the bottle. I picked it up and felt a small electric surge move through my body. I did not know why, but whatever this vial was, it felt familiar.

"Edwin, there is something about the vial that activated something within me. It is like I recognize it." I handed the vial to him. "Do you sense anything?"

"That is strange. It feels like it has a slight electrical charge to it, but I am not sure what to make of it. I trust your intuition. What do you think you have found?"

"I believe this is what we are looking for."

Edwin brought in a field kit and grabbed one of the testing vials. He took the perfume bottle from me and dipped a cotton swab into the contents and placed it back carefully into a glass vial and sealed it. He held it up into the light and looked at it more closely.

"I can't wait to get this back to the lab," he said with excitement.

"Is that blood?" I asked him as the liquid turned into a deep red color as it loosened from the cotton swab with the liquid in the vial.

"It is blood, but there is something else in it. Since it was on the altar, perhaps some kind of oil. I will need to run tests to be certain."

"He viewed this as the blood of the Gods."

"It holds religious significance, especially with it being a part of his altar. It is not so unusual to have anointing oil along with religious ceremonies. I went to India long ago on assignment to work with the British military, and the women there would put a circle on their foreheads to reflect marriage, and for others it was to remember creation and to honor God. They could have used the oil for anointing or for laying of hands for healing or blessing if they were a holy person. Our troop went through a small town where someone of importance died, and they were doing a bloodletting ceremony in the streets. We only went through a few of the provinces, but each province was unique and had its own culture and dialect. Difficult to say until we know more about this man and his background."

"He was not from India, but if I remember correctly, it was near Iraq. Can you read this?" I asked, holding up the scrap of paper.

"No, but I can tell that the writing is Arabic. I remember coming across the newspaper article in Dr. Alden's files. He was from Syria."

"Yes, that was it!"

"I have been meaning to ask. How does a parasite spread like the flu?"

"The simplest answer?"

I nodded.

"Parasites can be contagious. They spread through tainted soil, water, and feces. Hypothetically, the parasite used the flu virus to spread and replicate. When we sneeze or cough, we spray small particles in a projected radius. The essence of any virus is survival. Invade, replicate, and spread before the body's natural defenses eradicate it. Our parasite invaded the virus to hitch a ride."

"A hitchhiker?"

"Indeed. Want to be naughty?"

"What did you have in mind?" I asked with a laugh caught in my throat over hearing Edwin, who was normally so serious, asking me if I wanted to be naughty.

"Let's go break into the library," he said with a mischievous grin.

I broke down in laughter. Through everything that has happened, breaking into a library with Edwin seemed like the funniest thing I had ever heard. I had forgotten what it was like to laugh. It felt lifting, and the bellyache was a welcome reprieve to the overwhelming weight that I carried on my shoulders.

I watched as he placed each item in a sealed container, and we got back into the jeep with our escorts and headed back towards the main town square to break into the library. Edwin fumbled with the locked double doors that led into the tall, two-story brick building. He chose the wide window instead. Watching this huge soldier of a guy try to crawl stealthily through a window was something you do not see every day. For a man that could move like a ghost and move swiftly, windows were not his strong suit.

I entered the building and took a deep breath, enjoying the old musty smell of books. This was my home away from home and it felt familiar, as it did foreign. Seeing familiar titles on the shelves brought familiar memories of reading at the table with hot chocolate or sitting on the bench in the town square.

I followed Edwin to the card catalog, and while he became easily lost looking for a specific set of books, I looked up one specific book and went into the stacks to find it. A copy of *Wind, Sand and Stars*. I knew it was a silly thing to do. It was just a book, but my heart needed something to hold on to that reminded me of Anders. I walked towards Edwin, who had a small pile of books laid out on the table. He searched through book after book, and then, after about forty minutes of searching, he finally found what he was looking for in the librarian's desk. He pulled a bible out of the drawer and swore to himself. He brought both books to the table, and he opened the encyclopedia to a map of the middle east. He pointed at a coastal region.

"This is where he got on the boat," he said, as his finger trailed back a few paces. "Based on what he said in the newspaper clipping, he would be from somewhere around here, assuming the information gathered about his aunt and uncle and their origins are correct. They come from a small farming village just outside of Aleppo. Major Stevens' intelligence states that there are ongoing archaeological excavations in this same region. I am not privy to any further information. Here is a photo that shows a sample of Arabic writing. This looks at least like what is on the paper."

"Hold on. What about that new guy that came in to replace Gillard? He said something about being a translator or something," Levi chimed in. "Someone either messed up his transfer, or he pissed off the wrong person."

"You mean Sol," asked Edwin.

"Yeah, that's the guy," he said, laughing. "He is useless here, so we put him to work in the mess hall peeling potatoes. If you brought in something for him to work on, I am sure it would make his day."

"Let's get out of here and go ask him if he can read what this means."

"You took a great deal of effort to find the bible, Edwin. Is there something there you wanted to point out?"

"No," he said, embarrassed. "This is for me. It has been a long time since God and I had a conversation, and I have gained something I thought I lost."

"What did you think you lost?"

"My faith."

CHAPTER 34

SOLOMON

The first snow of winter fell as we left the library. It was a welcomed sight to watch as two helicopters flew overhead carrying supply crates. With the colder temperatures, I was optimistic that there would be warmer clothing or additional blankets. I know our stay would not be much longer and the gear they had was enough to keep them just warm enough, but there would be icy toes and fingers by the time quarantine lifted.

"Well, lady and gents, we're back in business for a few days," Edwin said as he looked up. "Think of how much you are going to appreciate being warmer at night. Your chattering teeth will not keep me up all night tonight. We may also get a decent dinner."

"What do you think it will be, Johnson? Chef's surprise? Chili brick or beans with bread and canned monster meat?" Levi asked him, grinning from ear-to-ear.

"I do not even care at this point. I am sick of oatmeal."

"What happens after quarantine? We just up and leave?"

"Nobody told her?" Levi asked Edwin, his eyes wide.

"Told me what?"

"Have you ever heard the term cleansed by fire?" Johnson asked.

"They are going to destroy the entire town?! All of it?!"

"I am sorry, Viv," Edwin told me sympathetically. "I wish there was another way. The world must never know what has happened here, other than the story that is fabricated. If people found out what happened here, it would cause panic.

We cannot allow whatever remains of the parasite to escape this town. We have no way to be sure. It is better to be safe than sorry later on."

I sat silently the rest of the way to the camp. Lost in thought. When I thought about everything taken from me, it did not occur to me that there could be more. I thought I had nothing left to lose, other than my sanity and my child. *It will be as if it never happened. Lost in the realm of forgotten history. The entire town! My God!* When we arrived back at the camp, there was a flurry of activity unpacking the large crates as they removed the rigging that held the crates to the parachutes.

I followed Edwin into the mess tent. Just like they said, there was a man sitting cross-legged between a sack of potatoes, supplies, and the serving table with his back towards us. Edwin walked softly and stood behind him. He reached out and touched his shoulder, startling him. He yelled at the top of his lungs, jumping up and twisting himself around in a way that forced him to fall backwards into the sack of potatoes.

"Easy," Edwin said, as he held up his hands, backing up slowly. "We didn't come to harass you."

"Then what do you want?"

"We need your help."

"Well, we know our dinner involves potatoes," I whispered to Levi, who was standing beside me.

"Anything is better than oatmeal, right?" Levi chuckled.

"What do you need from me?"

Solomon slowly stood up, eying us both cautiously. He was not at all what I expected. His dark skin was a stark contrast to the light beige sack of potatoes, and he stood out like a sore thumb. Just like I did. I heard plenty of stories about people from the American Indian tribes serving in the military, but I never thought I would meet one. He looked just as I felt. Out of place. I remember reading the controversy regarding their service in the military, but in all honesty, their service continued to give me hope we may one day have a world where all people of color could come together and find acceptance.

"Would you mind coming to the lab to help us with something we're working on?" I asked him, reaching out my hand. "My name is Vivienne."

He looked from Edwin to me, back to Edwin, and then to my hand. He slowly outstretched his hand, not trusting anything in good faith. I did not blame him. He experienced difficult hardships, and he held that pain behind his eyes. It was not obvious, but it lay just under the surface. His eyes were a deep brown. They drew me in and reminded me of fertile soil just after the first spring rains. Why is life this complicated? How can we build a community if we cannot even create a bridge?

"My name is Solomon," he replied quietly, taking my hand. "You can call me Sol for short. Everyone else does."

"What would you prefer I call you?"

"I prefer Solomon, but you folks like to give nicknames. You are not exactly like them, are you? I have heard the rumors."

"Depending on what you have heard. I am a monster. We are still trying to determine what kind of monster I am if that helps to put you at ease. My mother was a negro, and my father was a white man. Edwin, could he sleep in Alex's cot?"

"Would you be comfortable with that, Solomon?" Edwin asked him. "Or do you prefer a sack of potatoes for company? Either way, I would appreciate your help."

"Thank you," Solomon said as he grabbed his gear, and he followed Edwin and me into the lab tent.

"Here," I said as I showed him his sleeping area. "We understand you are a translator. Could I have you look at something for me?"

"Of course," he said, his demeanor automatically perking up. "I speak several languages."

"Were you a code talker in the war?" Edwin asked him with peaked interest.

"Yes, one of many," Solomon told him. "They trained me

to learn many languages, create new codes, and to translate for powerful men."

"Wish me luck," Edwin said with a look of pretend fear crossing his face. "I have to go tell Johnson he's replacing Solomon on peeling the potatoes."

"I do not envy you, Edwin. Solomon, do you recognize this?" I asked, handing him the scrap of paper.

He took out his spectacles from his shirt pocket and looked at the paper.

"Where did you find this?" he asked, turning pale.

"In the town," I told him, curious about his reaction. "Do you know what's happening here?"

"Yes. My people have stories such as this, and it never ends well. Bad omen. The paper holds a language like Arabic. If I am correct, it says, the gates of the dead are open."

"Do you know what the drawing is?"

"No, that I do not know. You would need a historian or archaeologist for that information."

"Let me guess," I said with a tired giggle. "We are fresh out of both?"

"He did not manage that well," Edwin said with a small smile, coming back into the tent. "The chef assigned him to the mess tent for the rest of our stay. Let us hope he does not spit in our food."

"Maybe we can send someone else in for our food?"

"My thoughts exactly," Edwin said as he took in a long sigh, looking at the boxes he lifted on the table. "Are you both up for doing research? I know you are more than capable, Solomon. Vivienne, how about you? Are you ready to take on additional duties and help me sort out this mess?"

"No more potatoes," Solomon asked. "Count me in."

"Only for eating," I said, smiling. "I am ready, Edwin. I need to be a part of this."

I looked at the table by the microscope and noticed a closed vial and a petri dish on top of a note and a sheet of paper that were observations of Dr. Lindberg on the state of a corpse.

"What's this," I asked Edwin.

"Dr. Lindberg saved me time by examining the corpse of Mostafa. Based on his observations, there was evidence of dried blood coming from his eyes, nose, and ears, like the other victims of the parasite. The body had a similar substance that came from the body and covered the skin like a protective mesh, like the corpses we found in the town square. The doctor provided a sample, which did not disturb the corpse. He took the sample from his clothing, which is what is in the petri dish. The mesh like substance appears to act like a preservative oddly enough. The substance, while active, preserved the corpse from decaying further, which is incredible. He states it is an altered chemical process of preservation, and in the body's broken-down state of decomposition, this process has become isolated and is no longer an integrated function yet continues to form a specific function until its process breaks down."

"Why is that not happening with Laura?"

"Based on what we have seen with Laura, based on Michael's findings, he is right. Based on what I have been able to put together, the medication she was taking tricked the parasite. Now that the medication is out of her system, it is rejecting her, but she already began a state of change. She is an unexpected accident that is now stuck in a space between both states of change."

"What about Mr. Perkins?"

"That I cannot say. I would need to study him. There is just so much that we do not know!"

"What about my blood?"

"Your blood is remarkable. The parasite is a part of your cells. I had to repeat my test two additional times to ensure I was seeing everything correctly. The parasite is like a ghost within your cells. I can only theorize that the parasite mimicked the human cells and, as a result, became one with the host cells, enabling replication under its own control. The design of the cell was breathtaking. The difference between my cells and yours is the outer membrane is much thicker, containing multiple layers like a reinforced wall."

"So, what you are saying is..."

"It is a tricky little bastard. There is one other thing," Edwin said with seriousness. "The blood we could analyze from Mostafa's clothing reflected that he was undergoing the same process as everyone else, except amplified. When they brought Mostafa's body in, Dr. Lindberg was under orders to observe his body and report his findings without performing an autopsy. He felt his abdomen, and it felt as if his insides had imploded on themselves, causing his organs to liquify. We cannot confirm this, of course."

"My God," I whispered. "He wanted to die. Do you think he knew he would take the entire town with him?!"

"It's hard to say what was going through his mind," Edwin said, rubbing the top of his nose.

"What the hell are you two going on about?" Solomon said, slightly spooked. "What exactly did I get stationed into?"

"Edwin, where did they find Mostafa's body?"

"I'm not sure," he said sleepily. "Look at the reports from the town. You wanted to dive in, right?"

"Yes. Point me in the right direction."

"Well," he said, with a long, tired yawn. "The reports are in that box, or they are on the back of the truck. Take your pick."

I grabbed the box and took it to the small, adjoined tent with Edwin and I's cots. It was strange to be back in this tent without Anders.

"Solomon," Edwin said, pointing at another small box. "Would you look through those files and look for anything that stands out of the ordinary? I know this will not make sense now, but just do your best. We will switch boxes once we have finished with the ones we are on. Three sets of eyes are better than one."

"Sure, but at some point, I hope you all explain to me what's going on."

About thirty minutes in, Edwin brought us plates of thick potato soup with ham and a slice of crusty bread. The chopped carrots added color to an otherwise colorless dish. The fragrant smell of the ham tickled my senses, and I devoured it quickly as I continued searching through the papers.

"I found it," I explained, standing up quickly, almost dumping my remaining soup in my lap. "They found his body near the gazebo of the town square. No wonder it spread so quickly. Whose blood is this?"

"That's the mystery we need to solve," Edwin told me grimly. "We owe it to all those who lost their lives to find those answers."

Like being welcomed back home, I surrounded myself with files, notes, slides, and miscellaneous papers everywhere in an unorganized fashion. I normally was not an unorganized type, but now that I had a purpose again and I had the weight of the world upon my shoulders, the mess became less of a priority.

"What are you thinking?" Sol asked me as he rubbed his eyes. I was grateful for his help. He was already an expert at deciphering Michael's more cryptic notes and extremely messy shorthand, and he could help us decipher Alex's notes. Alex left a lot in a code that none of us could understand. Solomon told them it could take him a while to get it all worked out. He called Alex acutely paranoid. I did not have the heart to tell Solomon just how right he was. Alex had a reason to be paranoid. He died for this research.

"If this blood is the blood of a God, as Mostafa suggests, and there were rumors of an archaeological dig in the region that Mostafa was from, then the area is rich with history. We may have a point of origin, right? So, what would their legends tell us of ancient gods? There must be a connection."

"We would need to find someone that is from that region to give us the right information," Edwin said from the lab. He was busy now looking at his own research, but still listening in and adding to our conversation.

"The last article I read before coming here was about anti-Jewish attacks and riots in the Middle East. They forced Jewish immigrants to leave their homes for thousands of years in religious prosecution from Palestine, Syria, and surrounding Arab and Muslim led countries. The entire region and its people have faced extreme hardships. I doubt we will get any information out of the country. Not in a time of war, at any rate."

"Do you know of their myths or legends, Solomon? Anything that can help us?"

"No, not offhand," he said, as he sorted through more papers. "I am sure with the right resources we can find out. You are fresh out of archaeologists and historians, remember?"

"Vivienne," Edwin said excitedly. It was dark and my eyes were feeling strained attempting to read with a shared lantern as our sole light to maneuver through varied writing styles. "I would like to give you the honor of naming the parasite. I know it is not the honor you would expect of something that took so much away from you. You do not have to, but it is only right that as you are the sole survivor, it should be you that gives it its name."

I stared at the solid dark olive-green fabric of the tent, and I became lost in thought. I did not know if it was fatigue setting in, but my mind felt like it was traveling. I already knew the answer to my question, and yet I had to ask.

"Vivienne?"

"What if the parasite had a purpose to revive and reawaken our species?"

"I see the truth in it, and yet, that truth terrifies me. It would suggest that most of humanity would not survive."

"What if that was not the point? What if that was an accident? If the parasite was ancient, from one of those archaeological sites, it was looking for a bridge or an ark, you know, like the biblical story."

"That...," Edwin said, pausing and looking at me like

he did not know what to make of me. "That is a remarkably interesting hypothesis. That is one way to look at it. Like the biblical flood, when Noah preserved life aboard his ship. Interesting. Do you mean the parasite was preserved? To what end?"

"Yes, that is exactly what I mean, but to what end? I do not know. The right host gave it an opportunity to adapt. We just need to identify what it was looking for and why. The answers are within me. We just need to know how to unlock it."

"I feel like I'm missing something," Solomon said, looking confused. "You are becoming something? Are you... you are like the walking dead that the camp speaks of? I thought they were only tales told to scare me. You are saying they are real?"

"Yes, Solomon. They are very real."

"Are we in danger?"

"It depends."

"On what?"

"How much longer will they allow themselves to be confined? I know Michael is too smart to be held for too long. Edwin, you must see this as well."

"I do. We are taking precautions."

"I think I am scared now."

"Good," Edwin said seriously. "It is better to be scared. It will keep you aware of your surroundings."

"So, this parasite created undead?"

"Yes."

"Yet, you call yourself a monster because you are like them?" Solomon asked, as he observed me cautiously.

"No. I am something else."

"Caused by the same parasite?"

"Yes."

"The same parasite also wiped out an entire town?"

"Yes. Caught up?"

"I suddenly feel like peeling potatoes was the better end

of the deal."

"I do not blame you. What about BDX587, Edwin? BD stands for before dawn to remember all that came before the dawn of this day, and to honor and remember the number of lives lost."

"It is a well-suited name. How about we call it Dawn to make it easy in the lab?"

"What is it with you people and nicknames?" Solomon asked, shaking his head. "Are we talking about a parasite or science fiction? How does this parasite work?"

"Once you are involved, Solomon, there is no turning back."

"Understood. Explain it to me."

"It is a parasite that uses a virus to invade its host. It is like the chocolate inside of a wrapper as it seeks a catalyst. Stony Creek was suffering from a flu outbreak when released. Once it invades the host, its structure changes entirely by mimicking another virus until it can replicate and integrate with human cells based on its function, which we have yet to identify and understand fully. The overall process changes the individual on the cellular level."

"Have we truly contained it?"

"That is a question we cannot answer at this point. If more of this blood that contains the parasite is in the hands of others, it is only a matter of time."

"Doesn't that mean that Vivienne's blood is a dangerous thing?"

"The parasite is very much a part of Vivienne at a cellular level and appears to be in a dormant state," Edwin said, turning back towards his lab notebook.

"Would someone then consider it as predatory? It seeks and destroys until it finds a host."

"Yes," Edwin nodded solemnly. "I suppose you are right, but for all intents and purposes, it does not seek to destroy. It is not in its nature. Its instinct is survival."

"No living thing is innocent when faced with survival."

"Welcome to the project, Solomon. I have heard good things about you."

"You know of me?"

"Our project has had our eyes on you for a while, Solomon. It is not an accident that you are here."

I stared at Edwin, my eyes betraying my feeling of surprise. Just how deeply embedded into this project with Major Stevens was he?

"Dance with me, Vivienne," a voice called out into the night. "Vivienne!"

"Oh my God," I whispered. "Michael. I almost allowed myself a moment to forget."

"Shit," Edwin muttered. He grabbed a vial of the sedative and a syringe, and stormed out of the lab.

"Dance with me, my ballerina," Michael's loud voice demanded. He carried on for several minutes, attempting to bait me from his mock prison. "Dance, dance, dance!"

"Pin his legs down," Edwin yelled out, followed by Michael laughing in a deep, throaty way that sent chills up my spine. If the camp was asleep, they were awake now.

"Who is Michael?"

"He is an extremely dangerous man that used to oversee this mission. He ingested my blood, and he became something else. Something dangerous."

We both listened silently, occasionally looking at one another as we waited. The camp became quiet again, and I took in a deep breath, not realizing I was holding my breath. As I let out a long breath, my physical body released its tension from hearing his voice. I could not fight back the stinging tears that found their way to the surface. Solomon shifted in his cot as he looked at me.

"He hurt you," Solomon asked me knowingly.

"Yes," I whispered, lowering my head into my hands.

"I have heard strange stories about people gifted with an inhuman strength that could defy human nature when they endured horrific situations that moved them beyond the human experience. There are those that believe that we can tap into these abilities. The parasite allows you to do something similar?"

"Something like that."

"What will you become?"

I did not know how to answer him. He was but one of the many individuals that would enter my life and ask me questions I had no answers for. What will I become? I refused to allow myself the process of the transformation. I could feel the need to bend to it, to complete the process I started. I was not ready.

"I wish I knew."

CHAPTER 35

ENTER THE DANCER

Michael refused to communicate with anyone for the first twenty-four hours. Major Stevens, at first, advised me to stay away from him. That was not an issue, but to get the information we needed, I would need to play his own hand against him. I was Michael's addiction, and according to Major Stevens, his mental state was deteriorating quickly. He has become erratic and aggressive.

Edwin was deep in research after having found where Michael hid his own research. He kept his research in a crate that he kept with Laura to guard like an attack dog. Based on Michael's notes, he was onto a potential solution to help him stay alive by applying a sequence of electrical shocks to our mingled bloodlines. Edwin compared it to having a light switch turned on with a faulty fuse. He believed it was only a short-term solution. Michael was well past the state of change to where that may or may not even work. This posed the additional question of how long the body would survive after this procedure using my blood. Could the body withstand ongoing electrical shock treatments? How long before the body stopped responding? What would it take for Michael to just go away?

I was not as excited to hear about Michael's other research notes suggesting using reproductive science to create a series of hosts in which to have a steady supply of blood to rejuvenate his dying body. He was optimistic that the parasite would complete his transition into a super being. While anything was possible, he would have to act fast, considering that his state of transition was almost complete. Doc Lindberg examined him and labeled him as almost deceased. His heart continued to work, but it was at a reduced capacity, not enough to provide oxygen to critical organs and supply the body with critical function. Without the ability to have access to regular feedings of my blood, it was only a matter of time. He must have taken enough of my blood to last him a while, but for how long? How long could he survive without my blood? This question alone kept me up at night.

My nightmares did not help. When the thought crossed my mind that my blood could rejuvenate him from the extremes of death, it filled my mind with horrific images that haunted my dreams. In my recent dream, Michael's flesh hung from his bones, his eyes wide and crazed as he hunted me. I watched him reach his bony fingers around my throat, ripping into my neck as he devoured every drop of blood. He comes back to life, as he was before his transition into death, and he laughs wildly as he picks my lifeless body up and dances slowly. He looked deeply into my eyes, and his expressions changed.

"My love," he says in a seductive voice. "We will never be apart."

He then pulls me into him, bites his lip as his blood streams from his mouth, and then he kisses me, whispering that I will be his slave for eternity. I wake up screaming, feeling as if I am choking on his blood.

When he and Laura fed from me, what they did together felt more ritualistic than anything else. I once met a young man that came to the cafe every Sunday to have breakfast as he passed through town to see his folks two towns over. He was a psychology major who also studied shamanism and how it applied to modern times in the deep jungles of Mexico.

I remembered one of our conversations. There are religions or cults that believe in ingesting that which they want to absorb, ranging from voodoo to miraculous healing cults. If an individual had liver disease, then that person would have eaten raw liver from a healthy host animal to absorb its power. Blood is the elixir, and blood used in what he had called powerful magic was as old as civilization existed and used ritualistic behavior to become more, or to alter their perceptions.

Michael was more like the legends of the vampire, focused on blood to survive, yet pale and ageless. I dragged my mother with me to the *House of Dracula* movie a couple of years ago, and we laughed and laughed at how ridiculous it all was. Its release was a precursor to what would become of my future. Forever hunted by undead creatures because of the elixir the parasite created within me. If Michael was Dr. Frankenstein, then Laura became Frankenstein's monster and bride all in one. There was more to these tales than met the eye. Even on a subconscious level, urban myths and stories come from a basis of truth. Answers were out there. We just needed the time and the resources to gather them all.

I went from prisoner to bait in the blink of an eye, and Michael would see me for the first time since his capture. Being nervous was an understatement as I walked into the tent holding Michael in chains. He appeared composed, and not at all as scary as Dr. Lindberg had suggested. Although, it was safe to say I was not looking for a comparison. Michael's head tilted down towards his chest, as if he were sleeping. His hands were pale in his lap, and his chest barely lifted. If he was breathing, it was barely visible to the human eye.

"You have come back to me," he said in a low growl.

Hearing his voice terrified me! My heart went into my stomach, and my hands shook of their own accord. I took a deep breath, which caused him to raise his head slightly, and I placed my hands behind my back as a knowing smile formed upon his pale and sunken face. My anger rose, and my skin crackled. I imagined his entire body engulfed in flames. The entity within me unfurled, and her energetic tendrils stretched like a young baby bird ready to take to flight. I could feel her hatred matching my own.

"Hello, Michael."

Michael started screaming in pain. The guards drew their weapons, pointing them between Michael's head and my chest out of fear as I felt my body lift

"Hold your fire," the Major said loudly. "Keep your guns pointed at Dr. Alden!"

"No," I raised my hands up and raised my voice over his screams.

Without question, the men did as he asked. A part of me enjoyed watching Michael writhe in agony. In my blind rage, I imagined the flames engulfing him until they consumed him. Michael screamed out again in pain, responding to the flames that engulfed him from within my mind. He writhed on the floor as he tried to escape. My escorts grabbed him quickly and pinned him down.

"Please," he screamed at me, his eyes pleading. "No more!"

I am doing this! It took a moment to register what was happening. My anger had completely taken over. I took another deep breath and imagined the flames dying around him. Michael quieted, and he finally looked back up at me through the blood-stained tears streaming down his cheeks. My entity responded by withdrawing. I did not understand what was happening, but I could sense that her display against Michael had weakened her.

"You are not like me, Vivienne. You are not the monster. Being without you is torture enough."

I found myself strangely attracted to his porcelain features, which I knew would not last, but in his present state, he looked almost angelic and alluring. How easy would it be for him to manipulate and lure the others? It was only a matter of time. I knew better. I knew what he was capable of. I did not feel that we were prepared enough.

"What do you want, Vivienne?"

"I need information, if you're willing to provide it."

"What will you provide?"

I withdrew a syringe filled with my blood from my coat pocket.

"Would this suffice?"

Michael's eyes went wild, and his hands shifted, which caused the guards to raise their guns and point them at his head as my escorts held him down more firmly as he struggled. He looked at them amusingly, closed his eyes for a moment as if he were centering himself, and then he opened his eyes and stared directly at me, studying me in a way that caused me to be cautiously aware of the exit behind me. He was toying with all of us. I knew if he wanted to leave, there would be no stopping him.

"Very well," he said, amused. "Shall we have a conversation? Would you care to join me?"

As his bundled hands motioned for me to sit, I asked Edwin, who was outside, to come in. I was not doing this alone. He came back with a medium-sized barrel and sat at my side. I was still out of reach of him if he reached out for me, but I was within grabbing distance if he rushed towards me. Hopefully, he was aware enough to realize that this kind of reckless maneuver would not benefit him. He had much more to lose.

"Are you aware that you have changed? Do you differ from who you were before?"

"Yes," he smiled and leaned forward. "I have known for a while now. Ask me how long."

"How long have you known?"

"I became ill the evening after we captured Laura."

I let out a small gasp of surprise. That would explain why we all saw so little of him. It would also explain his degrading mental state and acting out of character. Although, during the initial stages, it amplified those hidden urges or desires that a person may feel based on his journal that we had recently found, along with his research that he had kept hidden. It stems from the madness and is like a drug. It removes an individual's inhibitions. It becomes an addiction to play out their fantasies that bring pleasure, an altered mental state. Drugs were dangerous enough. Imagine having someone promising you untold pleasures that await you, and all you must do is grab the vial with the label that says drink me. *Alice in Wonderland* tales filled her mind.

"Michael," I lowered my voice. "Do you find you want to do things you have never done before? That are sexual or perverse?"

"You may refer to me intimately as *The Dancer*," his smile spread across his face. "Call it a side effect of my nature. I wanted so badly to fuck you and then watch my men abuse you after I finished with you."

"You are a sick son of a bitch," I whispered as I fought back the tears.

"Yes," he gave a lop-sided grin. "You broke my heart, but see how I have forgiven you? I protected you instead of allowing them all to taste you. They all want to taste you. They touch themselves when the camp is dark, imagining your struggle as they lay on top of you and enter deep inside you until they fill you up."

I stood up and turned away from him. I knew I had to keep my level of focus and come at this hoping he would give us more information about his transition, but more than anything, I wanted to see his body turned into ash. His intelligence and manipulative demeanor remain. That much was obvious. I took a moment to regain my composure, and I sat back down.

"You good?" Edwin asked me, looking concerned. I nodded and looked back at Michael, whose smile widened. What I would not give to watch him suffer as all those he had manipulated, tortured, and murdered had suffered.

"How did your transition begin? Was it the same level of decay as Laura's, or was it more advanced? Is that why you needed my blood?"

"My transition was much more rapid than Laura's. I developed symptoms of rapid deterioration immediately within the first twenty-four hours."

"And?"

"It was then that I realized that my experiment had failed, and I was like Laura. Only part of the puzzle. Having watched Laura feed from your wrist that night at the cabin, I knew you were the key. Your blood became unlike anything I have ever experienced before. I am drawn to you like a bee to the pollen."

"How were you infected?"

"Are you sure that you want to know? It is quite the story. You may find it unsettling."

"Yes, I want to know."

"Remember," he said excitedly. "Remember that you agreed to my terms."

"Did I?"

"When we brought back Laura, she was under sedation and laying on top of an examination table restrained under chains."

His eyes took on a faraway aspect, yet his body came alive as he spoke.

"What happened next?"

"I found her incredibly attractive, and I had a secret desire to touch a woman as she slept. She was under sedation, and I could not help myself."

An erection grew in his pants as his hips moved back and forth. The frustration with the two men holding him was building, and Edwin, who stood at my side, was ready to take him down. I did my best to stay focused on what we needed from him. It seemed more important than his need to draw me into his madness and molest me by any of the means he could get away with.

"What happened next?"

"I opened her torn uniform, and she was pleasantly naked underneath. I fondled her breasts, at first with my hands and then shortly after with my tongue. Her skin was cold, and she was not moving. I could not help myself! She was so beautiful as she slept. I took her hand and pleasured myself. I wanted to finish myself in her beautiful and lifeless mouth."

"Did you?"

"Yes," he said as he moaned with pleasure.

I should have left when he started telling the story. He used my curiosity that there was something more, something else I needed to know. *Stupid.* He continued to win. I felt disgusted, shamed for staying, and I felt as if I were standing before him naked. He was right. I agreed to his terms without realizing it. This was a performance to show me he was still in control.

He lifted his chained hands and attempted to reach for me. Edwin reacted and blocked him, leaning down and punched him right in the face. I watched as Michael's head bounced off the ground as our team of escorts secured him. Michael continued with his story as if what had just happened was not a big deal.

"She woke up as I finished in her mouth. She asked me to kiss her. I did not realize that she bit her lip. She kissed me deeply, and then spit in my eye. She claimed me as her mate. Since our joining, she has reached inside my soul and fulfilled all my hidden desires."

"You manipulated her just as you have done with everyone around you."

"Yes, sweet Laura. She will soon be nothing more than dust, which I will be if you do not give me your blood. Vivienne, I need to be alive for our child. Our special child. Help me live and bring me back."

"What do you mean, special? What the fuck did you do to my child?"

"I only gave our child a piece of me," he said in all seriousness. "I needed to ensure that our child remained bound to the both of us."

"What did you do?" I asked, my anger building.

"I injected some of my blood into your womb."

"Why? Why would you risk the child to do this?! What if you destroyed our child?!"

"How can I destroy that which is already so much more? I bound our child to us in the same way I bound us together. It was a beautiful ceremony."

"What ceremony?" I asked as pure panic blinded my vision in white. I blindly reached out for Edwin for support.

"While you were dreaming, I proclaimed my love for you! I gave you all that I was as a man and as a husband. I took your blood and injected myself with it. I have also given you my blood, to both of you. This is our ritual, where you renew my life, and we celebrate our union by making love. Look at what our union has made," he said, gesturing towards my swollen belly.

How naïve I have been. I have lived my life in this fantasy world of wanting the ultimate dream of being whisked away in a passionate romance, and I allowed this man to enter my life and take everything that I was. Who was Michael Alden, really? Did any of us really know? I was not like a small child fearing monsters under my bed. I only feared what humans became when they claimed the darkness within them.

"Doc Lindberg, would you come in?" I said, holding up the syringe filled with my blood as Michael's focus went from me to the contents. Doc Lindberg walked in and looked at Michael with disgust. "Feed him."

I stood up, turned slightly, and looked back at Michael as he was receiving his injection.

"I never loved you, Michael," I said, giving him a taste of the truth. "How could I love a soulless monster like you? You will never know my child, and you will never, ever touch me again."

I tossed the ring he had given me at him as it landed before him in the dirt.

"Vivienne, no," he whispered. "Don't leave me."

"Consider this our divorce," I told him as I turned to climb the ladder and departed from the tent.

"Vivienne," he cried out angrily. "Vivienne!"

CHAPTER 36

THE LAST DAY

Finally, the day we have been waiting for has arrived. It is our last day here and we will leave in the morning. Tomorrow, I say my final goodbyes to this nightmare in the hopes of a future for myself and my child. To say that I was nervous about the road ahead of me was an understatement. I woke up this morning feeling so many emotions. Fear, anger, sadness, and when I thought I could not manage it anymore, they came on again like ocean waves and my heart, being the tide as its undercurrents, pulled me through all the emotions all at once.

Edwin was out much of the day on an urgent mission for the Major, which left Solomon and I to pack what remained up into boxes in an organized fashion and to ensure the equipment was secure. By the time we finished and helped in the mess tent, dusk was already on the horizon. I never want to see another potato, ever. If I see another unpeeled potato, it will be too soon. I did not want to eat the potatoes either, but I felt famished, and potato soup was the meal of the night flavored with a ham hock and beans. The Chef called it his version of shit in the pot. What Solomon described as throwing whatever was leftover into a pot and calling it a day. If we wanted to eat, we would have to suck it up and eat it.

I had just finished packing up what little belonged to me into a large light green duffle sized military bag when Edwin walked into the tent with a stride in his step.

"What's that all about?" I asked him with a smile. "You win the Nobel prize?"

"Not, yet! That will come soon enough. You will never

guess what I found out!"

"What?"

"You discovered the Chef's secret ingredient?" Solomon asked, laughing.

"No! Seriously?! What was it? Please tell me it is nothing terrible," I said, praying there were no more surprises.

Edwin laughed. "No, in fact, it is the exact opposite. It is amazing! It's bourbon! Sneaky guy is always happy, and when it is late at night, I like to snoop my way around the camp! I caught him hiding his stash."

I laughed. "Well, that explains why his broth was just the medicine I needed."

"We also did one last patrol sweep of the area, and we found something," Edwin said, his face turning serious.

"Oh, God! Please tell me it is not another dead body," I said as worry spread through me like a lightning strike. "Or it is not a dead body, and Mr. Perkins is back? I did not sense him. Are you going to tell me it is an undead dog you are keeping as a pet? I am going to stop asking, and I do not want to know. I should just walk away now and go right to bed."

I tried to poke light humor, because the truth of it was, I could not manage another death or round of unwelcome news. Not like this, and not right now. If it were Anders, I did not know if I would have the strength to fight another day if he did not exist in my world. Solomon looked at me strangely, like he could not figure me out. Edwin just crossed his arms in front of his chest and shook his head.

"No, no, no," he said, chuckling. "Solomon, can you bring in my guest, who's waiting outside?"

"Guest," I asked, confused, and then my heart leaped into my throat and tears filled my eyes. He could not mean...

The tent flap opened, and Anders walked in. His face filled with excitement.

"Anders," I gasped with shock as tears streamed down my eyes. "You are alive! Oh my God! Are you here?!"

He pulled me into his arms. He lifted my chin and placed

both hands on each side of my cheek. He breathed me in with a contented sigh and then kissed me gently at first and then, with a longing that made my knees weak. It felt like years had passed since we were together. It was so strange that life could change so much for someone in such a short amount of time.

I looked into his eyes, touching the beard that was now coming in at a fast rate.

"Come with me," he whispered into my ear, guiding me outside

"Where?" I asked, unable to take my eyes off him.

He handed me my coat and lifted the flap of the tent. I turned back when I heard movement inside the lab as Edwin began moving one of the larger boxes and gave me a little wink with a genuine smile. I mouthed the words *thank* you as I let Anders pull me away. Solomon stood there, looking as confused as ever.

"Who is this now?"

"He is the soldier that we all thought was dead, eaten alive by an undead monster nurse."

"Eaten? Monster nurse?"

"Do not worry, Solomon, old man. I will fill you in," Edwin was saying as we left. "You have catching up to do. The drama on this mission. Where do I even begin?"

"I'm afraid to ask," Solomon said in response, and I could picture the puzzled look on his face. I could not help but chuckle inside. Solomon may think twice about joining this project. Not that he had much of a choice. Nope, like me, he would be a part of this project for life. Regardless of how he felt.

When we were both outside, he grabbed my hand, and we ventured slowly and quietly through the camp. The men around the campfire said nothing to us and just nodded in Anders' direction with a smile on their face, and the evening patrol pretended to not even notice us. We made it out into the forest with only the moonlight and the twinkling skyline that reached into forever, guiding our way.

"Can I at least pretend that we're doing a jailbreak?"

He stopped and turned towards me. He tilted my chin up and pulled my bottom lip between his parted lips while his tongue explored my mouth, beckoning my mouth to open. I parted my lips slightly and allowed my tongue to reach playfully out to his as his beard tickled my chin. I stepped back and looked up into his slightly darkened face. I could feel the heat permeating from his body, and the sudden chill in the air made me want to curl up into his naked body and feel his warmth.

There were a few leaves left on the trees. The deciduous conifers were a golden yellow, showing off their color as they shed their needles. The forest green pine trees that thrived in the winter continued to fill the air with their wonderful scent. Regardless of where I went next, I knew I would miss the scent of the pine trees and the open fresh air. Edwin mentioned we were going somewhere that was underground, and that is all he could say. I took in the early evening air and breathed deeply as I looked back up into Ander's face.

"I thought I would never see you again," I whispered, allowing the tears to come freely. "I felt so lost without you."

"Nothing, not even death, can keep me from you," he whispered back, nuzzling into my neck.

I felt a surge of energy as my heart expanded and I looked upon Anders adoringly. I could see the life force in everything. I looked around the forest, witnessing with new eyes. The trees and their roots glowed, interconnecting together like an intricate ecosystem we would never fully understand. How strange it was that the mushrooms glowed even brighter, and not only existed within the trees but also in the very air we breathe. The air sparkled with life where there were mushrooms exposed above the earth. Like veins, they networked and joined as one. The veins pulsed like a heartbeat, and I could feel it like an energetic wave. Familiar and calming.

"My God," whispered Anders as he looked at me in shock. "You're glowing."

MELISSA HALBERT

I raised my hand up into the moonlight, and the familiar blue shimmered onto my skin like a glowing veil upon my skin.

"Are you afraid of me?" I whispered, fearing his rejection.

"No," he whispered, pulling me into his arms. "You're beautiful."

This time, I kissed him. I could feel his warmth all around me. I felt safe in his powerful arms.

"Was this your plan? Get me out into the middle of the forest to kiss me?"

"No," he said, with a small twinkle in his eye. I could easily see that what he had been through was more difficult than he let on. I only hoped that he could trust me enough to share his pain with me. "I have something even better in mind."

"Out here? Better than fresh air and being in your arms? What could be better than that?"

"Just a little farther," he said, dragging me behind him.

I was content exactly where I was, but his sense of urgency piqued my curiosity about where we were going. When we finally stopped, I looked around and gasped. We were at the clearing by the stream I had visited with Edwin. He set a small tent up near a campfire, waiting to be lit. It was so romantic, and very well thought out. He definitely had help to pull all this off. That explained Edwin's eye wink! I peeked inside the tent and sure enough, two sleeping bags lay nestled on top of a tarp with additional warm blankets, a lantern, and a bottle of apple juice.

"What happened to you?" I blurted out, taking the romantic energy out of the air. He kneeled by the campfire and lit it. "Shit. Sorry."

"No, it is okay. I understand. I am just not ready to tell that story, Viv. Not tonight."

"We've both been through so much. How can you want to be with me, knowing I am the reason they tortured you?"

"Hey," he said, coming up to me and pulling me into his

304

arms. "You have nothing to be sorry for. He manipulated you, and everyone else around him. If it were not for Laura helping me to escape so I could try to save you, I do not know what would have happened."

"Laura helped you?"

"She did. She even told me the best hiding places and where to find food. I do not even know if she understands what she is doing or why she is doing it, but she is very protective of you. Even though she and Michael had their fun torturing me, she knew I wanted to keep you safe. I like to think she took it easy on me, compared to what I watched her do to others. I can imagine Michael was not too happy when he realized what she had done."

"How did you know it was safe to return?"

"I snuck into the camp late one evening when I watched Michael leave to be with Laura. I wrote a message and put it in Edwin's jacket pocket. The big oaf, he does not check his pockets very often. I have been hiding in the small basement of the church this entire time. It is easy to get in and out of, and I set traps in the event Michael or his men came looking for me. Just enough to slow them all down."

"When you were in the camp, did you come and see me?"

"I did," he whispered, lowering his head. "You did not look like you were doing well. I could not wake you from your deep slumber. If I could have taken you away at that moment, I would have risked it all for you. I cannot control what has happened, and I cannot wish away the past, but what I can give you is right now."

"Kiss me," I told him, pulling him back into me.

"Yes, ma'am," he said as his head lowered to meet my lips.

I could feel the moonlight bathing us in its light. I wondered if he could feel how surreal and wonderful this moment was for me. We sat down on the soft moss-covered ground wedged between two giant boulders with the soft trickling sound of the water as the moonlight illuminated our surroundings and the roaring campfire glowing at our backs.

I laid down on the moss and looked up at the night sky. I raised my hand over my head and placed one of my hands in the water. If there was such a thing as magic, I could almost feel its origins locked away within the very essence of my being. Did that make me less than human? Or was I losing myself in a wonderful dream? Right now, I did not even care. Anders was alive!

Anders laid down beside me and situated himself on his side, with one hand propping up his head while the other caressed my arm. It was not an awkward silence, but a silence that suggested he was waiting for permission. An old sense of terror ignited my body, and I closed my eyes firmly.

I was not sure if I was ready to do this with him. Michael's assaults haunted my thoughts and my nightmares. I knew it was not the same, and I felt guilty for comparing that situation to this one, but my body responded before I could acknowledge what was happening.

I am in control of my body. Michael is not here. He is not here!

"Hey," he whispered as he caressed my cheek, and a shadow of concern crossed his face as the campfire's light danced playfully. "Are you alright?"

"I'm fine," I said as a tear rolled down my cheek. "It is just…"

"He tortured you."

"Not even death stops him. He just keeps coming back."

"Huh?"

"What he did haunts me, and I just do not know how to do this," I cried. "Not since everything he did."

"Shhhhh," he whispered, grazing my lips with his. "We will take this as slow as you would like. We have all night, and you are in complete control. We do not have to do this. Okay? We can just enjoy each other's company. Being with you is enough for me. That reminds me. I have something for you."

He reached into his pocket and pulled out a familiar

bracelet. My mother's pearl bracelet. He took my hand and placed it on my wrist.

"Anders," I said, tearing up as the words caught in my throat. "Thank you!"

"I love you," he said, lifting my chin gently and smiling softly. Those three little words brought forth all our emotions. In that vulnerability, we revealed more than just our pain. We revealed our frailty as human beings. I may be a monster, but in his eyes, he loved me, and that was enough.

"I love you, Anders!"

I kissed him deeply.

"Take me," I told him, giving myself permission to feel again without fear, allowing the burning desire that I had locked away to be free from its kept cage.

He slid in closer to me and put half of his body on top of mine. He caressed my cheek and softly kissed my neck. Moving his way to my chin and then to my lips. He kissed me deeply, using his tongue to explore my mouth, entwined with my own in an erotic dance.

"Tell me when to stop," he whispered as his kisses went down my neck.

Despite the cold, our body heat mingled with the roaring fire made up for the slight chill upon my exposed skin. He unbuttoned my coat and clumsily went after my jacket. I pushed him back and stood up and walked into the tent. Looking behind me, beckoning him forward.

As we entered the tent, I turned back around to face him. I took my time undressing slowly, button by button, and when the last garment fell from my body, he looked at me with a silent pleasure, taking me in and I let him. I wanted to fill all his senses.

He tore off his clothes quickly, with a sense of urgency that took me by surprise. Gently pressing into my body, he kissed the longing parts of my body that ached for his touch with an explorative thoroughness that left me breathless. He moaned loudly as I caressed his throbbing cock with my hand and opened my legs wider to greet him. His free hand caressed my warm mound as my back arched in response with a quivering release as pleasure moved throughout my body. He maneuvered himself gently between my legs, pausing long enough to gauge my response. I let my hands trail down his back as I pulled his hips towards me. He purred with longing.

"I want to make love to you," he whispered hungrily into my ear. I moved away from him and laid down on top of the blankets.

"Make love to me, Anders," I told him as I reached out my arms to him.

He came down upon me slowly, being careful of his weight, and looking into my eyes for approval. I smiled at him and then closed my eyes as I arched my back, grabbing his shoulders and drawing him into me. He took his time entering me slowly.

"Look at me, Vivienne," he whispered. "I need to see you."

My eyes locked with his in a way that amplified the intensity of our lovemaking. His wantonness to connect on a deeper level drove my longing for him to take every ounce of me until we were both working in the natural rhythm. Our bodies took over, innately knowing what to do. I watched the surrounding layers unfold before us as they lifted us up, floating like feathers in the wind into a realm where dreams blossom to create reality. I cried out as his hips built into momentum. My hips joined his until we both gave in to the craving of release pouring our souls into one another. We stayed there holding each other, knowing that this time we were safe from Michael. I loved just lying there listening to his heartbeat. The act was so simple. A single heartbeat that meant everything to me.

We talked until we saw the first rays of the coming dawn. Even though I was exhausted, I wanted to savor every moment with him.

"My unit is busy getting fuel and torches ready to burn

the area down by late morning. As far as anyone is concerned, it is a fatal environmental hazard and chemical fire ate up the town, and there was not enough time to evacuate the people. It will be a tragedy, but they have done this repeatedly, and in each case, time goes on and history forgets."

"I will never forget."

"When you remember, you honor them."

"I do not know where I'm going after this," I whispered. "How will we ever find each other again?"

"We will find a way," he said, kissing my forehead. "There are no guarantees, but I will not give up. Even if it takes a lifetime. I will find my way back to you. I promise."

I had a feeling that we were at a stalemate, at least for now, and leaving on terms that neither of us wanted nor could control seemed like the only way we could both move on. At least we could make a promise to one another, and we could long for that day we could be together. He was not part of the project, and Edwin had already sworn me to secrecy. I could not tell him more than he already knew. There was, however, something that I could tell him. He deserved to know.

"We should get packed up and head back to camp," he said, kissing my forehead.

"I do not want this moment to end."

"Neither do I."

"Anders, there is something that I need to tell you."

We heard a warning bell and men shouting. Anders and I looked at each other, our eyes panicked and wild, and we took off running through the forest. I knew it with certainty.

Michael has escaped!

CHAPTER 37

STANDOFF

"I have a bad feeling about this," Anders told me as we moved towards the camp.

"Wait, Anders! He is…"

As we approached where the stream was wider that led down into a deep rocky ravine, Anders turned to look at me and fell to the ground by an unseen force that moved so fast that I could not even see them. I could, however, sense him. It happened so fast. When their struggling stopped and he had Anders pinned down to the ground, my heart almost stopped.

"Michael," I pleaded. "Please, do not hurt him! Please."

"You will learn your place," he hissed as he hit Anders so hard that he passed out. "You allowed this filth to touch you again."

He stood up from Anders' body and sauntered towards me like a predator toying with a mouse before it started the killing strike.

"Michael," I said pleadingly, holding my hands up as I backed towards the deep ravine. "What do you want?"

"I want you away from him," he hissed as he pointed at Anders. "We are going to disappear and raise our family together."

I looked over at Anders, and my heart twisted in pain. He was bleeding from his forehead, and I could not reach him. No, if I wanted anything, I would have to play his game. Nothing would happen without Michael's approval.

"Okay, Michael," I said, slowly and holding up my hands. "Please, let me help Anders first. I will go with you without question or resistance. I will be yours."

"I do not trust you," he growled at me, and then paused, considering my words. "Make it quick."

He backed off and held out his hand for me to pass. I strolled past him, fearing that he would grab me. I made a wide arch around him, and as I did, he scoffed at me. I ran the rest of the way to Anders and dropped to my knees as I held his head in both my hands.

"Anders," I whispered. "Please, wake up."

I tore at my t-shirt under the jacket and ripped an oddly shaped strip of fabric, followed by another. I bunched the fabric up and placed it on his forehead, followed by tying the other strip around his head and applying enough tension to help the bleeding stop. He must have hit the rock when he went down. He had a concussion and needed to see Doc Lindberg.

"Anders," I raised my voice, and I watched his eyelids attempt to flicker as they shut again, and I could not rouse him.

"Enough," Michael yelled. "Ah, Phil, you have arrived. Please help our Ms. Vivienne up and let us prepare to leave. We are wasting time."

"Phil?" I looked over, shocked that he would help someone like Michael. "Why?"

"He is going to help me save my mother."

"You think he can do such a thing?"

"Come on, Vivienne," Phil said, avoiding my eyes. When he looked down at Anders, he glanced at me, and I saw the shame in his eyes.

"Phil, he cannot save your mother. He is lying!"

"You do not know that!" He exclaimed loudly, grabbing me forcefully by the arm and dragging me as he limped to follow Michael.

"He does not have that kind of power," I told him, shifting all my weight behind me, and forcing him to stop so that he had to look me in the eye. He could not carry me with his wounded leg, and that I could use to my advantage if I had to. Michael was the problem. Why could I not move like them? "Drag me if you must, Phil, but you should know the truth. You do not have to do this."

"It is too late for me," he said through gritted teeth. "I killed a man to help him escape. There is no going back for me."

"Then help me get away from him, please," I whispered, pleading with him. "Help me!"

He dragged me as Michael looked back and looked at us with annoyance and impatience.

"We need to scout ahead to ensure there are no patrols in our way," Phil yelled ahead.

"Yes," Michael said, and took off quickly.

"Hit me," Phil said, surprising me.

"What?"

"Hit me and run," he said with urgency. "Do it!"

I hit him as hard as I could, hitting him in the mouth. He staggered backwards, and I took off running as fast as I could towards the camp. My lungs burned as the frigid air rushed into my lungs. My legs were tiring, but I continued to run, even though my pace was slowing down. I prayed I had enough of a head start. I continued to zigzag through the trees, hoping Michael would not be behind me. I looked back a little too soon, and I tripped over a large root and caught myself just in time to avoid a more direct impact.

"Vivienne," Michael's voice screamed out into the night.

I screamed and ran as fast as I could, avoiding the burning feeling that had now extended out from my lungs, into my chest, and into my legs. I felt the sting of fatigue as it fought against the power of my will. I could see the lights of the camp as the morning sun broke through and the sky turned into a vibrant shade of pale blue and pink. My breathing became ragged as I gasped in quick breaths, trying to compensate for the fatigue and the speed I tried to keep up. It was no use. I heard his running footsteps hitting the earth, and I stopped, turning around to face him.

"Stop running," he growled. "You are mine!"

"I will never belong to you," I screamed at him. "Never!"

"If you do not stop now, he dies," he yelled. "I will kill him slowly and painfully while reminding him you abandoned him."

Shit. I stopped and turned around to look at his cat-like stance, ready to bolt if I tried to run again.

He walked towards me, slowly, his movements jagged and inhuman. I spotted movement in the trees, and I gasped as I watched as Solomon leaped through the air, taking Michael off guard, and hitting Michael in the head with such force that Michael went flying backwards.

Solomon dropped the large rock he was holding onto, grabbed my hand, and we ran.

"What are you doing?! You are taking us back to the ravine," I cried at him as I held my chest with my free hand.

"Trust me," he said, smiling at me and racing us through the forest, hopping over roots and large rocks. When we reached the ravine, Michael was waiting for us, with his back to the ravine. I doubled over, gasping for breath.

"You think you are so clever? You would deny me my prize? What was your plan? To throw her down the ravine so that you would deny me of her life force?"

"What?" I asked, backing away from them both.

"Not clever enough," he said, smiling his crooked smile. "I will enjoy killing you."

He walked up to me and grabbed me by my hair, and then pushed me down onto the ground, and dragged me away from the ravine. I laid on the ground, holding the back of my head. It felt like it was bleeding and like he had torn out a nice sizable patch of hair, but it was not. It just hurt like hell.

"Stay like that, my dear. I love you looking so pathetic and lost. You will barely be able to walk when I am through with punishing you."

"Are you planning on fighting me soon?" Solomon asked him, sounding bored.

"Solomon, what are you doing?" I yelled out as the

tears of overwhelm came in heaving sobs. "Please, no more! Michael!"

"You had your chance, you little bitch," he said as he slapped me hard across my cheek. "Their deaths are on your head! This lesson will ensure that you will not make the same mistake twice. Yes, small one. Let us fight."

"You will pay for what you have done to Edwin," Solomon told him and went into a defensive posture.

"Edwin?!" I asked, focusing on Solomon as the words became caught in my throat. "You... He... No, he is... is he..."

"Yes," Michael hissed at me. "He died painfully for taking my research and touching my things. I took him by surprise and killed him slowly."

"Oh, God... Edwin." My heart broke. Once Michael finished killing everyone I cared about, I would be completely alone.

Solomon stood tall and proud as Michael ran towards him, and right before Michael would have crashed into him with an impact, Solomon moved out of the way, jumping into the air, and rolling into a somersault near the ravine. I stared, enraptured, as I watched Solomon move as if he could fly. Who was Solomon, really? He was more than a translator and code talker.

Michael screamed in anger, turned, and headed straight for Solomon again. This time with more speed and running at an angle, hoping to counter his attempt to move again. As he grabbed a hold of Solomon, Solomon tilted his weight back and I screamed as I watched them both fall into the ravine.

"Solomon!" I screamed out, hoping to hear a response. My forehead touched the earth and my hands grabbed big handfuls of dirt and pine needles. "Solomon, I'm so sorry!"

"Oh, man, my head really hurts," I heard Anders moan.

"Anders," I whispered. I picked myself up enough and crawled over to him. I took it as a good sign that he was still moaning swear words and attempting to sit up. "Anders! Oh my God! Anders!"

I put my arms around him and cried into his chest. He put one hand on the back of my head. I looked up at him as he looked around, looking confused as he attempted to piece a sequence of events together.

"It was Michael," I told him through heaving sobs. "Solomon, he is gone. He took Solomon down into the ravine."

"Who is Solomon?" Anders asked, looking even more confused than ever. "Am I suffering from memory loss, too?"

"He did not take me anywhere, Viv. I took him," Solomon said, creeping up behind us, laughing.

"Are you… are you a ghost?" I asked him, not sure what to say to the man that stood before me with only a couple of scratches on his face.

"Some call me that, but I prefer just Solomon."

"How did you survive that fall?" I asked, still not believing that he was standing before me.

"I'm a sneaky bastard," he said with a sly grin. "When one learns how to walk in the shadows, one learns how to live in two worlds. The unseen is a comfortable home."

"I'm so glad you're alive," I told him, standing up and hugging him, smiling back through the tears. "Will you help me get Anders back to the camp?"

"We must move fast," he told me, placing his hand on my shoulder. "We have little time."

"What do you mean, we have little time?"

"Michael is not dead."

"God, what are we going to do?"

"The Major has a plan. It is already in motion. It was supposed to be Plan A, but it will have to do. Come, let us go."

Solomon helped Anders up, and we each took a side to help him walk back towards the camp. I could not help but continue to look over my shoulder every so often, expecting to see Michael behind us, ready to take his vengeance. I was so grateful that we made it intact without having to face Michael again, at least not yet. Doc Lindberg swore under his breath, as he made Anders lay down to rest. Anders was not having any of it and continued to invite the Doc.

"What do you mean, I just sit here and do nothing? If Michael is out there, you need to round up all the men and go after him, me included! Otherwise, he just keeps coming back! The bastard does not die!"

"Anders, calm yourself," the Major said with his hands up as he tried to calm him down. "Trust me, he cannot refuse the bait we have set."

"How do you even know that?" I asked him, curious. "We do not even know enough about his condition to understand what he is or is not capable of."

"He will need to feed, and they crave your blood more than anything else. Your blood is the bait."

"Excuse me, my what now? What are you going to do?"

"We have a man waiting to open vials of your blood. We made sure that anyone watching would see our man taking the blood vials into the town square. As soon as our sharpshooter sees any activity heading towards your blood, it will cause a sequence of events to begin. The first being ignition of fuel, and in a matter of minutes, we will leave this area and watch a chain reaction that will burn it all down while we are at a safe distance."

"That's no guarantee," I said to him, frustrated and throwing my hands up in the air. "Is that where Solomon disappeared to? He is part of the bait?"

"Solomon went off to track Michael to ensure he takes the bait. This does not change our plan," he said as he took a deep breath to calm himself, becoming frustrated by all our questions. "He is well trained, and he will make it out in time at our rendezvous."

"If he already knows I'm here, what will draw him to the bait?"

"It's our best shot," he responded heatedly. "He cannot take on an entire camp, Vivienne. Give me a chance to make this work!"

"Hey, hey, hey, Viv," Anders said, sitting up slowly with

his properly bandaged head. "He has your best intentions at heart. We all do. Trust me, none of us wants to risk another run-in with that asshole. If anything happened to you…"

"Fine," I sighed, taking Anders into my arms. "How are you?"

"I feel like I have a bowling ball in my head, but otherwise I am fine. I need to talk to you. Can you spare a minute?"

"Of course," I whispered, looking adoringly into his eyes. He gave the Major a nod, and the Major reached over and shook his hand.

"My unit is ready to start the fires. I am to rendezvous with them immediately now that the Doc has cleared me. As soon as I meet them at the rendezvous, we are moving out to our next assignment."

"What do you mean? So soon?"

"I am sorry. It is a soldier's life. Look, I keep my promises. I will find my way back to you. My heart tells me this is not the end, not yet."

"No," I told him, crossing my arms over my chest. "I refuse to let you go! How can you walk away after everything? Can I ask the Major to let you stay? What can we do?"

"The Major is the one that reassigned me," he said, taking his hands and holding my face, cupping it like he would a precious and fragile thing. I felt far from fragile and wanted to hit him for not trying harder. "He thinks it is best that we return to our duties. He has plans for me and promises me we will find one another again."

"Why would he reassign you? How could he make such an empty promise?" The emotions of the past few days caught up with me, and my tears resurfaced. "Anders, I just got you back. Please! Refuse to go!"

"Viv! You know I cannot. I cannot risk a court-martial. What good can I do for you behind prison bars? Military prison is not as comfortable as a civilian prison. Trust me."

"What if we do not get reunited?" I told him as I leaned

my head in, placing my ear to his chest to hear his heartbeat and wrapping my arms around him. "I do not know how to do all this without you!"

"What does your heart tell you?"

"I refuse to answer that."

"Viv, come on," he told me softly as he kissed my forehead, the tip of my nose, and lightly brushed my lips. "What does your heart tell you?"

"One day, you will be back in my arms."

"I am holding onto that as much as you are. I love you, Viv. You are in my heart, and I am never letting you go. Come here," he said, pulling me into his arms and kissing me deeply. I held onto him, not wanting to let him go as the tears rolled down my cheeks. I felt the loss of him, and I could barely stand it. Someone outside the Doc's medical tent called out his name, and he gently pulled me from him as he kissed the top of my head. "I love you, Viv."

I watched as he walked swiftly away, not looking back, and I felt a gaping wound form in my heart. The pain was something I had never felt before. It felt so final. I walked towards the mess tent where I would be under heavy guard until it was time to leave and cried.

My heart yearns for him. I long to feel his touch, and to feel that connection that makes me feel alive. To feel his lips pressed against my own. To feel his gentle caress as his fingertips move gently across my cheek, and to feel his strong, protective embrace.

I sat there for what seemed like forever, lost in my daydreams of Anders defying his orders and taking me away from all of this. Levi startled me by grabbing my shoulder.

"Vivienne, let's go!"

I followed Levi to a large, covered truck with benches in the back. Michael must have taken the bait. Within a matter of minutes, I watched as the remaining tents came quickly down with the last of the boxes loaded, and I looked around me in shock at how the landscape had changed with everything being torn down and quickly loaded into the trucks. It did not look like the same place at all. How strange.

We waited with anticipation as we sat in the back of the truck. Whispers surrounded me in idle conversation as they wondered where they would be off to next. We were waiting for a signal over the walkie talkie on when to move out. Soon, we would travel towards an unforeseen adventure, and the mystery was enough to rattle my nerves. I did not know what to expect. I wanted to run after Anders and beg him to run away with me, while the rational mind warned me to stay strong. It was nice to know that the naïve young girl within me still existed somewhere beyond all the death and loss.

Half of the troops split up. They took positions ahead and behind us in the event there were problems. They left us with just enough men to launch a decent sized counterattack in the event there were more problems with Michael, or anyone else. I am surprised by their level of efficiency and how they work as a unit to accomplish even the most miniscule of tasks.

There was chatter over the radio. In a flurry of activity, we knew it was time, and that they had started the fires. I immediately grabbed onto Levi's arm as our truck started up and we began our trek away from the town. My home.

"Showtime," he said, and patted my hand as the truck started up and moved forward. I looked out of the back of the truck.

I placed my hand into the pocket of my jacket. As I did, I felt the smoothness of paper, along with the rounded shape of a small metallic object. I did not even realize they were there. I pulled out the paper and my heart leaped at seeing Anders' handwriting.

I will never stop trying to find you. I love you!

As the truck carried us to a safe distance away from the town, I looked up in time to see the flames swallow the small town of Stony Creek. I watched as the remnants of my life became engulfed in the vibrant flames and black smoke thicker than the fog. I placed my hand on my lower abdomen, closed my eyes, and took in a deep breath. I never got to tell him. I felt the small flutter of the quickening even then. We are all prisoners of time, and one day, just maybe, he would find his way back to me and his daughter.

CHAPTER 38

BURNING EMBERS

As the fire reaches the outer reaches of the encampments, a newspaper burns amongst the wood embers, alive with dancing flames. The article reads:

Anti-Jewish Riots in Syria after U.N. Votes to Partition Palestine

Thousands flee as tensions continue to build after the United Nations General Assembly voted on November 29th to partition Palestine into two new states. Arab states choose to use military force under threat of violence and bloodshed to evict Jewish citizens. Will civil war erupt?

CHAPTER 39

POSTCARD PRETTY

A postcard lays beneath the journal pages for a vacation resort built near the original town of Stony Creek. The postcard shows two couples on vacation, sitting in an indoor swimming pool having an enjoyable time. The date is exactly one year after they buried the original town.

We can't always see what's around us. The realms of our perception are layers of dimensions that operate in harmony. We are in a constant state of change, transition, but the only question that always remains is the same.

What will you choose to become?

A NOTE FROM
THE AUTHOR

The National Sexual Violence Resource Center states that 1 in 5 women in the United States alone have experienced rape or the attempted rape at some point in their lifetime. 1 out 3 women experienced sexual violence between the ages of 11 and 17 years old. Sexual violence does not know gender, and it affects everyone.

If you or someone you care about has been affected by sexual violence or are a victim of domestic or partner abuse, please contact your medical provider and/or local authorities for the next steps.

Made in the USA
Middletown, DE
20 September 2022

10208504R00183